# "You're too good to be true. It must be an act."

"Awww, Nina." His hand slid up to cup her face. "People can be genuine."

She couldn't help but be enticed by the promise in Alex's eyes. Yet pain from past betrayals welled up, how her husband and her in-laws had so deeply let her down, worse yet how they let down precious Cody. "They can. But they usually aren't."

He stroked back her hair, tucking it behind her ear. "Then why are you even considering having dinner with me?"

"I honestly don't know." Her scalp tingled from the light brush of his fingers, his nearness overriding boundaries she thought were firmly in place.

Their gazes met, eyes held. She breathed him in, remembering the feel of his lips on hers.

Would he kiss her again? Because if he did, she wasn't sure she could say no to anything.

\* \* \*

**Pursued by the Rich Rancher**
is part of the Diamonds in the Rough trilogy:
The McNair cousins must pass their grandmother's
tests to ~~...~~ true love!

# PURSUED BY THE RICH RANCHER

BY
CATHERINE MANN

Published in Great Britain 2015
by Mills & Boon, an imprint of Harlequin (UK) Limited,
Eton House, 18-24 Paradise Road, Richmond, Surrey, TW9 1SR

© 2015 Catherine Mann

ISBN: 978-0-263-25265-1

51-0615

Harlequin (UK) Limited's policy is to use papers that are natural, renewable and recyclable products and made from wood grown in sustainable forests. The logging and manufacturing processes conform to the legal environmental regulations of the country of origin.

Printed and bound in Spain
by CPI, Barcelona

*USA TODAY* bestselling author **Catherine Mann** lives on a sunny Florida beach with her flyboy husband and their four children. With more than forty books in print in over twenty countries, she has also celebrated wins for both a RITA® Award and a Booksellers' Best Award. Catherine enjoys chatting with readers online—thanks to the wonders of the internet, which allows her to network with her laptop by the water! Contact Catherine through her website, www.catherinemann.com, find her on Facebook and Twitter (@CatherineMann1), or reach her by snail mail at PO Box 6065, Navarre, FL 32566, USA.

To Mustang and his special boy. Thank you for
changing my life and touching my heart.

# One

Nina Lowery just didn't get the cowboy craze.

Good thing she lived in Texas. All the cowboys made it easy to resist falling for any man after her marriage combusted. And never had she been more neck deep in cowboys than today as she accompanied her son to the week-long HorsePower Cowkid Camp.

Nina peeled the back off the name tag and stuck it to her yellow plaid shirt that was every bit as new as her boots. She knelt in front of her four-year-old son and held out the tiny vest with his name stitched on it.

"Cody, you need to wear this so everybody knows which group you're with. We don't want you to get lost. Okay?"

Silently staring, Cody kept his eyes on the ground, so she had a perfect view of the top of his blond buzz cut. He lifted his hands just a hint, which she took as the okay to slide his spindly arms through the vest, leather fringe fanning in the wind. The summer smell of freshly mown hay mixed with the sticky little boy sweetness of perspiration and maple syrup from his breakfast pancakes. Cody had them every morning. Without fail.

They'd been running late today, so he'd eaten his breakfast in the car, dipping his pancake in a cup of syrup. Most of which drizzled all over his car seat. But after waking up at 4:00 a.m. to get ready, then driving from San Antonio to Fort Worth, she was too frazzled to deal with the fallout of disrupting any more of his daily routine. Syrup could be cleaned later.

There were far tougher issues to tackle in bringing up Cody than combating a trail of ants.

She would do anything for her little boy. Anything. Including immersing herself in the world of boots and spurs for seven days. *Yeehaw.*

About a month ago, when her four-year-old's eyes had lit up during a field trip to a farm, she'd been taken aback. He'd been mesmerized by the horses. So Nina had devoted herself to becoming an expert on all things equine related, desperate for a means to break through the walls surrounding her autistic son.

Finding a pathway of communication was rare and cherished when parenting a child with autism.

Never in a million years would she have guessed this particular world would pique Cody's interest. Usually boisterous encounters spun him up, leaving him disoriented and agitated. Sometimes even screaming. Rocking. His little body working overtime to block the excess stimuli.

But he liked it here. She could tell from his focus and the lack of tension in his body. She'd only seen him this way while drawing. He was a little savant with crayons and paint, finding creative canvases from rocks to boxes and, yes, walls. She even had a Monet-esque flower mural down her hall.

Apparently he was a horse savant, as well.

She held out the pint-size straw hat and let him decide whether or not he wanted to take it from her to wear. Textures were an iffy proposition for him. The brush of a rough fabric could send him into sensory overload, especially on a day when there were already so many new sights and sounds, horses and humans everywhere. She sidestepped to make way for a father pushing his daughter in a wheelchair, the tyke's arms in the air as she squealed, "Giddyap, Daddy!"

Cody clutched his tiny Stetson in his hands until a long-legged ranch hand strutted past. Standing straight, his eyes tracking the man walking away, her son slid his hat in place and tilted it to the side just like the stable hand he watched. Nina breathed a sigh of relief. She'd made the right decision to come here.

The cowboy camp for special-needs kids was a clear fit for her son. The program had only started this summer, but was already receiving high acclaim. The wealthy McNair family had put their power, influence and money behind launching HorsePower Cowkid Camp on their hobby ranch—Hidden Gem. The bulk of their fortune, though, had been made in their jewelry design house that created rustic Western styles.

Cody toyed with the fringe on his vest, tracing the stamped jewel patterns imprinted in the leather. She reminded herself to stay cautiously optimistic. They'd only just arrived.

She'd learned long ago not to set unrealistic expectations. Life worked better when she celebrated individual moments of success, such as how Cody took steps toward that cowboy. A horse whinnied and her son smiled. That meant more than the hundreds of hugs she would never get.

"Cody, let's walk around and explore. We have a couple of hours to settle in before the first activity." She was used to rambling on to fill the silences. Her son did speak. Just not often. Rather than expecting Cody to answer, she was advised by the speech therapist to accept it as a pleasant surprise when he did and take heart in his advanced vocabulary choices.

Cody held up his hand for her to take and she linked her fingers around his. A rare reach-out. Her heart filled at the chance to touch her child. If Cody wanted the ranch experience, she would follow that broad-shouldered cowboy to the ends of the earth.

Weaving around the other families, she tried not to notice how many of the children were accompanied by two parents. She savored the feel of her son's hand in hers and charged ahead to a corral about ten yards away, on the periphery of the camper chaos.

Multiple barns, cabins and corrals were walking distance from the lodge. Some would call the lodge a mansion—a rustic log ranch mansion with two wings. One wing for vacationers, the other wing for the McNairs' personal living quarters. The place had expanded from a B & B to a true hobby ranch, with everything from horseback riding to a spa, fishing and trail adventures… even saloon-style poker games. They catered to a variety of people's needs, from tourists to weddings.

And now this special needs kids' camp, as well.

She refused to be wowed by the family's power.

She'd walked that path, been too easily blinded by her ex's charm. The thought of a wealthy life of ease with a handsome guy had seemed like a fairy tale and so she'd seen what she wanted to see. But her would-be prince had definitely turned into a toad, taking that fairy-tale ending with him.

Nina skirted past a half dozen children surrounding a rodeo clown passing out toy horses. Childish squeals filled the air.

"I wanna spotted pony."

"Please, please the brown one with a girl rider."

"I wike the one wiff sparkles on the saddle!"

Cody, however, kept his eyes on the cowboy. For the most part, she'd only seen chaps on men in after-shave commercials. Even in Texas they weren't common. This guy's leathers were dusty and worn, the type a man wore to work. A real man. Not an overindulged toad prince like her ex.

So okay, maybe there was something to be said for the cowboy appeal after all.

Cody's cowboy leaped over the split-rail fence in a smooth blend of instinct and strength, his tan Stetson staying firmly in place. He walked with loose-hipped confidence toward a wild horse pawing the ground, nostrils flaring. The animal clearly didn't like the sad-dle on his back and eyed the approaching man with wariness. The horse danced nervously, shifting uneasy weight from hindquarter to hindquarter, powerful mus-cles flexing. She felt her son's pulse kick in excitement. So in spite of the tremor of fear in her heart, she stepped closer to the corral.

She'd been thrown once as a child and hadn't been

a fan of horses since then. She liked to think she was a person who learned her lesson. Once burned. Twice shy.

Yet the man in front of her showed no fear as he spoke softly to the stressed beast, lulling with his hypnotic voice and gentle strokes. Her stomach gripped just as he slid onto the horse's back.

Pinning his ears back, the horse yanked hard on the reins. Now the animal was well and truly pissed.

Cody tugged his hand free. "Let go."

And she only then realized she'd been squeezing too hard. "Sorry, sweetie."

"Uh-huh." Her son walked closer to the fence, and a different fear took over. Her child had very little sense of danger.

She stifled her own anxiety and stepped closer. "Cody, we have to stay outside the fence to watch. We can't go inside and disturb the man's work."

"Kay…" Her son nodded, enraptured.

The cowboy urged the horse gently forward. The horse bucked hard but had no luck at unseating the skilled rider. His cowboy hat, however, went flying. The midmorning sun glinted off his head of thick black hair.

The kind of hair a woman could run her fingers through.

The wayward thought hit her as hard and fast as those hooves pounding the ground. She'd never bought into cowboy lore, especially after being tossed on her butt by that supposedly docile pony. Until now. At this moment, she couldn't take her eyes off the smooth flow of the ranch hand's body as he became one with the horse. He rode the frenzy without letting it take control of him, rolling naturally with the unpredictable movements. She understood the restraint and self-control it took to tap in to that Zen state in the face of such out-right terror.

She carried fears of her own. Of not being able to care for her son as a single parent. Of trusting a man again after the hell and betrayal her ex-husband had put her through before their breakup and then his death in a motorcycle accident.

Those fears were nothing compared to the terrors her son faced. And the roadblocks.

Somehow she could tell this cowboy understood that fear. Knew how to ride through the moment until peace returned. He had the well-being of the horse in his care in mind at all times. And Cody was mesmerized.

So was she.

Finally—she had no idea how long they stood watch-ing—the horse settled into a restless trot, circling the fenced area, snorting. Nina exhaled in a rush, only just now realizing she'd been holding her breath and secretly rooting for him.

Cody knelt down and picked up the man's hat, shook off the dust and held it out. "Mister. Your Stetson."

Her son's voice came out a little raspy from being used so infrequently. The cowboy tipped his face to-ward them, the sunshine streaming over...

*Oh my.*

He'd stepped right off some Wild West movie poster and into her reality. High, strong cheekbones and a square jaw, damn good-looking *power*. She blinked fast against the sting of dust in the air.

He guided the horse to their side of the fence, and her stomach flipped. Because of close proximity to the horse, right?

*Ha.*

She'd quit lying to herself a long time ago.

The cowboy dipped closer, extending an arm toward Cody. "Thank you, little man." His voice was like Southern Comfort on the rocks, smooth with a nip. "I'm guessing by that vest you're here for camp. Are you having fun?"

"Uh-huh." Cody nodded without making eye contact. "Spectac-u-lar."

Would the man understand? This was a special needs camp, after all.

The cowboy stroked a hand along the horse's neck. "I see you like Diamond Gem. He's a good horse, but too large for you. The camp counselors will start you out with pony rides and before you know it you'll be ready for the big leagues."

Cody shuffled his feet and tugged at the fringe on his vest.

"Thank you," Nina said. "Cody's not very talkative, but he understands all we're saying."

He looked at her, his eyes laser blue. A shiver of awareness tingled through her. Did all of him have to be so damn charismatic?

A dimple tucked into one of his cheeks. "I'm usually not much of a chatty guy myself, actually."

He'd done better with Cody today than her ex-husband ever had. Warren had been a charmer, sweeping her off her feet with extravagant gestures, making her believe in the fairy-tale ending right up until...*ribbit*. Warren was a shallow, spoiled mama's boy with too much money and too little ambition other than the next thrill. When life got real, when the day-to-day specifics of dealing with their son's autism added up, he'd checked out on the marriage. Then he'd checked out on life altogether in his reckless motorcycle accident.

Cody scuffed his little boots in the dirt, his mouth moving, repeating, "Rodeo man, rodeo man."

The cowboy dipped his head, then nodded. "Back in the day, I was. Not any longer."

Cody went silent, and Nina scrambled for something to say. For her son's sake, of course, not because she wanted another taste of that Southern Comfort drawl saturating her senses. "Then what was that show all about?"

"Just doing my job, ma'am. This was actually a low-key session," he said, his voice washing over her as he sat astride the horse, his muscular thighs at eye level... and his hips. Diamond Gem shook his head up and down, shaking the reins, a reminder that the horse, although calm now, was still unsettled. "Diamond Gem and I have been working together for a couple of weeks."

That was an *easy* session?

"Do you miss the rodeo days?" she found herself asking, unable to stop herself from thinking of all the regrets Warren had lamented over after settling down.

The dusty cowboy scratched under his hat, then settled it back in place. "Let's just say these days I prefer to spend my time communing with the animals rather than performing for people."

"And this horse? You were communing?"

"This fella was confiscated by local animal control for neglect and..." He glanced at her son. "And for other reasons. Releasing him into the wild where he would be unable to fend for himself wasn't an option. So he came here to us where we can socialize him. He's a little green and gun-shy, but we've made progress."

So he'd used the old skills to help this horse. Was he playing on her heartstrings as a part of some camp gimmick or was he as genuine as those blue eyes? She settled on saying, "That's admirable of you to risk breaking a rib—or worse—to help the horse."

The dimple twitched at his cheek again. "I may have enjoyed myself a little bit…" His eyes dipped down to the name tag stuck to her shirt. "Nina."

Her skin prickled and heat flushed through her at the sound of her name coated in those whiskey tones. What harm was there in indulging in a light flirtation with a regular guy? No risk. She was only here for a week. Although she could be imagining his interest.

It was probably just his job as an employee to be polite to the customers.

"Well, my son certainly enjoyed it, as well. Thank you." She backed up a step. "We should start unpacking or we'll miss the lunch kickoff."

"Wouldn't want that to happen." He touched the brim of his hat. "Y'all have a nice time at the HorsePower Cowkid Camp."

Her skin flushed, heating at the sound of his low and rumbly voice soothing ragged nerves. How strange to be lulled and turned on all at once. But God, how she craved peace in her life. She treasured it in a way she never would have guessed a decade ago.

And watching the lumbering cowboy ride away, she had a very real sense of how smooth and sexy could coexist very, very well in one hot package.

For the first time in months, Alex McNair was stoked about the possibility of asking out a woman. He'd been telling himself for months he needed to move on after his cousin got engaged to the only woman Alex had ever wanted to marry. But the one-night stands he'd been having lately didn't count as moving forward with his life.

He slung the saddle off Diamond Gem's back and passed it over to a stable hand. Diamond Gem looked sideways at Alex from the cross ties and let out a long nicker. He preferred to brush and settle his own horses, but his responsibilities overseeing the Hidden Gem Ranch interfered more often than not with that simple work these days. He missed free time in the saddle, but his MBA was needed here more than his equestrian skills.

And the number-one priority today? He was due to meet his grandmother for an early lunch. That took precedence over anything else. He didn't know how many more meals they would share, since she had terminal brain cancer.

With his grandmother's illness, he had to step up to fill the huge void left by their McNair matriarch. Which probably made this a bad time to think about starting a relationship, even a short-term one, but the woman—Nina—intrigued him. Her curly red hair and soft curves snagged his attention, and the memory of her berry scent lingered in his senses.

And the protective way she watched over her son drew him in at a time when his emotions were damn raw. He didn't want to overanalyze why she pulled at him. He was just glad as hell for the feeling.

It had taken him a long while to get over the fact that his cousin would be marrying Johanna. But he'd gotten past that. He had to. She would be in the family forever now. Family was too important for any kind of awkwardness to linger.

The family needed to stick together, especially with their grandmother's cancer. They needed to support her, and had to make sure the McNair empire ran smoothly through this time of transition. Giving their grandmother peace during her final days was their most important task.

Still, he couldn't stop thinking about the woman— Nina. He didn't even know her last name, for God's sake, but he sure intended to find out. He could see asking her to accompany him to his cousin's wedding. How far did she live from here? People came from all over for the camp, but the bulk were local.

Regardless, distance didn't really matter. Not to a McNair. He had the family plane at his disposal. And yet all that money couldn't give them the one thing each of them really wanted.

Their grandmother's health.

He strode toward the main house, veering off to the family's wing where he was to meet his grandmother on the porch. His boots crunched along pine straw, children's chatter and a banjo playing echoed in the distance. Branches rustled overhead. Some of those oak trees were older than him and he'd climbed those thick branches as a kid.

He neared the family porch where his grandmother— Mariah McNair—already sat in a rocking chair. A tray of sandwiches and a pitcher of tea waited on the table between the two rockers.

His gut knotted with dread over the day that rocker would be empty.

Her favored jean jumper and boots fit her more

loosely these days. And her hair was shorter now. For as long as he could remember, she'd worn it long, either in a braid down her back or wrapped in a bun on her head. But she'd undergone a procedure to drain blood buildup in her head a few months ago. Her hair had been cut short and shaved away at the surgery site.

That made it real for him. She was going to die sooner rather than later, and not of old age. That damn tumor was going to steal her from them.

"You made it," she said, clapping her hands. "Come sit beside me, load up a plate and let's talk."

"I'll clean up and be right back down." He worried about her getting sick on top of everything else.

"Now is better. A little dust and dirt isn't going to make me keel over. Besides, I've seen you messier."

"That you have." He swept off his hat and hunkered down into the rocker beside her, resting his hat on his knee, thinking of how cute that kid Cody had looked passing it back to him. "How are you feeling, Gran? Do you want more tea?"

He reached for the pitcher, noticing she'd only nibbled at the corner of a sandwich.

"I'm fine, Alex, thank you. I have the sunshine, a glass of sweet tea and one of my grandchildren here. All is right in my world."

But he knew that wasn't really true. She didn't have long to live. Months. Maybe only weeks. She'd been getting her affairs in order, deciding who would inherit what. Not that he cared a damn thing about the McNair wealth and holdings. He just wanted his grandmother.

He reached for a plate and piled on sandwiches, more to make her happy. His stomach felt as if it had rocks in it right now. "Thanks for lunch. It's a chaotic day with all the campers coming in."

"Stone surprised us all by starting that camp instead of taking over the jewelry enterprises, but in a good way."

Alex touched his hat on his knee. "That he did."

"His new life fits him. Johanna helped him see that path while she helped him with his inheritance test." Mariah set her plate of uneaten sandwiches aside. "Alex, I want to talk to you about *your* test."

"*My* test?" The rocks in his stomach turned icy. "I thought that was just a game to get Stone and Johanna back together."

At least he'd hoped so as time passed and his grandmother didn't bring up the subject of putting her three grandchildren through an arbitrary test to win their portion of the estate.

It wasn't about the money. It was about the land. A mega-resort developer simply could not get a hold of Alex's portion of the land. That, he definitely cared about.

"Well, Alex, you thought wrong. I need to feel secure about the future of what we've built. All three of you children have a stubborn streak."

"One we inherited from you."

"True enough." She laughed softly before her blue eyes turned sad. "Much more so than my two children."

Her daughter had been a junkie who dropped her child—Stone—off onto Mariah's doorstep. Alex and his twin Amie's father had been unmotivated to do more than spend his inheritance and avoid his wife.

Mariah had been more of a parent to Alex than his own.

He, Amie and Stone were like siblings, having grown

up here at Hidden Gem together. Once they'd finished college, they all turned their attention to home, working to keep the McNair holdings profitable even after their grandfather died. Each one of them had a role to play. Alex managed the family lands—Hidden Gem Ranch, which operated as a bed-and-breakfast hobby ranch for the rich and famous. Until recently, Stone had managed the family jewelry design house and store. Diamonds in the Rough featured high-end rustic designs, from rodeo belt buckles and stylized bolos to Aztec jewelry, all highly sought after around the country. And Amie—a gemologist—created most of their renowned designs, even though the McNair jewelry company was now under new management, an outsider his grandmother had hired.

Gran rocked slowly, sipping her iced tea, her hand thin and pale with spidery veins as she set the glass back on the table between them. "Now back to what I've planned for your test."

That damn test again. Stone had already passed his test to retain control of the jewelry business. Gran had made Stone work with Johanna to find loving homes for his grandmother's dogs. Yet once Stone had finished, he surprised them all by proposing to Johanna and announcing he didn't want to run Diamonds in the Rough after all. He didn't want the all-consuming ambition. The camp had been Stone's brainchild, shifting his focus to the family's charity foundation, investing his portion of the estate into a self-generating fund to run the HorsePower program while a new CEO assumed command as head of Diamonds in the Rough.

"Seriously, Gran? You're still insisting on the test? I assumed since Stone backed out and opted to live on his own portfolio you would pass the company along to Amie."

"And leave the running of the ranch to you?"

He stayed silent. The land. This place. He'd put his heart and soul into it. But that was his grandmother's decision to make. Money wasn't a concern. He had his own. He could start fresh if need be.

Except he didn't want to. He wanted his home to stay untouched by takeover from some mega-ranch theme park.

Mariah set aside her tea. "Alex, it's a simple test really. There's a competitor—Lowery Resorts—that has been quietly buying up shares of the McNair empire through shell corporations."

Alarms went off in his head. This was the worst possible time for someone to stage a takeover. Stockholders were already on edge about his grandmother's illness, concerned about the uncertain future of the McNair holdings. "A controlling percentage?"

"Not yet. But between my illness, Stone's resignation as CEO and his replacement still gaining his footing, some investors perceive a void. If our loyalties split or if they continue consolidating, we could be at risk of having our haven turned into a sideshow resort."

How the hell had this happened? His hands gripped the arms of the chair and he resisted the urge to vent his frustration. He bit back the words he wanted to spout and simply said, "How did they manage that?"

"When word first leaked of my illness, they moved fast and took advantage of investor fears. I should have seen that coming. I trusted old friendships. I was wrong. I need to move faster now. Time's too important."

He should have seen this coming. He should have

thought beyond his part of the family holdings. "We could have Stone return as CEO until the crisis with the Lowery Resorts passes."

"No, he doesn't want it, and I need to see the company settled with our new CEO, Preston Armstrong, in control before I can rest easily. The board and I chose Preston because we believe in him, but he will need time to gain investors' trust. So in the meantime, I need your help."

"You don't need to make it a test." He patted her hand, then gripped it. "Just tell me what to do for you and I'm here for you, for the family."

Smiling, she gave his hand a squeeze back, before her eyes narrowed with the laser focus that had leveled many in the business world. "The Lowery family has a vulnerability in their portfolio."

"You want me to exploit it?" His mind churned with possibilities he wanted to discuss with Stone.

"Convince the Lowerys to sell back a sizeable portion of those shares bought by their shell companies and I'll transfer all my shares of the ranch into your hands effective immediately."

He waved aside the last part of her words. "It's not about me accumulating a larger part of the homestead. It's about our family. I will not allow our land to pass into anyone else's hands."

She nodded tightly. "There's that old competitive spirit of yours. I was wondering if you'd buried it completely under that laid-back air you carry around these days."

"Hmm." He didn't like reminders of that side of himself. He picked up his tea and drank. There was still a lot of dirt inside him to wash away from those rodeo days. Things he'd allowed his parents to push him to do. Things he regretted.

"You need to be aware, the Lowery family is going to be resistant. You'll need to be careful and savvy in gaining the trust of the one chink in their armor. I've even given you a head start."

He paused mid-drink, then set his glass back down carefully. "What do you mean by head start?"

Her thumbs rubbed along the arms of the wooden rocker. "The vulnerable shares belong to the Lowery grandson. His widowed mother is the executor, and she needs to invest wisely for the boy's future—long-term."

A kid? A widow? A creeping sensation started up his spine, as if he were about to get kicked by a horse or run over by a stampede. "Gran, what have you done?"

"I investigated all the Lowerys, of course. And when I found out the grandson adores all things cowboy, I made sure a brochure for our camp landed in his mother's hands so we would have the chance to meet with them—away from the grandparents' influence."

*Ah, damn.* It couldn't be…

"In fact, I believe you've already met her and her son." She pointed a frail finger toward the corral, where she would have had a clear view of his morning activities.

*Crap.* He could almost hear that stampede gaining speed, ready to run him over.

"The lovely red-haired lady who watched you work with Diamond Gem."

# Two

The sun was low and warm, piercing through the barn windows as Nina sat at a long wooden table eating supper with the other parents. A country band played twangy children's songs, a group of young campers sitting clustered in front of the small stage. Cody rocked and flapped his hands in time, having already finished his macaroni and cheese. A little girl with a pink scarf over her shaved head spun in circles with a streamer. A little boy with cerebral palsy held his new friend's hand as they danced. Three children ran up to the stage clapping.

She'd spent the morning unpacking, then eating lunch and attending camp sessions with her son, followed by pony rides, arts and crafts. They'd made belts and jewelry. And not just the children, but the adults had been included, as well. She touched the bracelet

full of little charms, all Wild West themed, and a gem
that was also her son's birthstone.

Between the horses and the art, her son's two favorite
activities, Cody had been enthralled. The tiny sticker
jewels he'd glued to the belt made an intricate repeating
pattern that had even surprised the instructor.

Her son was happy, but tired from a good day. The
best she could remember having in a long time. And
she couldn't deny that her mind wandered back to the
morning and the dusty cowboy who probably hadn't
given her a second thought. But she'd kept looking for
him in the crowds.

And she didn't know his name.

She stabbed at her dinner salad, covered in strips
of tender steak. The big grill outside had been fired
up with a variety of meats, potatoes and corn for the
adults. She was wondering how the fee they charged
possibly covered such a high-end production. The Mc-
Nair family, or some of their wealthy friends, had to
be underwriting the expense. Her in-laws were always
looking for tax havens. As fast as the thought hit her, she
winced. She hated how cynical she'd become, but it was
hard to feel sympathy for people who wanted to write
a check rather than get to know their only grandchild.

Old anger and hurt simmered. She sliced through a
steak strip, took a big bite and reminded herself to enjoy
this great food and the break from always staying on
guard as the only person to watch over Cody.

A shadow stretched across her, giving her only a
second's warning to chew faster.

"Would you like some dessert?" Warm whiskey
tones caressed her neck and ears.

She set her fork down carefully and swallowed the

bite before turning around. Sure enough, her dusty cowboy stood behind her, holding a plate of blueberry cobbler—except he wasn't dusty any longer.

His chaps and vest were gone. Just fresh jeans and a plaid shirt with the sleeves rolled up. Her eyes were drawn to the sprinkling of dark hair along his tanned forearms. Masculine arms. Funny how she'd forgotten how enticing such details could be.

"Oh, hello, again." Why had she thought she wasn't attracted to cowboys?

"Dessert?"

She shook herself out of the fog before she embarrassed herself. "Not just yet, thank you. I'm stuffed from supper. I didn't expect the meal to be this good, so I snacked earlier."

He straddled the bench, sitting beside her. "What did you expect? Rubber chicken?"

The hint of man musk and aftershave reminded her of how long it had been since she'd had a man in her life. In her bed.

Shrugging, she twirled her fork in the sparse remains of her salad. "I thought since this is a kiddie camp, the cuisine would be all about catering to their finicky palates. And there certainly was plenty for my son to pick from. I just didn't think there would be such a lavish adult course, as well."

"Gotta keep the parents happy too if we want repeat customers." He cut the spoon through the cobbler and scooped a bite, his electric blue eyes on her the whole time.

She shivered with awareness. And she wasn't the only woman noticing. More than one mom cast an envious look her way.

"True enough. Well, um, thank you for checking on us…" Was this standard for all the customers? Something in his eyes told her otherwise. "I still don't know your name."

"Sorry about that. How rude of me." He held out his hand. "My name's Alex."

He said it with an intensity that made her wonder if she was missing something.

Shaking off the sensation, she folded his hand in hers and held back the urge to shiver at the feel of masculine skin, delicious. "Hello, Alex, I'm not sure if you remember but I'm Nina and my son is Cody."

"I remember," he said simply. "But it's still nice to meet you both. Officially."

She eased her hand from his before she made a fool of herself. "You must be tired after a full day of work."

"Truth be told, I'd have rather had more time outdoors rather than spend the afternoon at a desk."

A desk? She'd assumed…well, there were lots of jobs on a ranch. She should know better than to judge by appearances. It was better to get to the heart, the truth, straightaway. She glanced at Cody. "My son has autism, if you didn't already guess."

This was usually the point where people said something about being sorry and how they knew a friend who had a friend who had a kid with autism, and then they left. And that was the reason she made a point to blurt it out early on, to weed out the wheat from the chaff. Life was mostly full of chaff.

He mixed some blueberries with the vanilla ice cream and brought the spoon to his mouth. "You don't have to explain to me."

"Most people are curious and I can't help feeling the

need to tell you before Cody has one of his meltdowns." She wet her mouth with a quick sip of tea. "It's easier when people understand why."

"This camp is here to do what's easier for him, not easier for us."

His words surprised her, warmed her. "Thank you. That approach is rarer than you would think."

"Since Stone put this camp together, we've all become more enlightened." He dug into the crust covered in blueberries.

"This place is amazing, and it's only day one. I can't believe how much fun I had and how much I'm already looking forward to tomorrow."

He eyed her over his raised spoon. "You sound surprised."

"I hope you won't take this the wrong way." She picked at the knee of her jeans. "But I'm not much of a cowgirl."

"Really? I never would have guessed," he said dryly.

"What gave me away?"

"What didn't?" He pointed to her feet. "New boots."

"New shirt too." She toyed with the collar. "I'm trying to fit in for Cody's sake, but apparently I'm not pulling it off as well as I thought."

"You're here for your kid, helping him pursue his own interests. That's nice, no matter what you're wearing." His eyes held hers, launching a fresh shower of sparks shimmering through her.

Then he blinked and stood. Regret stung over his leaving, which was silly because she was only here for a week. It wasn't as if they were going to have any kind of relationship. Her focus should be her son. Just because this cowboy seemed down-to-earth and uncomplicated didn't mean a thing. Not in the long run.

He glanced back over his shoulder at her, and her thoughts scattered.

"Nina, it would be a real shame for you to miss out on the Hidden Gem's blueberry cobbler. How about I bring some by this evening?" He held up a hand. "And before you accuse me of being some cowboy Casanova with ulterior motives, we'll stay out on the porch where you can hear your son if he wakes up. And the porch will be very public, so there's no cause to worry about me making a move."

"Does this kind of service always come with the camp registration?"

"No, ma'am. This is just for you." He tipped his hat. "I'll see you at nine tonight."

He didn't have a plan yet on how to persuade Nina Lowery to sell her stocks to him. He was going on instinct with her, except right now his gut didn't want to maneuver her anywhere but to bed…or on a walk.

What the hell was his grandmother thinking bringing a woman and her special-needs son here under false pretenses? There were a dozen other ways this could have been handled, but all those honest means were no longer an option now that she was already here.

At dinner, he'd considered just coming clean with her right away. Then he'd seen her eyes light up when he'd come to sit with her. The next thing he knew, he was chatting with her, digging himself in deeper until it was going to be one heck of a tangle to get himself out. If he told her now, she would shut him down, which would be bad for his grandmother and quite frankly, bad for him. He wanted to get to know her better. Maybe if he understood her, he would know the best way to approach her.

He couldn't deny that she was skittish. That much he knew for sure, sensed it the way he sensed when a horse was about to bolt.

Damn.

She definitely wouldn't appreciate being compared to a horse, but he'd realized long ago, his instincts with animals served him well in dealing with people too. He needed to approach carefully, take his time, get a sense of her.

Learn more about her.

Then he would know how to proceed. And that didn't stop the pump of anticipation over seeing Nina. He secured the two bags in his grip—the promised dessert.

He scanned the line of cabins that held the campers. Most of the buildings were two-bedrooms. He'd searched through the paperwork to learn she was staying in number eight. Katydids buzzed a full-out Texas symphony in the quiet night, allowing only muffled sounds coming from the lodge's guest lanai. Guests had already begun to arrive for his cousin's wedding. Between them and the campers, the place would be packed by Friday.

Spare time was in short supply. Alex stood at the bottom of the three steps in front of cabin number eight, eyeing the pair of rockers on the porch, exactly the same style as the ones on his family's longer wraparound that held a half dozen rocking chairs and four porch swings.

Guilt pinched his conscience again.

His grandmother had always been a woman of honor and manners. He couldn't figure out why she'd come up with such an underhanded test for him. It just didn't make sense, and his grandmother had always been logical, methodical. Could the cancer be clouding her judgment in spite of the doctor's reassurance otherwise?

But Alex wasn't ready to lead the charge to declare her unfit. That was a step he simply couldn't take. He would ride this out, play along and hope like hell an answer came to him soon.

He stepped up the wooden stairs, his boots thudding. He rapped his knuckles on the door, not wanting to wake Nina's son. He heard her footsteps approach, pause, then walk again until there was no question that she stood just on the other side of the door. But it didn't open.

Definitely skittish.

Finally she opened the door, angling outside and making it clear he wasn't coming in. She wore the same jeans and boots from earlier but had changed into a formfitting T-shirt with "hello" in multiple languages. Her hair was free from the ponytail, flowing around her shoulders in loose red curls.

God, he could lose himself for hours running his hands through her hair, feeling it brush along his skin. "Cobbler's warm and the ice cream's still cold. Shall we sit?"

"Yes, thank you." She gestured to the rockers, studying him with a wary smile. "You didn't have to do this."

He stopped. "Do you want me to leave?"

She glanced back over her shoulder, her hair swishing, enticing. "You're already here and I wouldn't want to deny you your dessert. Have a seat." She gestured to the table between them. "I set out some iced tea."

He thought of his talk with his grandmother earlier,

the shared tea, so few moments like that left with her. "Sweet tea?"

"The kind that was waiting for me in the fridge, compliments of your staff."

"Sweet tea is Southern ambrosia." He placed the containers on the end table between the rockers.

"One of my favorite things about moving down South." She cradled the glass in her hands, those long slim fingers drawing his eyes to her.

He cleared his throat. "What brought you to Texas?"

"How do you know I'm not from another Southern state?" She set her drink aside and took the container with her dessert, spooning ice cream on top.

"I saw your application." He could confess that much at least.

Her delicate eyebrows shot up. "Is that ethical?"

"It's not illegal, and I can't deny I wanted to know more about you. I still do."

"I guess I'll forgive you. This time." She ate a bite of cobbler, a sensual *hmm* vibrating from her as she closed her eyes.

Her pleasure sent hot lava through his veins.

"For what it's worth, I didn't read much of your application." But only because he'd been interrupted. "Just enough to make sure I got the right cabin so I can learn the rest on my own, asking you, getting to know you better while you're here. Are your rooms comfortable?"

"The place is perfect. Hardly roughing it." Smiling, she dug into her dessert with gusto.

"Hidden Gem works hard to keep authenticity to the experience while providing comfort. It may be a hobby ranch, but it's not a resort." He joined her in eating even though he'd had some earlier. Sharing the food with her here in the dark night was…intimate.

"I can see the special charm of the Hidden Gem. And hear it."

"What do you mean?" He glanced at her, surprised.

"I can't believe how peaceful this place is. That's important for my son, keeping the stimuli manageable," she said matter-of-factly.

"For his autism?" he asked carefully.

"Yes, it's moderate." She nodded. "I'm sure you've noticed his verbal impairment. He's advanced academically, especially in areas of interest like art and reading. He's only four, but he can lose himself in a book. Reading soothes him, actually…I didn't mean to ramble."

"I want to know more. I apologize if I'm being too nosy."

"Not at all. I would rather people ask than harbor misconceptions, or worse yet, pass judgment without any knowledge." She sagged back in her chair, dessert container resting on her lap. "I knew something wasn't right from the start, but my ex-husband and his family insisted he was just colicky. Then his verbal skills lagged and he couldn't initiate even the most basic social interaction with other children… We had to face facts. I had get help for him even if that caused a rift with my husband."

Her maternal instincts, that mama bear ferocity, spoke to him. He admired the hell out of that, even as he realized his grandmother might well have underestimated how hard it would be to get this woman to part with those stocks unless she was 100 percent certain her son got the best end of the deal. "I'm sorry you didn't get the support you should have from Cody's father."

"Thank you." Her green eyes shadowed with pain mixed with determination. "Early intervention is so crucial. I had to be his advocate, even if the rest of the family wasn't ready to accept the truth."

He found himself asking, "And Cody's father?"

"My ex-husband sent child support payments." She set aside the foam container as if she'd lost her appetite. "But he didn't want to have anything to do with Cody."

"Sent?"

"He died in a motorcycle crash shortly after our divorce." Silence settled like a humid dark blanket of a summer night.

"I'm sorry." Such inadequate words for the mix of losses she'd suffered, not just through the death of her ex, but in how the man had let her down.

"I like to think with time he could have accepted his son and been a part of Cody's life." Her head fell back against the rocker, her red hair shifting and shimmering in the porch light. "Now we'll never have that chance."

Time, a word that was his enemy these days, with his grandmother's cancer. "Regrets are tough to live with."

And he would always regret it if he didn't help ease his grandmother's last days.

Nina shook her head quickly as if clearing her thoughts and picked up her dessert again. "Enough about me. I don't mean to sound like my life is some maudlin pity party. I have a beautiful son who I love very much. I have a great, flexible job and no financial worries. Moving on." She scooped up some berries. "Tell me about you? How did you end up working at the Hidden Gem Ranch?"

"My family has always lived here." He couldn't imagine living anywhere else, especially after spending so much of his childhood and teenage years being dragged around the country by his parents to participate in rodeos. "I guess you could say I appreciate the quiet."

"So you're a professional cowboy? Rodeos and all?"

He'd lived a whole career by eighteen thanks to his mother's obsession with trotting her kids out into competitive circles—him with rodeos and his twin sister, Amie, with pageants. "My rodeo days are long past."

"Because?"

He shrugged. "Too many broken bones."

She gasped. "How awful. Are you okay?"

"Of course. It's all in the past. Kid stuff." As a boy, he hadn't argued with his parents' insistence that he continue to compete the moment the latest cast was removed. He'd even enjoyed parts of the competition. Most of all, he'd craved his parents' attention, and that was the only reliable way to get it. But then his favorite horse had broken a leg during a competition and had to be put down. He'd lost the fire to compete that day, realizing he'd only been doing it for his parents. More than anything, he'd wanted to go home and commune with the land and his horses.

Time to change the damn subject. "What do you do in San Antonio?"

She blinked at the quick change of subject, then said, "I'm a translator. Before I married I worked in New York at the United Nations." She toyed with the Eiffel Tower charm on her simple silver necklace. "My husband worked at the stock exchange. We dated for a year, got married, moved back to his home state of Texas…" She shrugged. "Now I help translate novels for foreign editions."

Ah, the necklace and T-shirt made sense now. "What languages?"

"Spanish, French, German."

"Wow," he nodded, eyebrows lifting, "that's impressive."

She shrugged dismissively, her hand sliding back to her neck, stroking the Eiffel Tower charm. "Words are my thing just as horses and running a business are yours."

Words were her "thing," yet she had a virtually nonverbal son. "When you said you're a city girl, you weren't kidding. Do you miss the job?"

"I don't regret a thing," she said between bites of cobbler. "I'm lucky to have a job that enables me to stay home with my son. I don't have to worry about making the appointments he needs."

"What about help? Grandparents?"

"My parents help when they can, but I was a late-in-life baby for them, unplanned. They're living on a shoestring budget in a retirement community in Arizona. My ex's parents come up with different options, ranging from some cult miracle cure one week to institutionalizing him."

"You should have their support." Since weeklong camps had started in the spring, he'd seen how stressed many of the parents were, how near to breaking.

"I have great friends and neighbors. I told you," she said firmly. "No pity party."

"Fair enough," he conceded.

She stared down into her cobbler, the silence stretching out between them. Finally she looked up. She stirred a spoon through the ice cream on the side. "Do you always deliver dessert to the campers?"

The question hung in the air between them, loaded with a deeper meaning he couldn't answer. Sure, he was here for his grandmother, but he would have been here anyway.

He settled for answering honestly. "You're the first."

"Oh." The lone syllable came out breathy, the wind lifting her hair.

He reached to catch a lock, testing the fine red threads between his fingers before stroking it behind her ear. Her eyes went wide, wary, but with a spark of interest he couldn't miss. For a long moment that stretched, loaded with temptation and want, he considered kissing her. Just leaning in and placing his mouth over hers to see if the chemistry between them was as explosive as he expected.

But that wariness in her eyes held him back. He had limited time with her. One mistaken move and he wouldn't have the chance to make it right before she left.

He angled back, pushing to his feet. "I should let you turn in. Morning comes early here."

She blinked fast, standing. "Thank you for the dessert." She stacked the containers and backed toward the door with them clutched in a white-knuckled grip. "I assume I will see you tomorrow?"

"You most definitely will."

It was only dessert. Only a touch to her hair.

And just that fast, she was tied up in knots over a man she'd met this morning. A cowboy.

God, she felt like a cliché.

Nina stood at the sink and scraped the last bite of gooey dessert down the disposal before tossing the disposable container in the trash. And God, it would be so easy to stand here at the sink and watch Alex through the window as he walked away. She'd only known him for a day. She wished she could just call it physical attraction, but she'd enjoyed talking to him. Even liked the way he could let peace settle for moments, as well.

Maybe she was simply starved for adult interaction. Her only time with other grown-ups centered on Cody's doctors' appointments or therapies. Even his play group focused on children with special needs. She wanted to give Cody every opportunity possible. But she couldn't deny her life was lonely no matter what she'd told Alex about having friends back home. The only interaction she had with others was volunteering in Cody's pre-school program. Some said she should use that time for herself, and she tried. But it was easier said than done.

This week truly was a relaxing gift for her and Cody. She dropped onto the fluffy fat sofa. The cabin was cozy, comfy. A pink and green quilt—Texas two-step pattern on a brass bed. The whole place was an advertisement for Lone Star relaxation without being hokey. A colorful rag rug was soft under her feet. The lantern-style lamps and overhead light were made to resemble a flicker flame.

She should really finish unpacking and get some sleep.

Her well-traveled luggage rested on a pinewood bench. But her mind kept swirling with all the dreams she'd once stored in that case. She'd taken that suitcase with her to college, then New York City. The stickers all over the vintage piece advertised countries she'd dreamed of visiting. Warren had bought her a new set after they married, but she couldn't bring herself to throw the old ones out. After her divorce, she'd donated the honeymoon designer luggage to charity and reclaimed her old "dreams for the future" set. Those changes had felt like a reclaiming of her values and hopes.

Her cell phone chimed, interrupting her swirling thoughts. She leaned from the sofa to grab her purse off the coffee table. Her stomach leaped at the possibility that Alex might be calling. He had access to her number from her registration.

She glanced at the screen. Disappointment jabbed at her. Then guilt. She should be thankful her friend Reed was checking in on her. She and Reed had met at a play group for their children. A nice guy, a single father of a little girl with Down syndrome. His partner had left him over the stress of having a special-needs child. Nina understood the mark that betrayal left. They helped each other when they could, but they both had such very full plates.

"Hello, Reed." She propped her feet on the coffee table. "You're up late. Morning's going to come early for you getting Wendy to the bus stop."

Reed owned a bistro and took his daughter to work with him when she wasn't in school. Little Wendy loved the activity and charmed the customers.

"I'm not the only one up late," her friend teased back, his Northern accent so different from a particular cowboy drawl. "Did you lose your phone? I've been calling for a couple of hours. Just wanted to be sure you arrived safely."

"I was outside on the porch talking to…" She couldn't bring herself to tell him about Alex, not that there was much to tell. So she fibbed. "I was talking with another parent. Cody was asleep. The nights here are…idyllic."

"How did Cody enjoy his day?"

She grasped the safer topic with both hands. "He was enthralled by everything here. We're only a day into it, but I'm cautiously optimistic we're going to make a breakthrough here."

"I wish I could be there to see that."

"You have a restaurant to run."

"True enough. So tell me more about the camp."

What parts should she share with him? That she suddenly understood about the cowboy appeal? Or at least the appeal of one cowboy in particular? Reed was a friend, but not the kind of friend to whom she could say anything like that. "I was nervous coming up here that the camp would just be some overpriced excuse for parents to get a break. But it really is all about the children."

"Such as?"

"They had pony rides but let the parents lead the children around so they would feel more at ease. The menu is kid-friendly with a variety of choices so even kids with issues about texture will find something that works." And the adult fare was delicious, especially when delivered by a hot man who looked at her with hungry eyes. She hadn't felt like a desirable woman in so very long.

"That's awesome, really awesome. I'm glad you're getting this break and able to spend time with other adults. You spend too much time alone cooped up in your house."

True enough, but she didn't want to dwell on negative thoughts. She sagged to sit on the edge of the brass bed. "You must have called for a reason…"

"Can't I just check on you because you should have people looking out for you?"

"Sure you can, but I also hear something in your voice that worries me." She traced the pink and green pattern on the quilt.

"Your mother-in-law called. She'd gone by your town house and realized you'd left. She checked again this evening."

"What did you tell her?" Her mother-in-law didn't approve of her choice to keep Cody at home, and Nina knew she would just get blowback for choosing this camp. Her mother-in-law would come up with a million reasons why it was wrong.

"I said you went on a weeklong vacation with Cody. She wanted to know where. I told her to call you if she wanted details."

"Thank you." Sighing, she sagged back onto the bed, her head sinking into the pillows. "I appreciate that."

"Stop worrying. They're not going to get custody of Cody. There's no reason for a judge to pass over custody to them."

"Thank you again. I feel like I'm saying that all the time, but I mean it." She stared up at the ceiling fan slicing lazy shadows across the room, the distant echo of a band playing at the lodge penetrated the walls like a soft lullaby. "They just want to lock him away and control his inheritance. They don't love him. Not really."

"I know. And so will any judge who looks at the facts. When my partner tried to get out of helping with child support, my lawyer was on me 24/7 to keep a journal," Reed said with the unerring persistence that made him a force to be reckoned with in the courtroom. "Write a detailed accounting of your schedule and out-ings. Document. Document. Document. You'll have the facts on your side."

"Aye-aye, sir," she teased. "I will. Now you should stop worrying and get some sleep."

"You too. And be sure to take lots of photos of Cody."

"I will. And give little Wendy a hug from me. Tell her I'll bring her a present."

"Sure will," he said, an unmistakable affection leaking into his voice. He loved his daughter. "I'll be checking for text message photos."

"You're a good friend." And such a good man. They could have a great life together—except for the fact that they weren't attracted to each other. At all. Not a chance ever, since she wasn't a guy. "Good night, and thanks."

She disconnected the call, the taste of blueberries and the tangy scent of a certain cowboy's soap still teasing her senses.

God, on the one hand she had an amazing friend she could never sleep with. On the other hand she had a week with the hottest man she'd ever met. Too bad she'd never been the fling sort. But with the memory of Alex's touch still buzzing through her, she wondered if maybe she could be.

# Three

Alex propped his boots on the office desk, the morning routine stable noises wrapping around him. Except today he couldn't get into the groove. Thoughts of Nina Lowery had him tied up into hitch knots.

He'd spent most of the night on the porch in a hammock, staring up at the stars, trying to reconcile his blaring conscience with his shouting libido. By sun-up, he'd reconciled himself to the fact that he couldn't hide his identity indefinitely. He would tell her who he was today and take it from there. It wasn't as if he'd actively tried to pry those stocks from her hands, and she had no reason to expect he would.

And he was genuinely interested in her.

What did he intend to do with this relentless attraction? It would be so much simpler if they'd just met somewhere outside the Hidden Gem Ranch. Not that he left this patch of earth often.

He cranked back in his chair, peering out in the open barn area that was more like a stadium, used for parties. The kids had worn themselves out with a morning of nature walks and a wagon ride picnic. Now they were napping in the cool barn on mats, a wide-screen television showing a video for the spare few who hadn't fallen asleep.

He scanned the familiar walls of home. Like in all their stables and barns, custom saddles lined the corridors, all works of art like everything the McNairs made. Carvings marked the leather with a variety of designs from roses to vines to full-out scenes. Some saddles sported silver or brass studs on horn caps and skirting edges rivaling the tooling of the best old vaqueros. He'd explored every inch of this place, starting when he was younger than those kids sleeping out there.

And speaking of those snoozing kids…

This would be a good time to clear up his identity issues. That much he could do—and should do—before making any other decisions about Nina.

He shoved up from his desk and walked down the hall, angling past a table of drying art projects made of leaves used for papier-mâché. Nina sat beside her son, cross-legged on the floor with a reading tablet in her hand.

Snagging a bottle of water off the snack table, Alex made his way over to her. He sidestepped sleeping children. Every step of the way he enjoyed the opportunity to look at her. Her hair was swept up on top of her head, a couple of red spirals brushed her forehead and one trailed down her neck. His hands itched to test the feel of her hair between his fingers, to tug one of those locks and let it spring back. What was she reading?

He wanted to know that as much as he wanted to touch her hair again, and this time run his fingers through the wavy curls.

Alex squatted down next to her, extending the water. "You need to stay hydrated."

She glanced up from her tablet, her eyes flickering with surprise, then happiness. She was glad to see him.

"Thank you." She set aside her book and tugged open her canvas bag to reveal three bottles of spring water. "But I'm set for *agua*."

He twisted the top of his bottle for himself. "What are you reading?"

"*Madame Bovary*."

"In French?" He thought of her speaking multiple languages.

She tapped her temple. "Keeping my skills sharp."

Cody stirred on his nap mat.

Alex froze, waited until the boy settled back into sleep with a drowsy sigh. Hesitating for a moment, Nina rose carefully. Alex gestured toward the door, tipping his head to the side in question. She tucked away her tablet and pulled out a bottle of water. Why did he feel as if he'd just won the grand prize? She followed him to the open barn doors, the wind sweeping inside as the low drone of the movie filled the air.

She lifted her drink and tapped his in a toast. "I truly do appreciate the thought even though I brought my own."

"You're a planner." As was he. He liked the regimentation needed to run this place, enjoyed the challenge.

"I wasn't always, but I have to be now." She gazed back into the barn at her son with obvious love and protectiveness in her eyes. "My son depends on me."

There was a strain in the corner of her eyes. He wanted to brush his thumbs along her cheeks until she rested. "I'm sorry you don't have more family to help out. Family is…everything."

As if he needed a reminder of the stakes for him here.

An awkward silence settled.

He'd met a woman he wanted to be with and her family posed a threat to his way of life. If she even would have him in the first place. She seemed attracted, but wary as hell—with reason.

An older cowboy brushed past, clapping Alex on the shoulder. "Hey, boss, mind if I take the afternoon off to go to my daughter's spelling bee?"

Alex waved. "Enjoy. I've got this under control."

"Great. My wife will have my hide if I don't make this, and I gotta confess, I would have been there anyway." The older cowboy's smile spread. "I'll pull overtime tomorrow."

"No thanks needed. Just tell the little genius good luck from Uncle Alex."

"Can do, boss."

Alex winced at the last word. Boss. So much for telling her on his own terms. He hung his head, wondering how she would react to his identity being revealed. Hell, he should have told her last night. Or even fifteen minutes ago.

Turning slowly, he prepared himself, surprised at the disappointment churning in his gut. He couldn't blame his grandmother either. This was his own fault… Except he didn't find anger in Nina's eyes.

Just curiosity. "You said you wanted to talk?"

Apparently she'd written off the "boss" comment to him being a foreman of some sort. He had to clear this up or it was going to explode in his face. "Let's go somewhere quieter."

Away from people who would tell her too much before he was ready for her to know. He guided her into the warm sunshine.

"Um, sure." She looked around nervously. "But I need to keep Cody in sight."

"Of course." He took her hand and tugged her toward a corral a few yards away, the only spot with a clear line of sight to the barn but also out of the hustle and bustle of ranch workers and guests.

She looked around, leaning back on a split-rail fence. "What's all the activity outside about? Seems like more than regular work and tourists."

"We host major events around here, parties, rehearsal dinners and weddings." The last word made him wince. One wedding in particular.

"Even in the middle of the camp going on?"

"Even then. We have a lot of land, more than just this one space, and we intend to keep it that way." Which reminded him of his grandmother's test as well as the Lowerys and their plans to convert the place into some Wild West theme park. "We pride ourselves on people feeling their event is private."

She angled her head to the side, her high-swept ponytail swishing. "And which event are they working on now?"

"A large-scale rehearsal dinner and wedding, actually." His cousin's wedding to Johanna. Alex was over any feelings for her, but he wanted the damn awkwardness to go away. "I bet your city-girl imagination is running wild at the notion of a country wedding."

The corners of her lips twitched. "Are you accusing me of thinking in clichés?"

"If the square dance fits." He winked.

She laughed, the melody of the sound filling the space between them and filling him up, making him want to haul her close. He needed more time with her. He just had to figure out how to balance his grandmother's request with his wish to be with the woman all week, no interference muddying the waters.

"Nina," he said, hooking a boot on the rail as he leaned back beside her, "there are all sorts of things going on at this place, including events planned for the camp parents."

She looked at him through her long eyelashes. "I read every word of the brochures and registration literature."

He allowed himself the luxury of tugging a curl, testing the softness between her fingers. "You're not interested in a spa treatment while your son naps? Or a sitter after he goes to sleep?"

Her eyes fluttered closed briefly and then steadied, staying open. "I'm here for Cody. Not for myself. I can't just turn off that mom switch."

He got that. And he sure as hell didn't expect her to neglect her son. He understood how it felt to be a kid shuffled to the side. "What about riding lessons?"

Confusion shifted across her face. "Excuse me?"

"If you want to be a part of your son's world, how about experience it firsthand? Cody's sleeping and the stable is next door." He set aside their half-drunk water bottles on the split-rail fence and called to one of their gentlest mares. A pudgy, warm chocolate–colored horse walked toward them with slow, ambling steps. And sure, Alex knew he was delaying his real purpose for speaking with her today, but he couldn't resist enjoying what could be his last chance to spend more time with her. "Consider becoming acquainted with one of our horses?"

She looked at the horse and tucked her arms behind her back, shaking her head. "No, thank you. I don't think so."

He hadn't considered that even as a city girl she might not like the ranch. "Are you afraid of horses?"

"Not afraid so much as...uncertain," she said hesitantly, holding up her hands. "My son is fascinated, so I'm here for him, but I can't say I share his fascination."

He didn't sense a dislike of horses. Just nerves and lack of knowledge. The notion of introducing her stirred him. "We all have preferences. Even if you're not an equestrian fan, I can see you want to know more about your son's world. So for his sake, give this a try." He raised his hands and linked fingers with hers, wondering why he wasn't telling her about who he was. Instead he was touching her, watching the flicker of the sun in her green eyes, and he couldn't bring himself to change course, not just yet. "We can take it slow?"

Her throat moved in a gulp. "Meaning what?"

"Just get to know Amber." He guided her hand along the mare's neck, Nina's soft skin making him ache to touch more of her. "Check out the feel of her. She's a gentle sweetheart."

Gasping, Nina stroked the horse again, reverently almost. "Wow, I didn't know. I rode a little as a child, but I only remember how scared I was and how bad it hurt to fall off. I thought she would feel bristly, but her coat is like satin."

"You've truly never been around a horse before?"

And yet she'd come here for her son, even though the horse clearly scared her every bit as much as she entranced her.

"I can feel her heartbeat." Her awe and laughter stoked him.

He kept his hand over hers, his eyes locked on her gaze, watching her entranced by the animal. "She can hear yours."

Nina turned and met his gaze. She wanted him. He could see that clearly, felt her desire crackling off her skin and into him.

Unable to resist, he dipped his head and kissed her. Just a simple kiss because they were outside and anyone could walk up to them. But damn it, this was his last chance before he would have to tell her about his grandmother's plan, and then he didn't know if he would get another opportunity. The thought of never tasting her, never knowing the feel of her was more than he could wrap his brain around.

She tasted like fresh spring water and the fruit salad from lunch. Strawberries and grapes. His hands curled around her shoulders. Soft. Warm. Such a perfect fit. Sparks shot through him, damn near knocking him senseless, as if he'd been tossed from a horse onto his head.

God, how he wanted to haul her closer, but they were out here in the open. A good thing, actually, because he still needed to talk to her. He couldn't go further. In fact, he had already taken more than he'd planned. But damn, she was tempting. And if she booted him on his ass once she found out who he was, what would he do?

The sound of a little boy's screams split the air.

Nina's supple body went rigid in his arms.

"Cody," she gasped against his mouth, pulling back. "My son. That's my son."

Frantic, repetitive screeches grew louder by the second. Nina tore out of Alex's arms and raced back to the barn.

Nina bit down the well of nausea born of pure panic. The smell of hay and dust threatened to choke her with each breath. Instead of making out with a man she'd only met yesterday, she should have been watching her son. She searched the barn, following the noise and finding her son on the far side, in a line of children waiting outside the bathroom.

Relief almost buckled her knees. He was fine. Safe.

But he was definitely having a meltdown. He needed her and she wasn't there with him. Her fault. Irresponsible. And just the sort of thing her in-laws would be watching for to claim their right to have custody of her son.

What if they had one of their private detectives here watching her now? She'd tried to keep this trip quiet, but her in-laws were cunning.

Alex raced past her, his boots pounding the earthen floor of the barn, past the now-blank movie screen, to the line of children.

He knelt in front of Cody, not touching. "What's wrong, sport?"

Her son stomped his feet, faster and faster, crying. Two camp counselors backed away, giving Cody space and looking at her with a shrug.

She resisted the urge to rush forward. Startling movements could upset Cody again, and focusing on Alex seemed to be calming him for now.

"Not his turn," Cody insisted.

Alex angled closer, not touching but using the breadth of his shoulders to block out the rest of the world and reduce distractions. "Excuse me?"

Without looking up, her son pointed at a boy wearing braces on his legs. "Not his turn," Cody gasped, tears streaking down his blotchy face. "He cut the line."

Nina stepped up and whispered, "He's comforted by rules and order."

The camp counselor, a slim blonde woman, was already sliding in to restore order, gently and ably distracting the child who'd innocently pushed to the front of the line. Or maybe not innocently. Children were children regardless of disabilities or special needs. But Nina was beginning to see that these counselors truly had the skills to manage the special issues these children faced.

"Cody," the camp counselor said softly but firmly, "breathe with me. Deep breaths at the same time I do."

And within a couple of dozen slow exhales, Nina's son was back under control again. Crisis averted for now. In fact, looking back, the meltdown hadn't been one of his worst. The teacher had read the signs and acted.

Nina knelt beside the camp counselor. "Thank you so much." Then she glanced at Alex. "And thank you for reaching him so quickly."

She forced herself to meet his gaze, tougher than she would have expected from just a half-innocent brush of their lips. But there had been so much more in the moment than she could remember feeling…ever. Though she didn't have a lot of first kisses in her life, this one ranked up there as the very best.

And the most unexpected.

One she ached to have happen again. Soon. But not with her son around. God, she was a mess.

She drew in a deep breath for herself this time. "I should take Cody back to our cabin for a while." She stepped away, slowly. "Thank you for introducing me to the horse—Amber—and for the help with my little guy."

"My pleasure." His hand cupped her shoulder, re-igniting the sparks in her belly. "After your son falls asleep, would you mind if I stopped by again?"

What? Did he actually expect they would jump in bed together because of a simple kiss? Okay, not such a simple kiss. A brief kiss that packed more of a wallop than most full make-out sessions.

Did he use this camp as a pickup pool full of easy marks, needy, lonely moms? But how could she ask as much with so many people around them?

"Alex, I don't think seeing each other tonight is such a good idea."

"With dessert," he said carefully. "Truth. Nothing more than dessert, and I never got to tell you what I planned when we walked outside."

"Tell me now," she pressed, even though the thought of having him come to her cabin tonight was damn tempting.

He hesitated and there was something in his blue eyes she couldn't read. "It's too noisy here. Cody's still on edge…this isn't the time."

"Okay, but just dessert. Nothing more," she said carefully. Curious. Nervous. And yes, she wanted to see Alex again at a time when she could be sure her son was 100 percent safe and settled, because the times for her to be a woman were few and far between.

He touched the brim on his hat. "Nothing more… unless you say otherwise."

Alex tucked out of the kitchen, through the back door of the family's private quarters, carrying a container with two fat slices of chocolate-raspberry cake. He really needed to up his game if he expected her to forgive him for holding back on who he was—and if he wanted a chance in hell of a repeat of the kiss earlier. A kiss that had rocked him back on his boot heels.

Except he had no clue what tack to take with her, and he couldn't figure that out until he got to know her better. If she gave him that chance after tonight. And then there was the whole issue with his grandmother and the stocks…

Hell, this better be some damn good chocolate-raspberry cake.

He stepped out onto the back lanai, lit with brass torches to keep the Texas-sized mosquitoes at bay. He stopped short at the sight of Amie, Stone and Stone's fiancée, Johanna, all having a dessert gathering of their own. Any other time he would have been fine sitting with them. He would have welcomed the chance to smooth the waters, to prove he was genuinely okay with Stone and Johanna as a couple. They were meant to be together. He got that. Nothing he'd ever felt for Johanna came close to the intense emotion coming from his normally reserved cousin.

Amie waved her fork in the air. "Join us," the former beauty pageant queen said. "We've been waiting for you."

A family ambush? Great. "I'm on my way out for the evening. Rain check."

His stubborn twin just smiled and shook her head, her long black ponytail draped over one shoulder. "It can wait." Amie leaned to pull out a chair for him, a gray tabby cat leaping from her lap. "We need to talk."

He considered telling her no—not enough people told Amie no—but whatever she needed to say might have something to do with their grandmother.

Or God forbid, the upcoming wedding.

He set his container full of cake on the tiled table. "Make it quick. I really do have somewhere to be in fifteen minutes."

Stone had an arm draped over his fiancée's chair. "I heard Gran called you in for a special meeting yesterday."

Word traveled fast around here. How much did they know? Not much if they were ganging up on him this way.

"We just had lunch." The last thing he wanted were the details of his "test" going public. That wouldn't be fair to Nina.

"How did Gran look?" Johanna leaned forward, her fingers toying with the diamond horseshoe necklace Mariah had given her. "She went to the doctor today and it wore her out so much she wasn't taking visitors."

Alarm twisted the knot in his gut tighter. "She looked tired. But determined."

The tabby cat bounded off the lanai and Johanna shoved up from her chair to race after it, even though it was Amie's pet—a part of their ongoing battle about indoor vs. outdoor cats.

"So?" Amie licked her fork clean. "What did you and Gram talk about?"

Alex leaned back in his chair, arms crossed over her chest. "Why are you making such a production out of me having lunch with my terminally ill grandmother?"

Amie chewed her bottom lip. "We used to be able to talk about anything. We're twins."

Stone studied Alex through narrowed eyes and said softly, "Are you ditching us because of the wedding?"

Leave it to Stone to throw it out there. At least Johanna was still chasing the cat through the shrubbery. "I've made it clear I'm happy for both of you, and I mean that." Might as well go for broke. "In fact, I'm asking a new friend to come with me to the wedding."

"Who?"

"You don't know her." And Lord, he hoped Nina was still talking to him after tonight. He brushed his thumb along the top of the boxed dessert, his memory filling with that world-rocking kiss.

Stone relaxed back in his seat. "That's good to know. You're just so damn quiet it's tough to get a read off you, and we're all on edge with the new CEO stepping in and Gran's—"

Amie sat up bolt. "Gran gave you your test, didn't she?"

His twin always had been able to read his mind. Most of the time he could see right through her as well, but she had up walls today. He should have noticed before, but he'd been so wrapped up in himself. Damn it. "Amie—"

She stabbed her fork in the cake. "I knew it!" She clapped her hands. "My life is boring as hell these days, so spill. What's your test?"

Nuh-uh. His secret for now. He shoved out of his seat and grabbed the boxed dessert. "If you want to know, ask her. But I suspect if she wanted you two to know, she would have invited you to lunch." He stepped away, determined to share as much as he could with Nina to lessen the chance of this blowing up in his face. "Now if you'll excuse me, I have a date and I'm running late."

He was ten minutes late.

Gripping the arms of the porch rocker, Nina told herself it shouldn't matter. She didn't care. But she did. She'd spent the past hour since her son went to bed showering and changing into white shorts and a silky shirt that showed off her arms and legs. She'd put on makeup and dried her hair out, straightening the curls. All because of one kiss from a guy she would only see for a week.

And then?

What would life be like when she returned to San Antonio with nothing but memories? The thought chilled her.

She shot to her feet and yanked open the front door to go back inside. She refused to appear overeager—or heaven forbid—desperate.

Still, at the sound of his footsteps on her porch steps, her stomach lurched. Damn it. Pressing a hand against her butterfly-filled stomach, she realized she had to regain control. For starters, she had to be honest with herself.

Yes, she was attracted to him. Very. And clearly he was attracted to her too. She hadn't misread that. Plus, he was so different from her silver-spoon-born ex. Alex was down-to-earth, a regular kind of guy.

And he was knocking on her door.

Late.

She yanked a scrunchie off the table and pulled her hair back into a ponytail. If anything happened here, she needed to be back in control—and never let him know he'd rattled her.

She grabbed a magazine for good measure and folded it open as if she'd been casually reading before she opened the door.

Her stomach flipped again.

She stepped outside, a much safer place to be with this man who tempted her.

She took the dessert box from him and sat in the porch rocker, only to realize the pitcher of lemonade she'd prepared earlier gave away how eager she'd been to see him. She was revealing too much of herself too fast. It was time to level the playing field.

"Alex, what did you come to tell me?"

He blinked in surprise. "You sure do cut right to the chase."

"The sooner you tell me, the sooner I can have my dessert." She tried to add levity even as nerves tap danced in her stomach. Did he have to look so hot in jeans and a simple T-shirt, his Stetson resting on his knee?

"I think we've had some miscommunication." His work calloused fingers drummed along the brim of his hat. "And I don't want you to think I misled you."

An option she'd never considered broadsided her, sending a flush of mortification, anger and disappointment through her. "Oh my God. You're married." Her breath hitched as she gasped, inhaling faster and faster. She pressed her hands to her face. "I should have thought to ask. But you're not wearing a ring, and yes, I looked—"

His hand clamped around her wrist. "No, I'm not married." He pulled her hands down and held them in his. "Hell no, actually. Never have been."

"Oh." She laughed nervously, hyperaware of her hands clasped in his. "Are you trying to tell me you're involved with someone else—"

"I'm not with another woman."

Relief flooded her, so much she wanted to launch herself at him for another kiss, one much deeper than the public one earlier. A kiss where she wrapped her arms and body around him, feeling the hard planes of those muscles against her. *Oh. My.*

She needed to rein herself in and find out what he wanted to tell her first. "Not that it matters, since we just met and this isn't anything like…or…um…"

"And before you ask," he said deliberately, shoving aside the table between them and leaning in closer to her, "I'm straight."

His knee brushed hers, the warm denim against her bare skin setting her senses on fire. He'd angled so close she could see the peppering of his late-day beard and her fingers itched to explore the raspy terrain, get to know the masculine feel of him.

She clenched her fingers against temptation. "I wasn't saying… Um, I wasn't… Oh hell. It's okay by me if you're—"

He leaned in closer, his clear blue eyes holding her. "I'm one hundred percent straight and one hundred percent attracted to you."

The night air went hot and humid fast, heavy with innuendo and need. She wanted him. Her body was shouting that truth at her. She wanted to have a wild and passionate fling with this man. No complications. A simple cowboy she would only know this week. A man who was the total opposite of her privileged, spoiled ex-husband. A man she would say farewell to in a week and who could give her sweet memories to carry with her.

She squeezed his hands and said, "Okay, that's nice to know. Very nice."

"And that's why I need to clear something up before you hear from someone else. I'm not a hired hand at the ranch. I'm a McNair. My family owns the place."

# Four

Alex's revelation stunned Nina silent. She snatched her hands from his.

Songs of deep-throated bullfrogs filled the quiet void as she clutched the arms of her porch rocker. Of all the things she'd expected to hear from Alex, this was last on the list. In her experience in New York City and with her ex's family, millionaire bosses didn't run around in dusty jeans.

Betrayal bit like persistent mosquitoes. The sting lingered, itching even as she told herself it shouldn't matter. She thought back, though, and all the signs were there. She'd even heard him called "boss" and let herself hear what she'd wanted. She'd heard of the McNair family but didn't keep track of all their first names.

But the heir? The McNair who oversaw the Hidden Gem Lodge? He wasn't a regular, easygoing cowboy.

And he was now the last sort of man she could consider for a fling. "You're serious? Your family owns the Hidden Gem Ranch?"

"As well as Diamonds in the Rough Jewelers. Yes, my cousins and I have run the family empire together. The Hidden Gem is my domain."

"And the rest of holdings?"

"My cousin Stone was the CEO of Diamonds in the Rough before he founded the camp. My twin sister, Amie, works for the company as a designer. We all own a portion of the portfolio, but our grandmother is the major stockholder."

Squeezing her eyes closed, she let his words sink in. Had she been dense about the "boss" part on purpose because she didn't want to know the truth or had she just been so dazzled by this man she couldn't think straight?

Hook, line and sinker, she'd bought in to the whole cowboy fantasy. Except the fantasy wasn't true at all. Alex was a rich businessman just like her ex. She scratched her arms along those imagined stings. She should go inside and close the door on him and her feelings.

Instead she opened her eyes and asked him, "Why did you mislead me?"

Remorse chased through his eyes, at least she thought it did. She wasn't sure who or what to trust right now, not even herself.

He rested his hand carefully on her wrist, squeezing lightly when she didn't pull away. "You didn't recognize me and it's rare I get to hang out with someone who thinks of me like a regular Joe Shmoe. I like to think I'm a good judge of character, but there are still people out there who only see the money."

His explanation made sense. She wanted to buy in to it and believe she could indulge in a harmless flirtation this week—maybe more. Still, the oversight rankled. "I hear what you're saying, but it still doesn't seem right."

"Does that mean you're not open to more dessert together?" he asked with a slow drawl and a half smile.

Goose bumps rose along her skin, the good kind. Could she just go with the flow here? It wasn't as if he'd claimed to be rich when he wasn't just to impress someone, and she wasn't committing to anything long-term.

"Okay," she conceded. "Since you came clean so quickly, I think I can overlook your allowing me to get the wrong idea about you. If you'd kept the truth from me for weeks or months that would be a different matter."

"Glad to know we've cleared that up."

She eased her wrist away and considered her words carefully, honestly. "To be honest, if you'd spilled the whole 'I'm a McNair' at the start, I probably would have thought you were bragging or feeling entitled."

He shuddered in mock horror. "My grandmother would absolutely not allow that."

She studied him through narrowed eyes, trying to reconcile this new piece of information about him. "You're really not a ranch hand or a foreman? You looked like such a natural."

"I'm a hands-on kind of boss." He clapped a hand to his chest. "And I'm getting the vibe that the boss issue is a problem for you."

"I'm just...unsettled." Her rocking chair squeaked against the wooden porch floor.

He leaned forward, elbows on his knees working his

hat between his hands. "It's nice to have someone to speak with who isn't caught up in the McNair portfolio."

"Sure…"

"But you're still uncomfortable."

"I'm adjusting. You live over there—" she pointed to the mansion lodge "—and I'm more comfortable in a cottage." Although her son had an inheritance that entitled him to so much more. But until she knew what the future held for Cody, she needed to be all the more cautious with his investments in case he couldn't ever work to support himself.

"Yes, I live in the family's half of the lodge. It's sectioned off into private suites." He set his hat on the table and took her hand back again, holding tighter this time. "But that's just brick and mortar, logs and rocks. It's not who we are."

"And who are you, Alex McNair?" she asked, because the image of him as a coddled rich kid didn't fit what she was seeing in him and his hands-on attitude. However, she knew how well a person could hide his real nature. "Why did you feel the need to let me misunderstand your role here for two days?"

He linked their fingers, his eyes glinting in the moonlight. "Meet me for dinner tomorrow night and let's find out about each other."

"My son is here for camp. I'm here for him, not for…" She stumbled on the word and held up their linked hands. "For whatever this is you think we might do this week."

But hadn't she just been considering a fling? Still, she needed it to be her decision, and this wasn't the kind of impulsive choice she'd ever made before.

"You're interested too. We're both adults. What's

wrong with us enjoying each other's company for the week you'll be here?"

Company? Could he mean that word as innocently as it sounded, or was there a hidden innuendo? "Do you see this program as a way to pick up vulnerable women short-term, no strings, and you get to say goodbye at the end of a weeklong camp?"

"Whoa." His eyebrows shot up in shock. "That's a lot to unpack in one sentence. I'll opt for a quick answer, 'no.'"

"No, what?" she asked suspiciously.

"No, I do not make a practice of picking up any kind of vacationer coming to the Hidden Gem. In fact, this is very atypical of me." He rubbed the inside of her wrist with his thumb. "And the last thing I would call you is vulnerable. You come off as a strong woman in charge of her life."

She rolled her eyes. "Flattery. But thanks."

"You're welcome. So, are we having dinner together tomorrow or not? After Cody's asleep of course, and under the care of one of our certified child care providers. There's a dinner boat cruise that's nice, public. No pressure."

He made the offer sound so easy. "I'll think about it."

"Fair enough." His stroke shifted from her wrist to her sensitive palm. "I'll stop by at lunch tomorrow to get your answer."

"At lunch?" She wasn't even sure what she was saying; her brain scrambled at the touch that was somehow so very intimate without being overt. What a time to realize how very little human contact she had in her life anymore.

"I happen to have gotten a sneak peek at the itinerary

from a very reliable source, and the kids are roasting hot dogs for lunch tomorrow at eleven. By noon they'll be in a saddle polishing class. Meet me while your son is settled under the attentive eye of the instructors and we can talk."

"I can't promise he'll let me leave," she said, wanting to turn the tables on him but not sure how yet. "I don't want to risk another meltdown."

"Understood. I can be flexible."

She stared at him with suspicion, chewing her bottom lip.

"What?" Alex asked.

She gave up and blurted, "You're too good to be true. It must be an act."

"Aw, Nina." His hand slid up to cup her face. "People can be genuine."

She couldn't help being enticed by the promise in his eyes. Yet pain from past betrayals welled up over how her husband and her in-laws had so deeply let her down. Worse, how they had let down precious Cody. "They can be. But they usually aren't."

He stroked back her hair, tucking it behind her ear. "Then why are you even considering having dinner with me?"

"I honestly don't know." Her scalp tingled from the light brush of his fingers, his nearness overriding boundaries she thought were firmly in place.

Their gazes met, eyes held. She breathed him in, remembering the feel of his lips on hers.

Would he kiss her again? Because if he did, she wasn't sure she could say no to anything. Her body was on fire from just having him near and a few simple caresses. He angled forward and her heart tripped over itself for a couple of beats.

He passed the dessert box over. "Chocolate-raspberry cake. Enjoy."

His lips skimmed her forehead so briefly, so softly, her breath hitched and then he was gone, jogging down the cabin steps and disappearing in the tree line.

Drawing in a steadying breath, she released it on a shuddering sigh.

No doubt about it, she had a serious willpower problem when it came to this particular cowboy.

The next day at lunchtime, Alex angled through the different stations of children enjoying camp activities from saddle polishing to panning for gold in a sandbox to using hula hoops for lassoing wooden horses. His cousin Stone had told him the activities helped with motor skills and confidence. Cody looked more relaxed today as he worked on cleaning the little saddle resting on stacked bales of hay. Nina sat on a bale beside her child, the sunshine highlighting streaks of gold in her red curls.

He was still pumped over how well the conversation had gone the night before. He'd learned a lot about her, more than she might have intended to let on. She was a wary woman and someone had obviously hurt her in the past, most likely her ex-husband. That would be important to keep in mind if Alex wanted a chance with her. He needed to tread smartly.

Nina Lowery was a tactile woman. He'd gauged her responses carefully, watching her pupils widen with arousal as he'd stroked her wrist, then massaged her palm. Her senses were hungry and he intended to feed them.

Even now her fingers were testing the texture of everything around, flitting from the bale of hay to the stirrups on the saddle.

She hadn't booted him out on his butt. She'd actually given him another chance. He was skating on thin ice with those stocks in play. It wasn't as if they were entering into some long-term relationship. She made it clear she was leaving in a week and her son filled her life.

Knowing that made him want to pamper her all the more while she was here.

Alex stopped behind Nina, resting a hand on her shoulder. "Good afternoon, beautiful."

She shivered under his hand. But in a good way.

He let his touch linger for a second before he stepped over to Cody. "You're doing a great job there, cowboy."

"Make it smooth," he said, stroking.

The instructor, a special ed teacher from a local school who'd been glad for the extra income working at the camp, stepped closer. "Cody's doing a fantastic job. I think he's having fun."

The boy nodded, his hands circling repetitive strokes over the leather, cowboy hat perched on his blond head and protecting him from the sun. "Having fun."

Nina pressed her hand to her chest, emotions obvious in her expressive eyes. "I knew this was a good idea, but I had no clue how amazing equine-assisted learning could be for my son, for all these children."

"I'm glad to hear that. My cousin worked hard searching for professionals to employ. It's important to do this right."

"Well, he succeeded." Nina smiled over her shoulder

at him. "I'm impressed with the way they've combined physical and speech therapy. And they've blended balance, posture, hand-to-eye coordination and communication skills into activities that are fun, making it seem more like play."

He hadn't thought about it that way before, but it made sense. "Horses are herd animals. They seek connections and have a way of communicating, a bond, that goes beyond words."

"I can see that." Her gaze shifted back to her child. "Most of all, I appreciate the self-confidence and self-esteem Cody's finding in these classes in such a short time. It's impressive how the different stations are geared for each child's special need. They've approached Cody with sensory activities, without overloading him." She glanced back at Alex. "But that's not what you came for. Yes."

"What?" he asked, having lost track of the conversation. He was locked in on the sound of her voice and the berry scent of her shampoo.

"Yes, I'll accompany you on the dinner cruise."

"Excellent." He folded his arms over his chest and rocked back on his boot heels.

She looked at him quickly. "You're staying?"

"This camp may be my cousin's endeavor, but it's a part of the McNair empire, happening on McNair lands. I care." He shrugged. "And it's my lunch break. I'd like to spend it with you. If that's okay?"

"Sure," she said, her eyes wide with surprise. "We could take a walk? The counselors encourage parents to step away today. You know that, since you've read the itinerary."

"Guilty as charged."

She laughed softly before kneeling to talk to her son, detailing where she was going and how long she would be gone, as well as what to do if he needed her. Cody nodded without looking away from his task.

"Cody," she said, "I need to know you understand."

He turned toward her and patted her shoulder with a clumsy thump, thump. "Bye, Mom."

Her smile at the simple connection stole the air from Alex's lungs. Then she stood, spreading her hands wide. "Lead the way."

Victory charged through his veins. He cupped her elbow and steered her around the different play stations, the controlled chaos of childish squeals all around them. "After yesterday's incident I thought you might be hesitant to go too far away."

"I feel more confident today than yesterday. So, would you like to show me around the place?"

"Actually, yes, I have something I believe you'll enjoy over by the pool area." He steered her along the path back to the main lodge, tree branches creating a shady canopy. "You'll still be able to see your son, but indulge yourself, as well."

"I don't have my swimsuit with me right now and a swim is on the schedule for later. I'll burn if I go twice."

"That's not what I mean." He gestured to the rustic canvas cabana off to the side of the pool area. "We're here for a couples' massage."

"What?" Her voice squeaked. No kidding, *squeaked*. Nina cleared her throat and tried again. "You must be joking."

"Not at all." He grinned wickedly. "My first choice was to fly you to my favorite restaurant for lunch, but

I knew that would be pushing my luck. So I opted for something here at the resort you would enjoy for an hour."

Horrified that she could have so misread him, she held up a palm and backed away. "We are *not* going to have massages together. God, I can't believe I trusted—"

"Wait." He grabbed her wrist, chuckling softly. "I'm not that clueless. Sorry for teasing you a bit there. If you pull back the curtain, you'll see it's just shoulder massages and a light lunch. Simple. No need to take off our clothes…unless you want, that is."

Her hand lowered. She'd been played, but in a funny way. She crinkled her nose. "You *are* a bad cowboy after all."

He held up his thumb and forefinger. "Just a bit."

Alex escorted her past the luxury pool area. One side of the tall stone fountain fed a waterfall into the shallow end of the pool. A hot tub bubbled invitingly on the other side of the fountain. Her in-laws were wealthy, but in a more steel-and-high-rise resort kind of way. Nina respected the way the McNairs had preserved the look of their place, even if it meant limiting customers. He stopped outside the cabana just as the curtain swept wide.

An older woman stepped out, frail, with short gray hair. Nina backed out of her way, but Alex urged her closer.

"Gran," he said, leaning in to give the older woman a kiss on the cheek.

So this was the indomitable Mariah McNair. The flyers about the camp had included the story of the senior McNairs' romance and how they'd built their dynasty.

Mariah had run the business side while her husband, Jasper, had been more of the artisan. The photo in the welcome packet bore only a passing resemblance to the woman in front of her, a woman whose health was clearly fading. Although her blue eyes were every bit as sharp and vibrant as her grandson's.

"Alex." Mariah smiled, looking frail but relaxed, a sheen of massage oils glinting on her neck. "Introduce me to this lovely lady."

Something flickered in Alex's eyes, but Nina couldn't quite figure out what. "Gran, this is Nina Lowery. Her son, Cody, is here for camp this week. Nina, this is my grandmother Mariah McNair."

The McNair matriarch extended a thin hand, veins spidery and blotched from what appeared to be multiple IVs. "It's a pleasure to meet you, dear. How is your child enjoying HorsePower?"

"Nice to meet you as well, Mrs. McNair." Nina shook the woman's cool hand and found the quick return clasp to be stronger than she would have expected. "My son is having a wonderful time, thank you. I'm amazed at how quickly the camp counselors have put him at ease."

"I'm glad to hear that." Mariah tucked her hands into the pockets of her loose jean jumper. "Leaving a positive legacy is important." She nodded to Nina. "Nice to meet you, dear. You'll have to pardon me, but I'm going to take a nap now." She waved to a younger woman behind her. Her nurse? An assistant?

Mariah walked slowly away, the other woman hovering close to catch her if she stumbled.

The pain in Alex's eyes was tangible.

Nina's parents had been older when she was born, so her memories of her grandparents were dim, but she recalled the grief of losing them, first to dementia, then to death. Nina touched his arm. "It's tough watching those we love grow older."

Alex rubbed the back of his neck. "She has cancer. Terminal."

"Oh no. Alex, I'm so very sorry."

He glanced over at her. "Me too. Nobody is ever okay with losing a loved one, but to be robbed of the years she should have had left is…just…" He rubbed the back of his neck hard. "Ah hell, I think I'm more than ready for that shoulder massage now."

And suddenly it was the most natural thing in the world to tuck her hand in the crook of his arm. "That sounds like an excellent idea. You'll have to pardon me if I'm antsy. I've never had a massage before. Lead the way."

He swept the canvas curtain aside, to reveal a massage table, two massage chairs and a team of massage therapists, just as he'd promised. The grandmotherly pair waited off to the side in simple black scrubs with the Hidden Gem logo on the pocket.

The canvas walls were lined with Aztec drapes. The music of Native American pipes drifted through the speakers and muffled sounds outside. Cooling fans swished overhead.

Nina eyed the massage chairs warily, designed for her to straddle, her back exposed and her face tucked into a doughnut-style cradle. Warily, she smiled at the therapists before sitting. The leather seat was cool, but the cover on the face cradle was cottony smooth with a hint of peppermint oils that opened her sinuses with each inhale.

Alex sat in the chair beside her, face in the cradle,

strong arms on the rests. Her view of him was limited, but then every bit of him intrigued her. It had been so long since she'd had a man in her life, the masculine details made her shivery all over. The dark hair sprinkled on his arms made her want to tease her fingers along his skin.

Clearing her throat, she shifted her eyes away from temptation. A tray of finger foods as well as glasses of green tea and lemon water with straws waited on a long table in front of them.

Never in a million years would she have expected him to come up with this idea. She heard the light rustle of footsteps as each masseuse took her place and whispered softly, "I'm going to start on your shoulders now. Let me know if you require more or less pressure."

At the first firm touch, Nina all but melted into the chair. Wow. Just wow. "Alex, this is…unexpected and incredible."

"Unexpected in what way?" His voice rumbled from beside her.

"That you thought of this and that you're here too, I guess," she answered, the last word turning to a low groan of pleasure. She reached for the lemon water and guided the straw through the face cradle for a sip. The scent of massage oils filled the air. Sage, perhaps?

"A good massage was crucial back in my rodeo days if I wanted to walk the next day. Even once my years on the circuit ended, I found I was still addicted."

She'd seen him on the wild horse that first day, but hadn't thought about his rodeo days. She turned her head enough to sneak a peek, her eyes roving over his body, envisioning those strong thighs gripping resistant bulls. She also thought of the kinds of falls he must have taken. He'd mentioned broken bones and she couldn't hide a wince at the pain he'd felt. She noticed a tiny scar peeking out of his hairline along his temple. Had he gotten that from a bad spill?

The masseuse gently guided her face back into the padded cradle of the chair and kneaded the tight tendons along her neck. The stress of so many weeks flowed down her spine and away from her body. "This really is heavenly and just what I needed." Her mind went a little fuzzy with relaxation, and her eyes slid closed, voice getting softer with each word. "Funny how I never thought about how little actual physical contact I have in my life these days. Not even hugs…"

Every deep breath she drew filled her with the scent of peppermint, sage and Alex's aftershave. The relaxing massage, the tempting smells and images of this oh-so-physical man made her warm with pleasure.

There was something intimate about sharing this experience together, yet safe because nothing more could happen while they were being massaged. But during the dinner cruise tonight? And afterward?

She'd already broken so many personal rules when it came to this man. How much further could he entice her to go?

# Five

Alex knocked on the cabin door, a bouquet of wild-flowers in his hand, wrapped in paper and tied with some kind of string the lodge gift shop had called raffia. He'd even written a card for her, including a poem he'd found in French about a beautiful woman. He wanted to make the flowers special, more personal.

If ever a woman needed some pampering, it was Nina.

That instant during the massage when she'd com-mented on how rarely she was touched had been a seri-ous gut check moment of all the things she was missing in her life, down to the simplest—touches. He'd wit-nessed firsthand how hard she worked for her son, how she'd restructured her whole life to be his first and fierc-est advocate all on her own. Alex burned with the need to make her life easier.

At the same time, all this made him nervous after Johanna's rejection. And now with Nina, it meant even more that things go well. He wanted to get this right, all the way down to a French poem.

The door opened and he felt the wind knocked clear out of him as surely as if he'd been thrown off a bull. "You look…amazing."

His eyes swept over her, her red curls gathered up into a loose bunch on top of her head, one curl trailing down her cheek. She wore a simple black wraparound dress that brushed the top of her knees. He recognized the long gold chain from the ranch's jewelry store. His pulse ramped up at the thought of her going to extra trouble to prepare for their date.

"It's nothing fancy. I didn't pack with a dinner cruise in mind." She toyed with the link chain, stepping back.

"If this is simple, I'm not sure my heart can take anything more." Truth.

"Save the bull for the rodeo ring." She laughed, taking the flowers from him and burying her face in the bouquet. "Thank you, they're lovely. I'll put them in water while I get my shoes. Sorry I'm not ready yet, but you are early," she called over her shoulder as she walked to the kitchen.

His eyes held on the gentle sway of her hips. He ached to walk up behind her and brush a kiss along the vulnerable curve of her neck.

"I came early to introduce you to the sitter, who ought to be here in just a minute. I thought it would be best if I brought her by to spend time with Cody before he goes to sleep, in case he wakes up while you're gone." He peered out the window to check for the caregiver, then sat beside Cody at the kitchen table where the boy drew using an iPad program.

His little fingers flew across the screen tracing lines, picking and shading with different colors. His concentration was so intense his wiry body didn't move other than for his tiny fingertips. He wore cowboy PJs, and his blond hair was spiky wet from a bath.

Nina turned on the faucet and filled a hammered metal pitcher with water, the flowers already tucked inside. "That's very thoughtful—and insightful. Thank you. I had planned to speak with her, of course, but having Cody meet her is even better. Is she one of the camp counselors?"

Alex glanced out the window again and stood to get the door for their guest. "Actually I brought the best babysitter I know. The one I trust above all others." He tugged the door open and waved her inside. "This is my sister, Amie."

The impulse to ask Amie had surprised him. His sister had merely hummed knowingly, seeing right through him. But she hadn't pumped him for information about the date. She'd merely asked what time.

His twin rushed into the cabin in a swirl of perfume and some long shirt-dress thing. Funny how she always said she hated the beauty pageant days yet she still glammed up like the runway queen she'd once been.

She hugged her brother quickly before walking to Nina standing stunned at the sink. "I'm Amethyst—Amie. Nice to meet you, Nina." She approached Cody more slowly, carefully, aware and sensitive. "And this must be Cody."

Nina set the pitcher in the middle of the table and

tucked the card into her purse. "My goodness, thank you for coming. I'm sorry if your brother pressured you."

"Not at all. I love kids. Although I feel robbed not to get more time with Cody, since he'll be going to sleep soon." Amie angled her head to look at his drawing.

Nina pulled a list from the counter. "I expected to have him in bed before you arrived, but I wrote down my contact info and all his favorite soothers. He has a special weighted blanket—puffy blue—for bedtime or watching TV. It's a sensory issue."

Amie took the list and placed it on the table in plain sight. "Weighted blanket. Got it." She tucked into the chair beside Cody slowly, adjusting her whirlwind demeanor. She slipped a boho bag off her shoulder and set it gently on the table. "Cody, do you like cats? I'm the cat lady around here."

"Cats?" he asked without looking up from his art project that was taking shape into a herd of horses racing in a circle around a little boy. "How many?"

"I have four at home." She held up four fingers, then pushed down two fingers, talking as if he were looking at her. "But I brought two itty-bitty kittens with me."

Cody looked to the side, toward her but not at her. Nina smiled and Alex slid an arm around her waist, whispering in her ear, "I told you she's great with kids."

Amie carefully lifted two young kittens from her boho bag. The orange tabbies wore little sweaters made of socks and were cradled in a lined box. "They stay warm by keeping close to me. These are strays we found in the barn. Actually there were four. Johanna is bottle-feeding two and I'm bottle-feeding the other two."

She pulled out a couple of tiny bottles and raised her

perfectly plucked eyebrows expectantly as she waited for his response.

"Oh," Cody gasped, rocking forward on the bench for a closer look. "Kittens? I like kittens. Cat lady has kittens and I like kittens."

Alex chuckled. "Does Stone know he's taking bottle-fed kittens on his honeymoon this weekend?"

Amie glanced up, her long black braid swinging. "They'll be weaned by then, silly. I'll have the four until they get back."

Nina leaned in to sweep a finger down each fuzzy orange back. "Will you keep them?"

"I'm not that much of a crazy cat lady. I already have four of my own." Amie cradled one in her hand and positioned the mini bottle to its mouth. "We'll get them spayed and neutered and find them good homes."

Cody sat cross-legged on his chair, the rocking barely discernible as he ran one finger along a kitten's back just as his mother had done. "So soft."

Nina cautioned, "Be careful, Cody. Gentle."

Amie scooted closer. "Would you like to feed her? I'll hold the kitten and you hold the bottle."

"Yes, yes, yes." He held out his hand, wriggling his fingers.

"Cody," Nina said. "I'll stay to tuck you in."

"Feeding the kittens. I want to feed the kittens. Don't wanna go to bed yet." His words dwindled as he took the bottle, his eyes focused on holding the bottle to the kitten's mouth. "Then gonna draw pictures of kitties."

Nina touched the top of her son's head lightly, smiling her thanks to Amie. "That sounds wonderful, Cody. You're going to have a great time with Alex's sister."

Alex's sigh of relief mixed right in with Nina's. Her

body relaxed as tangibly as earlier when they'd gotten massages. The tension drained from him, as well. Bringing his sister here had been the right call. Nina and her son fit with his family a way that boggled his mind. Things were happening fast with Nina, and he had no desire to slow down, just keep going with the ride. He would deal with his grandmother's test later.

For tonight, he would have Nina all to himself.

Nina's toes curled in her simple gold sandals as she sipped a glass of merlot on the paddle boat dinner cruise. She had a closet full of lovely dresses from her New York City days, but they were all back at her house. Yet Alex's heated looks made her feel attractive.

Alive. Even in the simple way they sat in silence now, enjoying their meal under the stars. She swirled the wine in the glass, then set it back on the table as the paddle boat made its lazy way down the Trinity River, lights twinkling from houses along the shore. The dinner cruise had tables inside and outside. But she'd opted for the moonlight and a filet mignon, the evening so different from her daily life. She loved her son, but this was such a treat after so many peanut butter sandwiches.

Things had felt so easy these past two days. Exciting and restful all at once. Alex had a slow swagger approach to life that seemed to accomplish so much more than anyone else racing around.

His twin sister had that same gift, but with a Bohemian flair instead of the down-to-earth cowboy ways of her brother. Nina had been stunned to see Amie show up in a sparkly long shirt worn as a dress along with thousands of dollars' worth of bracelets and draped necklaces. She didn't look much like a babysitter. But she'd brought orphaned kittens, teaching Cody to connect with other living beings.

There was something unique, something special about this family. And they were drawing Nina in despite the wealth and privilege, despite all the things she'd swore wouldn't be a part of her life again.

The engine roared, shifting gears as the paddle boat angled around a bend in the river. The tables were bolted to the floor, even though the glide across the water was smooth. Electric sconces flickered like candlelight in the centerpieces. Seating was limited, exclusive, only a couple of dozen tables total. Each corner offered privacy and intimacy, with the strain of live music muffling other conversation. How many proposals had been made on this riverboat?

And where had that thought come from?

She searched for something benign to say so her thoughts would stop wandering crazy paths. "Your sister is nice. You two appear to be close."

"Very close. We're twins."

The slap of the water against the hull mixed with the ragtime tunes from the musicians.

"Right, of course there's a special bond between the two of you." She tore at a roll, pinching off a bite. "Where are your parents? I haven't seen them around."

His face neutral, he answered, "They travel a lot. My father is a trust fund baby through and through. He has an office and little responsibility. My mom enjoys the finer things in life."

"I thought perhaps your father had retired, since you and your cousin run things."

Alex choked on his water. "The notion of putting my father in charge of a lemonade stand is scary." He shuddered, setting his glass back on the table. "You'll see them when they come for the wedding."

She set her roll down carefully. "Excuse me?"

"At Stone and Johanna's wedding this weekend. My parents are flying in." He smiled darkly. "They're big on showing up for the parties and flying away to the next vacation when things are tough."

She reached for his hand to offer comfort, but he leaned back and took his drink again in a not too subtle avoidance of sympathy. That simple gesture tugged at her heart even more than his words.

He drained the rest of his wine and set his glass down again. "Do you have any siblings?"

She considered pushing the point, then shook her head. "I'm an only child with no cousins." She'd hoped to have a big family of her own, with lots of siblings for Cody. "My parents had me late in life. They'd given up on ever having a child and wow, I surprised them. I know they love me, but they had such a deep routine by the time I came along, I definitely upset the apple cart—"

She stopped short as a waiter silently tucked in to refill their wineglasses before slipping away.

Alex turned the crystal goblet on the table. "You mentioned they'd retired to Arizona. I'm sorry they aren't here for you now as you parent alone. The support of family would make life easier for you."

"We're doing fine on our own." How strange that she and Alex had more in common than she'd thought. Both raised by distant parents who didn't quite know what to do with their kids. But there was so much more about him she didn't understand and so little time for this fling of hers.

"What?" he asked, the clink of silverware echoing from the next table. "Do I have food in my teeth?"

"Sorry to stare." She laughed softly, the wine and night air loosening her inhibitions enough to admit, "I'm just pensive tonight. I'm curious. Why are you going to all this trouble to romance me when I'm leaving so soon? I believe you when you say you don't use the camp for easy pickups. So what's going on here?"

"Is there something wrong with wanting to spend time with you?" Her charmer cowboy had returned; the storm clouds in his eyes from mentions of his parents long gone. "I enjoy talking to you and honest to God, it's been a while since I've found someone who piqued my interest."

"And that's all there is to it?" She leaned both elbows on the table, resting her chin in her hands while she searched for answers in his blue eyes…

And within herself, as well.

He met her gaze dead-on. "I'm attracted to you. I don't think I'm wrong in believing you feel the same. So we're dating. We have limited time together, so I'm cramming a lot of dates into one week."

"That's true." The wind stirred, carrying the strains of music and hints of lovebird conversations from a couple of tables over.

He toyed with her hand doing that tempting little move massaging her palm. "And for two of those evenings I'm already committed to attending my cousin's rehearsal dinner and wedding. I'm hoping you'll be my date for both events."

In spite of the warm summer evening, her skin chilled. "Is that what this romance is all about? Winning me over so you'll have a date for the wedding?"

"No, God. Of course not," he answered with unde-niable sincerity. "I would have asked you out this week regardless."

She wanted to believe him, but then she'd believed her husband right up to the moment he rejected their child and walked out the door. "You can be honest with me. I prefer to know the truth."

"I am being honest about wanting to ask you out." He hesitated, jazz filling the silence until he continued. "And yes, it'll be nice to have you there to ease any awkwardness in my family. I briefly dated the bride."

"Ouch." Nina winced. "That could be uncomfort-able to say the least."

He waved a hand. "Stone, Johanna and I have all made peace about this. I just don't want others assum-ing things that aren't true. Any feelings I had for her were passing and are over."

She saw only honesty in his eyes, his words ringing true. And even if he did still carry a bit of a torch for the bride, shouldn't that be a relief? It would make this week less complicated. Nina could have her romantic fling with no worries of entanglement.

So, why did she still feel a slight twinge of jealousy? Pride urged her to make light of it. "If you need me as a shield of sorts, you don't have to go to all of this trouble. Just say so and I'll be your amorous date. I'll pick up an incredibly sexy dress and look adoringly into your eyes."

"Nina, stop." He held her hand firmly and stared straight into her eyes. "I want to be here with you. And I want you to be my date for the rehearsal party and wedding because I enjoy your company."

She scrunched her nose. "Forget I said anything. Let's talk about something else."

"No, I need to be honest about this and I need for you to believe me."

"Good, because honesty is the most important thing to me."

He glanced down for an instant before meeting her eyes again. "If there wasn't wedding, I would still be asking you out, pursuing the hell out of you, because you are a fascinating woman. And please, please find that incredibly sexy dress. Except it will be me and the other men there staring at you." He lifted her hand and kissed her knuckles. "Now, would you like to dance before they serve dessert?"

"Yes, I would like that very much." She squeezed his hand and stood, letting the music tug her along with his words. Because all those jealous thoughts and wondering what he might be up to didn't matter. Tonight was a rare treat. To be out and romanced.

The band segued into a slow song as if anticipating her preference...her need. The small dance floor already held four other couples, but everyone was in their own private world. She'd thought she had that with Warren. God, she'd been so wrong.

Shaking off thoughts of her ex, she stepped into Alex's arms, determined to enjoy the night and stop thinking about the future. The heat of his palm on her back urged her closer, until her breasts skimmed his chest. He tucked her near him, resting his chin against her temple, the rasp of his late-day beard perfectly intimate against her skin.

No words were needed and in fact, she didn't want to speak. She soaked up the manly sensation that had been so lacking in her life for so long, the scent of Alex's aftershave mixing with a hint of musk. The strong play of his muscles under her hands as they danced. Her body flamed to life. Embers so long buried she'd assumed them cold and dead were stoked to life, igniting a passion. And not just for any man. She wanted Alex. This week was her only time with Alex McNair, and she should make the most of it.

The absolute most.

Something had shifted in Nina between the main course and dessert. She'd become…intense. All he'd done was ask her to his cousin's wedding. She hadn't even read the French poem yet. She'd tucked it in her purse, and as far as he could tell, she hadn't taken it back out.

He walked silently beside her up the flagstone walkway to her cabin. She hummed the music from the boat but didn't speak and wasn't sure where they were headed next. Especially after that out-of-the-blue outburst of hers offering to be his arm candy at his cousin's wedding.

Her speech would be burned in his memories as one of his favorite moments in life. Ever. She was amazing. Sexy and funny. Loyal. They hadn't known each other long, but in two days she'd turned his world upside down until he couldn't stop thinking about her.

Although there was still the issue of her son's stocks. She didn't even appear to know Cody had them or she would have said something. Her not knowing would only make it harder for him to offer to buy them.

Alex was a businessman, a damn good one. He always had a plan—everything from a five-year plan down to a plan for the day. But with Nina, he'd been flying by the seat of his pants without even reins to hold on to. He wasn't normally impulsive, but Nina made him want to forge ahead, throwing away rationales and agendas. He would figure out the issue of his grandmother's quest later. It would all come together. It had to.

The creak of the rocking chair sliced through the night sounds. His sister sat on the front porch under the outdoor light.

The former beauty pageant queen spread her hands. "Welcome home. You should have stayed out later." She carefully tucked her padded box with kittens back into her boho bag. Long fingers that had once played the piano to accompany her singing now crafted high-end jewelry. "Cody was an angel. We fed the kittens. Then he drew pictures of them. There's one for you on the counter, and I hope you don't mind that I kept one for myself. He's a regular little Picasso."

Nina grabbed the banister and walked up the steps. "Surely it wasn't that easy."

"He woke up once, asked for a glass of water. He really wanted to feed the kittens again." She adjusted her back, bracelets jingling. "I didn't think you would mind, so I let him, and then he went right back to sleep. We had fun. Truly."

Nina took Amie's hands. "I can't thank you enough for making the evening special for him too. Change is difficult for him, but you made the night magical with your kittens. I wish I'd thought to take a picture."

"Don't worry. We took tons of selfies. I'll forward them to you. I mean it when I say I enjoyed myself. I'll bring the kittens by again." She tipped her head to the side. "I would like to do a sketch of him, if that's okay with you."

"Of course."

"Good. It's a plan. I have this week off work for the wedding, so I'll see you around." Amie swept in a swirl of elegance. "Good night, you two. I'm going to head back before I turn into a pumpkin."

His sister patted him on the face as she walked down the steps, brushing aside his thanks before she wound her way back to the main house.

He turned to Nina to ask if she and Cody would go on a ride with him tomorrow, but before he could speak, she kissed him. Not just a quick kiss or peck on the cheek. She wrapped her arms around his neck and pressed flush against him. Her mouth parting, welcoming and seeking. And he damn well wasn't saying no.

Moving her closer, taking in the give of her soft curves, he deepened the kiss, sweeping his tongue against hers. Tasting and exploring. Wanting. The chemistry between them had been explosive from the first moment he'd laid eyes on her. With Nina, he was alive in the moment—the future be damned.

A throaty moan of pleasure vibrated through her into him. This kiss was the kind a couple shared when there was going to be more. But while he'd known things were moving fast between them, he hadn't expected to move this quickly. Her hands slid over his shoulders, digging into his shirt, sliding lower.

Sweeping back her hair, he kissed along her jaw. "This is not the reaction I expected."

"Good." Her head fell back to give him freer access, the gold links of her delicate necklace glinting in the porch light against her pale skin. "The last thing I ever want to be is predictable."

He trailed one finger along the path of those gold links, lower down her throat and collarbone, all the way to the curve of her breast. A slow shiver went through her, and it was all he could do not to put his mouth on the leaping pulse at the base of her throat.

"You're so incredible. You damn near bring me to my knees." Even if he hadn't come close to understanding her yet... God, how he wanted to.

She toyed with the top button of his shirt, as breathless from the touches as he was. "What if I said I don't care about your money and I don't have room in my life for another person? But I'm okay with having a fling this week?"

His body shouted hell yes, but his brain insisted this was too good to be true. And what if he wanted more than a week? How had she turned the tables on him so quickly? "You're really propositioning me? For the week only?"

"You may not believe me, but I don't do this kind of thing often." She nibbled her bottom lip. "But there's chemistry between us. With this window of time away from the rest of the world, it seems meant to be. For now."

He looked for doubt or hesitation in her green eyes and found fire instead. Pure fire. "When do you propose we start this fling?"

She wriggled closer, backing him toward the cabin door. "What about now?"

# Six

She was actually doing this. Having her first official fling.

Sure, she'd been married, but she'd dated her husband for nearly a year before sleeping with him and he'd been her first. Her only. Even the thought of Warren threatened to freeze her with nerves, so she pushed away those memories. Nothing would steal this opportunity from her. This was a fantasy getaway with a fantasy-worthy man, a slice of time away from the real world. She deserved this. Needed it, even, with a physical ache she hadn't known was there until Alex made her feel all that she was missing.

Nina reached behind her to fumble for the cabin door without ending the kiss. She was an adult with few chances to feel like a woman anymore. Right now, with Alex's hands cupping her bottom, she wasn't sure she'd ever felt like this before.

He nibbled her bottom lip. "I'll get that."

Before he finished the sentence, he'd swung the door wide, his hands returning fast to her bottom. He lifted her until her feet dangled and he walked her across the threshold. One step at a time, he moved deeper into the room until the backs of her thighs hit the sofa and he lowered her, leaning with her and stretching out over her. All of it so fluid they never broke contact. Her nerves hummed with arousal from the weight of him. His hands tangled in her hair as he kissed her deeply, thoroughly.

Her body ached for release. Not just release, because she could take care of that alone, but the completion that came from sex. From a man's hands on her body. From this man's hands.

He angled up onto his elbows, murmuring against her neck. "I don't want to crush you."

Her fingers skittered down his back, tugging his shirt from his pants. "I like the feel of you on top of me."

In particular the warm press of his muscular thigh between her legs. She arched her hips ever so slightly. Pleasure rippled through her.

Alex picked up on the nuance and nudged closer. "And I like being here."

She purred her approval against his mouth. "Thank you for the flowers."

The wildflowers' sweet perfume mingled with the rustic air of the log cabin. And there was that note she'd never gotten to read. What had he written to her?

Alex stroked her hair back from her face. "You deserve more pampering."

"You've pampered me to bits today."

"I have plans for tomorrow, if you're game."

"Let's focus on the right now."

"And what is it you need, Nina?"

"More of this." She skimmed her mouth over his. "And this…" She tucked her hands into the waistband of his slacks. "And this…"

She writhed against his leg, the pressure giving the perfect stimulation to the aching bundle of nerves. His growl of appreciation sent molten desire pumping through her veins. She met him kiss for kiss, stroke for stroke, exploring the feel of his hard-muscled body. She kept waiting for him to steer them toward the bedroom, but he seemed content to make out—with some seriously heavy petting. His hand smoothed aside the top to her wraparound dress, his fingers tucking inside her bra. The rasp of his work-roughened fingertips sent sparks shimmering along her skin, her nipples pulling tight.

She couldn't remember how long it had been since she indulged in just old-fashioned necking. He was stroking her to a fever pitch, her body moving restlessly under him.

"Alex," she whispered, "let's move to the bedroom."

Or to the spa tub in her bathroom. Her imagination took flight, the naked visions in her mind bringing her closer to the edge. Still, Alex didn't move to leave the sofa. In fact, his head dipped and he captured her nipple in his mouth, rolling it with his tongue and teasing gently with his teeth. Her back arched into the sensation, pressing her more firmly against his leg.

Bunching the hem of her dress in his hand, Alex skimmed against her panties. She thought about her mismatched bra and undies, wishing she'd indulged in some new lingerie at the gift shop instead of a necklace.

Then she felt the full attention of his eyes focused on her as he dipped inside her panties. The intensity in his eyes relayed how much he wanted to make this happen for her. That care aroused her every bit as much as his skilled fingers stroking her until she couldn't hold back the orgasm exploding inside her. She bit her lip to hold back her cries of completion as he caressed every last aftershock from her. With a final shiver, she sagged back against the leather sofa, her body melting into the cushions with the bliss of completion.

Her breath came in ragged gasps and she dimly registered him smoothing her clothes back into place. Then he stood and cool air washed over her. She elbowed upward and he touched her shoulder lightly.

"Shhh, just relax." He kissed her on the forehead, pulled the unopened card out of her purse and set it beside the pitcher of flowers on the coffee table. "Good night, Nina. Lock up after me."

Before she could collect her stunned thoughts, he'd left. Shock chilled the pleasure as she lay on the sofa, her arms sprawled and one leg dangling off the side. What the hell had just happened?

She gathered her dress together and sat upright. Alex was definitely the most confusing man she'd ever encountered. Not that she was doing any good at understanding herself these days either.

She swept aside her tousled curls and reached for the card on the coffee table. She popped the seal and withdrew a folded piece of paper, not a card at all. But a poem written in French. Her eyes scanned and translated…the romantic words about an ode to a beautiful woman.

Her fingers crimpled the edges of the paper as the words soaked into her brain.

She'd just convinced herself to have her very first fling. But she'd indulged with a gentleman bent on romancing her.

Walking away from Nina took every ounce of self-discipline Alex possessed. But the night had spun out of control and he needed time and distance to plan his next move with her.

He jogged down her porch steps, putting space between him and the mind-blowing image of her sated on the sofa. Yes, he wanted her—so damn much his teeth hurt—but he hadn't expected her to offer a fling. And he certainly hadn't expected to start caring about her and her son. Ducking under a low branch, he made faster tracks through the trees on his way back to the lodge, glowing just ahead.

Pursuing a relationship with Nina was a train wreck in the making. Eventually she would find out about his pursuit of the shares in Cody's trust fund—the details of which his grandmother had emailed to him this afternoon. So much so he felt like a damn financial voyeur. His grandmother could lose the company if he told Nina now and she walked away.

It wasn't just about keeping the ranch for himself. He would do anything to make Gran's final days peaceful. Now he'd put all that at risk by starting a relationship with Nina. And he couldn't deny the truth. He didn't regret pursuing her, not for a second, and he had no intention of stopping.

He halted midstride, his eyes narrowing. Turning on his boot heels, away from the house, he walked toward the stables instead. With luck a midnight ride would burn off the steam building inside him.

Because the next time he faced Nina, he needed to be absolutely calm and in control of himself.

"Horse rides, Mama. Horse rides," Cody chanted the whole way from lunch to the afternoon activity, clutching Nina's hand so tightly her fingers went numb.

The sun baked the ground dry as she led Cody from the picnic area to the stables. Nina's nerves were shot. She hadn't slept the night before, tossing and turning, wondering why Alex had walked away from her. She hadn't heard from him or seen him all morning. She wondered if they were still on for their plans he'd mentioned the night before. He'd said he wanted to see her and she'd agreed.

She absently chewed her already short nails. Her son had been wound like a top since he woke up. For the past few days they'd ridden ponies and worked on their equine skills. Today, he would ride a larger horse.

Nina's stomach was full of butterflies. She knew he was ready, but still. She tried not to let her own fear of horses taint the experience for him.

As she neared the corral, children clustered around their counselors, each camper wearing a different color shirt according to the group. Cody broke free and raced to his teacher. His confidence was already growing. And his joy. Even an inkling of joy from her pensive son was pure shimmering gold.

Parents had been encouraged to step back today, so Nina stopped by the split-rail fence.

"Hello, Nina?" Amie's voice called to her through the masses.

Nina searched the faces down the line along the rail. She angled and walked past other parents until she reached Alex's sister, standing with another woman. Part of Nina winced at the possibility Amie might ask about the date, but another part of her insisted this was an opportunity to learn more about Alex. And hopefully figure out her own feelings in the process.

"Hello," Nina said. "Thank you again for babysitting last night."

"My pleasure, truly." Amie set her sketch pad on the corral railing and hooked arms with the other woman. "Let me introduce you to Johanna Fletcher, soon to be Johanna McNair. You wouldn't know she's supposed to be the pampered bride. She insists on working in the stables right up to the day before the wedding. Johanna, this is Nina Lowery. Her son is that adorable little blond-haired camper over there—the one I told you I want to draw a sketch of today."

Nina stifled a gasp as she realized this was the woman Alex had mentioned briefly dating. Curiosity and something greener prompted Nina to study the leggy, down-to-earth woman. Johanna and Amie were total opposites, yet there was a scrubbed-clean glamor to Johanna in her frayed jeans, worn boots and baggy T-shirt.

Johanna laughed, swishing her blond braid over her shoulder. "The substitute vet tech doesn't arrive until then. I'm here for my animals. Stone knows that."

Nina shook off the jealous thoughts and searched for something to say. "This camp you and your fiancé have started is simply amazing."

Johanna's smile beamed. "We both consider ourselves lucky to have the means and opportunity to make a difference for children."

"Well, you certainly have made a difference for Cody. I'm grateful your staff was able to fit us in at the last minute when I called on Wednesday."

Johanna's forehead creased for a moment before she smiled again, stepping back. "Well, I should get to work. Amie, we can talk about the extra guests later." She waved quickly. "Nice to meet you, Nina."

Nina waited until the vet tech was out of sight before turning to Amie. "Did I say something wrong?"

"Not at all. I think she was just confused over how you got into the camp last week. There's usually a long waiting list."

"Oh, good, I was afraid I'd made things awkward, since she dated Alex."

Amie arched a perfectly plucked eyebrow. "You know about that? Not many do."

"He mentioned it to me."

"How interesting that he told you." Amie leaned back against the rail, her turquoise and pewter necklace glinting in the afternoon sun. "She and Alex went out once, purely platonic, though, because she was still on the rebound from a breakup with Stone. She also didn't want to cause trouble between the cousins. And truth be told, she never really got over the crush she had on Stone. Clearly."

"Crush?"

"She practically grew up here. Her father was the stable vet tech before her. Johanna has loved Stone for as long as I can remember. Sometimes romance happens slowly over years." Amie toyed with her turquoise necklace, her eyes pensive. "And sometimes that connection happens in an instant."

"My parents were the love-since-childhood sort." She remembered her plan to find out more about Alex and asked, "What about yours?"

Amie's smile went tight. "They met in college. My mother always said the second she met him, she knew he would be hers. My father was considered a catch and my mom is quite competitive."

How did a person respond diplomatically to that? "From the tone of your voice, I take it to mean competitive isn't a good thing."

"Not in her case." She snorted inelegantly. "She may truly love Dad, but she sure loves his money. It's weird to think how she likes the wealth but carries this huge chip on her shoulder, insecure from feeling that she never accomplished anything on her own. So she pushed us to find the success she felt she'd been cheated out of by living the life as a cossetted queen with a sugar daddy."

Whoa. Nina rocked back on her boot heels. "That's… unfortunate."

"Don't feel sorry for her. You haven't met my mom." Amie crossed her feet at the ankles, her brown riding boots immaculate. "Have you ever watched that reality show series about babies in beauty pageants? That was my life. From the beaded gowns to the questionably adult dance routines to pixie stix poured into cola to keep me awake at nap time."

"For real?"

"I have shelves of tiaras and trophies to prove it." She straightened and struck a quick beauty queen pose. "I

CATHERINE MANN                                               101

even have a special row for my fake teeth she had made when my baby teeth fell out."

There was something sad about not enjoying the precious gap-toothed smile of an innocent child. "It doesn't sound like you were on board with those plans."

"I'm only marginally messed up by her stage mom ways." Amie waved aside Nina's concern. "I went to college and double-majored in art and business. I wasn't summa cum laude, but I finished on time. I have a job. Alex is the one who had it far tougher than I did."

Nina's stomach clenched. "What do you mean?"

Amie glanced into the corral where children were being lifted onto placid mares and ponies. "Have you ever watched the rodeo circuit? It was sure nothing like that. Before the age of eighteen, my brother had broken more bones than an adult football player. Or at least it seemed that way. And to keep our parents happy, he kept climbing right back on again."

Nina pressed a hand to her tight throat, thinking about her son's joy today and envisioning Alex as a child being pushed by adults. "I'm so sorry. For both of you."

"Don't be." Amie shrugged an elegant shoulder dismissively. "We didn't starve. We weren't abused. We lived a life of privilege and accolades. I just wanted you to understand why sometimes we're a little bit off when it comes to relationships and expressing our feelings."

Nina wasn't sure what to say in response, looking around nervously, seeing a pigtailed girl with muscular dystrophy benefitting from the rhythm of the dun-colored pony she rode. The girl smiled from the saddle, her eyes dancing with each step of the pudgy pony. An older boy missing an arm worked on his balance riding a surefooted mare. Kicking up a steady stream of clay, the blue roan mare walked around the pen, seemingly sensitive to the needs of the boy.

Alex and his sister downplayed themselves and their lives, but this family clearly worked to use their money and power for good. And this clearly good woman was sharing so much about herself and their family. Nina felt like a fraud.

"Alex and I have only known each other for a few days," Nina blurted out.

"Right." Amie picked up her sketch pad off the rail and backed away one poised step at a time. "Like I said, some fall faster than others." With a wave, she spun away, sketch pad under her arm.

Nerves clustered in Nina's stomach over the mention of relationships and commitments. No surprise, since her ex had trounced her ability to trust. This was supposed to be a fling.

And yet she couldn't help searching the grounds for a glimpse of him.

A rush of warm air over her neck gave her only an instant's warning before…

"Good afternoon, beautiful."

Alex braced his hands on Nina's waist as she turned fast to face him. Waiting to touch her again had made for a torturous twelve hours. He'd always considered himself a methodical man, but in a few short days this woman had flipped his world upside down.

His late-night ride hadn't helped him find any answers for balancing his grandmother's request and his driving desire to pursue Nina for more than just one night. Until he came up with the right approach for ad-

dressing the stock purchase, he wanted to do everything in his power to win her over, not just physically.

Her eyes were wary as she met his. "Thank you. I
wondered where you were this morning."

"Taking care of business for the wedding." He
stroked her waist lightly. "Now I have a couple of hours
this afternoon free to spend with you."

Her chin went up. "If you think we're just going to
pick up where we left off after you walked out without—"

He tapped her lips. "I have other plans for the day
and hope you're amenable."

"To what?" she asked warily.

"A tour of the McNair property while your son's
busy with his lessons." Maybe then she would understand how important the ranch was to him, and then
she would understand how this legacy compelled him.
"Amie is staying nearby in case Cody needs anything.
She said it's the perfect opportunity to sketch him."

"You've thought of everything." She looked around.
"Are we going on a drive?"

He shook his head slowly. "Your son is riding today.
I think he would be proud to see his mom give it a go,
as well."

Her nose crinkled. "You're playing dirty pool, using
guilt on me.

"Is it working? Because your chariot awaits, beautiful lady." He stepped aside, gesturing behind him.

Her eyes went to the large bay-and-white horse behind him. The gelding was tied to a rail post swishing
his tail from side to side. Nina studied the horse in-
credulously.

"Do you actually expect me to ride him?" Her voice

squeaked, her wide eyes still fixed on the bay. Not surprisingly, the gelding's tack was gorgeous. The light tan saddle contained an elegant inlaid depiction of a horse herd at a full-out gallop. The cantle, skirt and fender were plated with etched silver, complementing the plates of silver ornamentation on the bridle. Alex and the bay looked like a scene from an old Western movie. Yippee-ki-yay indeed.

"I thought we could both ride together and that would make you feel more secure in the saddle." Had he pushed too hard? It had seemed like a good idea this morning.

She glanced over at her son, then back at the horse. The gelding was calm enough that Nina didn't run screaming in the other direction.

Chewing her lip, she nodded tightly. "Okay, sure. If Cody can conquer his fears to step out in public, I can do this."

Alex slid his hand behind her neck. "Nina, you are so damn incredible."

"Yeah, yeah, whatever." She grabbed his arms and tugged him toward the horse. "Now hurry up before I change my mind."

With a cowboy whoop, he grasped her waist and lifted her over the split-rail fence. He took his time setting her on her feet again, letting her slide down the length of his body. The press of her soft curves and the swing of her red wavy curls had his body on fire in an instant. He didn't regret walking away last night, but he sure as hell looked forward to the day he wouldn't have to.

"Nina, this is Zircon. He's an American paint." He stroked the white horse with brown markings. Zircon's

nearly solid brown face was interrupted by a long cres-
cent stripe below his right eye. Zircon shook his head,
a rumble that radiated all the way to his tail. He looked
lazily at Alex, tongue hanging out of the right side of
his mouth. "He's solid and sweet as you can tell. I trust
him with a second rider, but we'll keep it short for him
and for you. Are you ready?" Alex touched Zircon's
tongue and the horse came to full attention, tongue
back in the cheek.

Alex waited for her verdict. She glanced at her son,
clearly in his element, atop a horse. And sure enough,
Amie sat with her back against a tree, sketch pad in
hand.

Alex gripped Nina's elbow. "He's fine. Happy. He'll
be busy for the next hour on a scripted walk to the creek
and back. What about you?"

"Yes, let's do this before I lose my nerve." She
pressed her hand to the horse's body and slid her foot
into Alex's linked fingers.

She was tense and not particularly pliable, but he'd
helped worse. He hefted her up and secured her, quickly
mounting up behind her.

Zircon stood steady. Not a move. "Good boy," he
praised softly before sliding his arms around Nina, his
cheek against her hair. "How are you doing?"

"You have experience if this horse freaks out.
Right?"

"Of course." He breathed in the berry smell of her
shampoo as he clicked for the horse to start forward.

"Okay, good." She grabbed the pommel and horn
fast. "You know there are a half dozen women around
here who are green with envy—and not afraid of
horses."

"Where? I don't see anyone but you." He slid a palm to her stomach and urged her to lean into the circle of his arms. "You still aren't relaxing. Why don't you grab a chunk of mane with one of your hands? It'll help you connect to Zircon and you'll gain some more balance."

"Truthfully?" she said through her teeth. "I'm trying to figure out why you're doing this, since you left last night when I made it clear you could stay."

Her right hand moved toward Zircon's mane. She twined her fingers around the locks of bay-and-white mane, her breathing easing ever so slightly.

"You did." He rested his chin on her head, looking out at the grassy stretch of earth, the creek, the trees that had lived here longer than he had. Zircon walked on calmly, responding to the slight pressure in Alex's legs. He started to angle the horse toward the open field. Toward where he and Nina could talk. He was torn between this woman and his obligation to this land. "And there will come a day when I take you up on that."

"But not last night." Her back went starchy stiff against his chest.

"There's a difference between thinking you're ready to take a step and actually being ready." Arm wrapped around her, he urged her closer.

The press of her bottom against him was sweet torture. The roll of the horse's steps moved Nina's body against him until he throbbed with arousal. A low growl slipped between his clenched teeth.

She laughed softly. "Serves you right."

"Well, damn. I think I irked your feelings. Sorry about that." He chuckled softly. His arm slid up just under her breasts. "I guess we'll have to…talk and get to know each other better."

She tipped her head, her expression quizzical. "Talking would be good. Tell me more about what it was like growing up here."

"Well, my grandmother believed we needed to learn every inch of the farm firsthand." He guided the horse around a fallen tree and into an open field of bluebonnets. Zircon's ears flicked back and forth. "We shadowed the staff. Sometimes it was fun, sometimes not so much. She said she didn't want any spoiled trust fund babies taking over the family business."

"Good for her."

He nudged Zircon to the left past a fat oak, birds flapping from the trees up into the clear Texas sky. "One summer she got us all chickens and we learned to start a chicken coop."

"Seriously?" She relaxed against him, laughing.

"To this day we call that 'the Summer of Eggs.' We had to collect them and learned how to cook the eggs as well—scrambled, fried, then graduating to omelets and quiche."

"I like that your grandmother had you boys learn, as well."

Did she know that she'd loosened her grip on the horn, and one hand had slid to rest on her thigh? He didn't intend to point that out. Her shoulders and body started to move with Zircon's gait and not against it. Nina was a natural when fear wasn't her main focus.

"She and my grandfather built this business from the ground up." As the words rolled from his tongue, he realized his reason for bringing her here. It wasn't about riding a horse. It was about hoping she would understand his motives. Hoping that she would be able to forgive him for holding back part of his reason for seeking her out. "The ranch is actually Gran's. My grandfather was the jeweler/craftsman. Together they blended that dream into an empire." Alex's neck kinked with nerves as he considered how far to take this conversation.

"That's lovely, seeing their differences as strengths to be blended."

"You said your husband grew up pampered."

"Did I?"

"I believe so. You mentioned his wealthy parents and their need to control." He swallowed hard before venturing into that damn dangerous territory. "Would that be the Lowerys of Lowery Resorts?"

She glanced back in surprise. "Yes, actually they are. Cody too, since he inherited his father's portion of the holdings."

Alex forced his hands to stay loose on the reins. "And you're the executor or are his grandparents?"

"I am, and God," she sighed, sagging back into a slump, "the weight of that worries on me. The doctors still don't know exactly what the autism means for his future. Will he be able to support himself? Live on his own? I don't know the answers, so I have to be very careful with that money. He could have to live off the investments for the rest of his life."

Her words hammered at Alex with a reality he hadn't considered until now. He'd been so busy thinking about what was best for his grandmother and the ranch, he hadn't given a thought to worrying about that four-year-old boy. This wasn't about the McNairs versus the Lowerys. This involved a sick old woman and a special-needs child who might never be able to support himself. That truth sliced clean through him.

They were well beyond the bluebonnet field and

walking through a rocky, unstable area. Zircon's ears were pinned back. Guilt weighted Alex's shoulders down and dimmed the beauty of the day. So much so that he lost track of the path in the land he knew as well as his own hand.

So much so that he didn't see the arc of the rattle-snake between the horse's hooves until it was too late.

# Seven

Nina's heart leaped to her throat.

She felt the horse coil beneath her, almost mimicking the motion of the rattlesnake. Zircon's muscles exploded forward and he reared back. Ears pinned flat against his head, the paint pawed the air. Alex banded one arm around her to hold her secure and the other held the reins. He said something, some kind of command to Zircon, but she could only hear the roaring in her ears and the hammering of her heart as the world tilted backward.

She was going to die. Fall off the horse. Break her neck. Make her son an orphan. She'd stepped outside her comfort zone and would pay the price. A scream welled in her throat. She squeezed her eyes closed to fight vertigo, every muscle in her body tensing. She grabbed a fistful of mane, holding so tightly that her knuckles were bone white.

Zircon's hooves slammed down again, jarring her teeth, pushing her forward and off balance. She tried to stabilize her body weight on Zircon's neck but barely caught her breath before the horse bolted forward. She slammed back against the hard wall of Alex's chest, knocking the air from her lungs.

"Alex!" she choked out.

"Stay calm," his voice rumbled against her ear. "Hold tight and remember to breathe."

Faster and faster, the horse galloped along the path, then off. Zircon's gait was hurried, erratic. The horse was hardly running in a straight line and his ears were still pinned in fright. Earth and dirt flew past her vision. They raced through an open field, toward a creek. The wind whipped through her hair, but she hadn't been tossed off. She wasn't dead from a broken neck.

Yet.

Alex had her locked firmly against his chest, and her heartbeat raced as fast as the horse. "It's okay, Nina. I've got this. You're all right. Zircon will run himself out. We just need to stay seated."

She heard him and slowly began to believe him. Her nerves battled with a long-buried urge to enjoy the ride and ignore the risks. Just live on the edge. Which was exactly what they were about to do as Zircon readied to cross the creek. The horse pushed off the thin creek's bank. Instinctively Nina shifted her hands up the horse's neck, grabbing its mane and leaning forward into the jump.

Zircon went flying over the creek and landed smoothly on the other side. Had she squealed or screamed again? She didn't know, but the world was sparkling. This felt like flying.

The drumming of the hooves reverberated through her as Zircon nimbly galloped around fat oak trees. They approached another clearing. Alex gathered the reins and pulled the horse's head to the right. Zircon's head turned sharply and his legs followed. Nina watched the horse's nervous eyes soften. Alex kept the horse turning to the right. The circle became smaller and smaller. Bit by bit, the horse slowed. Then stopped, snorting and pawing at the ground.

Alex slid from the saddle and lifted her off, setting her quickly on the grass before kneeling beside his horse. His hands skimmed along the front legs, left and right.

Nina covered her mouth. How could she have forgotten about the snake so quickly? "Is he okay? Was Zircon bitten?"

Alex shook his head. "It doesn't appear so, thank God. The rattler just spooked him." He glanced over his shoulder. "Are you all right?"

"I'm fine, only a little surprised. And very grateful no one was injured, especially Zircon." She reached out tentatively and patted the horse's neck, the satiny coat soothing to the touch. Frothy sweat pooled beyond the horse's ears and around the bit.

Rising, Alex stood beside her again, stroking her cheek. "I'm so damn sorry that he went out of control so fast."

"You kept us all safe. And truth be told, once I got past the initial startle, I actually enjoyed the ride. I didn't expect to feel like that."

"Like what?" He stepped closer, his hand drawing her nearer.

"My skin tingled all over," she said with only a sliver of space between them.

He smiled, the corners of his eyes crinkling. "You're a horsewoman after all."

Laughing softly, she angled closer, her nerves igniting at the simple brush of her breasts again his chest. "A horsewoman? That's taking things a little far based on one ride."

He tapped his temple. "Trust me. I have a sense for things like this."

"Perhaps next time we ride we can take things a little slower and see how it goes."

"You're willing to ride again?" he asked with clear undertones.

"Absolutely I am." Her body damn near ignited with thoughts of last night, of taking things further. "In fact, I'm looking forward to it."

"You're going to be sore after today's experience." His hands slid down her back, lower, pressing her hips to his.

"Probably. Where's your masseuse?"

"I was thinking of something else to relieve tension later tonight, if you're game."

While she wanted to be with him, she was confused after his departure the evening before. Things were moving so fast, and she was the one who'd wanted that, wanted a fling, but she needed to understand *his* intent better. She needed to make sure they were on the same page. "About last night—"

"Things moved fast, I get that."

"They did, and I have to confess I'm not used to that. So maybe I sent some mixed signals. I was married, but my life has been focused solely on my son since then.

This week has been…different. I guess what I'm trying to say is that I didn't want you to leave," she admitted. Since she was living on the edge today, she might as well go for broke.

"I didn't want to go."

Finally she asked the question that had plagued her through a very sleepless night. "Then why did you?"

He tugged his hat off—how had that stayed on through the crazy ride?—and thrust a hand through his hair. "It's difficult to explain, other than to say this week doesn't seem like long enough."

"But it's all we have." She hadn't considered more. Even the thought of being vulnerable in yet another relationship made her feel as if the world had tilted again. She backed away from him. "I have a life and a home in San Antonio."

Although that life felt mighty far away at the moment.

He slammed his hat back on his head. "You're right. Forget I said anything. Let's live in the moment."

The tension in her chest eased and she leaned against him. "One day at a time. I like that."

She arched up on her toes to kiss him, enjoying the way their mouths met with familiarity, fitting just so. His arms slid around her, his hands warm and strong palming low on her waist. Her breasts pressed to the hard wall of his chest, and her mind filled with memories of the night before, of his touch, his intuition about just how to set her on fire.

Her senses, still so alive from their mad dash, burned all the hotter. "Alex…"

"Nina…" he whispered in her ear, his beard stubble rasping against her cheek. "I want you here, now, but we're too close to the camp and there are other riders out."

She gasped, jerking away. "Oh my God, the kids are out riding." She pressed a hand to her forehead. "How could I have forgotten?"

"But we have a date for later." He pulled her back into his arms and traced her bottom lip. "I told you, I have a plan for reducing tension. Trust me?"

God, how she wanted to. "I'll see you tonight after Cody goes to sleep."

Eight hours later, Alex held his hands over Nina's eyes, hoping she would enjoy his idea for their evening together. He'd brought dinner to her and Cody first, enjoying the chance to get to know her son better. They'd eaten barbecue and played with toy horses Alex had brought as a gift until Amie arrived to babysit again.

Nina had smiled more broadly over his present to her son than she had over the chocolate strawberries he'd brought for their dessert. He couldn't help being drawn to her devotion to the boy after the way his own parents had ignored their children except for when he and Amie were trotted out to perform.

He wasn't going to have many more opportunities to be alone with Nina with his cousin's wedding right around the corner. Even the small family service would still take up all their time over the weekend, relatives pouring in left and right. Not to mention the bachelor party and rehearsal dinner.

Thoughts of family were the last kind Alex wanted right now.

Nina had made it clear she only wanted a week together, and that was likely all they would have once she knew how badly his grandmother wanted her son's shares in the McNair Corporation. He'd considered just offering an exorbitant amount of money for them, but their own finances were tangled up in investments. Selling them off to liquidate cash would be unwise fiscally, and unfair to their own investors. He was caught in a loop of damned if he did and damned if he didn't.

So he did the only thing he knew to do. Focus on letting Cody have the best camp experience possible. Get to know the child better.

And pamper Nina for whatever time they had together.

She clasped his wrists. "Where are we going?"

"Almost there," he said, stopping in front of the sauna attached to the family's private pool house. "Are you ready for more relaxation?"

"I think so."

He lowered his hands and opened the door to the small cedar room. A tray waited with water bottles beside a stack of fat towels.

Everything had been prepared as he'd ordered. "This is our family's private sauna. No one will bother us here. I thought you might be sore after being jostled around on Zircon. Your choice, though, if you'd rather not."

She turned in his arms to face him, smiling. So easy to please and so at home in the places he loved best. She fit in here seamlessly. "I think it's a fabulous idea." The emerald green of her gauzy blouse made her eyes sparkle. "You have a knack for knowing just what I need. But I'm curious, what do *you* need?"

Her provocative question hung in the air between them.

His eyes fell to the deep V of her shirt, which had

been drawing his gaze all night long. A long lock of hair had slipped loose, the curl pooling just above her breast as if it were providing a path for his touch. "I need you, Nina. Just you."

He walked her into the sauna, the temperature still moderate. For now. His temperature? Definitely notching higher the longer he looked at her.

She stroked along his shoulders, her touch making his skin tighten everywhere. "I've got to know, though, are you going to walk out on me again?"

"Not unless you ask me to." He kicked the door closed, sealing them inside the low-lit cubicle.

For good measure, he went back and locked it.

"Doubtful." She arched up on her toes to nip his bottom lip. "I'm warming it up fast." She winked at him. "I think we're both way too overdressed for this sauna idea of yours."

"I'd like to help you with that." An understatement.

She lifted her arms in an unspoken invitation for him to peel off her loose blouse. He swept up the gauzy fabric and tossed it aside on the bench, his eyes never leaving all the creamy pale skin he was unveiling.

His breath caught in his throat at the sight of her breasts in white lace. High, luscious curves. "You look every bit as beautiful as you felt last night."

He'd been reliving those moments in his head all day long. Even more, he'd been looking forward to making even more memories with her tonight.

Her fingers walked down his shirt. "You don't have to shower me with compliments."

"I want to…if I spoke as many languages as you do—" he tugged the zipper on her jeans, down, down, revealing white bikini panties "—then I could tell you again and again how beautiful you are, how much I want you, how often thoughts of you distract me at work."

"You have quite a way with words no matter what language you're speaking."

She worked free the buttons on his plaid shirt, one at a time, her knuckles grazing his skin and tempting him to toss aside restraint. Then her cool hand slid inside his jeans and restraint was absolutely the last thing on his mind. She curved her hand around his throbbing erection and he bit back a groan as she stroked.

Growling low in his throat, he eased her down to sit on the bench and knelt in front of her, tugging her boots off one, then the other. Her new leather boots were starting to have a worn-in look, as though she belonged here. In his house. In his arms.

She flowed forward, sweeping aside his loose shirt, then leaned back again, eyes roving his chest with obvious appreciation. Kicking aside his own boots, he tugged his wallet from his pocket and pulled out two condoms, then placed them on the bench.

Her pupils widened with desire.

He peeled off his socks and shucked his well-worn jeans before standing naked in front of her. Her smoky smile steamed over him hotter than the sauna. She trailed her fingers down his chest, down his stomach, gently brushing his erection. He throbbed in response, her touch sweet torture. She trailed her hand lower down his thigh, muscles contracting at her caress. Urgency pumped through his veins.

Lifting her hand, he pressed a kiss to the inside of her wrist, feeling the pulse beat hard against his lips. Then he stepped back to turn up the heat on the sauna, coils heating the stones, a water fountain trickling down to send bursts of steam. Bottles of oils lined a rack before the fountain—eucalyptus, citrus, birch and peppermint.

Choosing eucalyptus, he drizzled oil over the stones before turning back to her. Anticipation curled through him. Finally he had her all to himself, naked, alone, his for the taking. They'd been building to this moment since the first time he saw her. And in spite of all the reasons they didn't stand a chance in hell at having more, he couldn't stop wanting her.

He reached to the stack of fluffy white towels in the corner and spread two out on the bench. He reclined her back, using an extra towel to make a pillow. He stretched out over her. Flesh to flesh. His eyes slid closed for a moment.

Then thoughts gave way to sensations. The scent of her berry shampoo. The creamy softness of her neck when he pressed his lips to her pulse. She hooked her leg around his, her foot sliding up and down the back of his calf. He finally gave in to the temptation to taste her, along her shoulder, nudging aside a bra strap, then the other, baring her breasts to his mouth, his touch. She arched up with a husky moan and he reached underneath her to unhook her bra and toss it aside.

Sweat beaded along her skin, glistening. Perspiration streaked down her neck, then between her breasts. One droplet held on the tip of her nipple. He dipped his head and flicked his tongue, catching the droplet and circling, laving. Her head fell back and a moan floated from her lips.

Nina nibbled his earlobe. "No more waiting." She passed him a condom. "We can go slow after. And from the count of what you pulled from your pocket, you're intending there to be an after."

"At least that much," he vowed. "And whatever else you want."

"Perfect," she purred, trailing her fingers down his arms and guiding his hands to hurry up.

He tore open the wrapper, and her hands covered his as she helped him sheathe himself. She hitched her leg higher, hooked on his hip, bringing her moist heat closer. His forehead fell to rest against hers as he pushed inside her. Her breath came faster and faster, flowing over him. He thrust deeper, deeper still and her hips rolled against his, inviting him to continue. He thrust and she moved with him, synching into a perfect, driving rhythm that had him clenching his teeth to hold back. She'd said they could go slow next time—and there would be a next time—but he wasn't finishing now until he'd satisfied her.

The steam billowed off the rocks, filling the small room, air heavy with the scent of eucalyptus and sex. Perspiration gathered on his forehead, a droplet sliding off to hit the towel under her. Their slick bodies moved against each other, his pulse hammering in his ears. He swept her hair from her face, capturing her mouth and soaking in the feel of Nina.

Just Nina.

He braced himself on one elbow to keep his weight off her and slide his other hand between them, caressing her breasts and lower. He stroked the slick bud, circling and teasing, her purrs of pleasure urging him to continue. Just when he thought he couldn't hold out any longer, her gasps came faster and faster. Her fingernails dug into his back, scratching a light but insistent path as her head flung back. She cried out in pleasure, her orgasm pulsing around him, clasping him tighter and hurtling him over the edge into his own release.

His arm gave way and he lay fully on top of her, thrusting through the final wave of ecstasy. His breaths shuddering through him, he buried his face in her neck and rolled to his side, holding her close. Already hungry for the next time and wondering how long he could keep her here and the world at bay.

Because more than ever, he was certain that a week with Nina would never be enough.

Tucked to Alex's side, Nina trailed her fingers along his muscular arm, the scent of eucalyptus steaming through the sauna. She was already nearly halfway done with the weeklong camp. Then she would have to walk away from the Hidden Gem—from Alex.

This place was like a fairy-tale getaway, a Brigadoon, too good to be true and destined to disappear when she left. Alex made her want things she'd decided were not meant to be. Scariest of all, he made her want to risk her heart again and she didn't know if she could take another betrayal.

A sobering thought at a time she was determined to live in the moment.

She slid her hand down to link fingers with Alex. "We should get dressed soon and head back. Your sister must be getting sick of babysitting Cody."

"No hurry." He kissed their clasped hands. "Amie adores Cody and she owes me."

"For what?" she asked, hungry to know more about him.

A smile tugged at his mouth. "When we were seventeen, she didn't want to win the Miss Honey Bee

Pageant—and given how many pageants she'd won in the past, it wasn't arrogant of her to assume she would run away with that crown. But back to that time. She didn't want to go because the Honey Bee Queen had to attend the county fair and she wouldn't be able to attend homecoming."

Nina drew circles on his chest, perspiration clinging to their skin. "What did you do?"

"Nothing awful. We went boating the day before the competition, and we stayed out so long we got sunburned. I told Mom the engine stalled. Amie looked like a lobster. Mom made her compete anyway. Just slathered her in more makeup. Amie got second runner-up."

"Seriously?" The story was funny and sad all at once.

"Scout's honor." He held up his fingers. "I offered to cut her hair, but she nixed that, so we opted for the sunburn instead. I was never sure if she opted out of the haircut idea out of vanity or because Mom would have just bought a wig."

"People call you quiet and reserved, but you're really quite funny."

"I guess I have my moments." He kissed the tip of her nose, then picked up a hand towel and gently—methodically—wiped the sweat from her body. "So I take it you approve of the sauna?"

"Very much. Is there anything Hidden Gem doesn't have? Seriously, sauna, massage therapist, airplane, catered dinners, even that well-stocked gift shop, so there's no need to leave for anything. This is like nirvana."

His smile faded. "There are others who would say this place should be modernized."

"In what way? There's every convenience possible."

She couldn't imagine anywhere more restful or entertaining.

"There are no theme parks or casinos. A high-rise could fit a lot more people into the space, make more money, attract big acts to perform."

The mention of high-rise tourism made her think of her in-laws, the last people she wanted intruding on this moment. "You can't possibly agree with that. It would take away the authenticity and the charm."

"It's good to hear you say that."

The fierce intensity of his kiss took her breath away and made her wonder about the reason for his sudden shift in mood.

She gripped his shoulders, questions filling her mind. But before she could ask, a cell phone rang, jarring her. Not her ring tone. His. Sounding from his jeans on the floor.

He murmured against her mouth, "Ignore it."

Oh, how she wanted to. "It could be your sister. Cody might need me."

"You're right. Of course, we can't ignore it. I should have thought of that too."

Rolling from her, he sat on the edge of the bench and scooped his jeans from the floor. Nina stroked his broad back and traced the light scratches she'd left along his shoulder blades.

He answered the cell phone. "Amie, is something wrong with Cody?"

Alex clicked on the speakerphone and Nina sat up beside him, concern and maternal guilt chilling her warmed flesh.

"No." His sister's voice was tight with nerves. "Not at all. He's fast asleep."

Nina relaxed against him, resting her cheek on his shoulder, her hand on his chest.

"Glad to hear it," Alex said, sliding an arm around Nina. "Then what's up?"

"Prepare yourself," she said with a heavy sigh. "Mom and Dad are returning home from their trip a day early. They've already landed in Fort Worth but didn't want to make the drive out to the ranch tonight. They'll be here first thing in the morning."

His jaw tight, he turned off the speakerphone and brought the receiver to his ear. "We'll need to band together to keep things calm for Gran…"

Curiosity nipped. He'd mentioned issues with his parents, but his reaction seemed…strong. It was only a day early. Surely that wasn't a big deal. But the muscles bunching along Alex's back told her otherwise.

Nina pulled a towel from the stack and wrapped it around herself. But there was no escaping the sensation that her Brigadoon was fading.

# Eight

Alex hadn't eaten breakfast yet and he already had indigestion.

He paced restlessly around the family lanai, brunch prepared, he and his sister waiting with Gran for their parents' arrival. The morning sun steamed droplets of water off the lawn from the sprinkler system. Making love with Nina had been everything he expected and more. He'd always been such a methodical man. But the instantaneous combustion between him and Nina rocked him back on his boot heels. And before he could get his bearings, his parents opted to put in an early appearance.

His mother had a way of being less than pleasant to the women he dated, which was strange, since Bayleigh McNair wasn't what anyone would call an overly adoring parent. Regardless, he didn't want Nina subjected to that, especially not now while they were still finding their way around whatever it was they had going.

A persistent crick pinched at his neck. He should have been better prepared for his parents' arrival and how he would handle them meeting Nina. They'd been due in tomorrow anyway, but he'd been taking things one day at a time this week. That sort of impulsive living wasn't his style.

Gran reclined in a patio lounger sipping tea, her breakfast untouched on the small table beside her. His indomitable grandmother was so frail she looked as if a puff of wind would whisk her away. He needed to make sure this breakfast—the whole wedding weekend—went smoothly. No drama. This was his family and they were at their best for his grandmother.

Stone's mother would be a wild card. Her behavior was always hit or miss depending on if she was using drugs or fresh out of rehab. Thus far she'd been clean for six months. If she followed past patterns, the fall was due any day now.

Maybe it wasn't fair of him to expect Nina to put up with his family's volatile dynamics, especially since weddings always multiplied drama. Except after last night with Nina, he couldn't bring himself to waste even a minute of the remaining week. He needed to persuade her they had something special—because he was going to have to come clean with her about the stocks soon.

Why couldn't Nina have come to one of the other camp sessions? Although she wouldn't be here at all if his grandmother hadn't orchestrated Nina's arrival. He couldn't imagine never having met her. So whatever it took, he would get through these next few days and maintain the peace for his grandmother.

And figure out a way to keep seeing Nina after the camp ended.

First, he had to get through welcoming his parents. They kept a suite here as well but were rarely in attendance. They preferred penthouse hotels around the world.

A limousine cruised up the oak-shaded entry road, turning toward the private drive and stopping near the lanai. While the others drank mimosas, Amie drained her simple orange juice and refilled the crystal flute. Stone and Johanna—lucky ducks—had bowed out of breakfast claiming a meeting with the caterer.

Clouds drifted over the sun as the chauffeur opened the door and Alex's mother stepped out in a flourish. Bayleigh McNair believed in making an entrance.

His mother breezed up the stairs. Collagen-puffy lips and cheek implants had changed her appearance until she looked like a distant relative of herself. Not his mother yet eerily familiar.

Alex stepped beside Gran's chair, wishing his presence alone could keep her safe and make her well. Her hand trembling, Gran set aside her teacup with a slight rattle of china, watching her grandchildren protectively. Alex patted her shoulder.

His father stepped alongside his wife, wearing a crisp suit as if he'd dressed for work. Ironic as hell, since Garnet McNair carried an in-name-only title with the company, some kind of director of overseas relations. Which just meant he could pretend he worked as he traveled the world. Mariah only requested he wine and dine possible contacts and charm them. On the company credit card of course. His parents were masters at wringing money out of Gran.

She was a savvy businesswoman, so Alex was certain she knew her son's game. And equally certain it had to break her heart, given how hard she and her husband had worked to build the family business. It was no wonder she felt the need to put her grandchildren through tests before handing over her empire.

Bayleigh swept up the lanai stairs—perfect. There was no other word to describe his mother. Not a hair out of place. Makeup fresh, a bit thicker each year. And always, always, she stayed almost skeletally thin—thanks to hours on the treadmill and a diet of cottage cheese and coffee. What the treadmill couldn't fix, she took care of with liposuction and tummy tucks. The rest of her was beige—blond hair, tanned skin, and off-white or brown clothes depending on the time of year.

He often wondered how his mom managed to keep those white outfits clean with kids around. Gran was always dusty and never minded if they'd just eaten chocolate ice cream when they gave her a hug.

Gran and Nina had a lot in common.

Bayleigh's heels clicked across the tile as she briefly hugged each of her children, leaving a fog of perfume in her wake. She dabbed her eyes with a tissue as she swooped down on her mother-in-law. "Mother McNair, how are you feeling?" She kissed Gran's cheek and then sat in a chair next to her. "I'm just so glad you're still with us for the wedding."

"No need to start digging my grave yet." Gran didn't show any irritation, only a sardonic smile of resolution. "I've got some life left in me yet."

Garnet knelt beside his mom. "Mother, please, let's not talk about unpleasantries." He took her hand in his. "I'm glad to see you looking so well, enjoying the sunshine." She glanced up at the sky. "Well, what little bit is peeking around the clouds."

Her smile turned nostalgic. "You look so much like your father, Garnet. I miss him every day even after all these years."

Although her son hadn't inherited much in the way of work ethic from his mother or father, Alex had heard his grandmother blame herself for pampering her children. He didn't agree. Not completely. She might have been indulgent in those days, but his father and aunt should have taken responsibility for their own lives. Alex passed his mother a cup of black coffee.

Bayleigh cradled the cup and inhaled the scent as if filling up on the smell alone. "We came early to help, since the bride doesn't have a mother of her own. And Mother Mariah is so very ill. Of course we all know Stone's mother can't be trusted to show up sober. So I thought I should come a day early to make sure all is in order."

Bayleigh sipped her coffee.

Garnet stayed silent, not surprising, and filled a plate with quiche and fruit. The sound of crunching footsteps sounded just before Stone jogged into sight from around the corner of the house.

Stone took the steps two at a time up to the lanai. "Sorry I'm late. Johanna is still working out details with the caterer. She'll be here when she's through. Thank you for coming, Aunt Bayleigh, Uncle Garnet." He swept his hat off and kissed his grandmother's cheek before loading up a plate of quiche, two danishes and melon slices. "I'm starving. Glad y'all saved me some food."

Amie sipped her crystal flute of orange juice. "Good

thing you got here before Aunt Bayleigh drank all the coffee."

Bayleigh scowled. "Amie, must you be unpleasant?"

"Always," his sister answered without hesitation. "Mother, Johanna and Stone are adults. I believe they can manage to plan a small wedding on their own."

Bayleigh set her china cup aside. "Well, I imagine if they're not set on impressing anyone, that's just fine."

Amie's eyes narrowed. "Then Johanna and Stone will exceed your expectations."

Garnet cleared his throat and slid a hand along his wife's back.

"Forgive me, Amie." Bayleigh patted her daughter's knee before picking up her cup again. "I'm just getting antsy to plan a wedding for one of my children, but neither one of them shows signs of settling down. I hope you don't wait too long, daughter dear. Your biological clock is ticking."

"Mother, you surprise me. I thought you were concerned about me wrecking my figure." Amie's barb was unmistakable and there was no stopping the mother/daughter battle once it started rolling.

Bayleigh eyed her daughter over her coffee. "Amethyst, your pageant days are long past."

Alex's twin shot blue fire from her eyes at her mother. "Maybe I should look into a sperm donor."

Their father's mouth twitched, but he didn't look up from eating his food while reading his morning news on his tablet. "Don't rile your mother. The weekend's going to be long enough as it is."

Stone set down his fork long enough to say, "Alex has been seeing a single mother here with her son at HorsePower Cowkid Camp."

Alex grasped the change of subject with both hands, grateful to steer the conversation onto relatively safer ground—ground that wouldn't upset Gran. "Hey, cousin, that's no way to treat the man planning your bachelor party."

Not that he was really all that stoked about the party, which surprised the hell out of him. All he really wanted was to find Nina and Cody.

Amie laughed softly. "She would have figured it out soon enough anyway when you showed up at the rehearsal dinner with your redheaded bombshell in tow."

Alex shot his twin a glare. "You are not helping, Amie."

"A redhead." Bayleigh winced. "Well, if you have ginger children we can always fix that with a quick trip to the hair salon. Tell me more about her."

Alex didn't like the gleam in his mother's eyes one bit. Protective urges filled him. "Are those storm clouds overhead? Maybe we should move brunch inside."

His mother patted her hair. "Not even the threat of drenching will distract me from finding out more about this woman. You didn't answer my question, son."

"Mother." Alex leaned forward. "Her name is Nina and you *will* retract your claws and leave her alone. Don't pretend you don't know what I'm talking about. No interfering in my personal life. Period."

"Of course." Bayleigh pressed a hand to her chest with overplayed innocence. "I just want grandchildren. I dream of the days I can buy little smocked dresses or tiny cowboy boots."

"That subject is also off-limits," Alex said firmly. "As is your intent to choose their mother. I mean it."

His father looked up from his iPad for the first time. "This week's going to be interesting."

His grandmother's keen blue eyes took in all, and he hated that she'd witnessed the sparring, even if it was par for the course with their family gatherings. Alex wondered if maybe there was more to Gran's test than he'd originally thought. Could this be some sort of reverse psychology? Maybe she didn't want the stocks? Or had plans for another way to get them?

Could she be testing his honor to make sure none of his father's screwed-up values were running through him?

Damn, that stung.

He'd always been the different one, not a part of Diamonds in the Rough. But he'd thought his grandmother respected how he'd channeled his own work ethic and values into turning Hidden Gem into an asset to the empire and a tribute to their land.

Hell, he didn't know what to think right now. He just wanted to get this breakfast over with so he could spend time with Nina.

Rain pattered on the barn roof, and Nina cradled a cup of coffee with rich cream and two spoons of sugar. Sitting at a rustic picnic table in the café corner area, she'd been eating a pastry while watching her son. The children were scattered throughout the stalls that had been set up petting-zoo style. Each kid had been partnered with his or her choice of a pony, donkey, dog, chickens or even a rabbit to brush, hold or pet. Four stalls down, Cody ran a bristly brush along a miniature donkey, a teacher close at his side, instructing.

Nina wasn't needed now. Her son was enjoying independent play. She should be happy and go back to her cabin to read or nap with the rain soothing her to sleep. She'd certainly gotten very little sleep last night. She set down her coffee with a heavy sigh.

Her stomach had been in knots all day over the influx of McNairs and what that did—or didn't—mean in regards to her relationship with Alex. Whether making love or just talking, she'd enjoyed being alone with him. Solitude would be all but impossible now and she felt that she'd been robbed of her last few days left for a fling.

Except if it was just a fling, she shouldn't be this upset.

Thunder rolled outside, and Nina looked at her son quickly to make sure he wasn't upset. Some of the other children covered their ears, one squealed, but Cody was lost in the rhythmic stroking of the donkey's coat.

The barn door opened with a swirl of damp wind, and Alex ducked inside, closing the door quickly. He shook the rain off his hat, scanning the cavernous space. His eyes found hers in an instant and he smiled, his gaze steaming over her in a way that said he was thinking of last night too. She started to stand, but he waved for her to stay seated as he walked past her to her son.

Alex nodded to the teacher and let her angle away before taking the teacher's place beside Cody. Nina threw away her coffee and padded over silently, curious about what he intended to say.

And yes, eager to be near him.

Alex picked up a second brush, smoothing it over the donkey too. "I wasn't much of a talker either when I was younger," he said softly. "I know it's not quite the same as what's going on in your mind. But I wanted to let you know I understand that even when a person is quiet, he still hears. That's part of what I enjoy most about the animals here, in the quiet with them, it's easier to hear."

"Yes." Cody's little hand smoothed steadily. "My mommy broughted me here."

"You have a smart mommy. But I don't know you as well as your mom does. So, while I know you're listening, I can only guess what you would be interested in hearing. For all I know, I could be boring you talking about fishing when maybe you prefer soccer. It's okay for you to be quiet, but I would appreciate a hint on what you would like to talk about."

Cody set aside the brush and stroked the donkey's neck. "Donkey's nice."

"You like activities with horses, ponies, donkeys? You're okay with me talking about them?"

"Uh-huh." He kept rubbing the donkey without looking away.

"Okay, then. My cousin Stone has a quarter horse named Copper. My sister, Amie, has an Arabian named Crystal." He listed them in a way that Nina realized gave Cody a connection to each McNair. Since Cody loved the animals, he would have positive associations with the person. "My favorite is the Paint, named Zircon. My grandmother has this thing about naming every person and animal after a gemstone. She likes themes and patterns."

"I like patter-ins," Cody whispered, drawing the last word out so it had a third syllable.

"Okay, let's talk about the gem pattern names. People call me Alex, but my name is Alexandrite and my sister Amie is Amethyst. My grandmother even had dogs that had similar names."

"Dogs?" A spark lit in Cody's eyes and he tipped his head toward Alex. "Where are the dogs?"

"My grandmother is sick, so new families are taking care of three of the dogs. My cousin Stone has the fourth dog named Pearl, and my sister takes care of Gran's cats."

"Can I pet the doggy?"

Alex grinned. "How about puppies? Someone dropped a box of border collie mix puppies on our land a couple of weeks ago. They must have thought we would be a good home for them since one of our ranch hands has a border collie that works with him. Would you like to see the pups?"

Cody nodded quickly, eyes wide. "Uh-huh."

Nina's heart all but squeezed in two as Alex went out of his way to lead Cody to the pen of fuzzy border collie mix puppies tucked in the office. She stayed out of sight so as not to disrupt the moment. Two puppies played tug-of-war over a toy. Another flopped back over belly catching a ball, ears flopping. Alex showed her son different ways to play gently with the small fluff balls. Cody had such little time with male role models.

Alex made her ache and yearn for things she'd thought she could never have again. The ranch was well equipped for taking care of puppies and kittens who needed homes, and even helping struggling young moms and special-needs children, but she had to remember for her and for the puppies—Hidden Gem was a temporary stop. Only the McNairs stayed here. Like the puppies, Nina and Cody would be moving on to a different home and this place would be just a nostalgic memory.

An hour later, Nina took photos of her son riding a mechanical bull—with the bull set on a very slow speed to buck and turn. She could already envision one of these images reproduced onto a large canvas in her living room, surrounded by smaller photos from throughout this incredible week.

Would Alex be in any of those pictures? Could her heart take that kind of bittersweet reminder?

The rainstorm had ended a few minutes ago and since Cody was the last of the children to take a turn on the mechanical bull, the head camp counselor called out, "Line up, by your groups. Blue ponies here. Yellow ponies there. Green. And then red."

The children raced toward the door in a loose cluster, pent-up energy radiating off their little bodies. A girl in a wheelchair whizzed by, pumping the wheels faster and faster, pigtails flying.

Nina felt Alex's presence a second before he put his hand on her shoulder.

"Who are you sending the photos to?"

"A friend at home." She held up the cell phone. "Reed and I met at a support group for single parents with special-needs children."

"Reed?" His jaw flexed. "Should I be jealous of this guy?"

"No, we're just friends. Good friends who try to help each other, but we're only friends." She tucked away her phone before taking his hand, wishing she could do more. But anyone could walk in, and children were within eyesight. "I wouldn't have been with you this week if there was someone else."

"Good, I'm glad to hear that." His thumb slid around to stroke the inside of her wrist. "Did you get your turn on the mechanical bull?"

She blinked in surprise. "Um, no. That activity was just for the kids."

"I own it." He patted the saddle. "Do you want to try?"

"I'm not going to put on some *Urban Cowboy* sexy ride show for you."

He grinned, a roguish twinkle in his blue eyes. "I wasn't proposing anything of the sort—especially not with kids nearby. But even the mention is filling my mind with interesting ideas." He squeezed her hand. "For now, how about a regular slow ride?"

Somehow he made even that sound sensual. Irresistible. She approached the mechanical bull tentatively, touching the saddle.

Alex's hand fell to rest on her shoulder. "There are different speeds. We take this as slow as you want to go."

She glanced back at him. "Are we still talking about the bull?"

"Do you want us to talk about something else?"

Her stomach flipped and she looked away. "I guess I'm riding the bull."

"All right, then. Climb on. Grab hold and we'll start her slow."

"Okay, but no pictures." She stepped into the stirrup and swung her leg over, sitting, half sliding off the other side before righting herself with a laugh. "I never was much of one for carnival rides."

"Let me know if you want to stop." He turned the knob, setting the bull into a gentle rocking motion that started to turn.

"I tossed my cookies once on the Ferris wheel," she confessed as the bull circled.

"I know where the mop is."

"An almighty McNair mops floors?" she teased, trying not to think about the day they'd ridden the horse together.

He increased the speed. "Gran brought us up with down-home, work-ethic values. We had jobs on the farm as kids and teenagers, just like everyone else, and we had to start at the bottom, learning every stage of the operation."

She gripped tighter. "What did your parents have to say about that?"

"Not much as long as the big money kept flowing their way."

"Your father didn't work?" That seemed so atypical compared to what she'd seen from Alex working up a sweat on the ranch in addition to his desk work running the place.

"My father has an office. He makes business trips, but does he work? Not really. I guess Gran wanted to make doubly sure the grandkids turned out differently. And we did. Although we always thought Stone would run the company, he decided to run a nonprofit camp instead."

She read rumors of a new CEO outside the family being hired to run Diamonds in the Rough, but she hadn't paid more than passing attention. "That must have been a huge disappointment to your grandmother not to be able to pass along her legacy to her children."

"It was—and is. But she's happy about the camp. Who wouldn't be proud of this? It's amazing, innovative and rewarding. I just want her to be at peace in her final days." Shadows chased through his blue eyes.

"All that parents want is for their children to be happy and try their best."

His eyes met hers. "Not all parents."

"Are you saying your grandmother—"

"Not my grandmother. My parents." Looking down, he scuffed his boots through the dirt. "Let's talk about something else. Like how's that bull feeling? Ready to take him up a notch? If you can still talk, it's obviously not going fast enough."

She shook her head quickly. "I think it's time to stop."

He switched off the controls and the bull slowed, slowed and finally went still. Alex reached up to help her down. "I'm going to miss you tonight while I'm at the bachelor party."

She slid down the front of him, enjoying the feel of their bodies against each other, her mind firing with memories from the night before. "I thought men lived for those sorts of things."

"I would rather be with you tonight." His warm breath caressed her neck.

She pressed her cheek to his heart for just a moment, listening to the steady thud. "That's really sweet of you to say."

"My thoughts are far from sweet." He growled softly in her ear, "I'd love to see you after the party if it's not too late."

His words rang with an unmistakable promise and she didn't have the least inclination to say no.

# Nine

Alex knew he was in trouble when he couldn't stop checking his watch for the end of the bachelor party. He wanted to spend the evening with Nina and Cody. But he owed Stone this traditional testosterone bash. Stone was more like a brother to him than a cousin, so for now, thoughts of Nina and her son needed to take a backseat.

The party was being held in a private lodge behind the Hidden Gem ranch house. Cigar smoke filled the room along with round poker tables. A buffet full of food and a bar stocked with the best alcohol and brews stayed stocked throughout the night. Country music piped through the sound system, a steel guitar still audible over raucous laughter, the clink of glasses and the whirr of a few electric card shufflers at work.

Garnet, Stone and Preston Armstrong, the new company CEO, sat with Alex at one table. Four more tables held longtime employees from the Diamonds in the Rough Jewelry and the Hidden Gem Ranch. Stone had insisted on the bachelor party being held the day before the rehearsal dinner, not wanting any of his friends to be nursing hangovers at his wedding.

Preston threw his cards down, gray eyes tired from concentration. "Fold. This is the lamest bachelor party ever."

Alex laughed, tossing turquoise and white chips into the middle of the table. The chips clinked and fell haphazardly in a pile. "You're just pissed because you're not winning."

"You could have a point there," Preston conceded, shoulders sagging.

Stone passed new cards to the remaining players. "My orders for the evening. Nothing but booze and cards."

"Not even a movie?"

Stone grinned devilishly. "Haven't you heard? I'm saving myself for marriage."

"Yeah, well, what about the rest of us?" Preston barked.

Stone shrugged, finishing his drink. He rattled the leftover ice in his glance. "Have your own bachelor party, and you get to make your own rules."

"Not going to happen," Preston insisted, palms up as he pushed back from the table. "While y'all finish this hand, I'll use the time to become reacquainted with the bar."

Garnet tossed in his hand. "I'm out too. Another drink sounds good."

Alex looked at the two pairs in his hand and slid a few more chips to the middle of the table. "I'm happy for you and Johanna." He paused to look at his cousin across the table. "I hope you know I mean that."

"That's good to hear," Stone answered, his voice hoarse with emotion. Stone's features flattened as he stared at the pile of chips, avoiding Alex's gaze. "You mean as much to me as any brother ever could."

"I'm sorry it even had to be said. She and I were too much alike to ever be a couple. Any feelings I thought I felt were more habit than anything else."

Because Alex knew now that anything he'd thought he felt for Johanna paled in comparison to what he felt for Nina.

"Well, loving a woman is rarely easy." Stone peeled his eyes up toward Alex.

Alex rubbed the cards in his hand. The plastic of the cards hummed, seeming to drown out all the other sounds of the bachelor party. "I'm learning that."

Stone set his cards facedown. "The mom with her son here at the camp?"

"Forget I said anything. And for God's sake, don't let anybody say anything more to my mother." Alex tipped back his drink. While it looked as though he had been slamming back vodka all night, his drinks had all been water. He wanted a clear head for later. He wanted to enjoy Nina. Their time together was short and he didn't need a single sense dulled. "This is about you tonight, cousin."

Stone pushed his cards into the middle. "Well, damn, then let's bail and go riding. You and me, like old times."

Now, that sounded a helluva lot more appealing than sitting here. Alex scraped his chair back, but had to ask, "Is it fair to leave Preston stuck with my father?"

"Preston's the boss now." Stone stood, his smile widening. "That's the beauty of having found my own path, cousin. Johanna and I answer only to ourselves and each other."

"Good point."

They clinked glasses, drained the contents and left the party. And Alex couldn't help thinking how damn important family was to him.

Even more important than the ranch? Or were they inextricable? Hell, if he knew the answer.

Stone and Alex hadn't been on a night ride in years. When they were kids, they used to steal away, ride deep into the night to get away from their respective parents. There was something calming in taking to the trails together, even if they didn't speak a helluva lot to each other.

Alex glanced over at his cousin. "Are you ready?"

Stone was preparing to mount Copper, his sorrel quarter horse.

"I bet you I can still whup your ass from here to the creek," Stone said, steadying himself on Copper. He tightened the reins, creating a curved arch in Copper's neck. The horse was sheer power.

The quarter horse danced with anticipation, sock-covered legs shifting from side to side, issuing a challenge.

"I doubt that. You're rusty these days." Alex absently stroked Zircon's neck. Zircon turned his head to nuzzle Alex's knee.

"It is my bachelor party, you know," Stone said dryly.

Alex smiled lazily. "All right. On my mark, though."

Stone nodded, urging Copper next to Zircon.

"One. Two. Three. Go."

Zircon leaped forward, seeming to read Alex's thoughts. That was what had always made horses easy for him. The nonverbal communication. The unexplainable connection.

From the corner of his vision, he could see the glint of Copper's tack. Stone was a stride ahead of him. Collecting his reins, Alex opened up Zircon's pace.

Zircon's ears pinned back as the horse surged forward. Finally Alex gained on his cousin as they drew closer to the creek. Memories of riding with Nina, of kissing her out here in the open on McNair land filled him. He had to see her tonight. No matter how late. Even if just to slide into bed with her and listen to her sleep.

The sensation of the gallop reverberated through Alex's bones. Shaking his thigh. Wait. The buzz wasn't from the connection of hooves and ground. It was his cell phone vibrating. *Damn.*

"Stone," he called out. "Hold on. Someone's calling."

As Alex slowed Zircon to a walk, the familiar ringtone replaced the hammering of hooves. Amie's ringtone. Amie who never called this late at night unless it was important. Or if there was trouble.

Hands shaking, Alex retrieved the phone from his pants. Stone slowed Copper, his face knotting with concern.

Alex took a deep breath. "Hello?"

Amie's voice pierced through the receiver. "It's Gran. She's got a horrible headache and the nurse is concerned. You know Gran never complains. We have to take her to the emergency room. It's faster than calling an ambulance. Please, you have to get here. Now."

"Stone and I will be right there." Alex looked at his cousin. "We've got to get to Gran. Something's wrong."

Stone nodded, his jaw tight with worry. Both men turned their horses back toward the barn. This time, they raced for another reason. For family. And Alex could swear Zircon burst quicker than he ever had before.

While she waited for Alex, Nina stretched out in her bed reading a Spanish translation of an American romance novel, work and pleasure all at once. She'd quickly become accustomed to having adult conversation at night and missed him.

And yes, her body burned to be with him again.

She glanced at her cell phone resting on top of the quilt. He'd said he would text when he was on his way so he wouldn't startle her. He was always so thoughtful, and the way he understood Cody made it tougher than ever to think about the end of the week. A lot could happen in the next few days.

Look how much already had.

Her cell phone vibrated on the bed—she'd been afraid to keep the ringer on for fear of waking up Cody. She scooped up her cell and found an incoming text. From Alex.

Delayed. Gran has severe headache. Going to ER.

Nina's fingers clenched around the phone, her heart aching for him. She texted back quickly.

So sorry. Prayers for your grandmother.

She wished she could do more, say more, have the right to go with him and comfort him. It was obvious his grandmother was like a mom to him. He spoke so highly of her and clearly admired her. Alex had to be going through a lot. How amazing that he still had so much to give both her and Cody this week between the wedding, his work and his grandmother's declining health.

Nina clutched the phone to her chest, flopping over to her back to watch the ceiling fan blades swirl. Had she been wrong to cut herself off from dating for so long? Did she even know how to answer that question when she couldn't even imagine being with any man other than Alex?

This was becoming such a tangle so fast when she'd been determined to never again to make an impulsive decision, to allow herself to be swept off her feet.

The phone hummed again and she pulled it up fast, elbowing to sit up. Hoping that it was Alex with good news.

Except it was an incoming call from her friend. "Hello, Reed."

"Hope I'm not calling too late."

"Not at all. I'm just reading, feeling lazy." She turned off the e-reader and set it on the bedside table. "Is everything okay at home?"

"I had to call. Those photos of Cody are incredible." Reed's favored eighties radio station played in the background. "I'm signing Wendy up. They had to put her on the waiting list, though. You sure were lucky to get a slot."

Nina thought back to her flurry of packing and preparation when the surprise slot and discount fee came open so quickly. "They told me there was a last-minute cancellation."

"And a waiting list a mile long."

She sat up straighter. "I don't know how to explain it, but I can put in a good word for you with the McNairs. I've, uh, gotten to know them this week."

"That would be fabulous, sweetie. Thanks. I wouldn't ask for myself, but it's for Wendy." He paused. "You're doing okay, then?"

"Cody's thriving. I'm doing great, enjoying the change of scenery." She used to travel often with her UN job. She missed that sometimes, and that made her feel guilty. It wasn't Cody's fault. The support group where she'd met Reed and learned to cope had changed her life and saved her sanity. "Wendy will love it here and so will you."

"Glad to hear it. Well, keep those photos coming. Night."

"Night," she responded, disconnecting and flopping back again. Her thoughts swirled and she felt she was missing something in her exhaustion.

She couldn't account for how she'd gotten the slot this week, but she knew everything about meeting Alex McNair felt as though it was meant to be, each day more perfect than the last. She was tired of being wary and cautious. Her time with Alex had been a personal fairy tale and she wasn't willing to question that. He was different than her frog-prince ex-husband. Alex had to be.

Sleep tugged at her and maybe a bit of denial too, because she just wanted to enjoy her remaining days here and let the future wait.

With only the moonlight in his bedroom to guide him, Alex tugged off his shirt, which still held the scent of smoke from the bachelor party and a hint of the antiseptic air from the hospital. The ER doc had diagnosed Gran with dehydration. An IV bag of fluid later, they'd released her to come home under the care of her nurse.

Or rather she'd insisted nothing would keep her from making the most of the wedding weekend with her family. She would check with her doctor every day and she already had round-the-clock nurses staying at the house. But she was dying and no amount of meds would change that.

Anger and denial roared through him. He didn't want to stay here and he didn't feel like sleeping. He yanked a well-worn green T-shirt from the drawer and tugged it over his head. The grandfather clock in his suite chimed three times in the dark. Regardless of the time, he had to see Nina.

He opened the doors out to his patio, leaped over the railing and jogged across the lawn toward her cabin. He had a key. She'd given him one for tonight right before he left. The full moon shot rays through the oak trees, along the path. Most of the cabins were dark. The only sounds were bugs and frogs. He took the steps up to Nina's two at a time and let himself inside quietly.

He checked on Cody first. A buckaroo bronco lamp glowed on the dresser. The boy slept deeply, his blond hair shiny in the soft light, his room cool and his weighted blanket on top of him. Nina had told Alex once that the cocooned feeling helped her son with serotonin production or something like that he'd meant to read up on.

He closed the door carefully and stepped into Nina's room. She was beautiful, princesslike even. Her bold red curls piled around her neck. Causal. Desirable. She was asleep on top of the covers, her cell phone in her left hand and her e-reader on the bedside table. She had on a light pink *C'est La Vie* T-shirt with a picture of the Eiffel Tower. The shirt barely covered her thighs. He thought about taking her there. To Paris. To Rome. And so many other places. To bed.

If she could forgive him for his half-truths this week.

Sitting on the edge, he eased the covers back. "Nina, it's me."

"Alex," she sighed, her voice groggy as she rolled toward him to portion of the bed with the quilt pushed aside. "How's your grandmother?"

Her concern was apparent, even if she wasn't fully awake. Damn.

"Gran is at home resting peacefully in her own bed. She was just dehydrated from the summer heat." He tugged the covers over Nina, kicked off his shoes and slid into bed beside her. "I hope you don't mind that I'm here. I know it's late, but I missed you."

"So glad you came." She cuddled closer, her arm sliding around his waist. "Missed you too."

Her warm soft body fit against his, the sweet smell of her shampoo filling every breath. He stroked her back in lazy circles, taking comfort in touching her. Hell, just being with her. His body throbbed in response, but she was asleep. So he gritted his teeth and tried to will away the erection.

Easier said than done.

She wriggled closer with a sleepy sigh. He bit back a groan. Maybe coming here and expecting he could just sleep hadn't been such a wise idea after all.

Her leg nestled between his. The soft skin of her calf added fuel to his already flaming fire. He ached to be inside her, to hear those kittenish sighs of pleasure mixed with demands for more. She was a passionate, giving lover. He wondered what it would have been like if her last name wasn't Lowery and she'd just been a regular mom bringing her son to camp.

She slid her hand down his side over his hip, wriggling against him. Was she dreaming? The thought of her having sensual dreams turned him inside out. But he couldn't take advantage of her that way.

Then her hand slipped around to cradle his erection.

He grasped her wrist and willed himself to move away. "Nina, you're dreaming."

Her eyelashes swept up and she smiled at him. "Dreaming? Not hardly."

Her voice was groggy, although she was very obviously awake. She unzipped his pants and wrapped her fingers around the length of him. His eyes slid closed and he allowed himself a moment to enjoy the sensation of her touch. The outside world would be intruding soon enough. This could well be his last chance alone with her before she dumped him—or his family scared her away.

"Nina…" he groaned, his arms going around her as he rolled to tuck her beneath him. "I need you."

"How perfectly convenient," she murmured in a husky voice, "because I've been dreaming of you and I need you too. Now. Inside me. I've been thinking about you all night long."

He fished out his wallet and tossed a condom on the bed before sweeping her underwear down. She kicked them aside with an efficient flick. And his whole body shouted to thrust inside her. But he needed to imprint himself in her memory—her in his own—in case this was their last time together.

No. It couldn't be their last night together. He refused to entertain the possibility.

He kissed along her jaw, her neck, then lower, between her breasts and lower still. Her breath hitched as she picked up his intent seconds before he nuzzled between her legs. He blew a light puff of air over her and she shivered, her fingers sliding into his hair, tugging lightly. She arched up as he stroked and laved. Each purr and moan and sigh from her had him throbbing with the need to take her. Her head thrashed back and forth on her pillow, her pleasure so beautiful to watch.

Then she tugged at his shoulders, scratching, urging him breathlessly, "So close. I want to come with you inside me, but I can't hold out much longer."

He didn't need to be told again. Pressing a final intimate kiss to her, he slid back up her body, nipping along her stomach and her breasts. Her hands impatient, she took the weight of him in her palms stroking, coaxing until he growled in frustration.

Smiling with feminine power, she sheathed him with another arousing stroke. He covered her, settling between her thighs, waiting even though holding back was pure torture. Finally she opened her eyes and looked straight at him. Holding her gaze, he pushed inside her velvety warmth with a powerful thrust. And damn, he was glad she was near her own release, because his was only a few strokes away. He moved inside her, again and again, her legs wrapping around his waist, drawing him deeper.

The bed creaked and the ceiling fan blew cool gusts over his back. But even blasts from the air conditioner couldn't stop the heat pumping through his veins. He saw the flush of impending release climbing up her neck, and he captured her mouth, taking her cries of completion, his own mixing with hers.

Perfection. Nina. Coming undone in his arms.

Rolling to his side, he held her to him, the aftershocks rippling through them. The night sounds of bugs and frogs sounded along with a gentle patter of a rain shower starting up again. He smoothed his hand over her hair, her face tucked against his chest until eventually her breathing returned to normal, then slower as sleep grabbed hold of her again.

So much weighed on his heart—between his grandmother's illness and the impossible position she'd put him in. He couldn't wait another day to unburden himself, even if he knew Nina was sleeping. And yeah, maybe he also needed to test out the words to find a way to tell her when the time was right. "Nina, I need to tell you something."

"Mmm," she answered, her eyes closed. Her arm draped limply over him.

He knew she likely couldn't hear, but still he confessed everything his grandmother had asked him to do, how torn he felt, how much he wanted her... And the unheard words didn't make him feel any better. So he just held her until the sun started to peek from the horizon. He needed to leave before her son woke. Alex had to prepare for his cousin's rehearsal dinner.

And for the proverbial storm that his mother brought to every occasion.

Nerves made Nina restless about her date with Alex. Her hand shook as she swept on mascara, leaning toward the mirror and praying she wouldn't end up looking like a clown this evening. She had tried out a makeup tutorial from the internet to update her look since she didn't get out much these days. Winged eyeliner. Classy and timeless but she would have to watch the sweat this weekend.

It was only a date. She was just Alex's plus-one for his cousin's rehearsal dinner. Except it wasn't just any party. It was a McNair affair, an exclusive event.

And Nina was sleeping with him. They'd gone beyond a one-night fling. And he'd left her the sweetest note on her pillow, in Spanish this time. Not perfect, but perfectly adorable. He'd complemented her beauty while sleeping and said she would be in his thoughts all day. She'd already tucked the note into her suitcase along with the card he'd given her with the wildflowers.

So yes, she wanted to be at her best and only had the limited wardrobe she'd packed for a children's cowboy camp.

She'd taken two hours this morning to race around and find new dresses to wear to the rehearsal party and the wedding, and an outfit for Cody tomorrow. She'd thought she misheard Alex when he said he wanted her son to attend the wedding, and she was more than a little nervous for her child. But Alex assured her it would be a casual affair with a Texas flair Cody would enjoy. There would even be three other children there.

It was almost as if she belonged here. With Alex.

A dangerous thought. They'd only known each other a few days. But she damn sure intended to leave an indelible impression on his memory.

She clipped on a brass bracelet with Spanish inscriptions, another acquisition from Diamonds in the Rough, and smoothed her loose chevron-patterned sundress. She admired her freshly painted toenails peeking out of her strappy sandals and stepped out of her bedroom into the living room, then stopped short, her heart squeezing at the sight in front of her. Alex and her son, both catnapping.

Cody curled up on the sofa, hugging his blanket and wearing new puppy dog pj's she'd picked up for him during her shopping spree this morning. The actual wedding rehearsal had already taken place and she'd skipped that to prepare her son before Alex came by to pick her up.

Alex snored softly in the fat leather chair, his booted feet propped on the ottoman. Her gaze skated from his boots, up muscular legs in khakis, past a Diamonds in the Rough belt buckle, to broad shoulders in a sports coat. A Stetson covered his face. He looked so much like his cousin Stone it would have been easy for someone to mistake the two men for each other. But she would know her man anywhere.

Her man?

When had she started thinking in possessive terms like that? And after such a short time knowing him?

They'd stolen late-night dates, but his days had been taken up with work and she'd focused on Cody's camp—other than keeping her cell phone in reach at all times, treasuring each quick call or text from Alex.

Oh God, she was in serious trouble here.

He tapped his hat upward and he whistled softly. "Nice!"

"Thanks," she said, spinning, the skirt rustling along her knees, "I guess it's time?"

"The sitter is already warming Cody's supper in the kitchen." Standing, Alex walked toward her, eyes stroking her the whole way. "And I queued up his favorite videos, since he'll probably be up late because he napped."

She stepped into the circle of his arms. "Is there anything you haven't thought of?"

"I sure hope not. I'm doing everything in my power to ensure that this evening is as pleasant as possible to make up for having to spend time with my mother."

"She can't be that bad." Certainly not as bad as Nina's in-laws. They'd been distant while she was married, but grew outright hostile after her divorce. And now? They barely acknowledged Cody existed. They rarely spoke to her. "I'll be fine."

He squeezed her arm. "Okay, then. But if you need me to rescue you from her, give me a sign. Like tug on your earlobe."

Laughing, she hooked arms with him, then ducked her head in to say hello to the sitter before they left. One of the camp counselors had agreed to watch Cody.

After a short walk to the open air barn full of family and friends, Nina found herself searching for his parents. Curious after all she'd heard. Alex went straight for them as if to get past the introductions and move on. An older couple stood together under an oak tree strung with white lights. The pair was easily identifiable as his parents by the resemblance. Although their idea of casual sure came with a lot of starch and spray tan.

"Mother, Dad," Alex said, placing a possessive hand on Nina's back, "this is Nina Lowery."

Bayleigh McNair was a beautiful woman, no question—except for her beady eyes, which moved around quickly, assessing without ever meeting Nina's gaze. "Lovely to meet you, dear. How long have you and my son been seeing each other?"

"Mom, I already told you she's here with her son for Stone's new camp." His hand twitched ever so slightly, even though his voice stayed amiable.

"So you just met this week." Eyebrows raised, Bayleigh looked at Nina as if she were a gold digger.

Indignation fired hot and fierce. How unfair and judgmental. And Nina had no choice but to keep her mouth closed and be polite. "We met my first day here. I thought he was one of the ranch hands. Can you imagine that?"

"How quaint." Bayleigh half smiled.

Amie joined them, the feathers on her skirt brushing Nina's legs. "Mother, you're being rude. Stop it or I'll wear white shoes after Labor Day."

Her mother sniffed, looking offended. "No need to be obnoxious, dear."

Alex's father folded her hand in his. "Nina, it's lovely to meet you. And your last name, Lowery... If I remember correctly, you married into the Lowery Resort family."

"Yes, sir." She shook his hand briskly, then twined her fingers in front of her. She wasn't comfortable talking about money the way these people were. That was her son's money, her ex-husband's wealth. She'd grown up in a regular middle-class neighborhood.

Garnet clapped his son on the shoulder. "That's mighty big of you, son, letting the competition in here this way."

Nina frowned. "Competition?"

Bayleigh swatted her husband's arm. "Leave the poor girl alone before Amie threatens us again. You heard Alex say she's here with her child, you know, for that *special* camp. For *special* kids."

Nina bristled. That last comment went too far. Digs at her were one thing. But her son was off-limits. Was this woman that clueless or deliberately baiting her?

Alex's father hooked arms with his wife to steer her away—thank heavens. "We should check on Mother. Inside."

Bayleigh patted his hand. "I know it's so hard for you to see her that way."

Garnet's chin trembled and he leaned on his wife. Amie cursed softly and walked into the barn full of tables and a dais.

Alex's jaw flexed and he hung his head, sweeping his hat off to scratch a hand through his hair. "I am so damn sorry for my mother's behavior. It's inexcusable." He dropped his hat back on his head. "I wouldn't blame you if you wanted to leave now."

Nina rocked on her heels. "I have to confess, she's a lot to take in all at once, but I'm fine. There's plenty to celebrate here and other people to meet. Let's have fun."

"That's diplomatic and kind of you." He caressed her shoulders, comforting and arousing at the same time. "Is there something I can do other than gag my parents?"

As angry as his mother had made her, Nina could let it go. The woman was superficial and catty. However, Nina's mind was quietly turning over the "competition" thing Alex's father had mentioned. What had she missed? She thought about how Reed had insisted spots at this camp were impossible to come by. Had someone in the McNair organization wanted to keep the competition close?

Certainly there was no way Alex would know about her relation to the Lowerys, was there? She shook off the suspicion.

Alex was clearly hurting now over his mom's behavior, and it wasn't fair to blame him for his mother or take out her frustration on him. "I know your parents are grieving too. People are rarely at their best when they're hurting."

His hands slid up to cup her face. "That's more generous than she deserves. More generous than I deserve too, because I should have given you a stronger warning."

"You're not responsible for your parents." Now that her anger had faded to a low simmer, she saw the pain they'd caused him. "Are *you* okay?"

He folded her hand in his. "I'm a big boy. I know my parents. I just want better for Gran, especially now."

"Your grandmother *has* better. She has *you*." Nina took in the angles of his face, touched by the wind and sun, nothing affected or fake. "And she has Amie—I like your sister."

His mouth twitched. "She's a character."

"From everything I've seen of Stone and his fiancée, they've made your grandmother very happy with their wedding. And I assume seeing you there with a date on your arm will reassure her, as well." Another suspicion blindsided her, one she hadn't considered. "Is that why you've been pursuing me? To make your grandmother happy by having a date at the wedding?"

He hesitated, then shook his head. "I'm not sleeping with you to make my grandmother happy." His throat moved in a long swallow. "But there is something important I need to tell you once we're alone."

# Ten

The three hours since Alex had said they needed to talk had passed at a torturous snail's pace. Nina wondered how much longer she could hold out waiting to hear what Alex needed to tell her. Good or bad? But if it had been good, wouldn't he have told her right then?

Her mind raced with darker possibilities. Had she allowed herself to get too excited over him? Overanalyzed his gestures? Made too much out of a few days?

She swiped sweat from her brow, searching for the restroom to make sure her mascara and eyeliner hadn't dripped into raccoon eyes after all the dancing she'd done. The live country band had started their first set with a Garth Brooks classic and Nina had thrown herself into the fun with both feet, telling herself to enjoy every moment she could before her time with Alex ended. She'd had fun, but after almost an hour on the dance floor, Nina was certain she looked like a train wreck.

She slid around tables full of guests enjoying after-dinner drinks and coffee. The desserts were all shaped and decorated like jewels. The event was lavish but personal, and touching, reminding her of all she'd once dreamed of having when she started her life with Warren.

Her imagination had been running wild all evening through dinner. Coveted camp slots? Lowerys competing with McNairs? A grandmother who wanted to see her grandchildren settled before she died.

Nina's instincts shouted that something was off, but she couldn't figure out exactly how she fit into the picture. And this wasn't the first time Alex had said he wanted to talk to her. Her heart beat faster, her chest going tight.

She tugged open a door and instead of a bathroom she found an office, with a desk, chairs—and Amie sprawled on the rust-colored velvet sofa. Her eyes were closed, but she was clearly awake. Tear tracks streaked through her makeup.

Nina stepped into the room and closed the door quickly behind her. "Amie?" she asked, walking to the sofa. "What's wrong? Are you all right?"

"Hell no." She peeked out of one eye, dragging in deep breaths. "But I will be."

Kneeling, Nina touched her arm. "Is there something I can do? Get you a tissue? A drink?"

"How about a pair of lead shoes, preferably men's size twelve?" Amie said bitterly, sitting upright and swinging her feet to the floor, tucking her feet back into her high heels.

"Ouch. Sounds bad." Sounded man-bad.

"Nothing I can't handle. I'm usually better at controlling my emotions, but there's so much going on…" She eyed the dartboard, strode over with determination and grabbed a handful of darts from the tray and plucked three from the target. "Next best thing to lead shoes? A dart, right in the face."

Nina winced. "Um, I'm not sure that's legal."

Amie backed away from the board. "I'm not going to stab him literally. Just imagine his face right there…" She lined up the toss. "…Bull's-eye. Every time. Rage does funny things like that."

"Remind me never to make you mad." Nina raised her hands in surrender, offering Amie a playful smile.

"Ah, honey." Amie turned fast and gave Nina a hard hug, one of the darts in Amie's fist scratching a little against Nina's back. "I would never hurt you. You're too nice."

"Do you mind if I ask which man made you mad? Family?" She saw a no and finished, "Or someone else?"

"Someone—" Amie pitched a dart "—else." She launched another.

"I'm sorry. I know how much it hurts to be betrayed by a man." Nina's ex-husband had left a river of pain in his wake, one she was still fording.

Amie avoided Nina's eyes, charged up to the board and pulled out the darts one at a time. "You're a strong, beautiful woman. Don't let anyone in my family walk over you."

Nina's nerves gathered into a big knot of uncertainty about Alex's secret. She churned over a million possibilities, but regardless of which one was true, they all led to the same ending.

Alex was going to break things off with her. Of course he was. He'd clearly just needed a date for the night. He had something to prove to his mother. To Johanna. Nina was just arm candy.

She'd wanted a fling, and Lord, she'd gotten it. This one week and one week only. And it was over. Her stomach plummeted worse than when Zircon had spooked.

What a time to realize she wanted more. What a time to realize how easy it would have been to have a life here with Alex.

Alex guided Nina out onto the dance floor, having ached to have her in his arms all night long. He had feelings for her that were about more than sex. He cared about her. Admired her even.

And he had to be honest with her, even if that cost him the ranch. He wanted his grandmother to be happy, but he couldn't do that at the expense of his honor. Seeing the strength and commitment—and love—Nina showered on her son made Alex realize he needed to man up.

"Let's dance outside, where it's less crowded," he said, clasping her hand and steering her into a dance under the lit oak trees.

The night was beautiful, the air cooler and the music a little quieter outdoors. Two people sat on a bench talking, and another couple danced, but none of them were close enough to overhear.

She was stiff in his arms, reserved and dodging his gaze. His mother had clearly done damage as usual. God, where did he even start?

"Nina—"

"Go ahead," she blurted out, her legs brushing against his.

He paused, angling back to look into her eyes. "Go ahead and what?"

"Go ahead and break things off with me. That's what you wanted to tell me, isn't it?" she asked, her face void of expression. She'd already built a tall wall between them. "You don't have to make this any more awkward than it already is. We had a fling and it's over. You don't need me to be your plus one at the wedding tomorrow. Dance with your sister, enjoy your family."

He pressed his fingers to her mouth. "That's not what I wanted to say at all."

A flicker of uncertainty sparked in her green eyes. Something that looked like cautious hope. "Then what is it?"

"I owe you an apology for not being up front at the start."

"I thought we discussed that already. You hid the fact that you weren't just a ranch hand. But we moved past that." Her fingers clenched, bunching his shirt in her hands. "It was a minor misunderstanding."

This was tougher than he'd expected but long overdue. "When my grandmother's cancer was first diagnosed, stock prices dropped because of concerns about the future of the holdings. My cousin and my grandmother thought they'd tracked the purchasers of those stocks to make sure no one group amassed a portion large enough to risk gaining control of the company."

Her eyes went from wary to resigned. "Something went wrong."

"Lowery Resorts has been buying up McNair stocks."

Her feet stopped moving altogether. His words hung between them, his gut heavy with guilt.

"My in-laws." Her hands fell to her sides; her fists clenched.

"In a sense. Your son's trust fund uses the same investment broker. He used shell corporations to buy up stocks for your son as well as your in-laws. The stocks that went to your son slipped under our radar."

"Until now." She sagged to sit on a rustic wooden bench. "It's no accident that I'm here, is it?"

He sat beside her, his hands clasped between his knees. "No, my grandmother made sure you received the brochure and the scholarship."

She met his gaze full on, her chin set but her eyes glistening with unshed tears. "And your role in this?"

"My grandmother wants me to encourage you to sell those stocks back to us."

Her eyebrows pinched together. Her face was impassive. The wall from earlier sprang back in full force. Damn. "Why didn't you just say that from the start? We could have negotiated."

"We didn't think you would agree." How had this ever made sense to him? He should have known this was a train wreck in the making from the start. He should have passed it over to the lawyers and accountants and let them handle it. Emotions screwed up business. "It's a great time to buy but not a good time to sell. In all honesty, it wouldn't be in your son's best interest to sell."

"Why is there an issue with having other stockholders?"

"Think about the resorts your in-laws build and look at Hidden Gem." The thought of his home being turned into a tourist trap made him ill. "We have a problem."

"More than one apparently." Sighing, she blinked fast and slumped back against the bench. Her mouth opened slightly, allowing a breath of words to escape. "How much of what we shared was even real, Alex?"

"God, Nina, how can you even ask that? My grand-mother not only wanted me to persuade you to give up those stocks, but she led me to believe my inheritance depended on it, like a test to prove how badly I wanted my piece of the family business. But I couldn't do what she asked. I pursued you in spite of her test. I'm being honest with you now. I never wanted those stocks to come between us." He reached for her only to have her flinch away. His worst nightmare come true. He'd told her the truth and she hated him for it. Not that he could blame her. It sounded awful when he laid it out. If he could only make her see he cared about her. About her kid. It wasn't about the stocks anymore. It never had been. He was falling for her and her son.

Footsteps sounded behind him, and Nina looked over his shoulder, distracted. He glanced back to find his sister racing toward them, a ringing purse in her hand.

"Nina, you left your bag back on the sofa. The sitter has been trying to reach you. She called me too."

Nina shot to her feet, her eyes wide with alarm. "Did Cody wake up? I need to go to him."

Alex knew his sister well, and even though she appeared poised, he could see the signs of blind panic. Something was wrong, very wrong. He stood beside Nina.

Amie clasped Nina's hands. "No, it's not that. I'm sorry to have to tell you this, but Cody is missing."

Alex's nightmare just got a whole lot worse.

"Cody!" Nina shouted into the night, her voice hoarse, her heart raw. Holding a flashlight, she walked alongside Alex into woods.

The staff was checking every inch of the lodge and the cabins. The family and guests were searching the grounds. She was running on fumes and fear. Other voices echoed in the distance shouting her son's name, but she knew too well even if he heard, he very well might not be able to open up enough to answer.

Her world was collapsing. Her son had wandered off. The sitter had put him to bed, and she was positive he hadn't gone out past her. His window was open. And he was gone.

Nina had been frantic and tried to bolt out to begin searching, but Alex had remained calm, held her back and reminded her that an organized approach would cover more ground faster. Ranch security had been notified and a grid search was under way.

Knowing that everything possible was being done hadn't made the last hour any less horrific. She'd allowed herself to be charmed and distracted by a man who was only using her, and now her child was in danger. She would never forgive herself. Served her right for believing she was in another fairy tale.

Alex swept his larger spotlight across the path leading to the creek they'd once soared over on a horseback. Nausea roiled. The thought of her son drowning…

She bit back a whimper.

Sweeping the spotlight along the creek, Alex stepped over a log. "We'll find him. We have plans in place for things like this, grid searches and manpower. We'll find him before you know it."

"This is my fault." And there was nothing anyone could say to convince her otherwise. She walked alongside the water, shallow, probably not deep enough to be a worry, but everywhere was dangerous to a boy with little understanding of fears or boundaries. "I should have been with him tonight."

"It's impossible for you to be with him every minute of every day," Alex pointed out logically. "The sitter has excellent credentials too."

And yes, he was right. But that meant nothing to a mother in the grip of her worst nightmare. "That's not making me feel any better."

"This kind of thing happens even when there's a houseful of adults watching." His spotlight swept over a trickling waterfall, no sign of her son. "You can't be attached at the hip."

"Intellectually I know that. But in my heart? I'll never forgive myself."

A rustling in the woods drew her up short. She struggled to listen, to discern...A rabbit leaped out of the brush and scampered away. Disappointment threatened to send her to her knees. Alex's arm slid around her to bolster her.

She drew in a shaky breath and regained her footing. "You can relax. I'm not planning to sue the camp. I just want to find my son."

"Nina, God." He took her arm. "Lawsuits are the last thing on my mind. I'm worried about Cody." His voice cracked on the last word.

"I shouldn't have said that." She pressed her fingers to her throbbing head. "I'm terrified and on edge."

"Understandably so." Having reached the end of the creek, he turned back, sweeping the light ahead of them, up along trees with branches fat and low enough for a child to climb. Owl eyes gleamed back at them. "Later we'll figure out if there's fault and if so, that employee will be dismissed. Right now we can only think about one thing."

"I appreciate that you're able to keep such a cool head." She swallowed down her fear and forced herself to think about the search for her son.

"You know, Stone and I wandered off once."

She realized he was likely trying to calm her by making aimless conversation, but she appreciated the effort, grounding herself in his deep steady voice. "Really? Where did you go?"

"Into these woods." His footsteps crunched as he backtracked toward the ranch again. "We planned to live off the land like cowboys, catch fish, build a fire and sleep in a tent."

"Obviously you made it home all right."

"A thunderstorm rolled through and drenched us. We got sick on the candy we packed, since we didn't catch a single fish." Flashlights from other searchers sent splashes of light through the trees, voices echoing. "And we had so many mosquito bites Gran made us wear gloves to keep from scratching."

"What gave you the idea to try such a dangerous thing?" she asked, on the off chance that would give her some insight to where her son might have wandered off to.

"We were boys. Boys don't need a reason to do stupid things," he said dryly.

"While I can agree on that," she answered with a much-needed smile, brief, then fading, "I think something made the two of you run off."

Alex sighed. "Stone's junkie mom had just threatened to take him again, and when I asked my parents to file for custody, they said no," he recounted with an emotionless voice at odds with his white-knuckled grip on the massive flashlight as they drew closer to the corrals. "Gran even asked them once too. But no go. Anyhow, that day, we decided for twenty-four hours we would be brothers."

His story touched her heart with a sense of family she'd never had, and while it didn't excuse his keeping secrets from her, she could sense the conflict he must have felt over the stocks and the ownership of a place that meant so much to him.

She leaned against the corral rail, her flashlight pointing downward. "Thank you. For trying to distract me while we search—"

Alex held up a hand. "Shhh…Nina. Listen."

She straightened, tipping her ears to catch sounds carried on the breeze, to parse through the people shouting for her son, the four-wheeler driving.

And puppies mewling.

She gasped. "Puppies. He's—"

"With the puppies," Alex finished, already sprinting toward the barn where the children had played with livestock.

Where he'd shown Cody the litter of puppies.

They'd checked here earlier and hadn't seen him. Could they have missed him? Or maybe he hadn't made his way here yet when they came through the first time?

Nina raced past him and yanked open the barn door. "Cody? Cody?"

Alex waved to her. "Over here. Asleep behind bales of hay holding a puppy."

She tore across the earthen floor, dropping to her knees and soaking in the sight of her son curled up around the fuzzy black puppy. He wasn't with all of the puppies. He just had one and they'd missed him. Somehow they'd overlooked him, but she wasn't going to second-guess. Not now. She was so damn grateful to have her child safe. Tears of relief streaked down her face, mixed with pent-up emotion from the entire week. She slid down to the ground, unable to escape reality.

She'd found her son—and now she needed to leave.

# Eleven

Perched on the edge of Cody's bed, Nina tucked her son in for the night. He stared back at her as he rhythmically touched the top of his blanket, completely unconcerned. She should never have left him this evening. Shudders pulsated as her thoughts wandered on what could have happened. But Cody was here.

Safe.

She didn't take that gift of safety for granted for even an instant. This evening could have ended so horribly. She should be happy. Relieved. But she was still so shell-shocked by Alex's revelation and the hour of terror looking for her son that she could barely function. Nina let out a breath she didn't realize had been locked in her chest.

She smoothed Cody's hair and he let her touch him without flinching. "Please don't wander off without telling me, okay? I know it's difficult for you to talk, but this is important. I need to know where you are."

"Want that collie puppy," he whispered, and pulled a piece of paper from under his covers. He'd drawn a puppy playing in the barn. The detail was stunning, capturing the border collie perfectly. So much talent.

If only they'd found that picture earlier, it would have steered them right to him. "We'll get a puppy when we're home, okay, sweetie?"

Cody sat up, hugging his puffy blue blanket. He shook his head. "Want a puppy here."

Her heart tugged at all the things she couldn't give him. "Oh, my sweet boy, it's beautiful here and I love your pictures so very much. But we have to go home."

His eyes darted from side to side, stopping to stare at the outfit on his dresser. Fresh blue jeans sat beneath a brand-new yellow cowboy shirt. A brand-new kid-sized Stetson hat rested on the top of the pile. Pale tan rope circled the base of the hat, the ends joined by a silver horse charm. New brown cowboy boots with a matching fringe vest sat next to the clothes. "The wedding. I have new clothes. We gotta go to the wedding. With the kitty lady."

His jaw jutted.

She could see him ramping up and needed a way to calm him. "We'll go to the wedding. You will get to wear your new outfit."

"Okay, okay."

"But I need you to promise me you won't wander off like that again. You could have been hurt. I was very scared for you. I need you to say the words, Cody. Promise me."

He avoided her eyes, but he nodded, lying back down again. "Promise."

"Good boy." She patted the blue blanket. "It's time to go to sleep. Night-night. I love you so much."

She could speak multiple languages, but words were so hard to find to get through to her precious child. What would she have done tonight without Alex's support?

Ah, Alex. The heartbreaking cowboy. Now, there was a touchy subject. Her stomach tightened as her brain tried to make sense of her conflicting emotions.

Backing away from Cody's bed, she adjusted the Buckaroo Bronco lamp on her way out. She closed the door softly. Sagging back against the panel, she let the tears flow, wishing the pain could be uncorked so easily.

A movement deep in the living room snagged her attention and she saw Alex rise from the sofa. Had it only been a few hours ago he'd come here to take her to the party? She'd dressed with such hope and silly expectations from a tube of mascara.

He walked across the floor and wrapped his arms around her. She pushed against his chest in a half-hearted attempt to make some kind of point. To get back at him for seeming so perfect and being so very flawed. Even worse, dishonest. Was he really just another frog-prince?

Crying harder, she pressed her face against his chest to muffle the sounds so her son wouldn't hear. She twisted her hands in his shirt.

Her legs buckled and his arms banded tighter around her. He smoothed her hair and mumbled words against her head. He backed closer to the living area until he sat in the fat armchair and pulled her into his lap. She continued to cry, not the hard racking sobs anymore, but the silent slip of tears down her cheeks. His hands roved up and down her back rhythmically.

As she shifted, her face brushed his. Or maybe his brushed hers and their mouths met, held. She should pull away. This was a bad idea for a thousand reasons that would only lead to more heartache. But this was her last chance to feel his hands on her, his mouth. She didn't want lies, excuses or half-truths. She didn't even want to talk. She wanted this. This man might not have what she needed from life, but she would take this moment of pleasure for herself before she left. She'd come a long way from the woman who'd married Warren and hoped for the best.

She looped her arms around Alex's neck as she wriggled closer. Neither of them asked if it was right or wrong. Their bodies spoke, communed, and his hands clasped her hips, shifting her until she straddled his lap. He bunched her dress up, his fingers warm on her skin, twisting the thin barrier of her underwear until the strings along her hips *snapped*.

Without breaking their kiss she fished in his pocket for his wallet and found a condom. With sure hands she unbuckled that rodeo belt and unzipped his pants. He growled his approval against her mouth.

Then frenzy took over and she lowered herself onto him. Inch by inch. His hands on her hips, her hands on his shoulders and yes… Her head fell back as their hips rolled in sync. Faster and faster. The heat and need built inside her, all the pent-up emotion from the night, crushed dreams and disappointment leaving her raw.

Soon—too soon and yet not soon enough—she felt

the rise of her orgasm building, slamming through her, riding the wave of all those emotions. She sank her teeth in Alex's shoulder to keep from shouting out. His hands clenched in her hair, his fists tight as she felt his release rock through him.

In the aftermath, she kept her face tucked into his neck while he stroked her back. Even though she would be attending the wedding tomorrow, she knew…

This was goodbye.

Wedding photos and receiving line complete, Alex was finally free to mingle before dinner and dancing kicked into high gear. He knew more about weddings than most men. After all, the Hidden Gem hosted them on a regular basis. And he focused on every damn detail tonight to keep from thinking about the hole in his heart over losing Nina. Last night had put him through the emotional wringer—from their fight, to Cody wandering off, and then to making love with Nina in a frenzied moment that had goodbye written all over it.

Damn straight he needed to think of something else to keep from walking away to lose himself in a bottle of booze in the solitude of his suite. So he focused on every detail, making sure the wedding and reception went off without a hitch.

And damned if he wasn't too aware of Nina and Cody's presence anyway.

Even knowing she'd only attended because her son had been emphatic about it didn't stop the rush of pleasure having them here. The kid was something else. Who'd have thought he would dig his heels in on wearing his new clothes and attending a cowboy wedding? Cody looked as though he belonged here, at Hidden

Gem Ranch, with his cowboy outfit. Guilt struck at Alex, rattling through his chest. He had to focus.

The vows Johanna and Stone had spoken were from the heart, the ceremony in the chapel brief. One grooms-man and one bridesmaid—Alex and Amie. The bride wore a simple fitted lace dress with a short train. The loose, romantic waves of her hair complemented the airiness of her dress. Elegant. Understated. Her lone bridesmaid wore a peach-colored dress in a similar but simpler style, to the floor without a train.

Stone and Alex wore tan suits with buff-colored Stet-sons for when they were outside. This event was about the bride and groom, their style, making memories on their day.

At the end of the service, as Alex escorted his sis-ter out of the church, he felt the weight of Nina's gaze, felt the hurt he'd caused her. More guilt. More shame. And he didn't know how the hell to make it right and he didn't know who to turn to for guidance.

Silently he and Amie walked to the barn where the rehearsal dinner had been held. All of the decorations from the night before were still in place, plus more. Gold chandeliers and puffs of white hydrangeas dangled from the barn rafters. Strings of lights crisscrossed the ceiling, creating an intimate, dreamy atmosphere. Bouquets of ba-by's breath and roses tied with burlap bows graced all the tables. The inside had been transformed into rustic ele-gance, with gold chairs and white tulle draped throughout.

There were rustic touches as well. At the entry table next to the leather guest book, seating cards were tied to horse shoes that had the bride and groom's names engraved along with the wedding date. A cowbell hung on a brass hook with a sign that stated Ring for a Kiss.

A country band played easy-listening versions of old classics.

But Alex was in no mood for dancing. Not if he couldn't have Nina in his arms. She'd made it clear last night after she'd booted him out of her bed that she was leaving right after the wedding. She'd only stayed this long for Cody. Alex poured himself a drink and found a table in the far back corner. Isolated. He would have to move up front with the family soon enough. For now, he could be alone with his drink and his thoughts.

"Mind if I join you?" His father stood beside him.

"Um, no, not at all." He gestured to an empty chair. "Have a seat, but Gran will insist we move up front to the main table soon."

"Then we might as well enjoy this as long as we can." Garnet tipped back his drink. "You look like you could use some support—or advice. Woman troubles?"

"There's nothing anyone can do." Alex sipped the bourbon, watching Nina and Cody talk to the bride. The little boy touched the bridal bouquet with reverence.

Memories of walking the ranch looking for Cody gut-kicked Alex all over again. He'd never known a fear that deep. Or a relief so intense once they'd found him.

Rattling the ice in his glass, Garnet followed Alex's gaze before studying his son hard. "People think your mother married me for my money and that I live off my inheritance. And they wouldn't be totally wrong on either of those points. But you know what, son?"

Alex met his father's piercing gaze—the McNair blue eyes—and finally saw a little of Gran in there. "What, Dad?"

"It's none of their damn business. Bayleigh and I may not live our lives the way others would, but it works for us." He thumbed his wedding ring around his finger. "We have a happy marriage. I did learn that from my parents. Pick the right person for you and to hell with everyone else's expectations. This is your life."

Alex wasn't sure how to apply the advice to his own personal hell, but he appreciated his father's effort. "Any reason you never thought to have this kind of father-son talk with me before now?"

"You didn't need it then." Garnet shrugged, adjusting his bolo tie. "Now I believe you do."

"It's not that simple with Nina." There. Alex had said it. Acknowledged that he and Nina were—or had been—a couple. He wanted her in his life.

"Sure it's every bit as simple as that. Buy the stocks from her. Pay more than they're worth and give that boy some extra security." Garnet's practicality sounded more and more like a McNair by the second. Maybe everyone had underestimated him. "So what if the ranch has to scrimp on mechanical bulls for a while? Big deal."

"You make it sound so easy." Very easy. Doable.

"Because it is." Garnet set aside his drink. "Your grandmother only said get the stocks back in the family. She didn't say who had to buy them. If you need me to chip in, consider it done."

And Alex could see his father meant it. He was offering to help. Alex clapped him on the shoulder, the advice solidifying in his mind with utter clarity. "Thanks, Dad. Really. But I think you already gave me what I needed most with your advice."

"Then what's holding you back?"

"I need for Gran to be at peace with this. Ever since I met Nina, it's stopped being about the ranch. It's about giving Gran peace."

His father nodded, gesturing to the front of the room where Gran held court with the bride, Amie—and Nina. Family. That was what meant the most to Gran.

This plan might not be what she'd had in mind, but his grandmother had always respected leadership and honor.

And love. There it was, no hiding from the truth anymore. Yes, it was impulsive and fast, but he'd never been so sure of anything in his life. Alex loved Nina. He loved her son as well, and he intended to do whatever it took to become their family.

Nina twisted her hands together, nervous at the attention from the McNair matriarch. Sweat began to build in her palms. Did the woman know her plans had been uncovered? Mariah was so fragile; it was easy to see how a person would do anything to make her final days as drama-free as possible.

Then again, damn it, if that had been the woman's goal, why come up with elaborate tests for her grandchildren to prove their loyalty to the family? Mariah's process of inheritance seemed to invite problems. Frustration simmered, balancing out the empathy. Nina's emotions were a huge mess today.

Mariah took Nina's hand in her cool grasp, her skin paper thin and covered with bruises from IVs. Despite her frailty, Mariah's grip was firm, confident. A true businesswoman. "I'm so glad your son was found safely."

"I appreciate all the help searching. This week has been a dream come true for him. I understand I have you to thank for getting him into the program."

Mariah's eyes went wide at Nina's frank approach—

and then she smiled sympathetically. "I'm sorry that life has to be so difficult for you."

"Life is hard for everyone in some way, ma'am. I love Cody. I have a good job in my field that allows me to stay home with my son. My life is good."

Life is good. This was what Nina had repeated over and over to herself as she dressed for the weekend. She desperately tried to convince herself that she didn't need anything else besides Cody and work. Tried to tell herself that was all she wanted. That it was enough.

"Then why are your eyes so sad?"

How could she tell the woman about the doomed affair with Alex? She couldn't. "My in-laws will use the incident with Cody getting lost to try and take him away from me. They think he would be better off in a hospital, coming home on holidays and weekends. And they want control of his inheritance from his father."

What was it about this woman that made Nina spill her secret fears?

"That has to be so incredibly frightening for you. They sound like they're using the issue of institutionalizing him as a power play."

Nina nodded. "They are." She looked at the deathly ill woman in front of her and saw complete clarity in her eyes. Nina didn't want to burden her, but honesty might allay Mariah's concerns about those stocks more than all this behind-the-scenes game playing. "Ma'am, with all due respect, if you wanted Cody's stocks, why didn't you just approach me and give me a chance to be a reasonable businesswoman?"

Mariah's pale blue eyes went wide and she gripped her cane. "So Alex has told you." She smiled, bringing color back to her pale face. "Good for him."

*What?* "I'm confused. You wanted to keep this a secret but you didn't?" Nina didn't appreciate having her life manipulated, regardless of how ill the older woman was.

"I want to apologize for bringing you here under false pretenses. My grandson is so introverted. He communes with the animals more than people, and that's a part of what makes him so successful at running the Hidden Gem. But he also needed a nudge outside his comfort zone. I hoped forcing a meeting between the two of you would help him move forward with having a life that doesn't center on work 24/7. Life's too short, too precious." Mariah leaned closer. "You must realize by now that the crush he had on Johanna was born more out of convenience than any real passion. When I see the two of you together—" her eyes twinkled with life "—now, that's passion."

How could Nina tell Mariah the test backfired? They'd broken up. He'd lied to her…for a few days. Then come clean. Could she forgive that? After her marriage, she had issues on that front, no question. But Alex had shown more compassion and honor in a week than her ex had displayed in their entire marriage.

Mariah squeezed Nina's hand and continued. "I took advantage of your desire to help your son. That was wrong of me."

"You were desperate to do anything for your family. I understand that feeling." As Nina said those words, she felt the truth of them settle deep in her soul. Life wasn't about black and white, right and wrong. It was about flawed humans doing their best, one day at time.

Now if she could just find a way to make Alex understand that her love for him was every bit as strong as her love for her son.

If he could understand that, they would be able to find a way to work through this tangle.

Together.

A box in his arms, Alex knocked on Nina's cabin door with his boot. Moonlight sparkled through the branches overhead. Now that he had his compass firmly planted, he'd accomplished a lot in a few short hours, busy as hell setting things into motion all while seeing his cousin off at the end of the wedding. But then a rancher was a multitasker by nature. He didn't want to waste another second. He had to win Nina over and keep her in his life.

Hopefully forever.

She opened the door, her hair wet from a shower, wearing pj shorts and a loose shirt. And she'd never looked more beautiful.

"Mind if I come in?"

She stepped back, opening the door wider to reveal packed suitcases by the sofa. Her vintage bag sported large stickers displaying sites from around the world. "We need to talk."

God, he hoped that was a good sign.

"Let's sit on the sofa. I have a few things to show you."

Her face gave nothing away as she padded silently beside him. Either she was egoing to boot him out on his butt. Or, if she somehow still had a shred of hope for their relationship, she was going to make him work for it.

Fine. Ranchers were well versed in hard work. He

was putting everything on the line tonight now that he knew exactly what he wanted.

"Nina, I realize I royally messed things up between us. I should have been honest from the start. I let my fear for my grandmother cloud my judgment, and that's the last thing she would want."

She rested a hand on his arm. "I understand—"

No way was he giving her a chance to let him down easy or tell him she'd already called a cab. He plowed ahead, situating the box he'd brought beside him. He needed to bring out everything he had. Now.

"I'm not sure that you do understand just how much you mean to me and how much I value the woman you are, but I'm hoping this will show you." He reached into the box and pulled out a book. "This is from the family library. It contains the French poem I gave you on our first date."

He set the leather-bound edition on her coffee table.

She traced the gold lettering on the front. "I thought you looked up the poem on the internet."

He would have laughed at that if he wasn't still scared out of his mind she had one foot out the door already. "That certainly would have been faster. But the journey is well worth the effort."

Next, he pulled out a box of Swiss chocolates and a Violet Crumble candy bar from Australia. "These came from our gift shop, but they're just a sampling of places I want to take you and Cody. I know you've given up a lot of dreams for your son, Nina, and I'd like to give them back to you. I want to ride in the Swiss Alps with you and make love under the stars. I want to take Cody to Australia and show him a whole other kind of cowboy to enjoy."

He meant it too. He'd stuck close to home ever since leaving the rodeo circuit, finding peace at the Hidden Gem. But he wanted to see more of the world through Nina's eyes.

Her hands went to her heart, but she stayed silent.

"I also want Cody to learn to love the ranch here."

"He already does," she said softly.

"Good, but I want him to feel a part of the history of this place." He pulled out a heavy woven blanket. "This is a Native American blanket made by one of our local artisans, quite heavy, and I thought it might be of comfort to Cody. And even if the blanket doesn't suit him, I want this to be a symbol of how much I care for your son."

Tears welled in her eyes as she took the blanket from him and clasped it her chest. "Alex, you don't need to say any more. You've already––"

He touched her lips to quiet her, hoping maybe he was getting through to her. But he had a lot to make up for and he wasn't taking any chances on screwing this up too.

"I worked to pull this together tonight and intend to see it through because it's important to me that you know how much you mean to me, Nina." Deep inside the box, he withdrew a manila envelope. "This contains the proposal my investment broker just sent to yours."

She took the envelope and pulled out the papers, her hands trembling. She scanned the documents, then gasped. "Oh my God, Alex. Why did you offer to pay such a ridiculous amount for Cody's stocks? I thought you said your cash flow was tied up right now?"

"I did this because it's the right thing to do," he answered simply. "Cody is an amazing kid. I hope with every fiber of my being that with you as his advocate, he will have a future full of independence. But I know that's not a given. So I did what I could to help him."

She cocked her head to the side. "You really did risk your inheritance by pursuing me instead of taking your grandmother's 'test.' You're not trying to buy me off?"

As if that could even be done? He knew her better than that. This was a woman with deep values and a huge heart. "Nina, I would do just about anything for you. But this was for Cody, because that boy has come to mean a lot to me. Because I want the best for his future too."

A future Alex hoped he would be a part of.

She tucked the papers back into the envelope and set them on top of the blanket. "You didn't put your own finances at risk for this, did you?"

"I'll be fine. Hidden Gem will be fine. It's a done deal." His grandmother was ecstatic. Now he just prayed it was enough to keep Nina and Cody in his life.

She smoothed her hand along the envelope. "I don't know what to say to that other than thank you."

He rested his hand over hers. "You could say you forgive me."

She drew in a shaky breath. "I wish you could have been open with me from the beginning, and especially as we got to know each other, but I can understand how deeply torn you must have felt the effects of your grandmother's illness."

"You're too forgiving." His hands slid up her arms as he started to hope this could work out after all. "I have one more thing for you in the box. Are you still interested?"

She smiled. "Most definitely."

God, how crazy that he was nervous over this part when he knew with every fiber of his being it was exactly what he wanted. But then nothing had ever been this important. He reached in to pull out a dozen yellow roses.

"I know that red roses are supposed to signify love, but we're in Texas, and the yellow rose is our flower. I very much want you to be my Texas rose. Now. Always. Because in spite of my quiet tendency to keep to myself, I have fallen impulsively, totally in love with you, Nina Lowery."

The tears in her eyes spilled over and she launched into his arms, the flowers crushing between them and releasing sweet perfume.

Her mouth met his and she kissed him once, twice and again, before pulling back. "Oh God, Alex, I love you too. Your strength, your tenderness, the way you always put others first, which makes me want to be your champion, giving back to you the way you give to so many others."

His heart pounded with relief and happiness. How did he get this damn lucky? "I have a plan. We can see each other every week while we work out details. If you don't want to move I can look into opening a Hidden Gem in San Antonio."

She gasped. "You would do that for me?"

"For you, absolutely." He cupped her face in his hands. "I want what's best for you and Cody. We can figure that out together."

She set aside the crushed flowers and pulled out one long-stemmed bud that had survived. "Actually my job enables me to live anywhere. So I was thinking more along the lines of a long-term rental of one of the cabins. You and I could...date." She trailed the flower under her nose and then provocatively between her breasts. "Get to know each other better. Turn this fling into an all-out affair."

"Ah," he sighed, anticipation pumping through him. "I can romance you. Win you over."

"You've already won me over. Lock, stock and barrel, I'm yours." She traced a rosebud along the side of his face. "And *you* are mine."

\* \* \* \* \*

**"I still feel it's wise that we not spend any more time together than necessary,"** Kira said. **"If you need my help finding someone who can assist you, I'm willing to begin looking tomorrow."**

Tarek pushed off the desk and approached her slowly, his intense eyes trained on hers. "You would defy your king's order?"

If he came any closer, she might agree to anything. "I'm sure he would understand if I explained why I can't accommodate you."

His smile was somewhat devious and patently sensual. "You would tell him that we made love on the marble floor in my ballroom?"

That prompted several more images that Kira forced away. "Of course not. I'll simply tell the king my schedule is too full."

He stood in front of her then, a scant few inches between them. "Surely you do not believe he will accept that explanation."

Tarek tucked one side of her chin-length hair behind her ear. "Your eyes fascinate me. The dark blue color is extraordinary, yet it suits your overall beauty."

*Here we go again.* His charming tactics had sent her straight into trouble the last time, but she couldn't force herself to move away from him. "You can stop the compliments now. You've already had your way with me."

"I wish to have my way with you again."

# THE SHEIKH'S
# SECRET HEIR

BY
KRISTI GOLD

Published in Great Britain 2015
by Mills & Boon, an imprint of Harlequin (UK) Limited,
Eton House, 18-24 Paradise Road, Richmond, Surrey, TW9 1SR

© 2015 Kristi Goldberg

ISBN: 978-0-263-25265-1

51-0615

Harlequin (UK) Limited's policy is to use papers that are natural, renewable and recyclable products and made from wood grown in sustainable forests. The logging and manufacturing processes conform to the legal environmental regulations of the country of origin.

Printed and bound in Spain
by CPI, Barcelona

**Kristi Gold** has a fondness for beaches, baseball and bridal reality shows. She firmly believes that love has remarkable healing powers and feels very fortunate to be able to weave stories of love and commitment. As a bestselling author, a National Readers' Choice Award winner and a Romance Writers of America three-time RITA® Award finalist, Kristi has learned that although accolades are wonderful, the most cherished rewards come from networking with readers. She can be reached through her website at www.kristigold.com, or through Facebook.

I've said it before, but it bears repeating.
Here's to the happily-ever-after connoisseurs,
the lovers of love stories, the cherished readers
who make our efforts so worthwhile.
You are very much appreciated.

# One

As head administrator of the royal palace in the small, autonomous country of Bajul, Kira Darzin had grown accustomed to being summoned on a moment's notice by the king. But as she stood in the study's open doorway, waves of shock washed over her when her gaze came to rest on the undeniably handsome man seated near the desk.

With his neatly trimmed near-black hair, perfectly tailored steel gray suit, and dark Italian loafers, he could have been any successful billionaire. His masculine hands resting casually on the red brocade chair's arms, and the slight lift of his chin, gave him the appearance of an average arrogant autocrat. Yet, when Kira zeroed in on Tarek Azzmar's dark eyes, the power in his intense stare threatened to sweep her away, as it had already done one fateful night not so long ago.

She saw unmistakable confidence. She sensed deep secrets. She felt the pull of provocative danger. A place she had been before both with him, and with another man from her past. A place she vowed to never revisit.

She also noticed that his somewhat regal air made it seem as if he was the one holding court in the private office that belonged to Rafiq Mehdi, the official monarch of Bajul, who was oddly absent. However, Mr. Deeb, the king's personal assistant, stood not far away. When Deeb greeted her, his words sounded tinny to her ears as Tarek rose to his feet, revealing well over six feet of prime male.

With effort, Kira reclaimed enough calm to pretend she had never associated with the Moroccan mogul beyond a few social gatherings. A bald-faced lie. "It's a pleasure to see you again, Mr. Azzmar," she said through a polite and somewhat forced smile.

"The *pleasure* is all mine, Ms. Darzin."

His emphasis on the word unearthed several images in Kira's mind. Hot kisses. Naked bodies. One night of unbelievable passion. And six weeks since that experience, not one word from him.

That sour thought thrust her back to the business at hand. "What might I do for you two gentlemen today?"

Tarek presented the sexy half smile that had melted her resistance like warm chocolate from the first moment they'd met. "Perhaps Mr. Deeb should explain."

The balding, middle-aged assistant stepped forward and pushed his wire-rimmed glasses up on the bridge of his nose. "Actually, I am here representing His Excellency. Both he and Mr. Azzmar request your assistance."

She saw planning an elite soiree in her future. Lovely. "I'm sorry, but I was on my way out for an appointment when I received the message to stop by here. I didn't bring the upcoming schedule with me. If you'll give me a date, I'll begin planning the event immediately."

"This does not involve an event," Tarek said. "It would require your attention for ten days, perhaps even two weeks."

She couldn't imagine any project that would last so long if it didn't involve a special occasion or state dinner. "Do you mind giving me specifics?"

"Mr. Azzmar needs a personal assistant," Deeb began, "and King Mehdi has offered your services until a replacement can be located."

Surely they weren't serious. She glanced at Tarek and, from the all-business expression on his striking face, saw he was quite serious. Regardless, she would not bend to his will and instead, mentally ran through a litany of reasons to decline, minus the most important one—she was too vulnerable when it came to his charisma. "Considering my responsibilities with my position at the palace, I'm afraid that's impossible. Prince Zain, his wife and children will be returning in three days. And next week, Prince Adan's sister-in-law and Sheikh Rayad will be joining them. Someone has to prepare for their arrival."

"We have resolved that issue," Deeb added. "Elena has agreed to assume your responsibilities until you fulfill your duty to Mr. Azzmar."

She had a difficult time believing Elena, former governess and biological mother of the youngest Mehdi prince, Adan, would agree to such a thing. "She hired me as the director of the household so she could retire. It doesn't seem fair to ask this of her."

Deeb scowled. "Our king gave the order and Elena still adheres to his directives."

Kira stifled a retort involving what the king could do with *this* directive. "And I have no say in this matter?"

Before Deeb could respond, Tarek took a step forward to address the royal attaché. "Might I have a word alone with Ms. Darzin?"

Deeb nodded. "Of course. I will return to my office should you require further assistance."

As soon as Deeb left out the door, closing it behind him, Kira turned to Tarek and frowned. "Would you please explain why you didn't reject Rafiq's request in light of what happened between us?"

He leaned back against the desk and folded his arms across his chest. "I made the request, not the king."

Unbelievable. "Why would you want me as your glorified secretary with all the other candidates available among the palace staff?"

"No secretarial work will be involved, and no other candidates intrigue me as you do."

Kira crossed the room to the window, putting much-needed space between them and stared a few seconds at the mountainous terrain before facing him again. "You mean no other candidates have slept with you, correct?"

"I do not recall any measurable sleeping that night."

Neither did Kira, but she did remember one important fact. "True, and then you suddenly disappeared. I assumed you had moved back to Morocco."

"What would the logic be in that since I have recently completed my estate here in Bajul?"

She supposed her hypothesis hadn't made much sense. Then again, neither had letting their relationship go so far during the time when the royal family had been in the States for their cousin Rayad's wedding to Piper Mehdi's sister, Sunny. If she'd only been focused on her job, they wouldn't be having this conversation.

"I just found it odd you haven't been around the past six weeks." And somewhat hurtful, not that she dared admit that to him.

"Actually, I have been traveling abroad."

She almost asked if the *broad* had a name but recognized that word probably wouldn't be a part of his vernacular. "Backpacking in Europe?"

That earned her a confused look. "Completing a multimillion-dollar business venture."

Just what he needed—more money. Kira bit back the snide comment for the time being. "Regardless, I still feel it's wise that we not spend any more time together than necessary, particularly for two weeks. If you need my help finding someone who can assist you, I'm willing to begin looking tomorrow."

He pushed off the desk and approached her slowly, his intense eyes trained on hers. "You would defy your king's order?"

If Tarek came any closer, she might agree to anything. "I'm sure he would understand if I explained why I can't accommodate you."

His smile was somewhat devious and patently sensual. "You would tell him that we made love on the marble floor in my ballroom?"

That prompted several more images that Kira forced away. "Of course not. First of all, we had sex with no love involved. Secondly, no one needs to know that I had an interlude with a palace guest unless I want to lose my job, which I don't. I'll simply tell the king my schedule is too full."

He stood in front of her then, a scant few inches between them. "Surely you do not believe Rafiq Mehdi will accept that explanation."

Not exactly. "All I can do is try. If he rejects my excuse, then I'll think of something else." A spontaneous trip to Canada to visit her parents seemed like a viable explanation.

Tarek moved closer, reached out and tucked one side of her chin-length hair behind her ear. "Your eyes fascinate me. The dark blue color is extraordinary, yet it suits your overall beauty."

*Here we go again.* His charming tactics had sent her straight into trouble the last time, but she couldn't force herself to move away from him. "You can stop the compliments now. You've already had your way with me."

"I wish to have my way with you again."

His motivation had become all too clear. "Is that what this is all about?"

Fortunately, he dropped his hand, causing her to release the breath she hadn't realized she'd been holding. "No. I sincerely do need an assistant I can trust. You are intelligent and personable and highly regarded by the Mehdis. However, I see no reason not to enjoy each other's company when you come with me to my private seaside escape."

That almost rendered her speechless. Bajul was located in the mountains, not a sea in sight. "You plan to take me out of the country?"

"Yes. Cyprus, where I am preparing to launch my latest venture, an exclusive resort. That is why I require your assistance."

Kira couldn't ignore visions of beautiful beaches, romantic sunsets and midnight swims. She also couldn't quell her suspicions. "What exactly would my role be?"

"I would like you to approve the final decisions on the resort's kitchen layout, as well as the interior design. You could also advise the hotel manager on hiring staff."

"My forte isn't interior design." Even if it was somewhat of a passion.

"Are you not overseeing the palace restoration that will begin in a few months? And do you not plan every palace event, including the food and décor?"

Clearly he knew all about her upcoming assignments. Too bad she couldn't say the same about his motives. "Yes, but—"

He pressed a fingertip against her lips. "Please know I will not force you to come with me. If you decide you cannot tolerate my presence for a mere two weeks, then I will seek other avenues. I do request you give my offer some thought."

She'd do nothing but think about it from this point

forward. And then she would tell him no. "When do you need my answer?"

"By tomorrow morning. My plane will be ready to depart in the afternoon."

With her thoughts spinning round like a carousel, Kira checked her watch. "Fine. I'll let you know as soon as possible. Right now I have somewhere I need to be."

His features turned stern. "Do you have a new paramour?"

"Doctor's appointment." As if *that* was any of his business.

Now he appeared concerned. "Are you not feeling well?"

Fatigued and edgy, but well enough to function. "Just a follow-up visit for a slight case of the flu I had a week ago," she said as she brushed past him and headed to the door. But before she could leave, Tarek called her name in a deep, chill-inducing voice.

She sighed and turned toward him again. "What?"

"Perhaps you need relaxation to recover from this flu. Cyprus is the premier place to do that very thing."

"You wouldn't worry I might expose you?"

He hinted at a smile. "You have already exposed me and I thoroughly enjoyed the experience."

That deserved an eye roll, which she gave him. "You're not helping your cause, Tarek. I won't agree even to consider accompanying you unless you promise to halt the innuendo and the thinly veiled seduction."

He tried on an innocent look, but it failed to impress her. "I can only promise that I will try. I do promise to make the journey worth your while."

His methods of making that happen concerned her most of all. "I'll keep that in mind. At the moment, I have to go."

He ate up the space between them in a matter of seconds, took her hand and kissed it. "Until we meet again."

*Don't hold your breath,* she thought as she hurried into the hallway. Wisdom dictated she refuse to go with him anywhere, especially to an exotic locale where she could forget her worries, and most likely would forget herself.

She needed to remember he was exactly the kind of man she'd strived to shun. And after tomorrow morning, when she'd tell him he could find someone else to do his bidding, she would have absolutely no reason to speak to him again.

"You're pregnant."

Balanced on the edge of the uncomfortable exam table, Kira tugged on her skirt hem and stared blankly at Dr. Maysa Mehdi, presiding queen of Bajul and resident village physician. "Excuse me?" she asked, her voice barely a croak.

Maysa scooted the rolling stool closer and flipped her lengthy dark braid back over one shoulder. "When I ordered your lab work last week, I had them add a pregnancy test, in light of your symptoms. That test was positive and all the rest were normal."

Kira pinched the bridge of her nose and closed her eyes against the sudden headache. "This can't be happening."

"I'm afraid it is, and it appears you are not pleased with the news."

Kira opened her eyes and exhaled slowly. "I'm shocked. First of all, I've been on the pill for years. Secondly, I've been exposed only one time in several years." And some exposure it had been.

Maysa opened the chart resting in her lap and scanned the text. "I notice here you have not requested a refill on your birth control in two months."

Guilty. "I suppose I've been so busy I basically forgot. And I had no real need for them." Until Tarek Azzmar slipped into her life like a thief of hearts and destroyed her self-imposed celibacy.

"Perhaps you were so busy that you forgot to take your pills prior to the time of your lovemaking?" Maysa asked.

Guilty again. "Yes, but only for two, maybe three days tops."

"That is all it takes, Kira."

She suddenly felt like an absolute fool. An unequivocal idiot. "Believe me, I never planned to be with this man."

Maysa smiled. "At times, plans go awry and mistakes are made. How will this man feel about the pregnancy?"

She had no clue how Tarek would react, or if she would even tell him. "I truly don't know. In reality, I barely know him beyond a few social functions. It was something neither of us expected to happen."

"If he is a man of honor," Maysa began, "he will accept the responsibility of raising a child."

If only she could claim he was a man of honor, but all signs pointed to the contrary. "I suppose only time will tell."

Maysa closed the chart and came to her feet. "I suppose you will learn soon enough. In the meantime, you'll need to take better care of yourself, including getting more rest."

As much as Kira had always dreamed of having a child, reaching that goal now hadn't figured into her immediate plans, especially when considering her duties at the palace. "I have no idea how to balance work and this pregnancy. And I can't imagine what my parents will say when I tell them."

Maysa frowned. "They would not welcome a grand-child?"

"Since my mother's Canadian and open-minded, she would be fine with it. My father, on the other hand, is from Bajul and quite the traditionalist. He would not be pleased to know his unwed daughter is giving birth."

Maysa rested a hand on Kira's shoulder. "If you determine the timing is not right for you, perhaps you should consider adoption."

Since she was an adopted child, a fact few people knew, she had mixed feelings about that option. "I don't know if I could hand over my baby to strangers."

"Some believe that is the most unselfish thing a woman can do for her child, myself included. Regardless, you do not need to decide immediately. I am going to prescribe prenatal vitamins that you should begin taking."

When Maysa turned to the counter and began scribbling on a prescription pad, Kira slid off the table and pressed her palm against the small of her aching back. At least now she knew why she'd been so tired and slightly nauseated. At least now she could explain the absence of her period. At least now she could formulate a plan for the future and decide if it would include the father of her baby.

It suddenly occurred to her that perhaps she should reconsider Tarek's offer. Not only would she get some rest, but two weeks might be enough time to determine if he wanted children, and hopefully whether he would be father material. If neither applied, she could decide where she would go from there.

As soon as she returned to the palace, she would seek out Tarek Azzmar and ask a few more questions about his proposition. Only then could she establish if spending more time with him would be worth the risk.

"Miss Darzin is here to see you, sir."

Tarek glanced up to find the young woman he'd recently hired standing in the doorway to his private study. He hesitated, surprised by the announcement. "Send her in, Adara."

After the servant disappeared, Tarek set the quarterly reports on the teakwood end table, rose from the club chair and waited for what seemed an interminable amount of time before Kira appeared, looking as beautiful as the first time he'd noticed her across a crowded reception hall.

After tugging at the hem of her blue blazer, she swept one hand through her chin-length golden-brown hair and surveyed the room. "It's nice to see you've completed all the décor."

"It is very nice to see you."

"Thank you," she said with cool formality. "Everything looks extremely different from the last time I visited."

The visit Tarek had not forgotten. The tour of the newly built, empty mansion had ended with a passionate encounter on the floor of the grand ballroom. "I still have some work to do on the third floor suites. How was your appointment with the physician, if you do not mind my asking?"

"I received a clean bill of health." She then strolled into the room and breezed past him to study the volumes of books on the shelves behind his desk. "You have very eclectic tastes when it comes to novels. I had no idea you were so interested in true crime."

He slid his hands into his pockets and approached her slowly. "Did you come here to approve my reading material?"

Finally, she faced him. "Actually, I came here to discuss the trip to Cyprus. I have a few more questions before I make my decision."

His optimism rose when he thought she might have reconsidered his proposition. "What would you wish to know?"

"You're certain we would be gone only two weeks?"

"Unless unforeseen issues arise. Granted, you would be required to stay only that length of time. Should you decide to depart earlier, I agree to accommodate your request."

She folded her arms beneath her breasts and attempted a smile. "Then you don't plan to hold me hostage against my will?"

Her assumption angered him somewhat. "I would never hold a woman captive." At least not in the literal sense.

"That's somewhat reassuring."

"Do you have more questions?"

"Yes. I still have concerns about your motives."

He could not fault her for those concerns. "Are you worried that I will attempt to seduce you? Perhaps persuade you to make love with me on my private beach, in my private pool or in my rather large steam shower?"

She pointed a finger at him. "That's exactly what concerns me most."

He opted to feign ignorance. "As it was when we made love the first time—"

"The *only* time we had sex," she interjected.

He hoped to change that soon, yet he would use gentle persuasion, not coercion. "As I was saying, I would never force you to do what you do not wish to do. And I assure you, my motives involve business, not necessarily pleasure, although I am not averse to that."

"You've made that quite clear, and that worries me," she said as she brushed past him and claimed the chair he had recently vacated.

Following her lead, he dropped onto the leather sofa across from her. His eyes followed the movement of her hand as she ran her palm down her thigh to smooth her skirt. He immediately imagined that hand on his body and then, with effort, forced the fantasy away. "Rest assured, if you join me, I will maintain my distance if that is what you desire."

"That's what I desire," she stated, yet her faltering gaze led Tarek to believe she was not at all certain.

"I will respect your wishes." Unless their incontrovertible chemistry dictated otherwise.

She appeared unconvinced. "Tarek, you're a brilliant businessman, but you're still a man. You possess two brains and if the situation arises, so will your secondary brain. You would have to maintain a great deal of control."

He would not attempt to debate her on that point. "You will have your own quarters at your disposal and you will have to endure my presence only during our business dealings."

She began to twirl the silver band on her right ring finger. "Look, I enjoy your company and I have since we first met. I'm just not in the market to enjoy it too much again."

Feeling satisfied over the admission, he inclined his head and studied her. "Then you did enjoy our encounter?"

She hesitated a few seconds. "I suppose I have to admit that I did, with the exception of the marble floor."

"That is why I allowed you to be on top."

"After you had me on my back."

"On your back so that I could quickly remove your clothes and run my mouth down your body to facilitate your—"

"We don't need to go there."

He could not suppress a grin. "Ah, but I already have,

and considering the sounds you made, I do not believe you were disappointed."

She quickly stood and sighed. "I'm not in the mood to take a journey down memory lane, so I'm going to return to the palace now."

Tarek came to his feet. "Shall I expect you on the plane tomorrow?"

When she did not immediately respond, he held his breath and hoped. "I'll let you know tonight, when you're dining at the palace."

He frowned. "I did not realize you were aware of the invitation."

She sent him a disparaging look before crossing the room. "It's my job to know everything about the royal family and their esteemed guests," she said on her way out.

After she disappeared, Tarek checked his watch, reclaimed his chair and picked up the phone to make his daily call to the other female in his life. If he did not do it soon, he would regret the oversight. A few moments passed before he was greeted with the familiar, quiet, *"Ahlan?"*

He opted to answer in English, not Arabic, to test her acumen, as he had since teaching her the language. "Did you receive my gift, Yasmin?"

"I did!" she said with the marked exubcrance of a typical five-year-old. "He is lovely."

That was not how he would describe the street-roving mutt. "I am glad you are pleased. Will you take good care of him?"

"Yes, I will. I promise to feed him and give him

water and take him for walks. What shall we name him?"

"That is entirely up to you, Yasmin."

"I will have to think about it. When are you coming home? Soon, I hope."

No matter what said he told her, he would disappoint her. "I told you about the new resort before I left Morocco. I still have much work to do on it."

"You are always working. I wish you would take me with you."

That would be impossible at this point in time. Very few knew of her existence, and he wanted to keep it that way. "Perhaps someday. In the meantime, take care."

"I will."

"I shall see you in a month when I return."

A span of silence passed before she said, "I miss you."

"I miss you as well, Yasmin." And he certainly did, though too much affection would serve neither of them.

As soon as he hung up the phone, Tarek began to contemplate his previous conversation with Kira and her erroneous assumptions.

*It's my job to know everything about the royal family and their esteemed guests...*

Little did Kira know, she was not privy to most aspects of his private life, as it had been with all friends and former lovers. Not only in regard to the child, but she was also unaware that he retained an important piece of the Mehdi puzzle. Only he held the key and no one else, not even the current monarch and his brothers. He harbored a great secret that might have died along with his parents, save an old man's conscience and overwhelming guilt.

Since gaining that knowledge, he had been bound by a pledge to keep the information guarded out of respect for his mother, yet he had grown weary of the pretense. He wanted answers. He demanded answers. He vowed to do whatever he must to gain that information, and he hoped Kira Darzin could aid him in his search.

From the minute he'd met her, he had sensed she would know much about the Mehdis, and he would continue to gain her trust in an effort to convince her to confide in him. That had been his primary goal in the beginning, until he had crossed the boundaries into ill-advised desire. He had not intended to be as preoccupied by her and he would do well not to let his base urges rule his rationality.

If his plan with Kira did not succeed, he would continue to covertly search for confirmation through every means possible, work his way into the royal sons' good graces, then he would properly introduce himself as the bastard son of the former king of Bajul.

Their brother.

# Two

Every evening at six o'clock sharp, Kira prepared to deliver her usual courtesy call. It was incumbent that she made certain all needs were met, though tonight that wouldn't be easy, considering she would have to face the father of her child. After she walked into the elaborate dining room, she found the lengthy mahogany table populated with the usual royal residents—King Rafiq and his wife, Maysa, along with the newlyweds, Adan and Piper—and one not-so-usual sophisticated man dressed in a beige silk suit, sitting to the right of Rafiq. Anyone who didn't know the Mehdis might mistake Tarek Azzmar as a relative, when in reality his only ties to the royals were big business, Middle Eastern roots and an abundance of good looks.

When Tarek leveled his gaze on her, Kira's thoughts

spun away like a desert whirlwind. She sincerely wanted to look away, yet it was as if he had her completely under some macabre magical spell. "Magical" would definitely describe his thorough kisses, his very skilled hands, his expertise at lovemaking, his obvious virility....

"Is there another bun in the oven, Kira?"

Taken aback by Adan Mehdi's query, Kira directed her attention to the youngest prince, her face splashed with heat. "Excuse me?"

He held up the empty basket. "We are out of bread."

Apparently, she was plagued by secret pregnancy paranoia. "I'll see to that immediately."

"And, Kira, if it's not too much trouble, I'd like more water, please," Adan's auburn-haired wife added as she leaned back in the chair, providing a peek at her rounded belly. "I'm so thirsty I think I'm giving birth to a trout, not a mammal."

Kira experienced a brief bout of envy when Adan and Piper exchanged a loving look. At least they had each other. At least Piper wouldn't be raising her baby alone.

Whether that would be the case for Kira when it came to her own child still remained to be seen. "I'll be certain to have the server deliver you an entire pitcher of water, as she should have done at the beginning of the meal. She's new and still trying to gain her bearings. I also believe she's a bit starstruck over her introduction to royalty."

Piper's grin expanded as she waved a hand toward Tarek. "I think she's quite taken with our guest."

Kira ventured a glance and discovered Tarek didn't seem at all disturbed by the conjecture. When he failed to reply, she focused on the eldest Mehdi son. "Is the dinner tonight to your liking, Your Majesty?"

"As usual, the fare is excellent," Rafiq replied as he regarded Tarek. "Would you would like more of the chicken kabobs, Mr. Azzmar?"

Tarek pushed his empty plate aside and leveled his gaze on Kira. "Not presently, but it was delicious. I particularly enjoyed the garlic yogurt sauce. Please give my compliments to the chef."

Adan presented his usual dimpled smile. "Perhaps you would like to deliver the message yourself and inspect the help further, Tarek."

Piper elbowed her husband, causing him to wince. "Stop it, Adan. I'm sure Tarek is more than capable of finding a date."

Adan grimaced. "Bloody hell, wife. I like it much better when your pregnancy hormones lead to pleasure and not pain. I was simply suggesting Tarek might be interested in keeping company with a woman who is obviously smitten with him."

"Your bride is correct," Tarek added. "I am very selective when it comes to female companionship. Although the server is attractive, she is much too young, therefore she does not hold my interest."

After the billionaire nailed her with another pointed look, Kira snatched the basket from the table and began backing toward the door. "I'll let the chef know you're all pleased with the meal and I'll send someone out with more bread and water. Good evening."

With that, she spun around and strode into the nearby kitchen, muttering a few mild oaths at herself over her inability to ignore Tarek. She mumbled a few more aimed at the businessman who seemed bent on keeping her off balance.

"Please take more rolls and water to the table immediately," she said to the recently hired, very pretty fresh-faced staff member. "And from this point forward, pay more attention to the family and guests' needs. Prince Adan requires more bread than most, and always make certain there is a pitcher of water close at hand in the dining room."

The young woman quickly took the basket, filled it with rolls, grabbed a water pitcher and scurried away, her brown ponytail bouncing in time with her gait. Kira then leaned back against the steel prep table while the chef remained at the stove, where Kira's own mother had once stood, preparing the finishing touches on dessert as several of the staff members engaged in clean-up. She rubbed both temples with her fingertips and closed her eyes against the beginnings of another nagging headache. The reason for that headache happened to be seated in the dining room, acting as if he practically owned the palace.

One arrogant man. One gorgeous egomaniac. One weakness she couldn't afford to have.

"Might I have a few moments alone with you, Miss Darzin?"

*Speaking of the sexy devil himself.* Kira's eyes snapped open at the deep timbre of his now-familiar voice. "Actually, I'm rather busy at the moment, Mr. Azzmar."

Tarek strolled into the kitchen as if he were king of the castle, hands planted in his pockets. "Then I would be happy to speak with you about our plans while you continue your duties."

Conversing with him in front of the staff could be detrimental on several levels. She could only imagine what they were already thinking. "I suppose we can discuss your needs in the corridor." And that sounded entirely too suggestive. "*Needs* as in your need for an administrative assistant."

"Ah, yes, that need." He swept a hand toward the opening to the hallway. "After you."

Kira rushed out of the room, unable to avoid the curious glances of the employees. She continued down the passage with the current thorn in her side trailing behind her and pushed out the doors leading to the courtyard. Once there, she turned and practically face-planted into Tarek's broad chest. "Do you mind giving me some space?"

He took a step back. "Is this better?"

*Better* would entail having the persistent man standing several yards away, not less than a foot in front of her. "As long as you don't come any closer, that will do."

His expression turned somber. "Do you fear me, Kira?"

"Of course not." Not in a traditional sense, yet she did fear the way he made her feel—vulnerable.

"Do you believe I would never do anything to harm you?"

"Yes, I believe that." He wouldn't, at least not physically, but he had dealt her an unsolicited emotional blow six weeks ago.

He released a rough sigh. "Then I must admit I am somewhat confused by your recent attitude. When we first met, I had several opportunities to attempt to seduce you, yet I did not. Instead, we spent many hours engaged in casual conversation, and only conversation, until the night we spent together. I assumed we had established a measure of trust between us."

"I thought so, too, until that night."

"Clearly I have been mistaken in my belief that our pursuit of pleasure was mutual."

"It was mutual," she stated firmly. "We were both consenting adults."

"Then why are treating me as if I am a pariah not worthy of your regard?"

He didn't understand, and Kira wasn't certain she could explain. Still, she had to try, and that entailed revealing how his careless *disregard* had made her feel. "That isn't my intent. What we shared was a mistake, not only because I crossed a line I shouldn't have crossed with a palace guest, but because you're clearly not the type of man to maintain a monogamous lifestyle. That became apparent when I didn't hear a word from you after that night, as if you'd had your way with me and tossed me aside."

A hint of anger flashed in his eyes. "You are making an erroneous assumption, Kira. As I have told you, I was seeing to business. I do not treat women as chattel."

"They why did you fail to inform me you would be leaving?"

"I was only honoring your request not to approach you again."

He definitely had her there. "True, but I didn't mean we should completely sever all ties. Your actions made me feel used."

He streaked a hand over his jaw and his gaze momentarily drifted away before he returned it to her. "My sincerest apologies, and I am sorry that you have so little faith that you would believe I considered our interlude as nothing more than a diversion. If you wish me to lie and say that I do not want you now, I cannot do that. I cannot promise that if you decide to join me, I will be able to discard my desire for you. If you have trouble accepting this, perhaps you should decline accompanying me to Cyprus. I prefer you not do that, but I will leave the decision to you."

As he turned to leave, Kira realized that if she rejected his request, she would be giving up the opportunity to know him better. To learn if he might be the kind of man who would be open to raising a child. She couldn't squander that opportunity for both her and their baby's sake. "Tarek, wait. We need to talk."

He faced her again and sent her a frustrated look. "I have said all that I have to say about this matter."

"But I haven't," she said as she strode to him. "I'm sorry that I've jumped to conclusions, and I do realize you were only following my instructions. If we can get past this, I would really like to start over and return to our original relationship."

"Which was?"

"Friendship." When he scowled, she added, "Unless you're not able to maintain a friendship with a woman."

"I would find it difficult to go back after what we shared, but I would be willing to try."

"And if that's true, then I'd be willing to go with you to Cyprus."

"You will?" Both his expression and tone reflected disbelief.

"Yes. We could spend the time together getting to know each other better."

Now he looked skeptical. "I am a very private person when it comes to certain aspects of my life."

"I'm not suggesting you show me a financial statement and I don't expect to rifle through your underwear drawer for secrets."

His expression turned hard, unforgiving. "Why would you believe I have secrets?"

His reaction took Kira aback and led her to believe he might be withholding something. But so was she. "Everyone has secrets, Tarek. I have no reason to ask you to reveal yours to me, unless you're doing something illegal."

He seemed to relax somewhat. "I assure you that all my business dealings are aboveboard and within the law."

"That is good to know." Now for the question that would seal her fate for the next two weeks, depending on his response. "Since I've laid out my terms, does the offer to join you still stand?"

"Yes. My driver will come for you at 4:00 p.m. and escort you safely to the airport."

She had less than twenty-four hours to prepare. Twenty-two hours, to be exact, to change her mind. But, with so much riding on this trip, she had to follow through. "I suppose I will see you tomorrow afternoon then."

"I am looking forward to it. Sleep well, Kira."

"You too, Tarek."

As neither of them made a move to depart, a tension as thick as smoky mountain haze hung between them. The craving to kiss Tarek settled over Kira, and to counteract that desire, she started toward the door to his back, intent on a quick escape. Yet as she brushed past him, Tarek clasped her wrist, halting her progress. "If I establish nothing else during our time together, Kira," he began, "I am determined to win your trust again."

Kira responded with a shaky smile and, after he released her, left him standing alone in the courtyard.

Trust between them was a slippery slope, for if Tarek Azzmar eventually learned what she'd been withholding from him, he would probably never trust her again.

She couldn't worry about that now. First, she had to finish her duties for the night and pack for the trip. Hopefully she wouldn't be disturbed.

"Are you busy, *cara*?"

Sequestered in her quaint but comfortable live-in quarters, Kira looked up from the suitcase to find sixty-something, Italian-born Elena Battelli hovering inside the bedroom doorway sporting her neatly coiffed sil-

ver hairdo, standard palace-issued navy suit and trade-
mark kind smile. "I always have time for you, Elena.
Come in."

"Good. This will take only a few minutes."

After placing the last of her clothing into the bag,
Kira zipped it closed, lifted it from the cream-colored
bench and set it on the floor at her feet. "All done. Did
I forget something when we met earlier today to go
over the schedules?"

"You covered everything in regard to business, but
I do have an important question."

"And that is?"

Elena strolled into the room and roosted on the
edge of the bed. "How well do you know this Tarek
Azzmar?"

*That* she hadn't expected. Time to bring out a half-
truth. "I've met him a few times during social gatherings. Why?"

"Several rumors have been circulating among the
staff that perhaps you and Mr. Azzmar are…how do I
say this? Lovers?"

If it were truly possible to swallow one's tongue,
Kira would have accomplished that feat following the
verbal bombshell. "You know how people talk, Elena,"
she said once she'd recovered her ability to speak. "Gos-
sip is as common as morning coffee in this place. You
can't believe everything you hear."

"Then why are you blushing, *cara*?"

Her hands automatically went to her flushed face
before she quickly dropped them to her sides. "It's em-
barrassing to think you're the butt of false hearsay."

"Then you and Mr. Azzmar are not romantically involved?"

"No, we're not." At least not anymore.

"Then he is not the father of your unborn child?"

Kira collapsed onto the bench from absolute shock. Did she already look pregnant? Had Maysa breached doctor-patient privilege and mentioned it to Elena? Both theories were utterly preposterous. "I have no idea where you would get the idea I'm pregnant."

After reaching into her blazer pocket, Elena withdrew a large white plastic bottle. "These fell out of your bag when you hurried out of the office following our meeting."

Kira remained frozen on the spot as she eyed the prenatal vitamins. She chastised herself for being so careless, or perhaps she'd subconsciously wanted Elena to find out. Consciously, she thought, for the time being, it was best to rack her brain for some plausible explanation that didn't involve the truth. "I've heard they're good for your hair and nails."

Elena presented a cynical smile. "I know several good herbal supplements that would suffice without expense. I also know when a young woman is concealing the truth from a presumed naïve senior citizen."

She should have known better than to attempt to pull the wool over the eyes of the wisest person she'd ever known. Resigned to the fact she couldn't wriggle out of this, and tired of denying a truth that should be bringing her joy, Kira collapsed onto the bench and sighed. "All right. I am pregnant. But I can't risk everyone knowing before I tell the baby's father." And her poor, clueless parents.

Elena pushed off the bed, claimed the spot beside Kira, and took her hand. "You are under no obligation to reveal the identity of the man who knocked you up."

Hearing "knocked up" coming from the woman's mouth sent Kira into a fit of laughter. Once she recovered, unwelcome and unexpected tears began to flow. They only increased when Elena handed her a handkerchief and patted her arm. "I don't know what to do, Elena. I'm so afraid of how Tarek is going to react to this news." A moment passed before awareness dawned that she'd let the truth tiger out of the cage. "And I'm sorry I lied to you about him in the beginning."

"That is understandable, *cara*," Elena replied, sincere sympathy in her tone. "This is not something that should be broadcast throughout the palace before you have spoken with the appropriate parties. You do plan to tell him while you're away together, don't you?"

She swiped the moisture from her cheeks. "I'm not sure I'm going to tell him at all. I agreed to this trip in part to find out more about him, and hopefully to gauge how he would react to the news. Maybe even to discover if he's fit to be a father to my child."

"Then you are planning to keep the baby?"

She couldn't think much past the upcoming two weeks and deciding whether to inform Tarek. "Maysa and I briefly discussed adoption, but I don't know if I could let my baby go. Does that make me selfish?"

"No, *cara mia*. That makes you a mother."

When Elena went silent, stared off into space and

smiled, Kira's curiosity overcame her. "What are you thinking about?"

"The day your parents brought you back to Bajul after their return from a lengthy trip to Canada. Most people assumed Chandra had hidden her pregnancy from everyone, but I suspected you were a precious gift they had received while they were away. Your mother confided in me not long after."

One more stunning revelation in a long line of many within the palace's hallowed halls. "You knew about my adoption?"

"Yes, I did, and I have kept the secret since your birth. You can trust me with yours as well."

She knew Elena's word was good as gold, but she wondered what other secrets the woman might be privy to. "Do you know anything about my birth parents other than they were very young? Mother and Father would never talk about them when I asked, and when I tried to contact my biological mother, she wasn't willing to speak with me."

Elena shook her head. "I am sorry I do not. I am also sorry they have not been forthcoming with that information, though I do understand their reasoning on some level. My son can attest to that. Adan spent his life believing another woman to be his mother."

Kira wrapped an arm around her shoulder and gave her a gentle squeeze. "You had no choice in the matter, Elena. From what you've said, you were following King Aadil's orders to keep Adan's true parentage concealed. At least the two of you now have the opportunity to know each other as mother and son."

"Yet we cannot live openly that way," Elena said. "Very few people know the truth, as it should be. Rafiq cannot afford another scandal after barely surviving his marriage to a divorcée with his authority intact."

And she could very well hand them another huge scandal if anyone learned that Tarek had fathered her child. Perhaps she should resign and move to Canada. No. She could not live off her parents' good graces, especially when her papa would be so disapproving of her unwed-mother status. But what other options did she have?

She was simply too tired to plan so far ahead. That fatigue filtered out as she hid a yawn behind her hand.

Elena got to her feet and patted Kira's cheek. "You need to sleep, *cara mia*. When I was expecting Adan, I remember nodding off in midsentence."

Kira rose and drew her into a quick embrace. "Thank you for listening to me. I'm honestly relieved that I have someone I can trust to talk to about this."

"You can always trust me, dear one. And should you need my counsel following your journey, I will be here."

"Thank you."

Elena then started toward the door, only to face Kira once more. "Since you obviously have decided to raise your child, I truly hope you find Tarek Azzmar to be an honorable man and a worthy father. As you have learned, every child deserves to know their legacy if at all possible."

With that, she walked out of the bedroom, leaving Kira to ponder her words as she readied for bed. Her instincts told her to trust in Tarek. Her past dictated she be overly cautious. Falling victim to a man with dishonorable intentions had taught her that hard lesson eight years ago. She sincerely hoped that the father of her baby proved to be the man she had at first believed him to be, and not someone who judged a woman for her lack of good breeding, led her on, then left her heart in tatters.

Only time would tell if the real Tarek Azzmar turned out to be a huge disappointment, or a pleasant surprise.

# Three

He was pleasantly surprised when she entered the plane, yet disappointed at her obvious aloofness when she muttered a greeting. She wore a somewhat sheer blue blouse and fitted white skirt rising a few inches above her knee, and that alone had him battling the urge to invite her into the onboard sleeping quarters, a request she would no doubt reject. He had to respect her friendship request for the time being, yet he could not be certain how long that would last.

Despite that, Tarek sent Kira a guarded smile as he showed her to the black leather seat and claimed the one set against the bulkhead opposite hers. They remained silent during takeoff, the lack of communication continuing as the pilot permitted them to move about the cabin.

As Tarek unbuckled his seat belt, Kira removed a magazine from the bag resting at her feet. "Would you like something to drink?" he asked as he stood.

"I'm fine, thank you," she said as she surveyed the area. "This is a very nice plane, maybe even a bit nicer than the Mehdis', although smaller. With all this black and white, it reminds me of a four-star boutique with wings. I'm surprised you don't have an onboard bartender."

"Due to the short duration of the flight, no attendants are necessary."

"Three hours isn't exactly short."

"It is not long enough to justify bringing along a full staff." In truth, he wanted privacy more than he had wanted someone waiting on him. "Therefore I will serve as your host. My wish is your command."

"Again, I have no wishes, but your hospitality is appreciated."

Frustrated, Tarek moved to the onboard bar, reached into the upper cabinet above the refrigerator and retrieved a bottle of wine that he had reserved for a special occasion. Apparently Kira did not see anything special about traveling with him. At the moment, he needed something to cut through the tension, even if it came from a glass of twenty-thousand-dollar French premier cru.

Once he returned to his seat, he found her flipping through random pages. "What are you reading?"

She paused and lifted the magazine from her lap, then set it back down. "Just something to pass the time."

"I have never had an affinity for tabloids."

That had earned him Kira's undivided attention and a scornful look. "It's not a tabloid. It features book and movie reviews and human interest stories."

"If one is interested in reading about adultery, illegal drug use and secret pregnancies involving Hollywood stars. Of course, the secret is soon revealed when paparazzi capture photos of the expectant actresses on the beach and release them to the general public. The concept sickens me."

She raised a thin brow. "The photos or the pregnant starlets?"

"Both, in a sense. It seems it is a rite of passage among the rich and famous to populate the world, with or without the benefit of matrimony."

"Now I understand. You're a traditionalist when it comes to marriage before the baby carriage."

She did not truly understand at all, nor would she without knowing his goal. "I am a pragmatist. It is immaterial to me whether someone marries or not before giving birth. I strongly believe that one should consider the atmosphere into which they are bringing a child. In my opinion, thrusting someone so young into the spotlight could be detrimental to their well-being."

Her gaze drifted away momentarily before she tossed the magazine back in the bag. "I suppose since everyone knows your business when you're in the spotlight, that's definitely a risk."

He took a drink of the wine and set it into the holder built into the seat's arm. "I would not wish to be placed under a microscope on a daily basis."

"But you have no problem having your face splashed

across financial publications. And yes, I've seen a few of those covers featuring your smiling face."

He briefly wondered if perhaps someone in the royal family had known of his existence prior to their introduction. "Where did you come by this knowledge?"

"The internet. I did some research before you visited the palace the first time."

"An order from the king?"

"No. I took the initiative on my own. I make a point to learn about guests of the royal family."

He relaxed somewhat. "What else do you know about my life?"

She shrugged. "Not all that much, other than you're in the top fifteen on the list of the wealthiest men in the world."

"Top ten."

"Forgive me for my ignorance. I also know that you are somewhat of a philanthropist. I read an article where you opened an orphanage in Mexico City a while back."

A pet project he had felt compelled to complete for personal reasons. "There was a need, and I had the means to fulfill that need."

"I'm sure the tax write-off doesn't hurt."

He bristled at her continual questioning of his motives. "I have global holdings in several countries with varying tax structures. I assure you that compassion, not company write-offs, drives my charitable efforts."

"I'm sorry," she said, sounding somewhat contrite. "I tend to be wary of men with an overabundance of money."

"Why is that?"

"Personal reasons."

He suspected he knew what those reasons might be. "Who was he?"

"I don't understand what you're asking."

The way she shifted in her seat and looked away indicated she chose to be evasive, confirming his conjecture. "Who was the wealthy man who broke your heart?"

"What makes you think this has anything to do with a man?"

"I can sense these things."

She sighed, then hid a yawn behind her hand. "Yes, my attitude stems from a former relationship. Actually, he was my fiancé. And if it's all the same to you, I'd rather not discuss it. I didn't sleep well last night and I'd like to take a nap."

He vowed to revisit the topic at a later time. "We have still have hours before we arrive in Cyprus. That should give you ample time to rest. You will find the sleeping quarters at the rear of the plane."

"I really don't need a bed to take a nap. I'll be fine right here."

He could think of more favorable ways to use the onboard bed. "If you are concerned that I might attempt to join you, put your mind at ease. I do not require any sleep."

"I highly doubt you'd want to join me to sleep."

He returned her unexpected smile. "You know me well."

"Not as well as I hope to know you before the end of this trip."

Though he found her comment somewhat curious, he decided not to assume too much. "If you're determined to refuse the offer of my bed, push the button on the right arm to release the footrest. The one to your left will recline the back."

After complying, Kira stretched out, turned on her side and closed her eyes. "Wake me up in thirty minutes."

Tarek finished off the wine and poured another glass as an afterthought. Rarely did he imbibe aside from the occasional social setting due to his need to remain in absolute control. Yet as he returned to his seat, he acknowledged the woman before him was as intoxicating as a shot of straight Russian vodka. In sleep, she looked innocent, yet he had experienced anything but innocence during their interlude. She had been a willing lover, exciting and experimental. Remembering those blissful moments now prompted a building pressure in his groin, causing him to bring his attention back to Kira.

With her upturned nose and the delicate line of her jaw, he saw little that indicated she would hail from Bajul, aside from the slightly golden color of her skin. Evidently her mother's Canadian roots had taken genetic precedence over her father's Middle Eastern heritage. Regardless, her beauty could not be denied and he had given up on doing that very thing.

During this adventure, he did hope to find out more about her, including the details of the miscreant who had emotionally destroyed her and filled her with distrust. More important, he needed to prove he was not the kind of man to fill a woman with false promises. Eventually he might take a wife and settle down, but not until he achieved his ultimate goal of building more wealth and power. Enough wealth and power to match the Mehdis. What better way to exact revenge for his denied birthright?

Kira awoke long enough to depart the plane that had been secured in a private hangar, only to enter an extravagant black limousine and drift off once again en route to Tarek's Cyprus home. She came back into consciousness a while later, mortified to discover her cheek resting on his shoulder. Had she snored? Drooled? Hopefully none of the above.

After straightening and scooting over, Kira adjusted the hem of her white pencil skirt, which had climbed up her thighs to a point that bordered on indecency. "I'm sorry," she muttered as the car navigated the drive. "I guess I needed more sleep than I realized."

"No apology necessary," he replied as the limo came to a stop. "I enjoyed having you so close. Granted, I was somewhat concerned that I might have to carry you into the house, although that would not have been a great burden."

Maybe not a burden for him, but a total embarrassment for her. "I'll endeavor to stay awake for the remainder of the evening."

When the driver opened the door, Kira realized the sun had already begun to set, yet enough light existed to witness the grandeur of the white, expansive estate with manicured tropical gardens and a four-car garage.

She accepted Tarek's offered hand as he helped her out of the car and followed him silently up the stone path. A man dressed in a white suit greeted them on the front porch, then opened the heavy wooden double doors wide. "Welcome back, Mr. Azzmar."

"It is good to be back, Alexios," he replied. "Please see to it that Ms. Darzin's luggage is delivered to her quarters immediately."

"As you wish, sir," the man said with a nod before making his way to the car.

Tarek turned to Kira and gestured toward the open doors. "After you."

When Kira stepped inside the foyer, she was taken aback by the ultramodern décor that directly contrasted with Tarek's newly built traditional mansion in Bajul. White and steel-gray leather sofas and chairs, accented with black and turquoise pillows, were set about the massive living room, accompanied by several tables comprised of glass and chrome. An enormous curved television hung above a fireplace surrounded by gray glass tile. Yet the most impressive sight lay beyond the open glass wall that revealed the panoramic view of the blue backlit pool, centered between two stone walls, and the Mediterranean Sea, which stretched out as far as the eye could see.

"Amazing," Kira said. "An absolute paradise."

"I am pleased that you are pleased," Tarek replied from behind her.

Pleasure wasn't her goal, a fact she had to remember before she let the atmosphere cloud her common sense. "I'm ready to work when you are," she said as she faced him.

"Tonight we will relax and simply enjoy each other's company."

That could involve going somewhere she didn't want to go. Correction. She shouldn't go. "I slept the entire trip, Tarek. I have no problem getting started on my duties."

"We will begin first thing in the morning with a visit to the resort. In the meantime, I will show you to your room, where you can freshen up before dinner."

She saw no point in arguing with him because she couldn't deny she was starving—both for food and for his touch. She could partake in one, but not the other. Not unless she wanted to forget her reasons for being there had nothing to do with falling into bed with him again.

After Tarek started down a corridor to her right, Kira followed behind him past several rooms, all the while recalling his perfect butt, which she unfortunately couldn't see now, due to the length of his gray jacket. But she had seen that tempting bottom before in all its glory, and his well-toned legs, his ridged abdomen and his impossibly broad shoulders. She remembered in great detail clinging to those shoulders before running her palms down his back, exploring the pearls of his spine before spanning the width of his rib cage, then traveling down to the curve of his buttocks and curving her hand between his thighs...

"I hope you find it to your liking."

Kira snapped back into reality when she realized

Tarek had opened the door to a room. Stepping forward, she peered inside to find her luggage resting on a copper bench at the foot of the king-sized bed covered in a silky white spread, and another set of glass doors leading out onto a private veranda dotted with aqua chaises and white wicker tables. And yet again, another stellar view of the ocean and a private beach.

"It's definitely to my liking," she said as she stepped into the suite. "But are you sure I'm not putting you out of your room?"

Tarek moved to her side, barely two inches separating them. "My quarters are on the opposite side of the house."

*Too bad*—her first thought. *A good thing*—her second. At least she wouldn't have to run into him on a regular basis, should she choose that course. Right now, after catching a whiff of his heady cologne mixed with the salty scent of the sea, she would like to do more than *run* into him.

Clearing the uncomfortable hitch in her throat, she turned to him and smiled. "Is there a bathroom nearby where I can take a quick shower before dinner?"

"As you wish," he said after making a sweeping gesture toward two bifold doors.

Kira followed his lead and peeked into the spa-like bathroom, equipped with a copper-tiled shower that had enough room and spray heads to wash an army all at once. And beside that behemoth shower, a jetted soaker tub butted up against a narrow window, which provided another incredible view of water and wide-open sky. "I suppose I can make do with this."

Finally, Tarek gave her a half grin. "If it is not up to your standards, you are welcome to use my facilities. As I believe I mentioned, I have a steam shower as well as a sauna."

Getting naked anywhere near this gorgeous man would be a recipe for danger. Sensual, hot danger.

Determined to put some space between them, she moved to the white marble vanity and ran her hand over the countertop. "Actually, I was joking. It's so huge I'm afraid I might seriously get lost in here. If I don't show up in an hour, please send a search party."

"Should you go missing for any length of time, I would not want the staff to see you in a state of undress. Therefore, I would seek you out since I have already seen you naked." Before she could respond, Tarek began backing to the door. "I will inform the chef to have dinner prepared in one hour."

"All right," she said. "Where do you want me to go?"

He sent her a smoldering look that seared her from forehead to feet and all parts in between. "I fear if I answer that with complete honesty, you will not join me for our meal this evening."

She frowned. "Where exactly is the dining room?"

"You will find it beneath the stars."

With that, he exited the bath, leaving Kira alone entertaining fantasies she had no good cause to have. She immediately returned to the bedroom to unpack her suitcase and select something to wear. After her lingerie was tucked into a drawer, she stuffed the bottle of prenatal vitamins beneath it, determined not to give away her secret before she had a chance to reveal it to the master of the house. *If* she revealed it. That still remained to be seen.

She then withdrew a lightweight, sleeveless violet dress from the clothing someone had already hung in the wardrobe and selected silver bangle bracelets with matching hoop earrings from the jewelry bag in her overnight case. A fitting choice for a romantic evening. She suddenly slammed on the mental brakes following that ill-advised thought. She wasn't looking for romance. She was on a fact-finding mission involving the prospective father of her child. She didn't want moonlight and roses. She wanted to remain grounded. She didn't need to be starry-eyed. She needed to see the real Tarek Azzmar clearly.

She also had to shower quickly in order to get something in her stomach before she became queasy, just another reminder of the baby growing inside her. Hopefully she wouldn't give anything away by eating like she hadn't eaten in a month.

Kira's appetite both surprised and pleased Tarek greatly. During their dinner on the veranda, she had consumed the majority of the cheese and olive appetizers, as well as the entire Greek salad, and had left only a scarce bit of the moussaka before pushing her plate aside.

He leaned back and studied her euphoric face. "Did you save room for dessert?"

She dabbed at her mouth with the black cloth napkin and sighed. "Heavens no. If I eat anything else, I won't be able to move."

When the server brought out a tray of baklava, Tarek

waved him away. "That will be all, Alexios. Tell Leda she has done an excellent job, as usual."

When the man nodded and scurried away, Kira turned her attention to the sky. "It's such a beautiful night."

The evening had nothing on her beauty. He strayed from decorum to glimpse her breasts, which were enhanced by the low neckline of her dress. He had not remembered them being so full, but on that evening when they'd made love, he had not taken enough time to inspect them. Perhaps he would have the opportunity to remedy that. Perhaps he would be fortunate enough to use his mouth on them, the tip of his tongue to...

"My eyes are up here, Tarek."

He had been caught red-handed stealing a questionable look. "My apologies. I was simply admiring your neck. I did not notice how delicate it is until you cut your hair."

"And you are an incredibly bad liar."

Luckily she had chastised him with a smile—a cynical one. "As you have pointed out in the past, I am a man with normal desires."

"Obviously you're a breast man."

Breasts, legs, buttocks. "I admire all aspects of the female body. I consider it a work of art." And if he could capture on canvas the way she looked now—her hair ruffling in the breeze, her slender hand supporting her cheek, her mesmerizing eyes—he would be a renowned artist, not a businessman.

"Speaking of art, do you think we could visit a museum while we're here? Or maybe make a trip to see the Tombs of the Kings?"

She was a master at changing the subject. Almost as good as he. "If time allows. I have much to do to ready the resort for its grand opening before summer's end. I hope that you will assist me in the endeavor."

Her frown did not take away from her beauty. "Surely you're not all work and no play."

He would gladly carve out time to play with her. "When it involves business, I am single-minded."

She leaned back and picked up her glass. "So you hang out in this house when you're not working? Not that there would be anything wrong with hanging out here. I mean, it's a beautiful place. How long have you owned it?"

"I do not own it. I have been leasing it the past eighteen months."

"That must be costly."

"Twenty thousand euros per month."

She sputtered on the water before quickly recovering. "You might as well buy it at that cost."

"If that is what you wish, consider it done."

Now she looked perplexed. "Why would you make such a large purchase based on my opinion?"

He had actually made an offer to the owner not long ago. "I would like to believe you might return with me in the future. Solely a pleasure trip of course, with ample time to *play*."

Kira rimmed her fingertip around the edge of the glass, inadvertently causing a tightening in his groin. "You're getting ahead of yourself, aren't you? We're not certain how well we will get along in the next two weeks."

He had no doubt they would get along well, at least from a physical standpoint. "If my memory serves me correctly, we spent quite a bit of time together since our first meeting. We have engaged in several enlightening conversations."

"Yet during those times, we talked about world politics and the weather, but not once did you mention anything about your upbringing."

With good reason. "I told you I grew up in Morocco and both my parents are deceased."

"What were your parents like?"

"They were decent people." He could say that with honesty about the man who raised him, yet he had his doubts about his mother after learning of her indiscretions.

"Do you have any siblings?" she asked.

That possibility was still open to verification, and something he was not prepared to divulge. "Would you like to take a swim?"

She sighed. "Would you like for once to tell me a little bit about yourself that doesn't involve your portfolio?"

To do so could create suspicion if he made one slip of the tongue. "I would prefer to spend the rest of the evening partaking of the pool."

"I don't want to get my hair wet since I just washed it."

"Perhaps a walk on the beach?"

"In the dark?"

"The full moon will guide us."

She pushed her chair back and stood. "Definitely a walk on the beach. And while we're at it, you can tell me exactly what you're hiding."

# Four

After discarding their shoes, they walked along the gray-sand shoreline side by side, without touching or speaking. Kira waited for a time for Tarek to break the silence and when he didn't, she took the initiative. "It's so peaceful here."

"Yes, it is," he replied without looking at her.

She opted to continue with lighter conversation in hopes of drawing him out. "When I was in college, we traveled to Barbados during summer break."

"We?"

He sounded oddly suspicious. "Yes. Myself and my former fiancé. His family owned a condo there. He had the entire place to himself the majority of the summer months because his parents preferred Europe."

"The man who wounded you," he said in a simple statement of fact. "He must have been wealthy."

She would provide some insight into that doomed love affair, but only a little. "Actually, he was a sultan's son from Saudi attending university in Canada. We were both in the hotel management program. Since I could speak Arabic, we made a connection, dated for a couple of years and became engaged before we broke up."

"Why did you part ways?"

She should have known he would ask and she would really rather not go into too much detail. That would completely ruin the mood. "Incompatibility."

"I thought you were a champion of honesty."

"I'm telling the truth."

"Only a partial truth. Was he unfaithful?"

She'd never found any proof of that, but there had been plenty of rumors before and after their breakup. "Look, I'd really rather not talk about it."

He paused and faced her. "I suspect he did have other women."

All the bitter memories came rushing back like the nearby waves hitting the shore. "Not that I was aware of at the time. If you must know, he found out that aside from the King of Bajul paying for my education, I had no blood ties to the royal family, so he cut me off completely. In other words, I wasn't good enough for him."

He sent her an oddly stern look. "The king financed your education?"

"Yes, out of appreciation for my parents' years of

service in the palace. He was a very generous man and like a second father to me."

When Tarek muttered something unflattering in Arabic, Kira's inquisitiveness kicked into overdrive. "Did you have some sort of falling out with King Aadil?"

"I never met the man nor did I ever attempt to meet him. However, I did not always agree with his archaic policies. I have already heard rumors regarding infidelity."

Her inherent loyalty to the Mehdis spurred her anger and she couldn't help but wonder if maybe he knew something about Adan's birth mother, Elena. Regardless, she didn't dare bring that up in case he didn't. "Talk is cheap, Tarek. Rumors are just that, rumors."

"I have often found they hold a modicum of truth, especially when repeated by many."

"Yet none of that stopped you from doing business with his sons."

"They are from a more progressive generation, and the water conservation project is a good investment."

His continuing focus on money disturbed Kira and reminded her of why they might not make a good match in the long run. As if he'd ever acted like he wanted anything more than an occasional conversation and some slap-and-tickle sessions. "I still find it a bit extreme to build a mini-palace in Bajul so you can oversee that project."

"I own houses in many places, including a villa in Barbados."

Of course he did. She saw the revelation as a means

to lighten the mood and move back into the present. "Do you visit the island often?"

"No, I do not," he said gruffly as he began to walk again. "I rarely have time for leisure."

So much for lightening the mood. She had to quicken her steps to keep up with him and with his long-legged gait, she might find herself having to sprint. "Are you angry at me because I happened to respect and like the former king, despite his faults?"

He stopped again and stared straight ahead, giving her a good glimpse of his stellar profile. "That is not my concern. I am displeased that you seem determined to dissect my past."

Her instincts had always been relatively good, leading her to believe she might be on the right track in regard to his secrets. "It's only because you seem so guarded about your life."

"As I have told you, I value my privacy. It is at times difficult to retain that privacy in light of my work."

That she could understand, but still… "All right. Keep your secrets and your privacy. It's neither here nor there whether you're open about your life, even when I just opened up about mine. Just remember, that doesn't bode well for building a true friendship."

He sent her a quick glance. "Perhaps I do not wish to be your friend."

For some reason, that stung her to the core. "Fine. We'll keep this strictly business since candor clearly isn't your strong suit."

He turned and took her by the shoulders. "If you require candor, then I will give that to you. I wish to be your lover again."

"Tarek, I—"

He pulled her closer, effectively quelling her protest. "I want to kiss you again, be inside you again, and I sense you want that as well."

Oh, how she did want that, but… "You're making this hard on me."

"You have made this *hard* on me in every sense of the word." He proved that point by moving her hand slowly, slowly down to his distended fly before sliding her palm back to his chest. "Seeing you tonight in that dress, watching you now and the way your hair ruffles in the breeze, only causes me to desire you more."

"You're trying to distract me from asking too many questions," she said, her voice sounding somewhat strained.

He brushed feathered kisses across her neck until his lips came to rest beneath her ear. "I am attempting to be candid."

"You promised you wouldn't do this." The lack of conviction in her tone, her inability to push him away, demonstrated her waning determination to resist him.

"I said I would *try* not to do this." He softly kissed her cheek. "Or this." Then he pressed his lips against hers, once, twice, before taking her mouth completely.

Kira internally debated the foolishness of giving in to him, all the while actively participating in that kiss. She readily accepted the gentle stroke of his tongue against hers, his palms roving down her back, the rush of damp heat when he pressed his erection against her pelvis. *Exactly what happened the last time*, she thought as he began to work her dress up to slide his hands inside the back of her panties. He kneaded her bottom, continued to press against her, as their kiss became deeper, more frenzied. If she didn't stop him now, they'd be making love not on marble, but on a bed of sand.

With all the strength she could muster, Kira broke the kiss and backed away, her respiration and nerves both ragged. "Tarek, we can't."

He swiped a palm over his nape. "Believe me, we could. In a matter of seconds."

"This isn't what I want." This wasn't what she had planned.

He narrowed his dark eyes and stared at her. "You are saying you do not want me?"

If she said that, she would be handing him a giant fib. "It's not about whether I want you or not. I just don't want to make a mistake I'll regret."

"Then you believe our need for each other is truly a mistake."

He had no idea how severe a mistake they'd made due to that desire. "I believe it's unwise to answer it again."

"Then I shall escort you back to your quarters," he said in a tone that revealed a hint of dejection mixed with irritation.

As they headed back to the house in silence, Kira couldn't deny her disappointment. On one hand, she did want to experience that intimacy with him again. On the other, she needed to maintain a clear head in order to establish if he was suitable to be involved in her child's future. If he would even want to step into the fatherhood role. She had no doubt that he would support their baby monetarily, but not necessarily emotionally. She refused to settle for less, even if it meant walking away from him for good.

Once they arrived at her room, Kira felt the need to say something to soothe his obviously wounded ego. "I really did enjoy our evening, Tarek, and I want you to know that any woman would be flattered to have your attention."

"But not you."

"Of course I'm flattered. I'm simply being cautious. Before I even consider being with you again, I have to be certain I'm not going to be hurt."

His features relaxed somewhat. "If you recall, we both agreed that our relationship would remain casual with no complications. What has changed?"

Everything. "I suppose I've learned I'm not the kind of woman who can engage in casual sex. I have to have more."

Now he looked concerned, as if his fight-or-flight reflex had kicked in. "How much more?"

"I need someone who appreciates me for who I am. I need to know that I'm not only a fling."

He swiped one hand over his jaw. "My lifestyle has not allowed me to consider settling into a serious relationship."

"Don't you want to someday have a wife and children?" She sounded almost desperate, even to her own ears.

He took both her hands into his. "I refuse to make

empty promises to you for the sake of having you in my bed. Yet since that night, I have thought of nothing aside from you. Nevertheless, if you cannot accept what I can offer to you at this point in time, an attentive lover who will treat you the way you deserve to be treated, with great care, then say so now and I shall not bother you again."

Not at all what she needed to hear. "You mean you want sex with no strings attached."

"Life is very brief. I endeavor to make the best of each moment. What better way to do that than to spend those moments with a remarkable woman?"

She leaned back against the wall next to the open door. "Are you trying to sway me to your side with pretty words?"

"Never doubt my sincerity where you are concerned. You are a remarkable woman. Highly intelligent and innately sensual. Your former lover was a fool not to recognize those attributes."

Common sense told her to let him go immediately. The child growing in her belly said she couldn't right now. Yet the loudest voice in her head came from her heart. The same voice that had cautioned her during all their lengthy conversations and heady flirtations—she could easily fall in love with him.

She would keep that voice quieted for the time being. "I understand what you're asking of me, and I can only promise I'll sleep on it." If she was in fact able to sleep at all.

He lifted her hands, turned them over and kissed

each palm before releasing her. "And that is all I ask. I will see you early in the morning."

Perhaps in the morning, she would see things more clearly.

As soon as the limo pulled into the drive leading up to the resort, the magnitude of Tarek's wealth finally hit home for Kira.

Perfection. Absolute perfection, from the white stone facade to the elaborate dual rock water features flanking the hotel's entrance. Three floors of rooms, all containing large balconies, fanned out on both sides of what appeared to be the main lobby. The manicured landscape would be described as lush and green and tropical, laid out precisely to her father's standards. Unfortunately, she couldn't express her favorable opinions to the proprietor since he'd departed for the resort long before her, according to Alexios. She couldn't help but wonder if he'd reconsidered and decided to shelve the seduction. That should give her some relief, but in reality, it gave her a sinking feeling in the pit of her stomach that had nothing to do with the pregnancy. As silly as it seemed, a part of her wanted him to persist.

After the driver stopped beneath the portico, he rounded the limo and offered his hand to help her out. Kira strolled toward the entry, expecting to be greeted by Tarek, only to see a woman emerge from the double copper doors. A classically beautiful, dark-eyed, golden-skinned woman dressed in an impeccably tailored white linen suit. Her shoulder-length raven hair had been styled in soft waves, reminiscent of a Hollywood icon from decades ago. Her makeup was equally perfect, as was her dazzling smile that almost seemed rehearsed. "Welcome, Ms. Darzin," she said as she offered a slender hand. "I am Athena Clerides, Tarek's business associate."

The goddess-like name fit her well, Kira decided, though she found it odd Tarek had failed to mention her during their many conversations. She also felt completely underdressed in her simple pink sundress and sandals. "It's a pleasure to meet you, Ms. Clerides," she replied as she shook her hand.

"Please call me Athena." Her accent hinted at her Greek roots and so did her striking features.

"As long as you call me Kira."

"Agreed. Now, if you will follow me, we will get started on your duties."

Evidently the taskmaster sent someone else to do his dirty work. "Is Tarek not here?"

Athena opened the door wide. "He is currently working on his own project. He has instructed me to have you look over the plans for the kitchen."

At least the woman didn't seem offended by the request. "I'm not certain what I have to offer you in that regard, but I'm willing to give my opinion."

"Obviously Tarek values your opinion," she said, the first touch of acrimony in her tone. "Now if you will please follow me."

Kira complied, trailing behind Athena as they walked through the high-ceiling lobby, complete with a gigantic purple Persian rug covering polished black marble floors—reminiscent of another marble floor.

She shoved the memories away and continued to survey the area. Unlike Tarek's beach rental, the décor was much more traditional, evident from the rich wood furniture and sofas covered in red, violet and gold fabrics. They continued through a lengthy corridor to the left and paused at an opening that revealed a large space, barren aside from a stainless-steel prep station centered in the middle of the room.

"This is it," Athena announced. "Or where it will be once the kitchen is complete."

"It's definitely a blank slate," Kira said. "Do you have some sort of blueprint for the layout?"

"Of course." Athena strode to the industrial island, picked up a notebook computer and held it out to Kira. "This is the current plan."

She studied the diagram before regarding Athena again. "Only one refrigerator?"

The woman looked at Kira as if she were daft. "A large refrigerator."

She studied the plan a few more moments before regarding Athena again. "Do you intend to serve wine?"

"Yes. We will be catering to travelers from around the world."

Well-heeled travelers, no doubt. "Then I suggest you add a wine refrigerator."

"I will take that into consideration, but the cupboards are scheduled to be installed this afternoon and the appliances delivered in the morning. It would cost money to make these last-minute additions."

As if the missing mogul would care. "I'm sure Tarek has a contingency in the budget to cover any added expense if the original layout needs to be reconfigured." Kira returned to the graphic to avoid Athena's glare. "Will the restaurant be serving only guests, or will it be open to the public?"

"Both."

That sent the mental wheels into a spin. "Then perhaps you should add another prep area next to the dishwasher since you have some wasted space. My mother always said you can never have enough room for food preparation."

Athena actually smiled. "That is a good suggestion, though it might not be feasible to have it here for a few more days."

Finally, they were getting somewhere. "A few more days shouldn't matter too much."

"Tell me, was your mother a cook?"

Kira handed the notepad back to her. "A chef. She worked for the former king of Bajul for many years. My father tended to the palace's gardens."

Athena lifted a thin brow. "Ah. You are the daughter of domestics."

She suddenly felt like that inadequate schoolgirl again. A commoner among royalty. Yet she would not let Athena's snobbery shatter her confidence. "Yes, I am, and very proud of my heritage. So much so I am following in their footsteps."

Athena leaned a narrow hip against the metal counter. "As a cook or a groundskeeper?"

Kira felt her internal temperature begin to rise. "Neither, actually. I'm the director of the household in charge of all the palace staff."

The woman's smile was entirely too snide. "How nice that your parents' humble lifestyle afforded you that position."

She felt puzzled by Athena's suddenly disagreeable demeanor, yet Kira wasn't beyond matching her condescension. "A degree in hotel management afforded me that position, as well as a recommendation from the current king."

"I see. Did the current king recommend you to Tarek?"

Every word that came out of the woman's mouth sounded like an indictment. "As a matter of fact, he requested I accompany Tarek here as a temporary assistant."

Athena looked as if she'd swallowed something sour. "Since the two of you appear to be on a first-name basis, exactly how are you assisting him?"

Kira suddenly understood the reason behind Athena's attitude. Jealousy, pure and simple. "Look, Tarek and I have socialized before and have become friends. If you're suggesting more exists between us, you're wrong." Aside from a baby, a fact that would remain hidden from this woman, and the rest of the world, for the time being. "If you have a problem working with me, then I suggest you take it up with him."

Athena's features seemed to soften somewhat. "I apologize for my suspicious nature, but I have worked alongside Tarek for many years and I know him better than most. He has an affinity for attractive women such as you."

Kira wagered Athena's and Tarek's relationship went

beyond the boardroom and into the bedroom. "How long have you been with him?"

"Eight years," she said proudly. "We have traveled the globe together, and since I am a Cypriot, I encouraged him to build this resort. Because he values and trusts my judgment, he agreed the venture would be a good investment."

Clearly Ms. Clerides had quite a bit of clout, and a very close relationship with her boss. Kira found that troubling on several levels that she would take out and analyze later. "Interesting. I'm sure you'll both be very successful in this and all your future endeavors. Is there anything else you'd like to discuss?"

Athena paused as if mulling over her response. "Yes. When did you meet Tarek?"

*That* Kira hadn't expected. "A little over three months ago. Why?"

Athena strolled around the table, her arms folded beneath her breasts. "That does explain his recent behavior."

"I don't understand."

She paused and leveled her gaze on Kira. "I suspected he had found another woman who had captured his interest. I do believe that woman is you."

Denial seemed the best course in this case. "I'm sure you're mistaken."

"I can assure you I am not." Athena hesitated a moment, as if again carefully considering her words. "I began to notice a change in him on his return trips from Bajul over the past few months. He seemed distant and distracted, when he has always been very attentive to me."

The truth about their relationship had now been officially confirmed, as far as Kira was concerned. "Excuse my intrusiveness, but I assume you and Tarek are lovers."

Athena appeared somewhat chagrined. "We *were* lovers until three months ago. He told me that our relationship had run its course and he was freeing me to pursue other options."

Unmistakable hurt filtered out in Athena's tone, leaving Kira in a quandary over what to say next. "I'm sorry it didn't work out since you obviously care about him."

Athena lifted her shoulders in a shrug. "Tarek is not the type of man who embraces a serious relationship. However, he is magnetic and very seductive, which affords him the ability to make a woman discard her convictions, along with her clothes. I caution you to keep that in mind."

Too late for that. "As I've said, Tarek and I are only friends."

"The heightened color on your face says otherwise."

Kira hated that her annoying blush gave away her feelings like a digital billboard. "Necessary or not, I will certainly take your caution to heart."

"And that will better enable you to protect your heart." She hesitated before adding, "Have you asked him about the phone calls?"

"Phone calls?"

"The one he makes every afternoon at the same time."

She hadn't been around him long enough to notice. "No, I haven't."

"Then pay attention and you will soon see it is part of his routine, and a mystery."

"Are you inferring he's speaking with a woman?"

"I suspected he is, but he has never been forthcoming. In all the years I've been with him, the identity of the party on the other end of the line remains a mystery. Perhaps you will be the one to solve it."

She had a few qualms about that. Tarek Azzmar might forever be an enigma. And if only she'd received Athena's counsel before that night six weeks ago. If Tarek rejected their baby, she would be heartbroken. "I suppose you should point me in the direction of Tarek now."

"You will most likely find him in the courtyard."

"That was certainly awkward, Tarek." And so was seeing him dressed in white painter's pants, sans shirt, displaying smooth warm skin on his remarkably strong back. He continued to carefully lay gray stone into the beginnings of a feature wall near the unfilled swimming pool, apparently too engrossed to respond to her comment.

*Please don't turn around*, she thought as he continued to go about his task, while she continued to shamelessly study his amazing physique. Much to her dismay, he failed to heed her silent request and faced her, showing to full advantage his ruffled hair, unshaven jaw, the slight shading on his newsworthy chest, the flat plane of his abdomen. Her gaze immediately came to rest on his navel, which was exposed by the low-slung waistband on the pants, before returning to his face. Of course, she immediately focused on his mouth.

After grabbing a rag from the nearby work table, he wiped his hands, then whipped out a scowl. "What is this awkwardness you speak of?"

For a moment, Kira couldn't remember what she had said when she'd come upon him looking like one hundred percent prime male. Fortunately, she recovered quickly when she recalled her tense conversation with his ex-girlfriend. "I don't appreciate you sending me into the lion's den with the lioness."

"Please explain."

Oh, she would. Gladly. "You should have informed me that you and Athena were lovers."

He tossed the rag aside and put on a somber expression. "She informed you of this?"

"Yes, because she assumes I'm her replacement."

He went back to cutting another stone. "And you said?"

"She was mistaken. She also warned me that you are the consummate heartbreaker."

That earned her another frown. "I prefer not to discuss this here."

Maybe not here. Maybe not now. But they would discuss it tonight.

Kira brought her attention to the intricacy of the wall and realized Tarek had talents she hadn't known about until then. In reality, she still knew very little about him from a personal standpoint, even if she did know what he looked like naked.

"Where did you learn to do this?"

He placed another tile—this one rust-colored—into the pattern. "I was schooled by the man who raised me."

"You mean your father?"

"Yes."

"Then why didn't you say that?"

He glanced at her over one shoulder. "He is the man who raised me, is he not?"

"Yes, but…" No need to argue a point she wouldn't win. "Was this a hobby, or did he make a living as a stone mason?"

"A meager living," he said as he faced her again. "His craft sent him to an early grave."

She could imagine the poor man being trapped under a stone wall. "Did he suffer a work-related injury?"

"He suffered from a weak heart that claimed him before his fiftieth birthday, as it was with his own father."

Kira's palm automatically went to her belly, an unexpected maternal gesture. "That probably causes you quite a bit of concern in regard to your own health."

"It does not."

In her opinion, he should be worried, yet Tarek would forever be a tough guy in her eyes. When it came to their child, she couldn't help but be troubled by genetic predisposition to disease. "What happened to your mother?"

His expression turned somber, as if he had been plagued by sudden and unwelcome memories. "She contracted pneumonia the year I turned ten and never recovered. She suffered from a weak will."

Kira swallowed around her shock. "That's a crass thing to say about the woman who gave birth to you."

"It is the truth, according to her husband. I barely remember her beyond a few select memories."

Odd that he couldn't seem to say "father." A very telling omission, and perhaps the reason behind his inability to commit. Maybe his father cheated on his mother. Maybe the man had been cold and distant. She could only hope that someday she would find out.

"I'm sure it's difficult to get past the grief over losing both parents so soon in life. I don't know what I would do without mine."

Tarek swept the back of one arm over his forehead now beaded with perspiration. "I am glad you enjoyed a stable childhood. Now if you will excuse me, I will finish here and see you at the villa later."

Talk about being dismissed in short order. She refused to let him get away with it the next time they conversed. "Fine. Hopefully you'll be back by lunchtime."

# Five

The sun had long since set before Tarek returned home. The troubling conversation with Kira had prompted him to remain longer in an effort to discard the bitter memories. In an effort to avoid her questions.

He had loved his mother greatly and had mourned her loss as any other devoted son would. He had respected her without fail...until he had learned of her deception and indiscretions. Since gaining that knowledge, he had concentrated on rising above his upbringing, and avoiding interpersonal relationships. He had built a financial empire that rivaled most. He had achieved this virtually alone.

Tonight, he would push those recollections away and concentrate on the one woman who could help him forget, if she would be willing to do that. To attain his goal, he would endeavor to answer her questions, at least those that he could answer. And perhaps he would ask a few questions of her.

After he entered the foyer, a person walking toward the end of the pool, cast in blue shadows, caught his attention. The curve of her hips and the grace of her movements left no question as to her gender. He had explored those curves before, and he wished to do so again. First, he must find out if she was still speaking to him.

After she executed a perfect dive and began to swim the length of the pool, Tarek strode through the open glass doors, claimed a nearby chair and waited for her to take notice of his appearance. He continued to wait an interminable amount of time until his patience began to wane. Before he could call Kira's name, she finally paused, climbed up the steps on the opposite end of the pool, grabbed a towel from a table and began drying off…slowly.

The swimsuit she wore barely covered her breasts and bottom, revealing a body designed to drive a man to the brink of insanity. He could not determine if she had yet to detect his presence, or if she was simply ignoring him. Regardless, he continued to watch her slide the towel down her thighs, well aware of what his perusal was doing to his libido. The pressure began to build until a painful erection strained behind his fly.

"I see you finally decided to come home."

Her comment thrust him out of his sexual trance, yet did nothing to remedy his current predicament. "My apologies for my tardiness. The time got away from me and then I had to shower and change before returning." He could use another shower now, if only to quell his lust.

After securing the towel low on her hips, Kira joined him and took the chair next to his. "Did you have dinner?"

"I did."

"With Athena?"

And so began the interrogation. "No. I dined alone at a small bistro near the resort. I assume you have eaten."

She rested against the back of the chair, revealing a clear view of her bare flesh, from her breasts to where the towel split at her thighs, adding fuel to the fire burning in his groin. "Yes, I did. A nice seafood salad, which I ate alone, too."

Touché. "Again, I apologize for not being here to share the meal with you."

"I'll accept your apology only if you're willing to explain a few things to me."

"I will try." That explanation could require several half-truths.

"What exactly is your relationship with Athena?"

"We have a business relationship. That is all."

"But it hasn't always been that way, Tarek. How serious were you?"

"Our liaison was solely for convenience. We spent quite a bit of time together and made the most of our proximity. Aside from that, there was no talk of permanency."

She swept a hand through her hair. "You might want to inform her of that."

"Athena has always known my expectations."

"Maybe, but did you know she's in love with you?"

He had suspected as much, though she had never said. "Athena loves the challenge and the chase. If I have wounded her, it would be limited to her pride."

She released a cynical laugh. "For such a smart man, you know very little about women."

"I admit women are enigmas, yet I do know Athena well."

"Apparently not if you haven't noticed all the signs leading to the aforementioned love aspect."

He was growing increasingly uncomfortable over the course of the conversation. "If you are referring to emotional entanglement, we agreed that would not be included when we became intimate."

"Tarek, most women are not wired like men. At times we're slaves to our emotions. That can lead to that most dreaded emotion, love."

"Love defies logic."

She sighed. "Love isn't supposed to be logical. It's about caring so much for someone you can't envision your life without them. Of course, a logical man like yourself probably has no clue what I'm talking about."

If she only knew the effort it required to reject those emotions, and how long it had taken to banish them from his life. "I am not without compassion, Kira, yet I am determined to keep grounded in order to succeed in life."

She appeared to be growing impatient with him. "You mean succeed at business, don't you, Tarek? Here's a headline. Life isn't only about building fabulous resorts, one larger than the other, to pay homage to the money gods. If you can't enjoy the fruits of your labor with someone you care about, what good is all the money in the world?"

"It is not only about the monetary gains. It involves the challenge of achieving a goal."

She came to her feet and released the towel again. "Speaking of challenges, I have a few more laps to swim."

"I will join you," he said as he stood.

"Knock yourself out, although I might be finished with my swim by the time you change." With that, she strode to the end of the pool and dove in.

He saw a way to remedy the lack of time, though it could cost him if Kira did not approve. He believed it to be worth the risk, and possibly rewarding.

After he toed out of his shoes and removed his socks, he quickly took off his shirt, slacks and boxer briefs. Kira continued to swim laps, presumably unaware he was completely nude when he dove into the pool. He swam to the shallow end near the steps to wait for her to reach him. Once she did, he clasped her wrist and brought her into his arms.

"What are you doing?" she asked as she pushed her hair away from her face.

"I am concerned you are exerting yourself too much."

"I'll be the judge of that, and how did you change so fast? Were you wearing your trunks under your pants?"

"I preferred not to waste time changing."

Awareness dawned in her expression. "You're naked."

He could not contain a smile. "Perhaps."

She reached around him and ran her palm over his bare buttock. "You really enjoy being the bad boy, don't you?"

"Perhaps," he repeated. "I am good at it."

She rolled her eyes. "Yes, you are. Do you mind if I get back to swimming now?"

He brushed a kiss across her cheek. "I can think of a more enjoyable way to exert ourselves."

When he kissed her neck, she murmured, "This isn't fair."

He suspected she would bring out the friendship-only argument. "It is fair because this is what we both want. I can tell by the way you are trembling."

"It's not fair because you're seducing a hormone-ridden woman."

Far be it for him to question that. He was simply thankful his theory had been wrong, encouraging him to proceed. He rimmed his tongue around the shell of her ear and whispered, "And I am a hormone-ridden man." He then took a major chance, took her hand and pressed her palm against his erection. "I want you desperately."

"I see your point," she said in a breathy tone. "Or maybe I should say I feel your point."

When Kira began to stroke him, Tarek realized he could not retain control if he did not stop her. He mustered all his strength, swept her into his arms and set her on the pool's edge. He kissed her then, slowly yet insistently, as he untied the string around her neck and unclasped the strap at her back. He waited for her protest and when she did not, he tossed the bikini top behind him and moved his mouth to her breast. As he circled his tongue around her nipple, she clasped his head and released a soft moan. As he moved his attention to her other breasts, she uttered, "I'm going to hate myself for this in the morning."

The comment proved as effective as frigid water on Tarek's libido. He refused to continue foreplay with an unwilling woman.

On that thought, he stood and ascended the steps, leaving her sitting there, her mouth agape. "What are you doing?"

He grabbed the towel and tossed it to her, then began gathering his clothes. "I am retiring to bed."

After covering herself in cloth, she climbed out of the pool and approached him. "Quite frankly, I don't appreciate you working me into a sexual frenzy, then stopping without any explanation."

After setting his clothing aside on the table, he pulled on his underwear to cover the fact he was not quite recovered. "As much as I would like to make love to you again, I cannot in good conscience continue and, in turn, be the reason for your regrets in the morning."

She sighed. "It's very difficult for me to fight this, but I don't want to complicate our situation more by making a wrong decision."

"Our situation does not have to be complicated. We are two vital people who enjoy intimacy."

She sent him a frustrated look. "But what happens

after we return to Bajul? Do we pretend our first night together and this trip didn't exist?"

Truth be known, he could not tolerate the thought of not seeing her again. He found her intriguing, fascinating, and since their meeting, she had never been a thought away in his mind. Yet he feared he could never measure up to her ideal of what a man should be.

"I would be remiss if I made promises to you that I cannot keep at this point in my life. Knowing that, should you decide you would like to explore further intimacy, I would welcome that decision. Consequently, you may rest assured I will not pursue you again."

"All right," she said as she started away then paused to face him again. "If you're okay with forgetting what transpired between us, so be it. But I, on the other hand, will carry the reminders with me for years."

After Kira disappeared into the house, Tarek dropped down on a chaise to ponder the puzzling comment. He despised the thought that he had wounded her so deeply that she would forever have his careless disregard imprinted on her soul. He hated that he had not seen through her guise about accepting a casual relationship. She still retained a certain amount of innocence, whereas he had become jaded when matters of the heart were involved.

He needed to stay away from her, yet never touching her again seemed unthinkable. More important, she had begun to stir emotions he wanted to ignore. Perhaps he could not love her for the long term, but he could find some way to prove that he was not the ogre she believed him to be. That he did value her. He would have to achieve that objective without a hint of seduction, and that mission would prove to be quite the challenge.

"He wants me to do what?"

Athena walked into the private elevator leading to the third floor and waited for Kira to enter and the doors to close before responding. "Tarek has asked that you select the finishes for the owner's suite."

Of all the strange requests. "Shouldn't he be doing that? Better still, shouldn't you? After all, you know him better than I do."

"One would think," Athena said. "But he insists you should take charge of this."

From Athena's slightly acid tone, Kira could tell the woman wasn't the least bit happy. "Fine, but I would really appreciate your input as well."

"My pleasure," she said as she threw open the wooden double doors with dramatic flair. "Here we are."

Kira stepped inside the massive suite, which was well lit due to the bank of glass doors, much like those back at the villa. The view of the surf hitting the private beach below was no less impressive. Aside from a huge king-sized bed with a bare mattress and a black bureau on one wall, the room was as empty as the kitchen. At least the walls had been painted white.

Athena crossed the room and gestured Kira to the double dresser. "These are a few samples the designer left for you to review."

Kira leaned over and studied the samples, then pointed at one opaque tile. "This is out because Tarek doesn't like green."

"Perhaps you know him better than you assume."

She sent Athena a weak smile over one shoulder. "Not really. I just remember him mentioning it in passing during one of our conversations."

"I am surprised since green is often associated with money."

Kira ignored Athena's cynical tone and turned back to the samples. "I believe the gray glass tile works well for the shower, white porcelain tile for the floor and Carrara marble for the bathroom vanity. The darker bamboo for the bedroom flooring would be a nice contrast."

"I agree," Athena said, actually sounding as if she did. "What would you suggest for the color palette in the bedroom?"

When Kira straightened, her head began to spin. "I think…I need to sit down."

Looking concerned, Athena surprisingly took her by the shoulders and sat her down on the bed. "May I get you something?"

"Some water," Kira croaked as she waited for the dizziness to subside.

"Did you have breakfast?" Athena asked.

She shook her head. "I had some pineapple juice."

"Then I will return with some proper food immediately. In the meantime, feel free to lie down."

After Athena left, Kira kicked off her sandals and stretched out on the plush mattress, one arm draped over her eyes. The lack of sleep certainly hadn't helped her predicament, nor had her and Tarek's interlude last night. She'd come so close to telling him about the baby, yet she'd lost her courage at the last minute. Maybe the time had come to let him in on the secret. Or not. She needed more time, a better opportunity. A more private place where they would be guaranteed privacy. She couldn't imagine anything worse than to have someone walk in on them when she was saying, "Oh by the way, Tarek, I'm going to have a baby...."

"Are you not well, Kira?"

Speaking of the prospective daddy. She uncovered her eyes to see Tarek standing at the footboard, holding a glass of water. "I'm fine. I didn't sleep well last night."

He rounded the bed, perched on the edge of the mattress and offered her the glass. "Perhaps you should return to the villa to rest."

Kira scooted up against the headboard and took a sip of water. "I've barely done anything today aside from picking out a few tiles, which leads me to a question. Why do you want me to decorate your suite?"

"I value your judgment."

"I still believe you should provide your input, in case I'm off base."

"As long as it is not green, I will be satisfied with your choices."

"You spoke to Athena."

He cracked a half smile. "How else would I have learned of your illness?"

"I'm not ill, Tarek. I'm...." She couldn't tell him here, or now for that matter. She needed more time to prepare. More time to know if telling him would be the right move to make. "I'm just a little fatigued."

Fortunately, he didn't look skeptical, but he did look

concerned. "Then you should definitely return to the house to rest. However, I do have a task for you this evening if you are feeling up to it. One I believe you will enjoy."

*Task* could cover a whole spectrum of possibilities.

"I'm positive I'll be fine by then. I do have a question, though. Does this task require wearing all our clothes?"

He hesitated, leading Kira to believe he was warring with himself over a proper response. "Yes, it does. Dress in formal attire and meet me at the entry no later than nine p.m."

Kira experienced a nip of panic over eating that late, and not having a thing to wear. "I brought only a few casual outfits and business suits."

He came to his feet and held out his hand. "Then I shall have something appropriate sent to the villa. Do you have a color preference?"

She allowed him to help her up, but continued to grip the water glass with both hands to quell the urge to touch him. "I'm sure I'll be happy with what you pick, and I'm almost certain it won't be green."

His smile arrived full-throttle, bright as the sun and sensual to a fault. "I will have Athena choose the dress."

Lovely. That meant she could be wearing metallic rags. "All right. Can you give me a hint as to what we'll be doing this evening?"

"I will say only that you will have a memorable experience."

Knowing him, and herself in his presence, she had no doubt about that.

* * *

"Exactly how well do you know Kira Darzin?"

Seated in his private office at the resort, Tarek continued to scan the expense report, intent on ignoring Athena's inquisition. "I see we've gone over budget on the kitchen redesign."

"Your newest protégée is to blame for that. I ask again, how well do you know her?"

He set the binder aside on the desk and leaned back in his chair. "She is not my protégée. She is serving as my advisor."

Athena began to pace the room like a captive animal. "I have known you to be a lot of things when it comes to women, but never naïve."

"What is your point, Athena?"

She paused to face him, her hands tightly balled at her sides. "I believe she is bent on sabotaging you by insisting on unnecessary changes to the resort's plans. Everything she has suggested will cost you more money."

Athena was more ruthless than he when it came to expenditures, even though it did not affect her bank account. "Why do you believe she would do this?"

She began pacing again. "Revenge, perhaps. I suspect you have angered her and she is attempting to punish you by targeting what you cherish the most. Your fortune."

He kept a choke hold on his anger. "These accusations you are making are absurd, Athena. The price of the alterations to the original kitchen configuration is minimal in light of the overall cost to build this resort. Your allegations stem from a personal vendetta."

She appeared shocked by his assessment. "I have no idea why you would believe that."

"Kira mentioned that you confirmed we were lovers. Perhaps this attack on her motivation is your retribution for the wrongs you believe I have committed against you."

"And your indictment tells me that this woman matters more to you than you care to admit. And since you have such faith in Ms. Darzin's abilities, perhaps it would be best if I resign my position, effective immediately."

Tarek shoved his chair back and stood. "You would leave in the middle of a project you encouraged me to begin?"

"Actually, yes. I'm certain you and your new charge will work very well together, until you tire of her as you tired of me."

He refused to wage a war of words with her. "I will see to it you receive suitable severance for your efforts."

Athena's smile was laced with sarcasm. "How generous of you. And as soon as you take off your blinders, you might want to pay more attention to your new lover's behavior. She could very well be harboring a secret that would not please you."

Before Tarek could offer a rejoinder, Athena rushed out of the room like a tempest and slammed the door behind her. He knew how Athena operated when she did not have her way. She would attempt to come back, apologize and return to business as usual. This time, he would not take her back, nor would he give any credence to her suspicions. He would sense if Kira was hiding something important from her. Unlike Athena, she did not have a deceptive cell in her being. She had demonstrated that to him through her insistence he be completely honest with her, and he had yet to answer that request.

No matter. He was more than ready to sever all ties with Athena, despite the hardship it would create on their deadline. This turn of events would change all aspects of his current project, yet he felt optimistic he had the answer to the dilemma—as long as he could demonstrate to Kira how much he needed her.

She needed to finish putting on her makeup, but first she needed to answer the summons.

As she tightened her white terry bathrobe, Kira crossed the room and opened the door to Alexios, who was clutching a vinyl garment bag. "Your attire for the evening, madam," he said.

She couldn't wait to see what Athena had picked out and, in some ways, dreaded it. "Thank you, Alexios. And tell Ms. Clerides I appreciate her assistance in choosing the dress."

He sent her a puzzled look. "Mr. Azzmar selected the attire, not Miss Clerides."

Even more intriguing. Apparently the rebuffed ex-lover had intentionally declined making the purchase. "I see. I'll thank him later. Is he here now?"

"He is currently placing his routine call to Morocco. He told me to inform you he will be awaiting your arrival at the entry."

"Thank you, Alexios. Tell him I shouldn't be too long."

"As you wish, Madam," he said before heading away.

Kira closed the door and pondered what the servant had said. Could that call be the one Athena had mentioned? Of course, logic said Tarek was speaking with the staff at the Moroccan mansion. Or that he had a silent business partner. Or another woman waiting in the wings.

She had no cause to be suspicious and hated that Athena had put those thoughts in her head, probably intentionally so.

Discarding her concerns for the time being, Kira laid the bag on the bed, unzipped it and removed one of the most beautiful full-length gowns she had ever seen. A shimmering fitted silver gown with a plunging halter neckline and an equally low back, along with a box containing matching high-heeled silver sandals.

She was admittedly floored by Tarek's choice and extremely surprised to find he'd chosen her correct size with both the dress and shoes. Maybe a lucky guess, but she predicted he'd had one of the staff check out her closet for reference.

After laying the gown across the bed, she returned to the bathroom to finish fixing her face, then pulled her hair back from her forehead and secured it with pins. Now for the finishing touch—putting on the one-carat diamond studs, the only souvenir from her previous relationship since she'd tossed the engagement ring at him during their breakup. Was that appropriate, wearing earrings another man had given her? Possibly not, but what Tarek didn't know wouldn't hurt him. Except for the whole baby issue.

She could spring the news on him tonight. Or not. She still needed to learn more about him, ask a few leading questions in light of what she'd recently learned, and then decide if he deserved to be a daddy. Wanted to be a daddy. The answer to both could be a resounding no.

Recognizing time was slipping away, Kira shrugged out of the robe and stepped into the dress. She then walked to the floor-length mirror hanging on the back of the door to do a closer inspection. No panty lines since she'd opted to go without them. No angle that made her butt look too big. No unsightly belly bulge. A perfect fit. A few weeks from now, she wouldn't be able to say that. A few weeks from now, her child's future would be resolved. She hoped.

She perched on the edge of the bed, slid her feet into the heels and grabbed the small black clutch. Now that she was appropriately dressed, Kira set out to find her billionaire prince and prepared to be wined and dined, minus the wine. Tonight she would pretend this fantasy date was the real deal. Tomorrow she would return to reality.

# Six

"Madam, your chariot has arrived."

After Alexios moved aside, Kira stepped out the door and confronted one more pleasant surprise. Not a chariot per se, but close enough. A white carriage, attached to a matched pair of gray and white dappled horses wearing purple feather plumes and piloted by a dignified driver, sat beneath the portico. Standing beside that fancy form of transportation was a gorgeous man wearing a black tuxedo and an overtly sensual smile surrounded by a slight shading of whiskers.

Once she had the presence of mind to move, she felt as if she floated toward Tarek, caught up in some surreal, romantic fantasy. She almost asked him to pinch her when he took her hand and helped her into the carriage. She almost pinched herself to make certain she wasn't dreaming this whole unexpected scenario.

Instead, when Tarek slid into the seat next to her, Kira kissed his cheek to show her gratitude. "This is absolutely wonderful. The dress, the transportation, everything. You're definitely off to a good start, but what's next on the agenda? Perhaps a moonlit cruise on the Mediterranean?"

He slid his arm through hers, as if they were on a real date, and grinned. "You will see soon enough."

Could the man be any more cryptic? "You could at least give me a hint as to where we're going."

"The resort."

She couldn't quell the disappointment over Tarek's type-A personality. "You apparently can't begin playtime before you do a little work first."

"In a manner of speaking, we both have work to do."

Wonderful. "If that's the case, our attire is probably overkill."

"Not necessarily. You will simply have to trust me."

Oh, that she could. When she'd initially met him, she'd sensed he was a womanizer but aside from that, believed he was trustworthy, at least on a business level. Now she wasn't at all certain due to his refusal to discuss any significant details about his past, but she'd give him the benefit of the doubt until proven wrong.

Kira opted to forget her cares and take pleasure in the ride. As they made their way down the winding road leading to the resort, she relished the feel of the warm breeze blowing across her face and studied the darkening sky. She thoroughly enjoyed the scent of

Tarek's exotic cologne, which reminded her of sandalwood incense. She truly liked the fact they were so cozy in this Cinderella coach, and was concerned that she could get carried away when Tarek began stroking her bare arm.

She imagined a few other strokes in less-than-obvious places. She fantasized about throwing caution to the wind just to experience his mastery one more time. She began to wonder if she'd entirely lost her marbles, as her mother used to say.

Before she had time to ponder her sanity any further, the driver pulled up to the resort and brought the carriage to an abrupt stop by the front doors. Tarek climbed out first, took her by the waist, lifted her out and set her on her feet. Yes, she had definitely stepped into a fairy tale.

Kira waited while Tarek handed their escort a roll of bills before they headed toward the entry, his palm resting lightly on her exposed back. Even that innocent gesture had her ready and willing to climb all over him like a sheet of human shrink wrap. Boy, was she in big trouble, and the night had barely begun.

"Where to now?" she asked as they walked into the lobby.

"The ballroom."

No surprise there. "I hope you're not suggesting we have a repeat of our first night together." Actually, she hoped he was.

He sent her a half smile. "The thought had crossed my mind, but we will not be alone tonight."

Evidently he'd arranged some social soiree without her knowledge or assistance. "Who's on the guest list?"

"You will soon see."

She actually saw nothing but a table for two near the far wall of the massive room covered in—of course—a white marble floor. Her heels sounded like tap shoes as they crossed to the table, where Tarek pulled out her chair. As soon as she was seated, a somewhat rotund man dressed in a white suit and black tie strode into the room. "Madam, Monsieur, I am François and I will be serving you tonight."

Tarek claimed the chair across from Kira's and tented his hands together on the table. "Has John Paul found the kitchen satisfactory?"

François let go a boisterous laugh as he unfolded one white cloth napkin and laid it in Kira's lap. "He is very honored to be the first to use it." After he unfolded Tarek's napkin and offered it to him, he added, "I will return briefly with the opening course."

"The kitchen was completed?" Kira asked, dumbfounded, after François left.

"Not completely," Tarek said. "The preparation table you requested will not arrive until tomorrow and there are still a few finishing touches that need to be made. Otherwise, it is quite adequate for meal preparation at this time."

She bent one elbow on the table's edge and supported her cheek with her palm. "It sounds as if you've already hired your head chef."

Tarek took a drink of water from a crystal goblet then set it aside. "He is actually auditioning tonight, and so is François. They are both employed at a five-star hotel in Paris that is owned by one of my competitors. If you find the meal and service satisfactory, I will entice them both away."

Kira leaned back in the chair and sighed. "You are clearly the greatest competitor of all if you're stealing employees."

"There is no true theft involved. If the price is right, most anyone can be bought."

That didn't hold true for her. "If you say so."

François interrupted the discourse by delivering two trays brimming with appetizers that included steamed mussels and cold-boiled shrimp, along with a variety of cheeses and fruit. Kira's tummy began to rumble despite the fact she'd had two snacks since lunch. At this rate, she would require maternity clothes, or tents, by her second trimester.

Regardless, she ate with abandon the luscious fresh salad, the array of fresh vegetables and the petite filet mignon accompanied by a lobster tail. She did skip the wine, but not the sorbet designed to cleanse the palate between courses. In fact, she'd barely drawn a breath before the *pêche Melba* arrived for dessert. Spun sugar and ice cream probably wouldn't help her expanding waistline, but at least the peaches were healthy. Sort of.

When she noticed Tarek staring at her as he had the last time she'd gorged herself, her face began to flame. "I'm sorry. I'm not accustomed to eating this late, so needless to say, I was starving."

"No apology necessary," he said. "I appreciate a

woman with a healthy appetite, though I am surprised you are still quite thin."

*Just wait a few weeks*, she started to say but thought better of it. "Honestly, I don't normally eat so much. Something about this island atmosphere makes me very hungry."

"It fuels my appetites as well."

His usage of the plural form of "appetite," led Kira to believe he wasn't only referring to food. "Well, that definitely quenched one of mine."

He sent her a knowing and somewhat smoldering look. "Then I suppose I do not need to ask if you enjoyed the fare."

"I would think that's obvious."

They shared in a laugh, the first one she'd heard escape from Tarek's mouth since they'd been there. If he knew the reason behind her ravenous behavior, he wouldn't be laughing.

François suddenly reappeared and gathered the empty dessert cups. "John Paul has asked if you found the meal satisfactory."

"You could say that," Kira muttered. "Let him know that as the daughter of a chef, I know excellent culinary skill, and he earns high marks on all counts."

The waiter executed a slight bow and regarded Tarek. "I shall let him know. Will there be anything else, Monsieur Azzmar? Perhaps the lady would like to sample a delicate chocolate liqueur?"

"No, thank you," Kira said, perhaps a bit too abruptly.

Tarek reached into his inside pocket, withdrew two

envelopes and handed them to Francois. "Tell John Paul I will be in touch soon with my offer for both of you. I am certain he will find it more than generous. In the meantime, enjoy the rest of your stay in Cyprus."

The man practically beamed. "I assure you he will be pleased to know that, as am I. Shall I send the others in now?"

"Please do."

She hoped "others" didn't involve more food. "You don't have more chefs to audition, do you?"

"Musicians."

As soon as he said it, a group of men arrived, carrying various instruments they began to set up on a slightly elevated stage at the front of the expansive ballroom. After they took their positions, they began to play a very familiar Billie Holiday tune.

She regarded Tarek with awe. "That happens to be my grandmother's favorite song."

He favored her with a soft smile. "Then it must be kismet they chose it. Would you like to dance?"

He apparently didn't value his toes. "It's been ages since I've done that, and I'm not very good."

"I am," he proclaimed as he stood, rounded the table and pulled out her chair. "A skill I had to hone due to the many social events I have attended during the course of my career."

At least he'd qualified his sudden burst of ego. "Then I suppose I'll have to rely on you to guide me."

"That would be my pleasure."

After she took his offered hand, he led her to the dance floor and pulled her gently into his arms. Although her heels gave her an extra three inches of height, making him only five inches taller than she was, she still felt petite and protected in his embrace.

She soon realized he'd been truthful when he led her through the steps with amazing expertise. She stumbled twice and muttered, "Sorry," each time. He responded with reassuring words. Before long, they seemed as if they had danced together forever.

As the music continued, they held each other closer, and closer still when the band played a sultry jazz number that reminded Kira of hot summer nights. "Hot" was the operative word when Tarek began rubbing her back, then pressed his lips against her forehead. She felt as if she might actually go up in flames when he moved to her mouth and kissed her in earnest without regard for their audience. Frankly she didn't care, either. She only cared about the soft glide of his tongue against hers and how much she had needed this. How much she needed more. But at what cost?

When Tarek ended the kiss, she practically groaned in protest. "We should leave now."

She didn't want the night to end and knew it wouldn't if she gave him the lovemaking go-ahead when they got home. "It's still fairly early."

"Yes, and our journey is not over yet."

"Are we going to watch the staff clean up now?"

He released a low laugh. "No. We have somewhere else to go."

"Where?"

He brushed another quick kiss across her lips. "That is a surprise."

"You're certainly full of those tonight."

"This surprise happens to be the best one of all."

A yacht. A white four-level yacht moored at the exclusive marina's dock, the likes of which Kira had never seen up close and personal.

She glanced to her left to discover Tarek looked very proud of the monstrous boat. "Is this yours?"

"It is," he said as he clasped her hand to guide her up the gangplank. "And as you mentioned earlier, we will be enjoying a moonlit cruise."

Clearly she'd become clairvoyant. "That sounds like a marvelous idea." And a chance to make a few more memorable moments before she lowered the baby boom.

When they reached the entry and Tarek opened the door, a gray-haired man dressed in navy-blue military-like garb greeted them with a smile. "Good evening, Mr. Azzmar," he said, his voice hinting at an Australian accent. "You've picked a beaut of a night for a ride. Hope you brought your bathers."

"We will not be swimming tonight, Max. We will enjoy the sea from the deck."

"That you will." He aimed his grin at Kira. "Who might this lovely lady be?"

She offered her hand to the presumed captain. "I'm Kira, Mr. Azzmar's personal assistant."

Max looked her up and down. "I'd be looking for another job if my boss made me dress that way for work. Not that I'm personally complaining."

"I believe it is time to set out," Tarek said. "Otherwise we will be taking a daylight cruise."

The man's pleasant expression indicated he wasn't at all concerned with Tarek's somewhat irritable tone. "Yes, sir. We'll be off right away."

After Max ascended a staircase across the way, Kira surveyed her surroundings. To her right, a series of white leather built-in sofas butted up to a bank of windows, accompanied by black tables and nautical-themed accessories. To her left, another staircase led upstairs and one led to a lower floor, both backlit in blue with glass guardrails. Beyond that, she spied what appeared to be another living area with black high-end furniture set out on the sleek white porcelain floor. She'd learned one important fact about Tarek. He liked black and white—and that seemed to suit his personality.

"How many bedrooms and baths does this house-sized boat have?" she asked.

"Three bedrooms on the lower deck," he replied. "Six baths. One on the swim deck, one on the bridge deck, one here on the main deck, and three attached to the bedrooms."

Kira couldn't imagine having to clean six bathrooms. She couldn't imagine how much the yacht cost, either, though she suspected probably in the millions. "I haven't seen a maid yet."

"I have a staff of stewards, but they have been dismissed for the night."

"Then it's just us and Max?"

"Correct."

Essentially they were completely alone except for the captain. No one to disturb them. That both excited and worried her. The way she'd felt in his arms on the dance floor hadn't dissipated in the least. "So what now?"

"I will pour us each a glass of champagne and we will enjoy it on the aft deck."

"No champagne," she said a little more forceful than necessary.

He gave her a quizzical look. "As I recall, we shared several glasses of wine in the past."

She searched her brain for a logical excuse. "True, but I'm opting for a healthier lifestyle. Also, I put on a few pounds lately so I've decided to lay off the alcohol." Of course, the way she'd eaten in his presence would most likely lead to the conclusion she needed to lay off food in general.

"I would not have guessed you had put on any weight," he said. "But far be it for me to involve myself in a woman's decisions when it comes to personal choices."

*Whew.* She'd definitely dodged a bullet for now. "I would love a glass of sparkling water if you have some available."

"I do. Follow me."

As Tarek walked into the second living area, Kira trailed behind him until he paused and rounded an elaborate built-in bar with silver quartz countertops and shelves full of premier liquors. She waited nearby while he opened the stainless-steel refrigerator to retrieve a bottle of the finest champagne a large sum of money could buy. After he filled a flute with the wine, he reached beneath the bar and withdrew a green bottle of sparkling water, poured some in a high-ball glass and topped it off with two ice cubes.

He handed her the glass, along with a small napkin embossed with his initials. "I have two more bottles, should you require more."

She sipped the water, then smiled. "Usually one is my limit, but I'm feeling somewhat daring tonight, so I might have two."

He rubbed his chin and returned her smile. "Living life on the edge is my specialty."

That attitude could affect their future as parents.

"Shall we go bask in the moonlight now?"

He rounded the bar, grabbed his drink and took her hand. "Yes, and perhaps be a bit daring."

Kira wasn't certain what he meant by that, yet she sincerely wanted to find out. Clearly her hormones had commandeered her common sense. But with the feel of his slightly callused palm in hers as he showed her to the veranda, the scent of his heady cologne, that gorgeous mouth framed by a slight blanket of whiskers, taking a sensual journey with him again wouldn't be a bad thing. Or would it?

She could throw caution to the trade winds, or come back to the land of realism. He had no idea she was pregnant. And she still had no idea how to tell him. Yet when he guided her to the deck, stood behind her and wrapped one arm around her waist, she only considered here and now, wisdom be damned.

"The view is stunning," she said as they watched the lights of the marina begin to fade in the distance.

He nuzzled the side of her neck below her ear and whispered, "You are stunning."

She sipped another drink to soothe her parched mouth. "And you, as always, are quick with the compliments."

Suddenly he dropped his arm from around her, prompting her to turn and meet his serious expression. "Never doubt my sincerity when it involves you, Kira. From the first time we met, you have invaded my fantasies on a daily and nightly basis."

She could relate to that, yet some serious issues between them still existed. "This is all a fantasy, too, Tarek. The dress and the dinner and especially the dancing. Tomorrow we'll be back to normal. You're the consummate global businessman on the fast track to continuing success while amassing a fortune. I'm the daughter of domestics who doesn't require all the finer things in life and yearns for a common life with a husband and kids. We are two very different people."

After setting his flute on a nearby cocktail table, he took her glass from her clutches and placed it beside his. He then returned to her and slid his arms back around her, pulling her closer.

"Do you not wish to travel the world before you *settle* into a domestic routine?" He made the word *settle* sound blasphemous.

"I've seen quite a bit of it already. I've also seen sheer happiness in the faces of the Mehdi brothers and their wives. Call me a fool, but I want to experience that, too."

His features went stony again, yet he didn't let her go. "What do you expect from me, Kira?"

*To be a father to our baby. To want what I want. To fall desperately in love with me.*

The last thought took her mind by surprise and her heart by storm. She didn't want his love. She wanted his respect and willingness to be involved in their child's life. She certainly didn't want to fall in love with him even though at times she thought she could be precariously close to going down that ill-advised path. But not knowing everything about him, and falling into that trap, could be disastrous.

Kira chalked the threatening fuzzy feelings up to a romantic evening with a sexy rogue and pregnancy hormones that had her emotions running amok.

"I don't want anything you're not willing to give, Tarek."

He feathered a kiss across her lips. "I am willing to give you all the pleasure possible. I wish us to be together again in every way. I want you not to concern yourself over the future beyond what we experience tonight. Life is too brief to discard what we have found together."

She rode the waves of confusing emotions. "You're referring to sex."

"I am referring to our undeniable desire for each other. I have never before experienced what I feel with you in my arms. It is very powerful, yet it leaves me powerless. No woman before you has done that."

He seemed bent on saying all the right things. "Not one?"

"No."

"Not even Athena?"

His frown deepened. "Definitely not. And now that she is no longer employed by me, you will not have to endure her again."

A total shock to Kira's already shaky system. "Did you fire her?"

"She resigned, with my blessing."

"Why?"

"She knew she could not compete with you."

Flattery could get him everywhere. Flattery had already immersed her in hot water one other time. She truly, truly didn't care about then, or tomorrow, only now.

On that note, she wrapped one hand around his neck, pulled him to her mouth and kissed him.

Kira soon found herself pressed against the railing, Tarek's hands roving over her bare back as he kissed his way down her neck, pausing to slide his tongue down the valley between her breasts. When he worked his way back up to her lips, he also worked her dress up her thighs and clasped her bare bottom.

He leaned back and grinned. "I believe you forgot something, or perhaps you were prepared for this."

"None of the above. I was trying to avoid unsightly lines."

"I am disappointed it was not the latter."

"Although I wasn't thinking about it at the time, it is very convenient."

His dark gaze bore through any resistance she might

still retain. "I want to touch you, yet I will not do so unless you convince me you want this, too."

She swallowed hard. "Yes, I want this."

"No regrets if we proceed?"

Maybe a few, but she didn't want to consider that now. "No regrets."

"Then show me exactly *where* you want me to touch you."

Kira suddenly felt self-conscious. "Here in wide open spaces?"

"Yes."

Maybe if they were completely alone… "What about Max?"

"He is piloting the boat. He cannot see us unless he decides to drive in reverse back to the port."

True, since they were at the rear of the yacht. But still… "Aren't you just a bit concerned about passing watercraft?"

He briefly kissed her again. "The possibility of discovery only increases the desire. You did say you wanted to be daring."

Kira couldn't believe how often her words had come back to bite her. She also couldn't believe the sudden surge of bravery she experienced at that second. The absolute high she felt when she shifted his hand between her thighs. The unquestionable heat and dampness when he began to stroke gently. For a moment, she felt as though her legs might not hold her, and as if Tarek sensed that, he circled his arm around her waist to provide support.

As the climax began to build, she tipped her forehead

against his chest and let the orgasm take hold, riding it out until every last spasm dissipated. She trembled in the aftermath, even after her respiration and heart rate returned to normal.

Tarek lifted her chin and covered her face with kisses. "You were obviously ready."

No kidding. "Obviously."

"Would you wish to go back inside now?"

Oh, yes. "As long as there is a bed available so we can finish this."

He seemed surprised by the comment. "As long as you are pleased, that is not necessary."

How dare he work her into a sexual frenzy and attempt to leave her high and not exactly dry. "Actually, it is necessary. I want to make love with you again completely."

His expression displayed his pleasure over her declaration. "If you are certain, I would like nothing better."

"I am." And strangely, she was, even knowing that inviting this kind of intimacy probably wasn't wise.

"Then we do not require a bed," he said in a low, deep voice that could convince a middle-aged spinster to hand over her virtue to him.

Kira started to argue that standing against the rail wasn't a banner idea, particularly in her condition, when he clasped her hand and guided her to a sectional sofa covered in blue stripes. He let her go, shrugged out of his jacket and set it aside, all while she awaited further instruction with barely controlled excitement.

"During our last interlude, we failed to use a condom in the heat of passion," he added, his hand poised on his zipper. "Although you did assure me you were protected against pregnancy, would you prefer we use one now to provide peace of mind?"

If she had known what she knew now, she would have insisted on it back then. If he knew what she knew now, this would all be over before it had begun. "I can promise you the pregnancy issue isn't a problem, as long as I can trust you're still okay on the safety front."

"As I told you that night, I have been judicious when it comes to my health. I would never put you in danger."

The conviction in his tone helped ease her concerns. "Then I suppose we should do what comes naturally."

His smile arrived slowly. "Then so we shall."

After he pushed his pants and underwear down to his thighs, he held out both hands. "Come to me."

Shades of the last time they made love. If she'd learned nothing else, she now knew Tarek's preference when it came to positions. She also questioned whether this aided him in avoiding too much intimacy.

Kira kicked off her heels, hiked up her dress, and straddled his lap. She guided him inside her, all the while keeping her gaze leveled on his. She recalled how good this had felt the first time, acknowledged how good he felt now. The guilt monster tried to rear its head, but she beat it down, determined to enjoy this.

She definitely enjoyed watching his face as he clasped her hips while she moved slowly, surely. His efforts at maintaining control showed in the tight set of his jaw and the way his brows furrowed.

Kira wanted him in that powerless state, so she took him deeper and witnessed when his fortress of self-control began to crumble. She was also primed for surrender when he slowed the pace.

"I want this to last," he told her in a harsh whisper. "I refuse to let it end too quickly."

"Are you strong enough to resist, Tarek?" she asked as she wriggled her hips.

"I have always been strong enough. Before you."

Kira had to admit that made her feel somewhat special, and empowered.

They engaged in a sensual war of wills, seeing who would give in first as they shared a smile and soft kisses. She so wished they could be closer, not physically but emotionally. She so wanted to mean more to him than only this. She didn't dare put any stock in that unless she wanted to set herself up for the ultimate disappointment.

A few minutes later, Tarek's respiration grew ragged while moisture beaded his forehead and finally, he closed his eyes. Every muscle in his body seemed to tense beneath her before he bowed his head, signaling his own climax wasn't far way. And then came the low groan followed by a long breath and few crude words muttered in Arabic that she understood well, thanks to being around the Mehdi brothers during her formative years.

He tipped his head back, his eyes still closed. "You win, yet I have never been so happy in losing."

Smiling, Kira laid her cheek against his chest and listened to the steady beat of his heart while he softly rubbed her back. Perhaps making love on a boat deck would be deemed casual and unconventional, but she

felt no less in tune with him. She waited for the remorse, for the internal lectures over letting this happen, and actively participating, yet they didn't come.
No matter what transpired between them in the days
ahead, or if he disappeared from her life for good after
learning the truth, she would cherish the memories.
And in a perfect world, when their child asked if they
ever loved each other, she wished she could honestly
say they did. Regretfully, she knew all too well a perfect world didn't exist.

Tarek had never been in love before, and he had
no intention of traveling that road. Yet as he watched
Kira, curled up beside him on the bed, her hands resting on the pillow beneath her cheek, eyes closed and
face slack with sleep, he experienced emotions he had
never welcomed, nor felt, until now.

In his life, love had come with betrayal. Betrayed
by his mother and the man he had known as his father.
Betrayed by a monarch who had denied him. Deep
in his soul, he believed Kira to be different. She demanded honesty and he felt as if he could place his
faith in her. Yet he also believed he could not offer her
a long-term future.

Tomorrow morning, his first order of business for
the day involved a request that would allow them more
time together for however long they had left. If all went
as planned, she would assist him in overseeing the completion of the resort. He would gladly offer her an opportunity to expand her expertise, even if he could not
offer her more, provided she did not refuse him.

# Seven

"That's impossible." And unrealistic for Tarek to assume she could extend her time in Cyprus and ignore her responsibilities to the royal family.

He scooted up against the headboard, giving Kira a bird's-eye view of his bare chest, which didn't help her concentration. "You would only be required to remain for another week to ten days," he said.

She pulled the covers up to her neck and sighed. "Rafiq would never agree to that."

"He already has."

She rolled to her side, her mouth agape. "You asked him before you asked me?"

"Yes. I had to make certain I had his permission before I spoke with you. He claims that Miss Battelli is thoroughly enjoying resuming her duties for the time being."

Elena would never let on if she wasn't. Then again, Kira might be out of a job when she returned. "At any rate, it's not fair to her to interrupt her well-deserved retirement just so I can continue to frolic about with you for another two weeks."

"I do not frolic."

She had inadvertently trampled on his manhood. "You know what I mean, so don't get your ego in a tangle."

He shifted to his side and extracted her grip from the gold Egyptian cotton sheet. "You would gain great experience overseeing the project." He rolled her hand over and kissed her wrist. "You would gain great pleasure spending more nights with me."

The memories of their lovemaking, both on the deck and in the bed at dawn, fogged her already hazy mind. The boat hadn't been the only thing rocking last night. "I don't have the experience Athena has."

"Perhaps, yet your talents are more far reaching than Athena's." He slid his palm across her belly, causing her to shiver slightly. "That does not include only your business acumen."

She should push that wicked hand away, but she didn't want to. "You're not playing fair."

He stroked the inside of her thigh with his knuckles. "You were not complaining about fairness this morning when I woke you."

No. She had mostly been moaning. "You're insatiable."

"You are responsible for that," he said as he made his way to his favorite target.

If he kept touching her, she couldn't be responsible for anything she might do next. "If we're going to get some significant work done today, we're going to have to get out of the bed at some point in time."

"Eventually." He nuzzled his face against her shoulder. "It is still early."

Kira glanced toward the nightstand to search for a clock but instead found a picture of a little girl who looked to be around five years old. She reached for the frame and turned it toward him. "Who is this?"

He immediately removed his hand and shifted to his back, one arm lodged behind his head. "Her name is Yasmin."

"Is she a relative's child?"

"She is no one's child."

This was both sad and confusing to Kira. "I don't understand."

"She is an orphan in Morocco. I learned about her from a business associate and agreed to be her guardian. She resides at my home in Marrakech."

Only one more surprising aspect of Tarek Azzmar's life. "I assume she doesn't live there alone."

"Of course not. I have a well-qualified French au pair and a very accommodating staff."

And a well-kept secret. "Why have you never mentioned her before?"

"As I have said, I prefer to maintain a certain standard of privacy."

The understatement of the century. "What is your role in her care, Tarek? Do you have an attachment to her, or are you only her benefactor?"

"I am very fond of Yasmin. I place a call to her every evening."

One mystery solved. "But you don't care enough to be a real father to her."

He flashed a look of anger before he left the bed to put on the robe draped on the chrome footboard. He then crossed to the window to stare out at the view, keeping his back to her. "This is why I did not mention Yasmin to you, or to anyone, for that matter. I assumed people would not understand, and clearly I have been correct in those assumptions."

Oh, but she did understand. Much more than he realized. The time had come to go quid pro quo and share a part of her past. First, she sat up and pulled her knees to her chest, taking care to remain completely covered. "I understand what it's like to be abandoned, Tarek."

The painful admission sent him around to face her. "Are you referring to your ex-fiancé?"

"I'm referring to my biological parents. I'm adopted. My mother couldn't have children."

He returned to the bed and perched on the mattress. "Obviously I have not been the only one withholding information."

If he only knew what she still withheld from him. But this newfound knowledge could be a good lead-in to telling him about the baby. "I personally haven't mentioned it to very many people because I consider my adoptive parents my real parents. They've been the greatest positive influence on me."

He sent her a fast glance before returning his attention to some unknown focal point across the yacht's cabin. "Do you know your biological parents' identities?"

"Yes. They were both Canadian and fifteen years old when I was born. Like Yasmin, I came to them through a personal connection. My parents were friends with a relative of my biological grandmother, who happens to be an attorney. She assisted in the arrangements for a private adoption."

He finally shifted so she could see his face. "Have you had contact with your birth mother?"

She shook her head. "No. It was a closed adoption, although I did locate my birth mother a few years back. She declined speaking with me by phone or in person because apparently she hadn't told her current husband and children that I even existed. She did send an email though."

The fury returned to his features. "Does this not anger you, knowing you have siblings you have never met and a mother who cared so little about knowing you?"

Disappointed would be much more accurate. "Actually, it did bother me a bit at first, but I respect her decision to maintain her privacy. I also called off the search for my birth father."

"Why?"

"Because I saw no use in bothering him when it's probable he doesn't want to be located, either. Besides, I grew up in a loving home with two wonderful, encouraging people. I came to the conclusion that those responsible for my birth played a very small role in who I am today. My mama and papa are completely responsible for giving me the foundation I needed to succeed, and that's all that matters."

Tarek pushed off the bed and began to pace. "I would be enraged if I were you. Everyone has the right to learn about those who have brought them into this world."

She was taken aback by the strength of his animosity. "Getting angry gets you nowhere, Tarek. You couldn't begin to understand unless you've been there."

He spun toward her. "Anger can be a motivator to succeed."

"Not in this case. Anger only makes you bitter if you remain rooted in past recriminations." She suddenly realized they'd gone completely off topic in terms of the little girl. "Now back to Yasmin. Apparently you have fond feelings for her or you wouldn't have a photo at your bedside."

"Yes, I care for her, but my time is limited due to my career. That is why I have carefully chosen people who can give her what I cannot."

Kira found his apathy discouraging. "You mean all you have to offer is money? Anyone can provide monetarily for a child, but nurturing is more important."

"She receives ample attention."

He didn't quite get it, and possibly never would. "But does she have enough emotional support? You may think you've saved her from a life of loneliness, but if she is attached to you in any way, then you are not saving her from anything every time you leave her behind."

He returned to the edge of the bed and ran both hands through his ruffled dark hair. "It is the only way at this time."

"Then why did you take her in?"

"She was a child in need. An innocent without a family."

Kira was slowly coming to the conclusion that perhaps he wasn't cut out for fatherhood. "I hope that you'll think about spending more time with her while she's still young. She needs a father, not a stranger looking after her."

He abruptly stood and headed toward the en suite bath. "We must ready for the day since it is growing late."

Kira worried it might be too late for Tarek to change.

Upon arrival at the resort, Tarek dove into the activity that normally gave him the most solace. Yet as he cut the stone for the wall, his mind kept turning to his conversation with Kira that morning. He had not been able to express how much Yasmin meant to him. Each time he left the child, he had to steel his heart in order not to stay with her. Perhaps he had done a disservice by taking her in. Perhaps he was still doing that by keeping her. Still, he could not fathom giving her away after two years.

For the first time in quite a while, someone had forced him to take a hard look at his choices. That same someone had caused him to question his decisions on several levels. Kira Darzin remained unaware of how much she had affected him in ways he had not anticipated.

"Looks like you're almost finished with that."

Tarek peered up from his handiwork to find the

woman who constantly invaded this thoughts and dreams standing nearby. "I still have much to do to make certain it is perfect."

Kira dropped onto a nearby bench and adjusted the hem of her aqua dress to her knees, as if she had been overcome with modesty. "At times, the beauty is in the imperfections."

He considered her absolute perfection, especially her haunting cobalt eyes that looked much lighter reflecting the noon sun. "Perhaps, but I am at times a perfectionist."

She gave the impression she was quite skeptical. "Only at times?"

"The majority of the time, if you must know."

"That's what I thought." She cleared her throat and briefly looked away. "I wanted to apologize to you about our conversation this morning. I didn't give you enough credit. Providing Yasmin with a safe place to stay is very magnanimous."

Yet she had inadvertently pointed out an obvious flaw in his character. "There is no need for that."

"Yes, there is. I have no right to judge you. Many men wouldn't give an orphan a second thought, much less open their homes to one. They would rather give money and let someone else handle it. You should be commended for your compassion."

He tossed aside the trowel and leaned a hip against the work table. "Save your commendation for someone who merits it. You were correct on several points. Yasmin does need a full-time father figure. She needs a man who deserves to be called papa."

"Is that what she calls you?" Kira asked, a note of awe in her voice.

"Yes."

"Then apparently that's how she sees you."

"It makes me somewhat uncomfortable," he reluctantly admitted.

"Why?"

"Because I believe I am not worthy of the endearment."

"Maybe you should work a little harder to remedy that."

She would not understand his reticence unless he explained further. "I fear she will become too attached to me."

Kira's frown deepened. "I don't view that as a problem unless you plan to send her away."

"I would never consider such a thing." His tone sounded unquestionably defensive.

She studied him for awhile as if trying to peer into his very soul. "Then maybe you're afraid you're going to become too attached to her."

Her insight astounded him. "Perhaps you are correct."

She crossed one leg over the other and leveled her gaze on his, as if preparing to analyze him. "What's the basis for this fear, Tarek?"

"Attachment leads to betrayal. You should know that as well in regard to your former fiancé." Now he had said too much.

She swept one hand through her hair as she appeared to ponder that a time. "That's different, Tarek. We're talking about a child. I'm going to guess that your parents somehow wronged you, or maybe you feel betrayed by your mother's death."

He had been deceived by his mother, yet not in the way Kira believed.

When a landscaper began planting shrubs nearby, Tarek thought it best to suspend the conversation. "Our privacy has now been disturbed so it is better we return to our duties. Did the table you requested for the kitchen arrive?"

Kira rose from the bench and sent him a slight smile. "Yes, and it's exactly what I was looking for. I'm about to meet with the designer and inspect the furniture in the restaurant. Would you like to go with me and give your seal of approval?"

He would like to go with her to another place that had nothing to do with the resort. "I plan to complete this project before day's end."

She did not appear at all pleased with that. "I hope you return to the villa tonight at a decent hour so we can finish this discussion."

As far as he was concerned, they had. "I should be there before sundown, yet I would prefer to spend our evening in ways that will not require discourse."

She started away before hesitating and facing him again. "It's really imperative we talk, Tarek. I have something important I need to tell you."

He could only imagine what that might be. Perhaps in her eyes he now seemed dishonorable due to his reluctance to permanently commit to raising Yasmin. Or perhaps she no longer intended to stay. Regardless, he would attempt to convince her that he wanted her by his side, for however much time they still had together. He had the means, and the methods, to make her forget they ever had this conversation, though he most likely never would forget.

The man was nowhere to be found. Avoidance, plain and simple.

Kira strode through the living area in search of someone who could tell her Tarek's whereabouts. She assumed their conversation earlier today had him running scared. Or at least running from her.

She reached the cook's kitchen—all stainless steel, granite and glass—to find the one member of the staff who seemed to have a human radar where his employer was concerned. "Alexios," she began, "have you seen Mr. Azzmar? He didn't come back for dinner and I was wonder—"

"He's taking a walk on the shoreline, Ms. Darzin," he replied without missing a beat folding the cloth napkins. "He told me to inform you of his location should you need to speak with him."

Oh, she needed to speak with him all right. And he knew it. "Thank you for another wonderful dinner tonight." Too bad she'd had to spend it alone. Again.

Kira made her way past the pool and through the gate that led to the private beach. The moon wasn't quite as full as it had been on their impromptu cruise, but it provided enough light to guide her way. She didn't have to walk far to see the silhouette of a man seated in the sand, his arms casually resting on bent knees.

After kicking off her sandals near a small rock formation, Kira approached him slowly and the closer she came, the better she could see his profile. *Handsome and rich*, her first thought. *Troubled and stoic*, her second. He seemed so immersed in contemplation, she almost hated to disturb him. But the mission she was on—sharing the information that might very well change their future—could no longer keep. She'd waited too long to tell him and worried that he wouldn't take the news well, even though she'd seen a nurturing side to him that both pleased and surprised her.

In a matter of minutes, she arrived at his side, claimed the spot beside him and hugged her legs to her chest. "You look rather pensive tonight."

"I have been reflecting on what you said to me this morning about Yasmin."

She regretted some of her comments, but others, not so much. "I didn't mean to intrude, Tarek."

His thoughts seemed to drift away momentarily before he began to speak again. "She is a very gregarious little girl. She possesses a free spirit and rarely goes anywhere without running." He paused to smile. "She is also quite the conversationalist. At times, I listen quietly to her only to hear the sound of her voice. She seems unaffected by the hardship that has befallen her."

The hint of emotion in his voice touched Kira deeply. "Children are resilient. They only want to be loved."

His expression turned suddenly somber. "Perhaps another family would better serve her needs, one with both a mother and father."

*We could have that family*, she wanted to say, but

stopped short of spilling her secret. "You don't give yourself enough credit, Tarek. You have inherent compassion and the capacity to love her more than you realize."

He glanced at her, then reached over and took her hand. "I sincerely appreciate your faith in me, yet I feel as if I am bereft of any true emotion. I am not certain I can change that."

She leaned her head against his shoulder. "Hearing you talk so fondly about Yasmin leads me to believe you already have. Or maybe those emotions have always been there and you're simply afraid to feel them. I'm really sorry that someone has hurt you that badly."

He remained silent as he rubbed his thumb back and forth over her wrist in a soothing rhythm. "It is warm tonight."

Leave it to him to talk about the weather when she was getting too close for his comfort. "It's a beautiful night. Just enough breeze to make it totally comfortable."

Without warning, he leaned back and took her with him. Without words, he kissed her thoroughly. She so needed to ask him to stop so she could tell him about their child. She also needed to protest when he rolled her onto her back and slid his hand beneath her top to cup her silk-covered breasts.

"Tarek, we still need to talk," she managed when he turned his attention to her neck.

"Later," he muttered as he brushed his knuckles down her belly.

Later seemed like a banner idea, especially when he

released the button below her waist and slid her zipper down. Much later, she decided as he worked the cotton shorts down her hips, taking her panties with them. She didn't have the strength to utter one protest when he moved over her, gently parted her thighs and kissed his way down her torso.

Now there she was, lying on a bed of sand, completely out in the open with her bottoms down to her ankles and Tarek working his magic with his talented mouth between her legs. The ultimate intimacy could prove to be her emotional and physical undoing. The tempered strokes of his tongue could send her straight to the three-quarter moon above them. The ensuing climax could very well cause her to actually scream from the pleasure.

Fortunately she had enough presence of mind to remain quiet except for a low moan when the orgasm took over. She couldn't recall ever feeling so grand and so ready for Tarek to complete this sensual journey.

She had to wait for him to shrug out of his white tailored shirt, which he spread out on the ground.

"Lay on this," he said as he took off his slacks and underwear.

As Kira stretched out on the makeshift blanket, Tarek joined her and guided himself inside her. He kept his gaze locked on hers while he moved lightly at first, as if bent on teasing her into oblivion.

She loved the closeness of his body, the feel of his weight. She loved the sound of his breath at her ear, growing more uneven with each passing second. She loved the power of his thrusts, the crude but sexy words he uttered until he didn't speak at all. She loved...him. She had no idea when it had happened, or why she would let herself be so vulnerable. She did know that despite his efforts to present himself as a man who wanted no emotional ties, a caring man resided beneath the hardnosed businessman.

After Tarek collapsed against her, Kira stroked his back and relished the feel of his weight. All too soon, he rolled over and draped an arm over his eyes. They lay there for quite some time beneath a host of stars, serenaded by the sound of lapping waves. She could stay here forever, shutting out everything aside from these few special moments. But the secret she held— the one she desperately needed to tell him—continued to play over and over in her mind.

Tarek transferred back to his side, rose above her on one elbow and smiled. "You are a most amazing woman."

She released a curt laugh. "First the boat, now the beach. I'm beginning to think I'm an exhibitionist."

"You are more daring than you would wish to believe."

Yet not quite daring enough to blurt out the truth. "I've never been that way before you. Actually, you're only the second man I've been with."

He looked both pleased and surprised. "I am honored. You are the first woman I have trusted implicitly."

The gravity of what she had to reveal weighed heavily on her heart. If she told him now, she would ruin the wonderful aftermath of their lovemaking. And when he kissed her tenderly again, she decided to wait until tomorrow to tell him she had been lying to him all along. With that revelation came the probability of a permanent goodbye.

# Eight

"Have you not told him yet, *cara mia*?"

Seated cross-legged in the middle of Tarek's king-size bed, Kira gripped the cell phone and instantly regretted calling Elena to check on the state of affairs at the palace. "No, I haven't found the right time."

"You have been there almost three weeks."

She found herself caught in the grip of shame. "Yes, but we've been very busy readying the resort. The grand opening is less than a month away."

"And I would estimate your pregnancy should begin to show around that time."

Kira realized Elena was right. Her waistbands had already begun to grow tighter and her belly had become much more rounded. If Tarek had noticed, he hadn't said. He'd definitely seen her eat like two-hundred-pound man, and naked on more than one occasion. "The signs aren't obvious unless you know I'm pregnant. And I promise I'm going to tell him very soon. At least before I return to Bajul next week."

"I believe it is imperative you do and soon. Now I have a question for you. Do you happen to know Tarek's mother's first name?"

"Actually, no, I don't. Why?"

"Someone I once knew a long time ago was acquainted with a woman by the last name of Azzmar."

"Was she from Morocco?"

"Yes."

"That's odd. I'd wager the chances of it being the same woman are slim, but it is a small world."

"Much smaller than you realize, *cara*. Please call me when you are on your way to Bajul. And if you don't mind, ask Tarek to stop by and see me when he returns to the palace. Perhaps we can make a connection between the two women."

That seemed like a strange request. "I'll ask him, but I make no promises. He's very guarded about his parents."

"I have no doubt about that. Stay well, Kira."

With that, the line went dead, and Kira's mind shot into overdrive. Elena's cryptic words could keep her guessing for the duration of her stay in Cyprus. Tarek's astounding lovemaking could keep her in a sexual frenzy as well.

As if she'd conjured him up, the breathtaking billionaire strolled into the room wearing a black shirt and tan slacks, along with a sinfully sexy look. "It is nice to have the remainder of the day off."

It was nice to see him after spending the morning with a cross contractor who didn't care for her suggestions. "We deserve it after working so hard the past few weeks." Busy weeks dealing with the resort pitfalls and wonderful nights spent in the throes of passion.

Hands in pockets, he approached the bed slowly. "How would you propose we spend the time today?"

Playing truth or consequences per her promise to Elena would be good. Kira patted the space beside her and geared up for the revelation she had put off for too long. "We could talk for a few minutes." *Or not*, she thought, as Tarek toed out of his loafers, pulled off his socks and began unbuttoning his shirt.

After he removed and kicked off his slacks and underwear, he stood beside the bed looking like a very proud Adonis. "We will talk later," he said as he crawled toward her like a sexy, stalking cougar. "At this moment, I need you very badly."

"I noticed." Boy, had she ever.

He rose to his knees, quickly divested her of the yellow sundress that didn't require a bra, slid her panties down to toss them over his shoulder and then gave her a long, lingering look. "I wish to have you this way all the time."

"That might be awkward when we're out in public."

He smiled as he circled her nipple with a fingertip. "Would you like to try something new?"

She managed to move the comforter from beneath her and Tarek, uncovering another set of exquisite silver sheets. "Are you suggesting perhaps we make love on the rooftop? We've already initiated your shower, this bed several times, the beach, the yacht, and oh yes, the supply closet at the resort. Lucky for us we didn't get caught."

He sent her a knockout grin before he kissed her senseless, using his wicked tongue in some very suggestive ways. "I suppose we could utilize the kitchen countertops here," he began after breaking the kiss, "but unfortunately dinner preparation has begun."

She wrapped her arms around his neck and smiled at his sudden show of humor. "Honestly, I like being on a comfy mattress."

"I was actually suggesting a new position we have not tried before." He rolled her to her side and whispered, "One that will only enhance your climax."

When he pressed his erection against her bottom, she looked back with him over one shoulder. "I'm going to trust you on this."

He draped her leg over his thigh. "You may trust that you will feel sensations you have never felt before."

When Tarek slipped inside her, Kira wholeheartedly agreed with his assessment. She keenly experienced every nuance of his body as he began to move in a steady rhythm, felt every gentle caress with heightened awareness as he delved between her legs with skilled fingers. She did miss seeing his face so she could witness that instant when he achieved his release, but his nearness almost made up for that piece of the sensual Tarek puzzle.

When he picked up the tempo, with both his thrusts

and touches, Kira quit thinking about anything as her orgasm began to arrive with the speed of a runaway locomotive. The first strong spasm hit, but Tarek didn't let up, bringing their lovemaking to new, wild heights. She felt the tension in his frame and heard the sound of his harsh breathing as he tightened his hold on her. By the time he climaxed with a shudder and a groan, Kira was as spent as she'd ever been in his arms, and more satisfied than she ever thought possible.

In the quiet aftermath, she realized all too well that this would soon be coming to an end, something she had known all along but hadn't wanted to accept. Even if Tarek opted to be a part of his child's life, he would never forgive her for not telling him sooner. He would probably want nothing to do with her after they left Cyprus. Only one way to find out, as painful as it might be.

After Tarek laid back and took her into his arms, Kira rested her cheek on his chest, her favorite place to be. A brief span of silence passed before she decided it might be best to lead into the disclosure with casual conversation. "I talked with Elena right before you came in."

He began rubbing the side of her thigh with slow, even strokes, refueling her hormones and hindering her concentration. "I hope all is well with the palace and you are not being summoned back to Bajul."

"Everything's fine," she said as she listened to the steady beat of his heart. "I do have a message for you from Elena, though. She wants you to stop by when we're back in Bajul and meet with her."

"For what reason?"

"Something about a Moroccan woman with your last name that a friend of hers once knew. She thinks you might have a mutual connection."

He suddenly stopped caressing her altogether. "I would be surprised if that were the case. There are several Moroccan citizens with my surname."

"That's what I told her, but I promised I'd pass the message on to you."

"I will see her if I can find the time when I return." His tone sounded strangely irritable, as if he found the request unpalatable. She couldn't imagine anyone not liking the former governess. Nevertheless, a subject change seemed to be in order. One that would aid in the transition to baby news.

"Have you spoken with Yasmin lately?" she asked.

"Earlier this morning," he said. "She is very pleased over the puppy I gave her, though he is a mixed breed that one of my staff found wandering the streets."

"Those are the best kind of dogs."

"Yasmin seems to believe that to be the case. She called to tell me she has named him after me."

He had given a child a dog, and that indicated he had good paternal instincts. The fact that the child had given the dog his name spoke to her fondness for her reluctant replacement patriarch. "I'm sure there aren't too many Tareks running around in the canine world."

"Not Tarek. She calls him Poppy, which she has called me when she's attempting to persuade me into allowing her to have a treat or stay up past her bedtime."

Just a few more indicators that he must be closer to

the little girl than he'd previously led on. "Sounds to me like she's quite smitten with you, too."

"She is a good-natured child."

She could be his real child if he'd only give fatherhood a chance. Maybe knowing he would soon have a baby of his own would prompt him to change his mind.

The time had come to make the announcement, and face the inevitable.

In an effort to get down to serious business, something she couldn't do while naked, Kira sat up and covered herself with the rumpled sheet, bringing about Tarek's groan of protest. If she only knew how to begin without blurting, "I'm pregnant." A plan started to form, one that involved guiding him into the information minefield without tossing a verbal grenade.

She grabbed a pillow from behind her and put it in a choke hold. "Have you considered maybe getting a playmate for Yasmin?"

He scowled. "A pet does not qualify?"

"I meant a human playmate. A brother or a sister. I grew up as an only child and know firsthand how lonely that can be, although I did have the good fortune to have the Mehdis as surrogate brothers."

He frowned. "I also grew up as an only child and I fared well. Since Yasmin is not officially my offspring, giving her a sibling would be impossible. You have also pointed out I do not carve out enough time for her. If I took in another orphan, I would be depriving them both."

Time to test the paternity waters. "Perhaps you

should consider finding someone special to share the child-rearing responsibility."

"As I have stated before, I have an exceptional au pair."

Could he be more obtuse? "*Special* as in a spouse. Since you're a couple of years away from forty, don't you think it's time to consider settling down? If you're like most men I know, surely you'd like to have a son who can inherit your fortune and carry on your legacy."

"I have that option with Yasmin."

"Yet you haven't made a move to adopt her and give her your name, although I sense you truly care about her. What makes you steer clear of anyone who gets too close to you?"

He pushed off the bed and began to pace. "Love comes with conditions and, many times, lies."

Kira clutched the covers tighter in her fists as her anxiety increased. "Who lied to you, Tarek? Another woman? Athena? Believe me, I know what it's like to be betrayed by a lover. But it's important to move on and not let that experience guide your choices and keep you closed off to all the possibilities."

He stopped and streaked a hand over his nape. "This has nothing to do with a lover, and it does not matter now. I prefer to leave the past in the past."

Stubborn, stubborn man. "That sounds good, but I don't think you're doing that at all."

"You do not know all there is to know about me, Kira."

"And you don't know all about me either, Tarek. Honestly, I've tried to tell you several times since we've been here, but you somehow always manage to distract me." She sighed. "Or maybe I thought if I avoided revealing everything it would somehow all go away. But this is not going to go away."

After slipping his pants back on, Tarek moved to the end of the bed and braced his palms on the footboard. "Are you wed to someone else?"

She found that almost laughable in the midst of a humorless situation. "Of course not."

"You have a secret lover?"

"No. Not even close."

"You have a secret child?"

"You're definitely getting warmer." And from the stern look on his face, she was poised to walk right into the fire.

"No more guessing games, Kira. Tell me what you have been keeping from me."

"I'm pregnant with your baby." There, she'd said it, and the sky hadn't fallen. Tarek's expression did, right before recognition dawned.

"How long have you known this?" he asked, his tone teeming with anger.

She'd dreaded this part most of all. "I confirmed it at the doctor's appointment on the day you asked me to come to Cyprus with you. That was part of the reason I agreed to make the trip."

"Yet you did not afford me the courtesy of telling me the news before we left."

The indictment in his tone made Kira shiver. "I wanted to get to know you better and try to find out how you would react. It's fairly apparent you are not happy about it."

He laced his hands behind his head and turned his back on her. "You assured me you were protected against pregnancy. Was that a lie as well?"

Her own anger reached the boiling point. "If you think for a minute I trapped you by intentionally getting pregnant, think again. When I heard the news, at first I was devastated, then confused. But once I became accustomed to the idea, I decided I am going to have this baby and love it and care for it whether you come along for the ride or not."

Without responding, Tarek began to put on the rest of his clothes. Kira wrapped up in the sheet and climbed out of the bed, intent on forcing him to express his feelings. "Don't you have anything else you want to say to me, Tarek?"

"I need to think," he said as he headed out the bedroom door.

On the verge of tears, Kira resigned herself to the fact that her biggest fear had been realized—Tarek Azzmar had no intention of being a father.

He had intended to return to the resort, yet several hours later, he found himself driving a newly purchased Porsche along the coastline with no definitive destination. Kira's declaration continued to occupy his thoughts as he turned back in the direction of the villa.

*I'm pregnant with your baby...*

Not once had a woman ever uttered those words to

him, even as an empty threat. Not once had he believed he would hear them spoken as the truth.

In spite of his ongoing shock, he needed to talk with her soon, even if he could not say what she needed to hear. Granted, he did have feelings for her more powerful than any he had ever experienced with any woman. Perhaps with any living soul, aside from Yasmin. Yet Kira deserved better than a bitter, broken man bent on revenge, and so did his unborn child as well as Yasmin. If he could not devote all his time to his charges, or be the kind of father Mika'il Azzmar had been to him, he would be doing his offspring a disservice.

As soon as he returned to the villa, Tarek handed over the car to a confused Alexios and entered the house to look for Kira. After a brief search, he found her seated at the bistro table on the terrace outside the master bedroom, the favored place where they had shared several intimate conversations and sexual interludes. Unfortunately, those late-night discussions had not included information he should have been privy to weeks ago. Logically, he could not fault her for the concealment since he, too, had been withholding his own secrets, yet he could not deny his continued anger over yet another betrayal.

The lies would soon come to an end.

Tarek strode through the open doors and claimed the chair opposite Kira, who seemed taken aback by his appearance. They sat in silence for a time, avoiding each other's gazes until Kira cleared her throat.

"Are you calm enough to talk reasonably now?" she asked.

Externally calm, yes, but not internally. "I am as calm as humanly possible under the circumstances."

She sipped water from a glass clutched in her delicate hand. "Look, neither of us expected this, but how we feel no longer involves only us. We have to decide how we're going to proceed for the baby's sake."

He would need more time to adjust to the reality of a child. "Rest assured, I will make certain you and the child will be more than adequately compensated. Aside from that, I have little to say at this point in time in light of your lack of warning." And one more betrayal in a long line of many.

She looked as distressed as he felt. "I wish I would have told you sooner, Tarek, but I didn't know how. Regardless, this is *our* child, Tarek, and I don't want your money. In fact, I don't need it. I'd rather be struggling and loved than rich and lonely."

He would endeavor to set her straight. "Wealth does not equal loneliness, Kira."

"Sure, if you don't mind buying friends."

She had touched a nerve with her veiled accusation, causing his anger to return with the force of a hurricane. "You have no right to judge my character after what you have withheld from me.."

She leaned forward and centered her gaze on his. "But isn't that exactly what you've done with the Mehdis, isn't it?"

"I consider them business associates as well as acquaintances."

"You've said several things that have led me to believe you hold them in disdain and that definitely includes their father. Of course, that didn't stop you from investing in their conservation project just so you could ingratiate yourself in the family. You even built your mansion in the shadow of the palace. I'm beginning to wonder if this is some sort of contest to see if you can outdo the royals who apparently have something you want."

If she only knew his real reasons for those actions and exactly what he did want from them—acknowledgment that he existed. "You may think what you will, but the project was a sound investment. The estate was an afterthought."

"A nice addition to your collection of estates, I'm sure," she said, her tone heavy with sarcasm. "And it's so ironic that the place is so large, yet you have no one to fill all those empty rooms. Why is that, Tarek?"

At one time he believed the size of one's home determined societal status. Now he was not as certain as he had been in the past. "I spent my formative years in a two-room bungalow where I slept on a cot in the living area. Perhaps that explains my obsession." At one time, he'd believed the size of one's home determined societal status. Now he was not as certain.

"Perhaps, deep down in a place you won't acknowledge, you hope to fill those rooms with family. Then again, that's probably wishful thinking on my part."

He had no desire to debate that theory, yet he needed to force her to understand their dire straits. "You have no idea what the implications of this pregnancy will be."

She took another drink of water, then pushed the glass aside. "If you're worried about losing your standing in the good old boys' rich club, don't. The Mehdis don't have to know you're my baby's father. I, on the other hand, have to worry about possibly losing my position and telling my parents their unwed daughter is expecting their first grandchild. But I know in my heart the royal family and my family will forgive me, whatever the future holds."

To think she would suffer the consequences of their actions troubled him, despite his anger. So did their child's true legacy.

"Again, I will make certain you will want for nothing."

She sat back and released a frustrated sigh. "Okay, Tarek. Toss me a few of your precious dollars every month and maybe set up a college fund for the kid, if that clears your conscience. But one day down the road, when our child grows up, he or she will begin to wonder about his or her father and why he abandoned them. I know that to be true because I wondered the same thing, even if I pretend it doesn't bother me."

Unbeknownst to her, he had felt the same way about his legacy. He still did, and the time had come to state the facts. "There is something you are unaware of regarding my heritage."

Her frown heralded her confusion. "You were born to common folk like me. What else is there to know?"

"I was born to a common mother, but I cannot say the same about my father."

"I thought you said he was a stone mason."

"I am referring to my birth father."

Her expression now showed her shock. "Are you saying the man you grew up with isn't your father?"

"No, he is not. He wed my mother when she was pregnant with me after my biological father abandoned both of us and never acknowledged my existence."

"Where is he now?"

"Dead. I might celebrate that fact, but unfortunately he took to the grave all the information I require about the circumstances that led up to my birth."

She sent him a sympathetic look that he did not want or need. "I'm truly sorry, Tarek, but maybe it's better you don't know the details."

"I demand to know the truth."

She released a weary sigh. "Well, I would like to know the name of this mystery man who's filled you with so much hatred."

For the first time in his life, Tarek would unveil the identity of the tyrant responsible for his abandonment. The bastard who had ignored his own son. The royal leader who had led everyone astray. "Aadil Mehdi, your revered former king of Bajul."

# Nine

As her mind began to reel, Kira's shock came out in an audible gasp. Any response escaped her at the moment, then suddenly reality hit home. "This baby is a Mehdi?"

"That appears to be the case," Tarek began, "though I would prefer it not be true. Nothing good can come out of being born into a family of scheming royals who do not know the first thing about earning a living."

Her loyalty to the royal family swiftly kicked in. "The Mehdi brothers are good men, Tarek, and their father was a strong, generous leader."

"He was an autocrat who ignored his country's poor."

Kira had acknowledged long ago the former king wasn't without faults or failures. "It's true he didn't make enough assistance available for them, but Rafiq, Zain and Adan have made great strides in that regard.

Evidently you're too bitter over their father's actions to realize that."

"We will see their true character when I inform them I am the illegitimate son of their former king."

That definitely did not sit well with her in light of her own situation. "Every child is legitimate, Tarek. I despise that label."

"Despise it or not, it still exists and many would see me that way."

She had so many more unanswered questions yet didn't quite know where to begin. "Exactly how did you discover this information?"

A hint of sorrow showed in his dark eyes, but the anger soon returned. "My presumed father told me right before he died. He forced me to swear that I would never reveal my true parentage to honor my mother's memory. Since that day, I have worked tirelessly to prove that in spite of the fact I was shunned and denied my birthright, I am as good as any prince."

That explained his obsessive drive when it came to getting ahead in the business world. "Are you going to tell them you're their half brother?"

"When I deem the time is right."

She didn't have the energy to ask what he meant by that, but she did see a problem with his plan. "If Rafiq, Zain and Adan knew the truth when you'd first met them, they would have probably welcomed you with open arms. But I can't guarantee they'll accept your subterfuge now."

"It is immaterial what they think of me. I do not need their approval."

Sometimes she believed she knew him better than he knew himself. Time to give him a hard lesson on self-awareness. "Their approval is *exactly* what you desire. You all but admitted it a minute ago. And I hope you tell them sooner than later, and that you have proof to back up your claims aside from a dying man's declaration."

"Not presently, yet I am sure someone in the palace is privy to my mother's affair and her lover's abandonment."

She had another disturbing epiphany. "Is that why you sought me out and established a relationship? Have I been some pawn in your ploy to gain information?"

His hesitation spoke volumes. "I would be disingenuous if I said the thought did not cross my mind. Yet when you continually demonstrated your loyalty to the Mehdis, I determined you would not be forthcoming with confidential details."

That gave her very little comfort. "I'm beginning to wonder if your relationship with me has been founded on revenge. What better way to get back at the family you believe wronged you than by seducing a woman who is like a sister to them?"

"I assure you that is not the case. When we met, I was not aware that you grew up with the Mehdis. Aside from that, I would not be surprised if one of the Mehdi sons is aware of my identity."

Kira shook her head. "I don't believe that for a second." She wasn't sure she could believe Tarek on any point. "They would have confronted you the moment you entered their house. In fact, they probably know nothing about your mother's involvement with their father, if it is the truth."

"Or perhaps they are attempting to avoid another scandal."

The palace had been plagued with scandal in recent times, including the revelation that Elena was Adan's biological mother and the former king's longtime lover—a fact that was still kept undercover for the most part—as well as the current king marrying a divorcée. But in comparison, this one could trump them all.

When Kira recalled Elena's peculiar questions regarding Tarek's mother, the mental light switched on. She didn't necessarily like aiding him in the cause, but she had to consider her own child's legacy. "I know who you need to ask about your mother's possible affair with the king."

"If you are suggesting I speak with one of the princes, I would prefer not to begin there."

"No. I'm suggesting you talk to their former governess. She served as the king's confidant for many years. If you're seeking proof, she'll have it if it exists. If it doesn't, what then?"

He rubbed his chin. "I will decide that after I speak with the king's former mistress."

Apparently the continuing secret hadn't been concealed as well as she'd assumed. "How did you find out about that?"

"Adan informed me that Elena is his natural mother and of the circumstances behind his birth. Obviously Aadil could not be loyal to one woman."

She despised the disdain in his voice, particularly

since he didn't know all the pertinent details. "Elena told me their relationship evolved after the queen's death. Her agreement to have Adan when the queen could no longer conceive was only that, an agreement. They never meant for the relationship to blossom the way it did. I do know they loved each other deeply."

"Another love built on lies."

Kira saw no end to his cynicism, and that made her sad. Still, she had one more thing to get off her chest, not that it would make a measurable difference. "Tarek, I love you, although believe me, that's been quite a challenge. I think I fell in love with you the day we took a walk in the garden and you told me about your years at the university and how hard you worked to succeed. You took my hand to make sure I didn't stumble over a stone, and I thought, now there's a true gentleman. But I refuse to stay involved with a man who is so steeped in resentment he no longer appreciates the value in loving someone unconditionally. My baby deserves more and so do I."

She paused to draw a breath. "Yes, I betrayed you by not being honest about the baby from the beginning, and you did the same by not telling me about your suspicions. But every time you cut yourself off from feeling any emotions other than rage, you're betraying yourself. Your baby needs a father who's not afraid to feel something other than anger."

He seemed to mull that over for a time before speaking again. "If I do discover that I am a true son of the king, perhaps it would be best if we wed to give our child a name."

Where had that come from? "Oh, sure, Tarek. Let's engage in that archaic practice of marrying for the sake of a child. Thanks, but no thanks. I would rather raise our baby on my own than be tied to a man who hasn't the first clue how to love someone unconditionally."

When Kira pushed back from the table and came to her feet, Tarek asked, "Where are you going?"

"To my room to pack." And probably cry. "You told me I could decide when to leave, so I plan to do that tomorrow. The resort is almost finished and the designers can take it from here. I wish you much success in your endeavors, and if you by some miracle decide you want to be a proper father to our child, send me an email and we'll make arrangements then."

"I would prefer a face-to-face meeting."

"I wouldn't." A personal encounter would take away her advantage and possibly strip of her strength.

Not waiting for Tarek's response, Kira rushed out of the room and retired to her quarters. She had no expectations when it came to Tarek Azzmar. She also didn't expect the tears streaming down her face would end anytime soon. She could foolishly hope that he might come around, or she could move on with her life without him.

Her hand automatically came to rest protectively on her belly. Sadly she would always have a little reminder of him, no matter what the future held.

"May we come in?"

Kira unpacked the last of her clothes before turning to discover sisters-in-law, Madison and Piper Mehdi, standing in the bedroom doorway. "You two girls are always welcome so feel free to come in."

"Girls" being the operative word in that instance considering the two closed the door and practically bounced onto the bed. "Thank you, Kira," Piper said, her palms resting atop of her T-shirt covered pregnant belly. "We had to have a break from toddler central. The kids are absolutely wild today. Sam's on a sugar high, thanks to his grandmother giving him two cookies."

"Mine are more than wild," Madison said as she tightened her blond ponytail. "I've never liked the term 'double trouble' when referring to twins, but that describes the way they've been acting since they awoke at dawn."

Kira cleared away the folded clothes from the club chair and set them on the bureau before claiming a seat. "How is the new governess handling everything since I hired her?"

Piper tucked one bent leg beneath her and twisted her elaborate wedding rings round and round on her finger. "I'm worried she might quit today."

Madison fell back on the bed and stared at the ceiling. "I'm worried Zain is going to start hounding me to have another baby. I just got the twins fully potty-trained."

Piper playfully slapped her arm. "You know you want another one. Or at least you like the procreation process."

"Yes I do," Madison said with a smile. "I can't imagine what would've happened if Zain hadn't stopped me from leaving and I had to raise the babies on my own."

150        THE SHEIKH'S SECRET HEIR

That struck a deep chord in Kira. She really had no place to go except for Canada and that could prove to be a disaster. "Luckily you didn't have to face that."

Madison's grin deepened. "True, and he got two babies for the price of one."

"Adan did let me leave," Piper began, "but I have to give him credit for coming after me in the States with his heart in his hands once he learned he couldn't live without me."

She certainly couldn't count on Tarek returning to profess his undying love. "And now he has a mother for his son and a new baby on the way. Both of you have done very well for yourselves in the procreation department."

Madison popped up like a jack-in-the box. "Since we're on that subject, did you do any procreating with Tarek Azzmar on your trip?"

If she didn't know better, she'd think both Madison and Piper were privy to her pregnancy. "I went on the trip to work, not procreate." That had happened before the trip.

After leaving the bed to press her palms against her lower back, Piper sent Kira a skeptical look. "Are you sure about that? I would swear you're practically glowing, or maybe that's a blush."

Kira automatically touched her flaming cheeks. "It's a little warm in here."

"Speaking of Tarek, go get the picture, Piper."

"It's not finished yet," Piper said.

Pointing toward the door, Madison told her, "It's finished enough. Now go fetch it from the hall."

Feigning a pout, Piper retreated out the door, muttering something about not being a dog. She returned a few moments later and held up a portrait of a thirty-something man. "As the official palace artist, my mother-in-law commissioned me to do this for her private collection. She gave me a photo of King Aadil in the prime of his life. Apparently it's her favorite and I can certainly see why. He was one good-looking king."

Kira could barely contain her shock over how much Tarek looked like him. Then again, she could be imagining things because she missed him so much. "That's absolutely some of your best work to date, Piper. She's going to love it."

"Don't you think he looks like Tarek?" Madison said, echoing Kira's thoughts.

Kira shrugged. "They're both of Middle Eastern descent and both nice-looking men. Aside from that, I'm not seeing it." However, she was telling one whopper of a lie.

"I think the resemblance is uncanny," Piper said. "Maybe he's Aadil's secret son."

Kira almost choked on air. "That is exactly how nasty rumors get started."

"True," Madison replied. "And when that happens, it's my job as the palace press secretary to explain them away, so stop it right now, Piper."

Piper rested the photo against the wall and reclaimed a spot on the edge of the mattress. "Seriously, Kira, we both noticed you and Tarek flirting months ago. Are you sure nothing happened between the two of you in Cyprus?"

Madison came to her knees and looked like a pooch begging for a bone. "Come on. We're all friends. Give us the dirty details."

For reasons that defied logic, tears began to well in Kira's eyes. "I'm sorry," she muttered. "It's just that…" She sniffed and decided to stop talking now before she started sobbing.

Piper scowled. "If that jerk did something to hurt you, I'm going to have Adan beat him up."

"I'll sick Zain on him, too," Madison added. "Not that I don't think Adan can hold his own, but Tarek is a really big hunk of a guy."

Piper's scowl melted into a grin over the faux pas. "You mean hulk of a guy."

"Both," Madison said.

That only made Kira want to cry more. "Since the two of you will probably find out sooner or later, Tarek and I did have a relationship for a while. But I'd appreciate it if you wouldn't say anything to the brothers. If they know I was fraternizing with a palace guest, I might be looking for a job. As it is, I'm worried they already suspect something's been going on."

Madison waved a hand in dismissal. "Don't worry about that, Kira. Men are obtuse when it comes to picking up signals unless it involves their personal radar."

Piper nodded in agreement. "And sometimes not even then. I practically had to tattoo my feelings to Adan's forehead before he figured it out."

An option Kira might entertain, if she ever saw Tarek again. "Just so you know, it's over between us. As nice as it was, it simply wasn't meant to be. He's not the kind of man who's searching for a serious relationship."

A shrill singsong sound had Madison pulling a cell phone out of her pocket and scanning a text. "It's the poor governess. She wants to know if it's okay if the kids have more cookies."

"Heck no," Piper said as she pushed off the bed. "We better get back to the nursery and run interference. It's time for Sam's nap anyway."

"I could use a nap," Madison said as she followed suit. "But knowing my little munchkins, that's not going to happen."

They both doled out hugs to Kira before heading out the door. "Kira, if you need to talk, you know where to find us," Piper began as she paused with her hand on the knob, "but sometimes life turns on a dime, so don't give up on Tarek yet."

Kira saw no good reason not to give up on him. She did see a valid reason to call him—the portrait. No, that wouldn't be wise. Besides, this was Tarek's paternity battle to undertake. As it was, she had enough on her hands with her own paternity issues. She had no idea how she would resolve the, but she did know she was weeks away—if not months—from successfully mending another broken heart.

For the past two weeks, the transition had come slowly but surely, and painfully.

Tarek had tried unsuccessfully to forget about Kira. How could he when everything reminded him of her? Every detail at the resort, every dawn, every sunset.

He had gone to bed alone, and awakened reaching for a woman whom he missed terribly, only to find an empty space where she had been.

Now he waited outside Elena Battelli's private quarters, seeking answers he required to move away from his past, as Kira had urged him to do. She had forced him to open old wounds, left him to bleed alone, and assess the direction his life had taken. He had not liked what he had discovered.

Tarek rapped twice on the mahogany door and waited for the woman to answer his summons, which she did immediately.

"Come in, Mr. Azzmar," she said with a sweeping gesture toward the small parlor. "Please have a seat."

Tarek chose the small blue sofa while Elena took the paisley chair across from him. "I appreciate you agreeing to meet me on such short notice," he began, "but I felt this could not wait a moment longer."

She studied him with keen eyes. "Kira told me you suspected Aadil was your biological father, so we will dispense with all pleasantries and get to the point. Was your mother's name Darcia?"

Hearing the name had a startling effect on him. "Yes, it was."

"Then I have something I must show you."

She pushed out of the chair, disappeared into another room and returned a few moments later holding a yellowed piece of paper and a brown portfolio beneath her arm. "She sent this to Aadil. Read it."

He managed to take the offered letter, unfolded it and began to scan the text written in Arabic. He immediately recognized his mother's script from cards she had given him during his childhood. The content itself verified the covert relationship and contained a demand that the king never contact her again.

He turned his attention from the missive to Elena who had reclaimed the chair. "There is no mention of my mother's pregnancy or anything about me."

"It's clear in the letter Darcia believed they could not be together permanently since he was promised to another. She perhaps saw no need to inform Aadil."

The fury he had felt for so many years returned. "Then I am no closer to learning if he was, in fact, my father."

"Not necessarily," she said. "One evening many years ago, Aadil told me that your mother was the love of his life and he intended to give up the throne for her. When he returned to Morocco, she had moved away from her parents' home and into your father's house. He managed to find her and when he discovered she was pregnant, he confronted her about the baby's parentage. She denied you were his child and asked him to leave. He always believed otherwise, but he never bothered her again and went on to assume his duties as king."

"Suspicion does not equal fact."

"But this does." She opened the portfolio resting in her lap, withdrew what appeared to be newspaper clippings and handed them to Tarek. "He followed every step of your rise to fame and fortune as if he were searching for proof."

Tarek flipped through the photos and articles featuring him then returned them to Elena. "This is not

proof of anything other than a man obsessing over the
son born to a woman he could not have."

Elena pulled one last piece of paper from the folder
and offered it to him. "Yet this is irrefutable."

A few seconds passed before Tarek understood what
he was reading—a DNA report containing his and the
former king's name. Most important, the test concluded
that the results were 99.9999 percent positive he was the
offspring of the former king. Still, he had more questions before he would let himself believe. "How did he
obtain my DNA?"

Elena lifted her frail shoulders. "He was a very powerful man with many connections. I actually did find
a written account from a private investigator outlining
an unnamed person he was following in Morocco and
that he gathered a paper cup the subject discarded in a
trash bin. I assume that subject was you."

The information was almost too much to digest.
"Then I suppose my mother had been truthful to her
husband."

"My guess would be that he rescued Darcia from
the shame of giving birth to a child out of wedlock.
That was looked upon unfavorably forty years ago. I
also think Aadil never sought you out to save you from
shame as well."

"I believe now that was most likely the case." And
as he considered that he would never know his biological father, a certain sadness replaced the ever-present
anger.

When Tarek offered Elena the paper, she waved it

away. "You've waited many years for confirmation, so you should keep it."

"Thank you. Now that I have the information, I will have to consider what I should do with it in regard to my recently discovered brothers."

Elena presented a kindly smile. "Of course you should tell them."

His intent all along, yet everything had changed, including his attitude toward them. "I am not certain they will forgive my deceit."

"Rafiq might be hesitant to welcome you into the fold, but Zain and Adan should have no issues with accepting you into the family. And if you'll notice the date on the report, Aadil received it the week before his death. I believe he sensed he didn't have much longer on this earth, and this was the last bit of unfinished business. If he would have known sooner, he would have shown you the same care and concern as he did for his other sons."

"I would like to believe that to be true."

"I would like to believe you have learned something from this journey in regard to your own unborn child."

He should not be surprised Kira had confided in her. "How long have you known about the pregnancy?"

"Since the day Kira found out. She needed a shoulder to lean on and a listening ear. Of course, I encouraged her to tell you, though I was surprised she waited so long to do so."

He could not fault her for that. "I am still uncertain how to proceed. In many ways I feel as though I am not worthy to be a father."

Elena leaned over and laid her hand on his. "It's true that any man can procreate, but it takes a special man to take on fatherhood. You will make many mistakes but the rewards are very great. And would you subject your child to what you have endured, spending a lifetime wondering about the man responsible for his or her birth?"

The woman possessed uncanny wisdom. "No, I would not."

She leaned back, looking quite satisfied. "Excellent. Now what are you going to do about your child's mother?"

He saw no easy answer to that. "I will support her in every way possible."

"Every way?"

"In all ways that she will allow."

"Do you love her, Tarek?"

He'd once thought himself incapable of that emotion. He had recently learned that was false. "It matters not how I feel."

He still could not form the word for fear it would make him too vulnerable. "I proposed marriage and she declined."

"Did you profess your love then?"

"I did not."

Elena muttered several Italian oaths, complete with hand gestures. "No wonder she didn't accept. I ask again, do you love her?"

He prepared to open himself up to the truth. "I have admittedly been miserable. I long for the day when I might see her again and finally express my true feelings for her, yet I worry that might never come to pass."

Elena scowled. "Poppycock. I will never understand why men are so stubborn that they cannot see what is right in front of their nose. You are in love with her and Kira loves you. She wants nothing more than to be by your side from this point forward. Would you deny her that? Would you deny your own child?"

No, he would not. Yet a serious problem still existed. "Before she left Cyprus, she also refused my offer of a meeting to discuss our child. She instructed me to send an email."

"Well, she deserves the opportunity to throw you out in person, or possibly take you back."

He longed for the latter but braced himself for the former. "I am at a loss as to how to accomplish that."

Elena chuckled. "Oh my, have you come to the right place. I happen to have some experience with playing Cupid."

He would welcome any assistance. "Do you have a plan in mind?"

"It would involve a bit of creativity and borderline deception."

He was growing somewhat concerned. "Deception has created our conflict."

She laid a dramatic hand below her neck. "This is necessary to achieve our goal. Kira will understand once she sees what she will gain."

"Then I will trust you on this."

Elena's expression turned somber. "First, I must

know you are ready to pursue a permanent relationship with her. If not, then we will not proceed."

"I am more than ready." Words he never thought he would say.

"Good. Now we will go over the details."

Something suddenly occurred to him. "Should I inform the Mehdi sons of my identity first?"

"Leave them to me."

Having Elena run interference would be to his benefit, though under normal circumstances, he would not allow someone else to fight his battles. "If you believe that would be best, I will agree."

"It would be best." Elena leaned forward, lowered her voice and said, "This is what we will do…."

"Are you busy?"

Seated at her office desk, Kira didn't bother to look up from the computer as she said, "Never too busy for you, Elena. What do you need?"

Elena pulled up a chair next to hers. "I was curious about your doctor's appointment."

She inputted the last budget item then shut down the program before turning her office chair toward her. "Maysa said everything is great. The baby's heartbeat is strong and next month I'll have my first ultrasound. I can find out the gender if I want to, but I'm not sure about that yet." She was sure about the disappointment over Tarek not sharing those moments.

"Have you heard from the father?" Elena asked, as if she'd read Kira's mind.

Annoying disappointment came back to roost. "Not a word. But I never really expected it."

Elena took a quick look at her watch. "If Tarek came to you and expressed his undying love, would you consider taking him back?"

In a heartbeat. "I see no reason to ponder that since it's never going to happen."

"One never knows, *cara*," she said as she checked the time again.

"Do you have an appointment, Elena?"

"No, but you do." She pushed out of the chair and patted her silver hair. "You have a meeting with Rafiq."

Kira did a mental rundown of her schedule. "Since when?"

"Since now. He sent me here to summon you to his study."

Wonderful. She had too much to do and too little left of the day. "Do you know what this is about?"

"I have a few ideas, but I feel it's best not to speculate."

Kira stood and headed toward the door. "I hope this doesn't take too long."

Elena muttered something in Italian from behind her as they headed to the king's private study. Once there, she rapped on the door and heard Rafiq tell her to come in.

The second she entered, Kira felt as if she'd walked into an inquisition conducted by well-dressed royals. Rafiq sat behind the desk, looking handsome and regal, as usual. Zain and Adan stood behind him, arms folded across their chests like sentries. Then her gaze tracked to the right of the Mehdi sons, where another man positioned at the window caught her immediate attention. To most, he would appear to be any handsome, highly successful mogul, but she knew him as the father of her unborn baby.

"What is this about?" Kira asked as soon as she could form a coherent sentence.

"That's what I'd bloody like to know," Adan said.

"I would as well," Zain added. "My wife and I plan to have dinner in the village and have a night away from the twin follies."

Elena came to her side and laid a protective hand on Kira's shoulder. "If you would be patient, all will be revealed by Mr. Azzmar in short order."

As if on cue, Tarek stepped forward and cleared his throat. "I have asked you here today to reveal that I have not been completely truthful to any of you."

Rafiq sent him a hard look. "We are well aware that you and Kira have been involved in a tryst."

Kira exchanged a concerned look with Tarek before she said, "I promise we had no intention—"

"We didn't have to be rocket scientists to figure out, Kira," Adan interjected. "You both practically drool in each other's presence."

"The staff members have also entertained suspicions," Rafiq added. "Nothing is sacred in the palace."

Kira's cheeks heated like a furnace. "I don't know what to say except I'm very sorry."

Tarek took a step forward. "You cannot hold Kira accountable for my actions. And my personal relationship with her is only part of the reason why I called you here."

Zain shifted impatiently in the chair. "Then could you please clarify immediately?"

Tarek paced the room as if gathering his thoughts before facing the brothers to speak again. "Investing in Bajul is not my primary reason for being here. It never was. I arrived here seeking information and as of this morning, I have found it."

Kira held her breath as Tarek launched into his suspicions about his mother's involvement with the former king, his presumed father's revelation and his need to know his true parentage. He concluded by saying, "With Elena's aid, I now have the proof I have required for most of my adulthood. I am Aadil Mehdi's biological child, and your half brother."

The Mehdi sons sat for a time in stunned silence, until Rafiq regarded Elena. "Is this the truth?"

Elena squeezed Kira's shoulder before answering. "Yes, it is. There is no doubt that Tarek is your father's son. His relationship with Tarek's mother happened before he wed your mother, and he remained unaware he had another child for many years. He managed to confirm that fact shortly before his death."

"Bloody hell," Adan said. "The man did get around. Is there any chance there are more Mehdis primed to crawl out of the woodwork? The last time we had one of these little soirees I learned the woman I always thought of as my mother was actually my mother."

"Hush, my child," Elena told him. "Tarek has not finished speaking his mind."

Kira saw a hint of self-consciousness in his expression before he resumed his steel persona. "I do not expect any of you to readily accept this rather shocking turn of events, but I do hope I have your blessing on what I am about to tell you now."

He turned toward Kira and held out his hand. "If you would please join me."

She strode toward him in a fog, her head whirling with possibilities, and took his offered hand. As they stood there before the king's court, she feared her knees might not hold her.

"As you know," Tarek began, "Kira and I have grown very close—"

"I'm sure that is an understatement," Zain muttered, earning a quelling look from Elena. "I am only saying that you are a Mehdi, and with that comes a certain amount of virility and lack of control." That earned Adan's chuckle.

Surprisingly, Tarek smiled. "Regardless, I recognize you are all very protective of Kira, and I want to be clear on my commitment to her. She is everything a man could desire in a woman."

Kira practically gasped. "You want a commitment?"

"I definitely do. I did not realize this until you had left me."

"I want that, too, Tarek, but—"

"Enough with the moon-eyed declarations," Rafiq muttered. "Get on with it."

Tarek turned his focus back to the brothers. "In the absence of her father, I am asking you for permission to propose marriage to her."

While Kira stood frozen on the spot, the brothers nodded at each other before Rafiq rose from the chair. "If you will treat her with the respect she deserves, you have our blessing."

Tarek turned to Kira, a satisfied look on his face. "Kira Darzin, will you honor me by being my wife?"

How badly she wanted to say yes, but she couldn't in good conscience. Not yet. "No."

# Ten

Tarek was somewhat stunned she was rebuffing him again, only this time in front of an audience. "You do not wish to be my wife?"

"I'm not saying I won't marry you. I'm saying my answer depends on your reasons for wanting to marry me."

His answer would require putting away his manly pride, he realized, when he glanced at the brothers who sat patiently awaiting his response, seemingly enjoying his predicament. "I vow to you that I will love you now and forevermore."

"You love me?" she asked, sheer wonder in her voice.

"I do."

Still, she did not seem quite satisfied. "And our baby?"

He sensed the sudden tension in the room. "I will love our child as I love you, and I will endeavor to be the best father possible."

Finally, she smiled. "Then my answer is a yes, I will marry you, Tarek Azzmar."

"You are with child, Kira?" Rafiq asked before Tarek could finally take Kira into his arms.

His future wife turned her attention to the king and frowned. "Yes, but we didn't plan that, either. Regardless, we're both very happy about it now."

"Cripes, we're going to have to expand the nursery," Adan groused.

Zain came to his feet. "Worse, we are going to have to replace Kira."

Elena stepped forward. "No need to worry about that. I will be in charge until we find a replacement...."

As the chaotic discourse continued, Tarek saw the opportunity to escape. He took Kira by the hand and said, "Come with me," As he led her to the door.

Before they could make a hasty exit, Zain called out, "Tarek, you will now be required to sit on the governing council."

Tarek raised his hand in acknowledgement and left out the door, closing it behind him. He led Kira down the corridor, and when they turned the corner, he seized the opportunity to kiss her thoroughly.

Once they parted, she looked at him with concern. "Are you absolutely sure about taking this step?"

More sure than he had ever been about any decision he had made at this juncture in his life. "I have not experienced such certainty for many years. Now, if you will join me upstairs, I have something I would like to show you."

She feigned a stunned look. "Oh my, Tarek. I realize the brothers seem to be fine with us, but do you think that's appropriate in the palace?"

He could not resist kissing her again. "That was not my intent, at least not presently. When we leave here later, I will give you an appropriate ravishing."

"I'm all for that."

They traveled to the second floor and paused at the door to the nursery, where the sounds of childish voices filtered into the hallway. "Let me guess," Kira said. "You've already set up a crib for our baby."

"I reserve that for our home," he said as he opened the door and searched for the little brown-haired, brown-eyed girl. He spotted her in the corner playing with a slew of stuffed animals and Zain Mehdi's twins under the watchful eye of a young governess. When he summoned Yasmin in Arabic, she looked up and favored him with a bright smile.

"Poppy!" she shouted as she ran toward him, her curls bouncing in time with her gait.

Tarek lifted her into his arms and turned to Kira. "This is Yasmin. Yasmin, this is Kira."

The absolute awe on Kira's face was worth all the gold in the hemisphere. "I am very pleased to meet you, Yasmin."

The little girl reached out and touched Kira's cheek. "You are very pretty."

"So are you, sweetheart. And you speak very good English."

Yasmin shrugged and pointed at Tarek. "He taught me. May I play now, Poppy?"

Tarek set her on her feet and knelt on her level. "You may, as soon as I give you a gift."

Yasmin rocked back and forth on her heels with barely-contained excitement. "Is it another puppy?"

"No, yet I believe you will like it." He withdrew one of the two black velvet boxes from his pocket. "Open this for me."

After Yasmin complied, her eyes filled with surprise when she saw the tiny silver band. "Is this mine?"

"Yes, it is." Tarek slipped the ring from the holder and held it up. "If you agree to be my daughter."

She pretended to pout. "I am your daughter, silly Poppy."

He pocketed the empty box and slid the band on her right ring finger. "Yes, and this makes it official."

She threw her arms around his neck and kissed his cheek. "I am going to show Cala and Joseph my ring now."

When she started away, he gently clasped her arm to halt her progress, took her by the shoulders and turned her around. "What do you say to Kira?"

"It is nice to meet you," she replied, followed by an exaggerated curtsy, then rushed back to her playmates.

Tarek escorted Kira back into the corridor and kissed her again. "I have arranged for some private time for us for a few hours. How do you suggest we spend that time?"

She stroked his jaw. "I can think of several pleasant things, but first I have to tell you that you giving Yasmin that ring meant so much to her, and me."

A long overdue gesture, in his opinion. "While we were apart, I arranged to adopt Yasmin so it will truly be official. However, I have put the process on hold since I would like to have you listed as her mother. I realize that is much to ask of you—"

She pressed a fingertip against his lips. "I would be honored to assume that responsibility, as long as Yasmin agrees."

"She will eventually, though it could require another mutt."

"I would hope loving her like my own would be enough to convince her to love me back."

He could not imagine any living being not loving an extraordinary woman such as Kira. "I am certain it will be, and we will tell her about the marriage very soon. Since meeting you, I have learned that being a good parent does not require blood ties. It involves caring and commitment and yes, making errors in judgment at times. I learned that long ago from my father, yet I allowed myself to forget those lessons."

She gently touched his cheek. "Do you think you can forgive your biological father for never acknowledging you?"

Before falling under Kira's positive influence, Tarek's answer would have been a definitive "No." "There is nothing to forgive. My mother gave him no choice in the matter. Unfortunately, when he finally made the effort to confirm that I was his son, it was too late. I do regret that."

She embraced him briefly and smiled. "Look at it

this way. You've gained an entire family. A somewhat eccentric family, but a loving family all the same."

"Yes, I have."

Her eyes suddenly went wide. "Oh no, I have to tell my parents about us and the baby before someone else does. I'm going to call them now but I left my cell phone in the office."

When Kira started away, Tarek clasped her hand to stop her. Apparently all the women in his life were bent on deserting him today. "Before you do that, I have a gift for you."

He withdrew the second box, opened it, and removed the second gift. "This is for you to make our engagement official."

Kira stared at the three-carat ruby and diamond ring, her eyes welling with tears. "It's beautiful, Tarek, but it's too much for a common girl like me."

He lifted her chin and kissed her cheek. "There is nothing common about you, Kira. You are an amazing woman deserving of all the best life has to offer."

She sent him a shaky smile. "I already have that in you."

After giving her one last kiss, he slipped the ring on her left hand, returned the box to his pocket, removed his own phone from his jacket and offered it to her. "You may call your parents now, and my wish is they will approve of our union."

"They will approve. Eventually." Kira took the cell and keyed in the number, a nervous look in her eyes. "Hi, Mama. I have something to tell you. I'm getting married."

* * *

"Now that your wedding day has arrived, dear daughter, I have something to give you."

After a final adjustment of the gold and diamond leaf headband securing the cathedral-length veil, Kira turned from the mirror to face Chandra Allain Darzin—the best mother anyone could ever want or need. She looked positively radiant and remarkably young in the cream-colored chiffon gown. "Let me guess. You're going to give me sage advice on how to keep my husband happy."

"Actually, I'm going to give you this." Chandra leaned over and withdrew a white box from her gold clutch, then opened it to reveal a dainty pearl bracelet with a small diamond heart-shaped pendant dangling from it.

"That's so beautiful, Mama. Was it grandmother's?"

"No. It's a gift from someone quite special."

Kira couldn't imagine who that might be. "Another relative?"

"The woman who blessed us with you. Your birth mother."

Tremors of shock ran through Kira, causing her hands to shake as she lifted the bracelet from the box to inspect it. "When did she give this to you?"

"Your eighteenth birthday. She sent it in the mail, along with a request not to open the box until your wedding day. This came with it." Her mother took out a folded piece of paper from her purse and handed it to her.

Since she didn't quite trust her own voice, Kira read the words in silence.

*Dear Baby Girl,*

*This special bracelet belonged to my great-grandmother. I wore it on my wedding day and I felt the need to pass it on to you since it has brought me luck in my marriage.*

*I feel you should know that when you were born, I was barely a child myself and ill-equipped to care for a baby. As hard as it was to give you up, I knew the Darzins were good people and could give my child the life she deserved. I realize this simple gesture will never make up for my decision to let you go, but it's the best way I know how to show you that you have always been in my heart, if not in my arms, and will never be forgotten.*

*With love and wishing you much luck,*
*Janice*

In that moment, any latent resentment Kira had directed toward her birth mother slipped away as her mother clasped the bracelet around her wrist. Any questions about whether the young woman responsible for her life cared at all, dissipated. The tears sliding down her cheeks were part relief, part sadness and in a large part, joy.

She shook off her melancholy and drew her mother—her real mother—into an embrace. "Thank you, Mama."

Chandra replaced the box with a handkerchief that

she used to swipe at her eyes. "You don't have to thank me, sweetheart. I had nothing to do with this."

"Maybe, but you had everything to do with who I am today. Because of you and Dad, I've learned the importance of forgiveness and the value of love."

Her mother sniffed then returned the hanky to her bag. "You have always been the absolute light of our lives, Kira. And you are such a beautiful bride. Now let's go find your father before he finds your young man and threatens him again."

After sharing in a laugh through the last of the tears, Kira and her mother walked arm-in-arm where she discovered her dad waiting in the vestibule, looking as if he might faint. When she heard the musical cue, she kissed her mother temporarily goodbye, then prepared to walk into her future with the man she adored and loved.

To the melodic strains of Bach's *Ave Maria,* Kira strolled down the aisle clinging tightly to her father's arm. She homed in on her mother seated in the first row, still dabbing at her eyes with the handkerchief. She then glanced at her papa and discovered he was looking rather misty, too. Sabir Darzin didn't cry, and at this rate she'd be blubbering before she reached the man standing at the front of the packed grand ballroom with the gleaming white marble floors. A gorgeous man wearing an immaculately tailored black silk tuxedo, a red rose pinned to his lapel and a welcoming smile on his face.

She barely noticed Madison and Piper, dressed in gold shimmering gowns, standing to his right, or their tuxedo-bedecked husbands, Zain and Adan, standing to his left. She did notice Yasmin walking ahead, tossing rose petals with abandon, and that Rafiq wore a white sash with the Mehdi family coat of arms embossed in gold as he waited to preside over the ceremony.

Before she stepped up on the temporary dais decorated with white roses, her dad paused, kissed her cheek and whispered, "I wish you luck, my precious daughter, and should this man not treat you well, I am not so old that I cannot take him on."

Kira returned his smile. "I promise that won't be necessary, Daddy, but thank you for the offer to defend my honor."

After he let her go, Kira held up the flowing floor-length white satin gown with the empire waist that somewhat concealed her growing abdomen and handed off her red-rose bouquet to Madison. She frankly didn't care what anyone thought about her pregnant-bride status. She only cared about her future husband, who held out his hand to her.

She came to Tarek's side and listened intently to Rafiq as he delivered a message regarding the responsibilities required for a successful marriage. After he finished, he instructed the bride and groom to face each other to deliver their own personal vows.

At that moment, every word she'd planned to say flew out of her brain, so she opted to speak from the heart. "Tarek, you were a pleasant, albeit unexpected, surprise. I choose you to be my husband for your compassion, your capacity for great love and your commitment to our children, present and future. The yacht doesn't hurt, either." After the spattering of laughter died down, she finished by saying, "I love you with all my heart, and always will."

Tarek looked down for a moment, and when he returned his gaze to hers, Kira saw unmistakable emotion reflecting from his eyes. He declared his love in Arabic, spoke his feelings about her in French, then concluded in English. "I stand before these witnesses and my family to vow that you will not want for anything during our life together. I look forward to waking with you by my side every morning, retiring with you each night and spending my days in pursuit of your happiness, for if you are truly happy, then so am I. I also vow to be actively involved in midnight feedings and diaper-changing, as ordained by my brother Adan."

Another bout of chuckles ensued, yet Tarek's expression grew serious. "What you have taught me has more value than any fortune. I love you, *rohi*."

*My soul…*

For Kira, that said it all.

"With the power vested in me as the king of the sovereign country of Bajul, I respectfully pronounce you husband and wife. And since you are clearly impatient to do so, you may now kiss your bride, Tarek."

Per Rafiq's final directive, Tarek put his arms around Kira and gave her a gentle, heartfelt kiss. Madison returned the bouquet to Kira before they left the dais and headed down the aisle to applause and well-wishes.

When they reached the hallway, Tarek guided Kira

into his private study and closed the door. He came back to her and drew her into a close embrace.

"Shall we begin the honeymoon now?"

Kira playfully slapped at his arm with the flowers. "We have to attend the reception first."

He nuzzled her neck. "They will not miss us as long as there is food."

And there would be a lot of food. Kira had been actively involved in planning the ceremony for the past month, when she hadn't been hanging out in bed with her fiancé. "Patience, my dear husband. We have plenty of time for that. After all, you'll have me all to yourself for three weeks on your yacht."

He grinned like the sexy devil he could be. "And we can be very daring."

"As long as no one sees my enlarging stomach."

He touched the place that housed their child with such sweet reverence, Kira almost cried. "This is for my eyes only. And you are still beautiful."

With Tarek, she sincerely felt beautiful. "Well, husband, now that we're married and we've moved Yasmin here, guess there's only one thing left to do, aside from the honeymoon."

He sent her a quizzical look. "What would that be, wife?"

"Have a baby."

"I swear this baby is never going to get here!"

As he smoothed his palm over Kira's damp forehead, Tarek had never felt so helpless in his life. "Soon, *rohi*."

"Very soon," Maysa said from her perch at the end of the bed. "I need one more push, Kira."

Panic was reflected in his wife's eyes. "What if I can't do that?"

"You will," Tarek said as he slid his arms beneath her for support.

Kira's low moan shot straight to his soul, but his baby's cry shot straight to his heart. He glanced toward the sound to see Maysa lifting the child up and saying, "It's a girl!" As she placed the baby on Kira's chest, Tarek witnessed her motherly instincts immediately set in, touching him deeply.

"My sweet baby girl," she cooed while the nurse covered the baby in a blanket. She then sent Tarek a worried look. "Are you disappointed she's not a boy?"

He laid his palm on his daughter's tiny back, experiencing an abiding love he never expected to feel. "Not in the least. Boys create trouble wherever they go. I am proud to have two daughters."

Kira touched his cheek. "Two beautiful daughters. I can't wait for Yasmin to see her as soon as she's finished with her lessons."

"She will be quite pleased we have given her a sister." As he was quite pleased that he had given her his name, and an outstanding mother.

Ignoring the flurry of activity and sounds coming from the hospital halls, they remained that way for a while, bonding as a family, marveling over the new life they had made. Tarek experienced an abiding love, an emotion he'd never expected to feel so deeply until he had allowed this woman into his heart, and his adopted daughter into his home, though he had once been reluctant to admit it to himself. That was no longer the case.

"We're going to take the baby now to weigh her and examine her," Maysa said, interrupting the emotional interlude. "We won't be gone long."

Kira seemed hesitant to let her go. "Hurry back," she said after she relinquished their child to the nurse.

Tarek pulled a chair up to the bedside and took his beloved wife's hand. "You were braver than most men."

Kira released a cynical laugh. "I turned into a sniveling, whiny wimp."

"Understandable since you were in pain."

"Yes, that was some pain. But now that it's over, what are we going to call her?" she asked.

A debate that had been ongoing for some time. "I believe we should go with what you prefer. Using our mothers' middle names."

Kira looked as if he had handed her the key to the universe. "Then Laila Anne Azzmar it is, although Yasmin will insist on calling her Annie."

"I have no issue with that."

Either name would suit her well. This life suited him well. He had come a long way as the son of two commoners who had learned he was the son of a king. He had built a fortune, achieved resounding success, yet nothing could compare to his greatest accomplishment—learning to love. From this point forward, he was prepared to continue this greatest of adventures with the treasured woman whom he loved with all that he was, or would be.

And as the nurse returned their beloved child and placed her in his arms, Tarek Azzmar, billionaire mogul, knew what it meant to be truly blessed.

# Epilogue

Kira had discovered a long time ago that Mehdi family gatherings were quite an adventure, though before she had been on the outside looking in. Before there weren't quite as many Mehdis, either. As she sat at a table beneath a copse of olive trees on the palace grounds, holding her sleeping six-week-old against her breasts, she took a quick look around and smiled at the scene. Yasmin and Cala were attempting to climb a brick retaining wall, ignoring the fact they were wearing party dresses. Joseph stood nearby, egging them on and calling them babies when they couldn't quite achieve their goal.

In the distance, Adan held his toddler son, Sam, while his wife, Piper, cradled their three-month-old, Brandon. And standing beside them, the formerly-widowed

Mehdi military cousin, Sheikh Rayad Rostam, had his hands full with yet another newborn son who carried his father's name, while his new wife, Sunny, looking exhausted, rested her head on his shoulder. Rafiq entered the picture, chasing after young Prince Ahmed, who'd just learned to walk, while Maysa trailed behind him, laughing. But Kira had yet to locate Tarek, who had disappeared twenty minutes ago.

Elena, Zain and Madison soon arrived with a tray of refreshments that they placed on the lengthy table nearby. After shifting Laila to her shoulder, Kira came to her feet and joined the group for the festivities.

She then felt two strong arms come around her from behind and a kiss on her neck. Missing husband found. "Where have you been?" she asked him when he moved to her side.

He took the baby from her grasp and held her against his broad shoulder. "I had to finalize the purchase on a new yacht."

"We have a perfectly good yacht."

He gently kissed Laila's cheek, causing Kira's heart to take a little tumble in her chest. "This one is child-proofed and has more cabins. We need extra room to house the children. I predict we will have a son very soon."

"I'll get right on that."

He had the gall to grin. "We can begin tonight."

"We can pretend tonight. I'd like to wait until this little one is out of diapers before we make another one."

"I suppose I can agree to that, as long as we do quite a bit of pretending."

She saw no problem with that. "When can I see the new yacht?"

"The *Kira* should be delivered to the port in Oman in ten days."

The man was still full of surprises. "You named a boat after me?"

"Of course. A beautiful watercraft should always carry the name of a beautiful woman."

She could so kiss him for that, and she did.

"Gather round, adults and many small creatures," Adan called out. "It is time to toast our good fortune."

Knowing the youngest prince, Kira expected anything to come from his mouth. She hooked her arm through her husband's and claimed a place at the table next to Elena, who smiled and patted Kira's back. For months, she had thanked the former governess, matchmaker and mentor for her role in bringing Tarek to his senses, though Elena had claimed every time she had only been doing her job.

As Adan held up his glass, everyone followed suit. "To children, the future of Bajul. And should anyone else in attendance be pregnant, please notify us immediately so that we might add another wing to the palace, or respectfully find another place to live."

As soon as the laughter died down, Adan continued. "And now, in the words of my dear Italian mother, *la Famiglia!*"

"To family!" everyone repeated in unison.

Kira looked around at the people surrounding her and felt completely immersed in love. This was an extension of her family. This was the place she wanted to remain. And when spring rolled around, her parents would be relocating to Bajul, her father's homeland, making Kira's world complete.

She then gave her attention to her children and realized the best things came in small packages. She'd learned forgiveness was always attainable in the presence of true love, and fate handed you gifts when least expected.

The greatest gift slid his hand into hers and looked as if she were the most important person on the planet. Her handsome husband. The man of her dreams, who possessed her heart. He might be the consummate billionaire mogul, but she could think of a billion reasons why he was the consummate man and father.

For Kira Darzin Azzmar, life didn't get any better than this.

\* \* \* \* \*

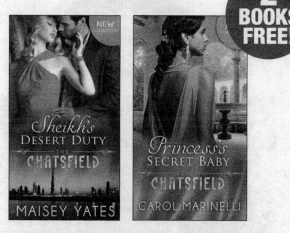